BREAKING
LUCKY

BRUCE MITCHELL

BRUCE MITCHELL
brucemitchellauthor.com

Printed in the United States of America
First Printing 2021
First Edition 2021

10 9 8 7 6 5 4 3 2 1

To my wife, Marilyn. Thank you for
Your everlasting support and honest feedback.

'The Royal Hotel Act says we judge people by their behaviour, not by the colour of their skin, and as long as our customers behave themselves and respect others, we don't give a rat's arse where they come from, or what colour they are–please excuse my French.'

Jim Thornton, 1918.

The Thornton Family

The Pioneers:

Mick Thornton (1808-1883)

> ➢ married

Cate Connor (1810-1890)

Children:

1. Michael (b.1835)
2. John (b.1836)
3. James (b.1843)
4. Margaret (1844-1858)

The Next Generation:

James Thornton (b.1843)

> ➢ married

Sarah MacDougall (b.1853)

Children:

1. James (Jim) (b.1880)
2. Catherine (Cath) (b.1887)
3. John (b.1890)
4. Danny (b.1895)

Table of Contents

Chapter 1

A Beginning

The Gallipoli Peninsula, Turkey. August 6, 1915.

An eagle soared on warm updrafts above the Aegean Sea, hunting mullet and wrasse. In the forests of Samothrace, a brood of hungry chicks nested high in a pine tree, waiting for her to return. She circled in a wide arc above warships and supply vessels scattered across the sparkling blue - their funnels belching black smoke. In the distance, the rugged cliffs of ANZAC Cove rose from a thin crescent of sand, and as the thump! thump! of artillery fire rolled across the water, she banked away from the commotion, and beat her wings further northward.

Nineteen-year-old Private Danny Thornton of the 4th Battalion, 1st AIF hunkered down in the mud, counting down the minutes to the 5.30pm 'zero hour' when the artillery barrage would cease, and he'd 'hop the bags' and go over the top with the Anzac force. A four-month veteran of the Gallipoli campaign, he'd waded ashore on April 25th and stormed across Anzac Beach under a hail of Turkish gunfire.

Thousands of men stood crammed together in the forward trench for the attack on Lone Pine. Some fixed their eyes eagerly on the parapet ladders, some gazed down at the dirt in silent prayer, some scratched a final letter they hoped would find its way home if they didn't survive. Danny's thoughts strayed to home-his loved ones flickered like a silent movie across his mind. Would he ever see them again?

The guns fell silent, and the bugle sounded the charge. Along the snaking trench line, the diggers shook hands and wished each other the best of luck. Danny took a deep breath, thumbed off the safety catch of his Lee Enfield .303 rifle and climbed the ramparts with his mates.

~   ~   ~

Upstairs at the Exchange Hotel, Orange, NSW Australia, 1895.

Sarah Thornton watched raindrops zig zag down the windowpane as the seconds ticked away to her next contraction. Outside, rivers of muddy water cascaded down Anson Street; heralding the end of the drought. *'Good rain for the farmers'* she thought, as another cramp hit her, right on schedule.

Edna Brown sighed and glanced at her watch. 'Your contractions are hotting up, darlin'. We'd better get this baby arse-upwards before your water breaks, or it'll be in there 'til Christmas.' She brushed aside a straggle of grey hair and pulled back the eiderdown. Edna had been a midwife longer than anyone could remember - she'd ushered most of Orange's townsfolk into the world. It was said that if the populace lined up on Summer Street on a dark night with nothing showing but their bare arses, she could name most of them with one eye closed.

Sarah's mother had told her each birth gets a bit easier, and after six children, she ought to know. But this little bugger of hers was breaking all the rules. Morning sickness stayed over for lunch and dinner, her veins bulged like fire hoses, and to top it off, the damn thing was upside down; a fact that thrilled James, as he was born arse upwards too, back in 1843. A "family tradition", he'd called it. Anyway, whether it was a boy or girl, she couldn't tell, but at 42, it was definitely her last. James would have to tie his willy in a knot.

Edna gently laid her hands on Sarah's belly, feeling the contours of the baby, getting her bearings. Sarah looked at those hands-rheumatic knuckles like knots on a tree, a battered wedding ring in the eroded groove of her finger. Old hands, but capable hands. Hands that had delivered Sarah into the world, 42 years before. Hands she trusted.

'Now darlin', I've done this more times than I can remember. It only takes a minute or two, and it'll feel like one of his little kicks. I say "his", because if it can't tell its arse from its head, it must be a man. You know our beloved Mayor, Sean Hetherington?' Sarah rolled her eyes and gave Edna a nod. 'I turned him round three times in his poor mother's womb, and three times he turned back again; which explains why he's such a stubborn bastard to this very day. Finally, I grabbed him by both feet, took the cord from around his little neck and brought him out safe; but now, everyone tells me I shouldn't have tried so hard.'

She pressed down gently and Sarah felt a warm ripple. Edna moved her hands higher and cupped a section of Sarah's swollen belly, thumbs pushing rhythmically in and out in a slow, careful downward arc. Sarah's insides bucked for an instant, then settled like a hand in a soft woollen glove. Edna smiled. 'That's the curtain raiser, darlin'; now let's get on with the main act.'

When Sarah's contractions were only 60 seconds apart, she could feel the baby moving downward to its first lungful of air. Edna's voice was a soothing balm. 'That's it darlin', you're doing fine. Not long to go now, the little bugger's on its way.' Sarah smiled through the pain of another contraction and continued to push.

Sarah's husband James was downstairs in the public bar, one ear cocked for any hint of progress upstairs. It was unusually crowded for a lunchtime - word had apparently gotten around that the missus was about to add another one to the family. Young Jim wiped a cloth over the bar and glanced at his father. 'You should do this more often, Dad, it's good for business.' James threw a bar towel at his son and pulled another beer.

The baby had ceased its rhythmic gyrations, and its crown emerged into the light. 'Alright Sarah, we have a mess of black hair down here, and I'm pretty sure it's not all yours. One more push, darlin', and the Exchange will have another Thornton to feed.' Sarah gritted her teeth and wailed loudly, and with a last desperate surge, felt the final, welcome release. 'We have one baby down here with ten fingers and toes, plus one other appendage, darlin'. It's a boy!'

A hush comes over the bar as Sarah's wail of pain drifts downstairs, and thirty or more knockabout blokes raise their heads and hold their breath, until the unmistakable cry of a newborn baby follows closely behind. A ragged cheer erupts and hands come from everywhere to slap James on the back. Jim shakes his father's hand. 'You better get up there, Dad; let us know if I've got a brother or sister.' James heads for the stairs.

He knocks softly on the bedroom door and pokes his head inside. 'Barmaid or cellarman?' Sarah beckons him in. 'It's a cellarman, love!' James grins and joins his wife and newborn son. A wizened pink face with enormous blue eyes stares up at him. 'Hello Daniel', he says, and kisses his son. Edna looks across at the three as she folds towels. 'With Sarah on the far side of 40 and that baby trying to walk down the birth canal, you'd better make his middle name "Lucky".'

And that's how Daniel 'Lucky' Thornton came into the world.

~ ~ ~

James and Sarah had lived above pubs for over twenty years, and the kids had lived nowhere else. The family couldn't sleep at night without the clink of glass and the low hum of a public bar rising through the floorboards. James started at the Wellington Inn as a 15-year-old apprentice cellarman back in 1858, and now had two pubs of his own–the Club House Hotel and the

Exchange Hotel on Anson Street, where the family lived. He was sturdily built, with broad shoulders and a crop of sandy-brown hair and eyes the colour of an evening sky. Born and raised on a cattle farm and fed on fresh air, good food and hard work, he had preserved his boyhood sense of wonder, and was an affable man; liking nothing better than good company, a good laugh and a cold beer.

It was a porcelain-blue day when he first saw Sarah at the end of a line of McDougall sisters, all curls and giggles as they bustled through the ballroom of the 'Exchange' in a flurry of petticoats and high-button shoes. She was nineteen years old, with a firm jawline, dark hair, narrow waist and pale blue eyes that sparked electric; and he couldn't take his eyes off her. The MacDougalls were well-to-do wheat farmers, and would have preferred a doctor or lawyer for a son-in-law, but with three daughters not yet wedded, the value of a publican in the family was not lost on the frugal Jock MacDougall.

They married under rainy skies at St. Joseph's Church, Orange in the spring of 1874; she was 21, and he was ten years older, almost to the day. Orange's gossip-mongers tut-tutted behind their teacups about 'James the cradle-snatcher' or 'Sarah's sugar daddy', but all could see that the newly marrieds were too much in love to bother with the jungle drums of the town.

Sarah soon became 'the missus' to the pub's workers and patrons as she embarked on a mission to turn a rough country pub into a clean, reputable hotel. Fresh flowers magically appeared on window sills, and the whole place took on a certain brightness. Some old lags complained the public bar wasn't dirty enough, and a couple of the local lads, slow-witted but quick fisted after a couple of beers, winced under the withering stare of the 'missus', and gradually drifted off to other watering holes.

While the pub business went smoothly for James and Sarah, starting a family was a different kettle of fish altogether. The doctors could find no reason for it - Sarah's plumbing was practically brand new, and James didn't seem to be firing blanks, but after a few years of dedicated practice, the game remained scoreless. With her usual determination, and more than a touch of Scottish superstition in her veins, Sarah sought the advice of the crystal-gazers of the town - quaint women in shawls who owned several cats and poked around in chicken's entrails, or drank more gin than was good for them.

She was advised to try an ancient fertility rite that held if the husband's underwear was cast onto the roof during a waning moon, and retrieved under the new moon, a baby would soon follow. James, while being a loving husband and at pains to indulge his wife, was also a practical man, pointing out that (a) the Exchange was a two-storey building and he had no hope of landing a pair of his long johns onto the roof, and (b) even if he could, he'd likely break his neck getting them down again.

In 1880, after further enthusiastic practice, Sarah gave birth to their first child, James junior, who for clarity's sake became known as 'Jim'. James senior was besotted with the arrival, and had no explanation for their reversal of fortune - but at the bottom of Sarah's battered old glory box lay a pair of ebony fertility statues, hand carved by a tribe on Africa's Ivory Coast, and said to aid fertility if rubbed. She never let on.

After another moderate drought, Catherine (aka Cath) arrived in 1887, and John a close third in 1890. By then, at 47 and 37 respectively, James and Sarah felt Providence had been more than kind to them, and with three kids, were glad to hang up their spurs; but once Providence had gotten into its stride, it was slow to pull up, and that's when Daniel (aka 'Danny') made his entrance.

~ ~ ~

A full moon blanketed the Exchange Hotel in silver on a frosty night in the winter of 1899. Blustery winds moaned along the veranda, rattling windows, but from John and Danny's room came a different sound - the wheeze of laboured breathing. Nine-year-old John ran to his parents' room and shook his father awake.

'Dad! Dad!'

James rolled over and blinked his eyes half open. 'What's 'matter, matey?'

'It's Danny–another attack–a bad one, Dad.'

James shakes himself awake and stumbles to the boys' room where Danny's hunched over his bed, a horrible rattling sound coming from his chest as he battles for air. The little boy looks up to his father in a silent plea for help - his face red from exertion. Sarah appears in the doorway, hair dishevelled and a small brown bottle in her hand, and laying the boy down on the bed, lifts his pyjama top and massages his heaving chest with mustard oil. 'This is a bad one love', she says. 'Get the pills, would you?'

James hurries to the bathroom cabinet. Sarah tilts the boy's head back and James places two 'Datura' pills on his tongue. Danny's lips turn blue; his eyes bulge in the effort to draw a feeble breath. Sarah massages his chest, speaking in a calm, reassuring voice. 'Danny sweetheart, push your stomach out and breathe slow and deep down into it. Don't stop. Slow and deep, slow and deep.' James looks on, feeling completely useless.

Ever so slowly the medication took effect, and Danny's breathing deepened, the colour coming back to his face as Sarah covered him against the night chill. His brow beaded with sweat from his battle for breath. 'I'll stay with him a while, love; you get some rest–you've got a day's work ahead of you.' James wrapped his dressing gown tighter. 'I'm wide awake now, love; I'll stay here.'

Later that morning, Doctor Parker closed the bedroom door and returned the stethoscope to his medical bag. 'You both did well to act quickly. This attack was the worst yet, and there's no end in sight.' He glanced at them both. 'Perhaps you should start thinking about Danny's longer-term future.'

Sarah's brows knitted in concern. 'Longer term?'

'Yes. His attacks coincide with the colder weather. We know asthma is an inflammation of the airways, but we don't know with any certainty what causes it. For some it may be dust, or pollen, or even cigarette smoke, but for Danny it seems to be the cold, dry weather. The attacks have worsened as he's grown, and I think it may be worthwhile moving him to the coast; somewhere where it's warm and humid, like Sydney. Orange has some bitter winters, as we all know, but for him it might have serious consequences.'

James grasped Sarah's hand. 'You mean it could kill him?'

'I don't want to be melodramatic about it, James, but yes, it's a strong possibility, based on last night's episode. We can't rely on Datura; in larger doses, it's a poison. Continuous use will have unwanted side effects.'

Sarah gazed out the window, thinking about her youngest child and the seriousness of his condition. She looked out over the roofs of Orange; the spire of St Joseph's Church, Duntryleague mansion, and the mist over Mount Canobolas to the south. She'd lived nowhere else. Moving the kids to Sydney? They knew no-one there; and what about making a living?

As if he'd been reading her mind, James squeezed her hand. 'Well, a pub is a pub wherever you live, and we can run one in Sydney just as well as we run them here.' Sarah smiled and thought to herself. *'Typical James, seeing the possibilities and excited about a challenge.'* She drew from his optimism and summoned up her own courage. 'We'd better tell the kids.'

That night James and Sarah broke the news to the family, and waited for the avalanche of protest. Nineteen-year-old Jim was the first to speak.

'Sounds to me like there's no question, Dad; Danny can't stay here any longer, and that's that. Sydney's full of pubs, so we can show 'em how it's done. And anyway, it can get pretty dull in the bush; Sydney has beaches, a racecourse, and plenty of girls.'

Cath shook her head ruefully at her older brother. At 12 years old she was top of her class and sharp as a tack, with an acerbic wit. 'And what makes you think the girls in Sydney would be interested in you, Jim Thornton? I don't see them kicking down your door in Orange.' Jim gave her a sneer, and she continued. 'Anyway, I agree; I hate the cold here. I want to ride the Manly Ferry and swim in the ocean.'

Sarah looked across at John and Danny. 'And what about you two?' John held his brother's hand. 'I have to take care of my little brother, and if he's going to Sydney, so am I.' A thoughtful look crossed Danny's face. 'If I'll be better in Sydney, I won't wake you up at night anymore, Johnny.' James looked around the table. 'Well, looks like that settles it. This will be an adventure; new places, new people, a new home by the sea. Lots of ways you can all get into mischief.'

~   ~   ~

James was one of three brothers, and the only one not born in Ireland - Michael and John Thornton, now aged 64 and 63, were born in Galway, and at six and five years old respectively, had arrived in Sydney Cove as free settlers with their parents Mick and Cate in October 1841.

Mick and Cate Thornton had the determination of an iron-bark tree. The winter of 1842 was at its coldest when they crossed the Blue Mountains on the back of a rattling furniture wagon with Michael and John, a clothes trunk, a one-pound note and a single dream–to have land of their own. Over the following years they turned that dream into reality. After back-breaking work and a few setbacks, Mick bought his beloved 'Gundungurra' property, and he and the two boys became leading cattle graziers and farmers in the Central West.

James came along in 1843, and steered a different course - into the hotel business, but the three brothers had remained close all their lives. Tonight they were celebrating a new direction for James–he was to journey back over those same Blue Mountains to Sydney, in a new chapter for the Thornton dynasty.

The three brothers sat at the kitchen table. Michael raised his glass. 'Here's to you and the family, Jimmy; make sure you have a keg of beer available when we come to visit.'

'There'll be one in the cellar with both your names on it.'

John refilled their glasses. 'You know, if Dad was here now, he'd still be telling us how to run our businesses.' He looked pensive for a moment. 'Hard to think that it's been, what, sixteen years now since he went, and Mum, nine. I sometimes think I'll turn round and see them sitting on the veranda with a glass of wine, looking over at Canobolas in the sunset.'

Michael replied, 'John - remember when you and I came back from Ballarat in '56? We had the arse out of our pants, and not a tenth of the gold we thought we'd bring home. We rode up to the homestead; thin, tired and filthy. Dad was on the veranda, and just looked up with a straight face as if we'd never left, and he said. 'Judging by the lack of a golden coach and horses, I'd say you blokes are looking for work. I'll be waiting on the southern boundary fence; there's a large hole to fix.'

Michael bent down to a canvas bag on the floor and pulled out a long object wrapped in calico. It was a 'nulla nulla', an Aboriginal club used for hunting and fighting, made of intricately carved hardwood and about one metre in length, with a bulbous clubhead at one end. It was clearly old and beautifully carved. James recognised it immediately. It was given to his father in 1842 by a

Gundungurra man named 'Galu' who rescued Michael when he became lost in the Blue Mountains.

'Dad pulled this from the ruins of the homestead, after the bushfires in '70. Aside from the chimney it was about the only thing that survived. We thought you, being the youngest brother, should have it. Take it to Sydney and hang it somewhere in Dad's honour. You never know, it might come in handy if there's a brawl in the bar.'

James hefted the old weapon with reverence. He remembered his father in his younger days, riding the perimeter fences of Gundungurra; the nulla nulla, strapped to his saddle in a leather sheath. His voice caught with emotion for an instant as he raised his glass in salute. 'Thank you both; I'll cherish it. Here's to Mum and Dad.'

Chapter 2

The Road Ahead

A locomotive stood at Orange railway station panting clouds of white steam like a bull about to charge. A railway porter loaded the Thorntons' luggage onto the train as young Jim boarded to locate their compartment. A scorching sun in a cloudless sky had James uttering the usual curses at the stiff collar of his dress-shirt.

The Thornton and MacDougall families were there in force to see them off—Sarah's parents Jock and Agnes and three of her sisters, James's brothers Michael and John with a few children, grandchildren, a cousin or two and three cattle dogs cavorting in the dust. Sarah hugged her parents with a tear in her eye, and James shook hands with his brothers while the rest of the entourage patted backs and wished them 'bon voyage'. The engine let go a shrill blast of its whistle, and the porter herded them inside the carriage as the train lurched forward into the morning sun, bound for Sydney in January 1900.

Their compartment was just big enough for six, with upholstered leather seats against walnut-panelled walls, brass luggage racks and a carafe of drinking water above the window, where Orange passed by as they gained speed along silver rails. James watched on as the family settled themselves in for the long journey. Sarah gazed out the window, no doubt, he thought, with trepidation about leaving Orange. Jim sat beside her - he'd grown into a strapping young man who could throw beer kegs around a cellar like no other. He was already taller than his father, with jet-black wavy hair and an olive complexion, hazel eyes and a smile that exploded across his face. He was quiet, well-considered, and slow to anger; useful qualities for managing a bar. He'd soon be 20, and one day he'd run a hotel of his own.

Cath's head was buried in a book, as usual. '*That girl will be an achiever*', he thought, '*and God help the man who tries to tame her*'. John clutched his precious bag of tin soldiers, fidgeting with the expected boredom of the trip, while Danny sat next to him, already drowsy from the rhythm of the train. It was Danny he feared for most - they gambled that the move to the coast would pay off, and his attacks would subside, but only time would tell.

And what of himself? He'd be 57 that year; he was still fit, could still throw a keg or two himself, and was looking forward to another career challenge. He'd found a pub in Randwick, 'The Royal Hotel', that was up for sale, and had paid a holding deposit pending an inspection. It was in a good neighbourhood, close to the city, and its books looked healthy. He'd have to sell both his existing pubs to pay for it, but he had a feeling it would be an excellent investment. Sydney was thriving as the colonies looked forward to federation, and he was certain that businesses like his would benefit.

The train took on water in Bathurst and approached the climb over the Blue Mountains. Low pasture land dotted with farmhouses and stands of she-oaks gave way to the big eucalypts, and soon they were climbing into the foothills through Lithgow, into the towering Blue Gums of Mt Victoria, toward Katoomba. The air sharpened as they climbed higher and the tree canopy closed over the railway tracks like a green cathedral. Through the open window they heard the piercing cry of whip birds.

Jim turned to his father.

'Hey Dad, isn't this where Uncle Michael got lost in the bush?'

'Yes mate, in 1842, just before I was born, but I've heard the tale many times.'

John and Danny were fast asleep, but Sarah and Cath were listening in.

'Tell us what happened, Dad.'

Michael was six years old and had wandered off, chasing a wallaby, and before he knew what he'd done, got himself lost in the bush. He walked for hours and ended up following a downhill track as the afternoon light extended long shadows into the valley. As he rested, he heard running water. Maybe he'd see people there? He was thirsty, and he hurried down the slope as the sound became louder. Suddenly the track widened into a flat clearing holding a small rocky stream. He stumbled to the water's edge and threw himself down to slake his thirst.

A little further downstream, standing at the edge of a wide, calm pool, stood a tall, lean Aboriginal warrior holding a long wooden spear. About 25 years of age, with shoulder-length black curly hair, he wore a dappled kangaroo skin cloak that hung almost to the ground. His dark expressive eyes watched Michael intently for a moment, then he swiftly gathered up his weapons, crouched low and crept toward the boy.

Michael didn't hear him coming. Having drunk his fill, he turned from the stream to see the warrior standing only a few feet from him like a dark statue. Michael let out a piercing yell and turned to run, but the man was too quick. He grabbed the boy's arm and swung him back. Michael's eyes were like saucers as he struggled vainly in the warrior's firm grip. He was petrified.

'Please don't kill me, mister!'

'Not gunna kill anyone, now stay still boy!'

'You speak English?' Michael said as he stopped struggling and stared up at the warrior.

'Probly better n' you do. Where d'you come from, boy? You lost? You come from up that way, up Bathurst Road?'

'Yes. My mum and dad stopped there last night. This morning I was chasing, um, I mean, hunting a wallaby near our camp and then I couldn't find my way back.'

'You hunting without a spear?—that wallaby's a lot smarter n' you, boy.'

The man pointed to where Michael came out of the bush. 'That blackfella hunting track up there. You show me where you come from. We'll get back to your camp.'

'Thanks, mister! I've never talked to an Aboriginal before. What's your name?'

'Name is Galu. And you?'

'Michael.'

They walked for a long time as Galu followed Michael's trail back out of the valley. It was almost dark when he found the spot where the boy had come down from the Thorntons' campsite.

'You came down from up there.' He pointed.

'How do you know that?'

He pointed to a faint impression in the scrub. 'Blackfella don't wear boots in the bush.' He bent down towards the ground and sniffed. 'And you did a wee here.'

Michael's face reddened. 'Are we far from mum and dad?'

'Not far–can smell smoke. Come on.'

Mick and Cate sat despondently by the fire, sick with worry. They'd called out and searched all day without a sign of their son. Without warning, a noise came from the darkness and Mick rose to peer intently through the gloom. The footsteps in the undergrowth were louder now, and they held their breath as they heard 'Dad!' And Michael came running out of the dark to his family. They clung to each other as tears streamed down Cate's face, and Mick whispered, 'Thank God, Thank God.'

Suddenly Mick looked up to see Galu standing at the edge of the clearing; the firelight gleaming against his lean *torso. Michael piped up: 'Mum, Dad, this is my friend Galu! He found me and brought me back!'*

Mick was stunned. He walked slowly to the tall Aboriginal and held out his hand. 'I don't know what to say.' He stammered, with tears in his eyes. 'You saved my son's life.' Galu shook his outstretched hand. 'Well, fish weren't bightin', and I felt like a bit of a walk anyway,' Galu said with a straight face, and Mick burst out laughing.

James continued. 'That night, Dad and Galu talked for a long time by the fire. Galu told him about the Aboriginal people losing their land, the massacres, the polluted creeks and billabongs and the diseases brought by the white man. After that, Dad would always do what he could to help the Aboriginal people by letting them hunt and fish on Gundungurra unhindered, and not harming the land. Mum gave Galu her St. Christopher medal, and Galu left his nulla nulla behind as a gift. We never saw him again, but he's been part of the family for over fifty years.'

~   ~   ~

Sydney was only 112 years old when James and Sarah made it their new home. In 1788, it was a disparate collection of souls thrown together by circumstance–an unlikely social experiment that could have gone horribly wrong. It was an infant society beneath a cluster of sorrowful tents, and grew to be a wild child - born from adversity and raised with a healthy disregard for authority. The gold rush filled its pockets with cash, and gave it a half-dose of bravado, and the isolation of the great southern land forced it to think for itself. As it matured to a young adolescent at the end of the nineteenth century, it peeked from behind a curtain into a new era, where technology and fading Victorian inhibitions gave it a glimpse of its own unlimited potential.

Destined to be the city's major thoroughfare, George Street grew from a dogleg bush track beside the Tank Stream, where the Eora people had fished and bathed for untold generations. In 1900 the old watercourse still flowed down to Sydney Cove, but was consigned to a stygian underground drain meandering between Pitt and George streets, as if unsure of which way it should go. Up on the surface, Sydney acted out its daily drama along the roads and laneways snaking an uneven pattern across the inner-city. Electric trams rumbled along narrow rails, commuters deftly swinging on and off like seasoned performers on the high wire. Carts, drays and carriages hurtled about, missing one another by inches, as if they'd rehearsed their moves for years. Women in Victorian finery gossiped outside store windows, and boys on bicycles showed contempt for the traffic as they weaved recklessly wherever they pleased.

A phalanx of disparate buildings lined the streets; some mean and withdrawn, some bland, some beautiful. The imposing General Post Office held court in Martin Place, with its towered bell dutifully marking time every quarter hour. Well-dressed ladies and gentlemen strolled the Strand Arcade, taking coffee at fashionable cafes, and the regal Queen Victoria Building sat comfortably atop the hill like an empress on her throne. Over in Hyde Park, separated by a maze of lawns and criss-crossed paths, St. James Anglican Church squared off against its larger rival, St. Mary's Cathedral, in a showdown of faith.

And Sydney had its darker side. The human crucible of The Rocks, the docks fringing Darling Harbour and the alleyways of Woolloomooloo harboured Sydney's unfashionable slums; a medley of the hungry and grimy, the forlorn and forgotten, the battlers and the bludgers, the swift and the dangerous. But it was from these narrow laneways and paint-peeled doors that Sydney was infused with a personality that had been slow-cooked since the early days - a self-deprecating stoicism that 'she'll be right, mate'; a strong sense of 'a fair go', a dry humour, and a very sensitive 'bullshit detector' - aspects of a personality which would see it through the rough times, and ultimately become part of a national consciousness.

~ ~ ~

Afternoon shadows crept across the tracks as the train pulled into Sydney Terminal station with a squeal of metal and a hiss of steam. A tide of passengers surged to the exits in a riot of chatter, scraping bags and exuberant shouts. James found a porter to help load their baggage on a sturdy cart and he led them out to Devonshire Street. The spires of the Sydney Exhibition Building in Prince Alfred Park captured a dying sunset, conjuring up images of a Cairo mosque. He marvelled at the vaulted roof that had witnessed so many of Sydney's flamboyant events. To the north, the city's heart reached up to a burnished sky, almost touching the clouds. Sarah folded her arm through his as they shared the realisation that they were in a new home—a strangely tantalising home that beckoned to them: 'Come. Come and unlock my secrets.'

Jim nudged the pair out of reverie. 'What now, Dad?' He asked, as the crowd of commuters passed them by like a swollen river. James scanned the street. 'The publican's supposed to pick us up. His name's Joe Hoskins, but I've no idea what he looks like.' They saw no sign of Joe or his wagon; just a lone woman seated on a two-horse dray.

As they looked about, the woman hopped down from the dray and ambled over toward them. She was in her fifties, stout and plainly dressed, with long grey hair in a single plait down her back and wearing work boots. She strode with purpose, extending her hand in greeting.

'James Thornton, is it?'

James shook her hand, puzzled. 'Yes, that's right.'

'Jo Hoskins from the Randwick Royal. Pleased to make your acquaintance.'

'Oh, I'm sorry, Jo, I was expecting…'

She smiled. 'A man? That's alright, it happens often. There aren't that many women publicans; a few, but not a lot; and it doesn't help when I'm called Jo, short for Joanna.'

James shook off his momentary embarrassment and introduced the family. 'My wife Sarah, Jim, Cath, John and young Danny.'

'What a fine family you have, Mr. Thornton.'

'Thank you. And please, call me James.'

'Alright James, let's get you lot to Randwick.'

They loaded the bags onto the trailer. James noted that Jo hefted even the heaviest bags with apparent ease and was no slouch when it came to securing a load of luggage with knots tied with the ease of a sailor. *Clearly*, he thought, *this Jo Hoskins is an unusual woman.*

James and Sarah shared the driver's seat with Jo and the kids piled onto the luggage in the back; Cath holding on tight to young Danny. They set off southwards along Elizabeth Street, weaving past trams crowded with peak-hour commuters heading home. They turned east onto Cleveland Street, and Jim, perched on top of Sarah's travelling trunk, cocked his head at a strange sound. He nudged his brother.

'Hey, did you hear that?'

'Hear what?' Answered John.

'I must be goin' mad–I thought I heard an elephant trumpeting just then.'

'I can't hear anything with the noise of all these trams.'

He turned to Cath. 'Hey sis–did you hear an elephant just then?'

'Yes, I did. Moore Park Zoo is up ahead.'

'How d'you know that?'

She gave her brother a sarcastic look. 'Well, brother of mine, if you'd spent more time reading about Sydney and less time ogling girls, you'd know that too. And I can tell you more-the zoo opened in 1884 on a spot known as 'Billy Goat Swamp'. Its elephants were donated by the king of Siam.' She punched him playfully on the shoulder. 'How about we ask Dad if we can go there? It's close to Randwick.'

Jim grinned. 'Alright–I'll take you all.'

As if in confirmation, the elephant trumpeted again, and this time they all heard it, despite the trams. The zoo was a favourite attraction for Sydney-siders for many years, until Taronga Zoo opened, overlooking the harbour on Bradley's Head. The famed elephants from Moore Park crossed the harbour on barges to their new home in 1916.

Jo turned the dray onto Randwick Road and they climbed the steady rise past the racecourse onto Belmore Road - Randwick's 'High Street', and as they neared a junction, she pointed ahead to a two-story building. 'There she is, James–the 'Royal'.

The pub straddled a corner block; one facade facing north and the other looking eastwards down the slope to Coogee Beach. Atop the crenelated roof was a brick and concrete inscription: 'Royal Hotel–1887'. It was an impressive building that dominated the intersecting streets, with a lacework wrought-iron balcony surrounding the first floor. James counted ten tall windows on one side of the upper floor, and on the ground floor, three entrance doors led onto the street. It was bigger than any pub he'd worked in, and he was eager to see it.

Jo drove the dray expertly down Soudan Lane to the doors of a carriage-shed and stable. 'I've reserved your rooms upstairs; how about a tour of the property? James nodded. 'That'd be good.'

Jo led them up the back steps, and at the end of a short corridor, the pub opened to a wide vestibule with four-metre ceilings. A wide stairway led to the first floor; and off to the right, the public bar ran the length of the northern facade and down the eastern side of the building. The bar was busy, with city workers stopping in for a beer on their way home. Two barmen were on duty, pulling beers and chatting to patrons.

James cast his eyes over the bar. The ceilings and walls were newly painted in a fashionable cream, and the floors were of hardwood. The bar was well constructed from carved red cedar; the surfaces clean and the shelves well-stocked. Bisecting the eastern wall was a large stone fireplace that would house a welcoming fire in the winter months. The rest of the ground floor contained a lounge/billiard room, guest dining room, and kitchen. Jim and Sarah glanced at James, nodding their approval.

They climbed the stairs to the first floor, containing six guestrooms and men's and women's bathrooms, a lounge/reading room and separate publican's quarters. James had never seen such a high standard of craftsmanship and design, and could see that the asking price for the Royal was a very reasonable one.

He turned to Jo. 'The place is immaculate–the best I've seen, Jo.'

'Thank you. It wasn't like this six years ago. The last bloke didn't have a clue about running a pub. He thought you just opened the doors, sold beer and made a fortune. I was lucky the building and its equipment were sound, because the place was filthy and knocked about. The clientele was small, turnover was low–the 'Royal' had the smell of death about it. I worked hard for three years to clean it up, get rid of the barflies and attract better customers. Now I've done that, I'd like to have a rest for a while, and let someone else carry on with it. The Thornton pubs have a good reputation in Orange, James, and I'd like you to be that person, if you agree.'

James had no hesitation. He liked this woman; she was experienced, talked straight and didn't pull punches. It felt right.

'Looks like have a deal.'

Later that night, after the luggage was unloaded and unpacked, dinner eaten and kids asleep, James and Sarah collapsed into bed. Despite the rigours of a long day, Sarah lay awake, thinking about the step they'd taken - pulling up stumps to live in Sydney. It had all happened so quickly. She'd been monitoring Danny closely, watching his little chest rise and fall, the way he breathed through his mouth, and she thought she'd noticed an easing of his chest with the humid Sydney air; or was it just wishful thinking? Time would tell.

'And dear me,' she thought, *'my exuberant husband.'* The thrifty Scot in her wanted to negotiate the price of the Royal. But James was a dreamer—and once he became excited about something, there was no holding him back. He knew the hotel business like the back of his hand, and she trusted his judgement, but a few quid saved would have been worthwhile. She could almost see old Jock MacDougall nodding his assent. *'My father's daughter',* she thought, as she drifted off to sleep.

~ ~ ~

The sun slanted low over Avoca Street as Sarah walked Danny and John to 'Our Lady of the Sacred Heart' Primary School. The two youngest Thornton kids had been uprooted from Orange and transplanted to Sydney like turnip seedlings, and the first day of school in 'the big smoke' would test the strength of their delicate roots. It was Danny's first ever day of school–his biggest challenge since conquering the toilet seat. He carried a school case that he could have slept in; reminding Sarah of a tiny travelling salesman. John, having reached the ripe old age of 10, was wise to the ways of the classroom, but now he was to be the 'new kid in class' for the first time. He'd checked at least five times that his fly was buttoned.

Sarah felt pangs of emotion at the last of her brood growing up so soon. *'Before I know it, they'll be young men.'* She'd been watching Danny's breathing, and was now sure there was an improvement, but made a mental note to tell the school about his asthma. They came to the school gate and Danny halted, eyes wide, staring at a group of nuns shepherding children across the playground.

'Mum! Look at the big penguins!'

John burst out laughing. 'They're not penguins, dopey. They're nuns; that's their uniform.'

Danny turned to his mother. 'What's a 'nun', mum?

Sarah stifled a giggle. 'They're your teachers, love. The "brides of Christ".'

'All of them?'

'Yes.'

He thought for a minute, with a puzzled look. 'Gee, Christ's got lots of wives; how come Dad's only got you?'

At the same moment Sarah struggled with that somewhat ticklish theological question, Cath was riding the tram along Randwick Road dressed in her St. Vincent's Girl's College uniform - a navy-blue dress with black high-buttoned shoes and a wide-brimmed straw hat. She felt quite the grown-up; assuming a pose of refinement as the stately buildings of Sydney Cricket Ground glided by. St. Vincent's was in Potts Point - a leafy headland jutting out into the harbour in the shape of a dolphin's fin between Woolloomooloo and Elizabeth Bay. The area's elegant Georgian mansions, with impressive names like 'Rockwall' and 'Tusculum', ignored 'The Loo' with its ramshackle buildings and fish markets, preferring instead to peer regally across to the Botanical Gardens and Parliament House.

Cath paused at the gate, staring across manicured lawns to the College's Dickensian spires and pitched roofs with a tremor of apprehension at being 'the new girl'. For a moment she thought of turning for home, until a voice interrupted her thoughts.

'Excuse me, are you Catherine Thornton?' She turned to see a girl her own age with thick curly black hair to her shoulders, pearlescent skin and expressive green eyes that held a twinkle of mischief.

'Yes, I am.'

The girl shook Cath's hand. 'I'm Charlotte Edmonstone, but everyone around here calls me 'Eddie'. I'm your official guide to St. Vincent's.' She glanced about for eavesdroppers and took on a conspiratorial tone; leaning towards Cath: 'Stick with me–the nuns will give you the sanitised version of what goes on here–but I'll give you the horrible truth, and set you straight on who to trust, and who to avoid like a creeping skin rash.'

Cath laughed. 'Lead on, Eddie.'

She took Cath's arm, and the two strolled down a pathway lined with maples. Girls were filing through the gates–youngsters laughed and chased one another round the trees while senior girls looked on with hauteur. Nuns passed under archways–their heads bowed in subdued conversation.

Eddie led Cath into a building draped with old ivy. Inside was a classroom lined with tall windows and furnished with ageing timber desks. Girls took their seats under the watchful eye of a nun as Eddie whispered. 'The nuns at "Vinnies" have the power to take control of your mind. You won't notice it, but suddenly, all your willpower will disappear, and you're under their wicked spell.' Cath giggled behind a hand as they continued down the corridor to a science laboratory with rows of timber benches, each with a small sink, curved water spigots and test tubes. Eddie waved an arm toward the equipment and resumed her conspiratorial tone. 'Some say that late at night, dead bodies stolen from the morgue are dissected in here. If you listen closely, you'll hear their ghostly moans.'

Their last stop on the tour was a kitchen where girls in white aprons were spooning 'White Wings' flour into bowls. Eddie tapped Cath on the shoulder. 'Here's where they teach us how to be dutiful wives, who cook, clean and dote on every word their husband might utter, and never have an original thought of our own.' She grasped Cath's elbows and locked with her eyes. 'Never, ever, come in here. You'll come out vapid, useless and totally boring.'

Cath took an immediate liking to this girl named Eddie.

~   ~   ~

The Royal's guest accommodation hosted a steady stream of travellers who turned up in irregular waves like a storm-surf at Coogee beach. They were a cross-section of Sydney's Victorian humanity: horse-owners, fancy goods importers, travelling salesmen with products and potions, land agents, brush-makers, saddlers, debt collectors with narrow eyes and sharp pencils, razor-strop manufacturers and gluemakers, to name but a few. They'd step off the tram with a frayed carpetbag and bloodshot eyes, brushing train-soot from their shoulders. Scratching their signatures in the guest ledger, they'd take their brass door-key and climb the stairway with the thud of travel-weary feet.

One of the Royal's permanent guests was Major Edward Finch-Hatton, known simply as 'The Major'. Having moved in when the pub opened in 1887, he was its longest-serving guest. A short, rotund man with a military bearing, he was approaching 70 years old, with snow-white hair, a florid complexion and an enormous walrus moustache. Hard of hearing, absent-minded and fond of a sherry, he walked with a silver-tipped cane that he'd tap on the wooden floor to gain the barman's attention. His grandfather had fought against Napoleon at the Battle of Waterloo in 1815, and his father faced

George Washington's troops at Gettysburg. The Major upheld the family tradition, serving in the Anglo-Afghan Wars as a fresh-faced private.

One afternoon, not long after the Thorntons took over, James invited The Major for a drink in the bar. At the duly appointed time, wearing his customary three-piece black worsted suit and silver watch and chain, the Major entered the bar-and consulting a small piece of paper from his pocket, called out to the clientele: 'I'm looking for a Mr. James Thornton!', at which James rose and beckoned the old man over to his table.

'Thank you for joining me, Major.'

He stared across the table at James. 'And who are *you*, sir?'

'James Thornton, Major–the publican.'

The Major's eyes widened like saucers. 'Gad! You used to be a woman!'

'Ah, no Major, that was Jo Hoskins; she sold the Royal to me.'

The Major glanced around the room. 'Damn fine club it is too. What's its name?'

'The Royal Hotel.'

'Damn fine club.'

'Ah, sherry, Major?'

'Yes, of course! And I'll have one as well, if you don't mind.'

James walked to the bar as The Major followed him with his eyes. 'Pick up your feet, Lieutenant, this is a parade ground, not a Shanghai bordello!'

James returned with the drinks. 'Service is a bit slow this afternoon; we're short-handed.'

'And who are *you*, sir?'

'James Thornton, Major.'

'Damn fine club. There were no officer's clubs in Afghanistan; too busy with the damn 'Ghilji's' in the Hindu Kush. There's nothing like a good bayonet charge to liven things up though, eh Lieutenant?'

'No, Major.'

'Damn fine club. What did you say your name was?'

~ ~ ~

Two doors down the corridor from The Major lived the other permanent guest of The Royal; the bohemian Minnie Fitzroy. 'Miss Minnie', as they knew her, was born into a farming family under the shadow of Mount Warning in the tropical northern coast of New South

Wales. Her age was indeterminate, but guesses ranged between 50 and 60, depending upon what time of day it was, and how many gins she'd consumed.

She grew up in a wealthy household and was educated at a Brisbane girls' boarding school, where she excelled at oil painting, and in the 1880s, travelled to Paris to study at the École des Beaux-Arts with the likes of Claude Monet, Paul Gauguin and Alphonse Mucha. Following a disastrous love affair with a young French woman from Montmartre, she left Paris and boarded a steamer at Marseilles, bound for Australia. She sailed through Sydney Heads in the 1890s and again fell in love, this time with the sparkling blue harbour; and she'd graced The Royal with her unique presence ever since.

Sarah and Miss Minnie met under rather awkward circumstances. The artist had been setting up her easel on the upstairs veranda to capture the roofs of Randwick against the backdrop of Coogee to the east, which under normal circumstances would not have been a problem, except that she painted in the nude. Mrs Eliza Pardy, who ran the grocery store across the road, strode into the bar one afternoon in high dudgeon, demanding to see the manager, and in a shrill voice, told of Minnie's indiscretions, predicting a downward spiral of depravity and moral corruption across Sydney. Interestingly, not a peep came from Bootmaker George Cherry in the shop next door to Mrs. Pardy, even though George would have had a slightly better view. Being a sensitive matter, James considered that Sarah was better equipped to resolve the issue, and she knocked on Minnie's door one bright Saturday morning.

She opened the door in bare feet, dressed in a pink kimono and nursing a glass of gin. Smoke from a long cigarette holder curled upwards to the ceiling like a genie from a bottle, and from somewhere inside, a scratchy phonograph played Puccini. Her bright blue eyes shone with an air of bemusement from a finely crafted face framed by dark curls. It was a face that had weathered the years well, with none of the frown lines that mark a regretted life. Her kimono followed the contours of a lithe, sensuous figure; which perhaps explained the silence from the bootmaker across the road.

'Mrs. Thornton, is it not?'

'Ah, yes; do you ah, mind if I come in?'

'Please do.'

Her room resembled a Gilbert and Sullivan stage-set. Canvasses of all sizes and in varying stages of completion leaned up against each other like drunks at closing time. An enormous easel was parked in the corner beside a stuffed and fully plumed male peacock, and a human skeleton wearing a fez stood casually beside a hat stand draped with coloured silk scarves. A dressing table held a mixture of pots of coldcream, potions, waxes and three long wigs; blonde, black and red. A heady fragrance of perfume, salt air from the open windows, and the aroma of oil paints pervaded the room.

'I'm Sorry to disturb you, Miss Fitzroy, but there's been a complaint from the grocery shop across the road.'

'Please call me Minnie.' She smiled mischievously. 'They don't like my paintings?'

'No, it's more a matter of you apparently painting naked on the veranda.'

'They prefer me to be naked downstairs?'

'They want you to put your clothes on.'

Minnie took a long pull from her glass. 'Well, I'm not surprised; I'll bet it was that old battle-axe Mrs. Pardy–she has a large stick up her ample arse.' She winked. 'I'll bet you haven't heard from the bootmaker - I believe he's hit his thumb with a hammer quite a few times already.'

It was Sarah's turn to smile. 'Mr. Cherry is getting on in years; it can't be good for his heart.'

Minnie swung an unexpected arm around Sarah's shoulders. 'I'm think I'm going to like you, Sarah. It's good to have a woman around here with a sense of humour.'

'So, you'll dress for your veranda appearances?'

'What about just a tiny slit up the sides of my kimono?'

'That could be negotiated.'

~ ~ ~

The summer of 1900 had come and gone, and by April the nights were getting longer and cooler, turning the maple trees in Perouse Road to gold. Jim manned the public bar on a quiet Tuesday night as the clock ticked towards closing time. Drinkers sat in knots of conversation under a listless cloud of tobacco smoke, and the occasional Hansom cab would jingle down the street through haloes of lamplight.

One table of middle-aged men had been drinking since the afternoon, and had become louder than the rest, spilling their drinks and erupting into shouts and the occasional raucous curse. One of them rose and staggered to the bar. He was a thick-set man in his early forties with a pock-marked face, wearing work overalls, a felt hat and a coarse woollen jacket. As Jim filled the glasses, the man jerked his head toward a pair of drinkers at a far corner table.

'D'you know it's against the law to serve alcohol to Abo's, mate?' He was referring to two Aboriginal men - stable hands at Randwick Racecourse and regulars at the Royal, sitting at their table, quietly nursing their beer.

Jim continued his pouring. 'I'm aware of what the law says.'

'Then why don't you get rid of the filthy buggers?'

Jim put the glasses down and regarded the man. 'Because there's another law here that takes precedence. We call it the 'Royal Hotel Act'. Have you heard of it?

The man shook his head with a vague look of confusion.

'It states that at the Royal, we judge a man by his behaviour, not by the colour of his skin, and as long as our customers behave themselves and respect others, we don't care where they come from or what colour they are.'

The man wore a sneer. 'That's bullshit. I've a good mind to let the coppers know what goes on here–you could lose your licence, you know.'

Jim slid the filled glasses across the bar. 'Sir, I couldn't give a rat's arse if you told the King of Persia. Now, seeing it's almost closing time, I'd appreciate it if you and your friends would finish your drinks, leave the bar, and don't come back.'

The man was taken aback for an instant, then scowled. 'You'll fucking regret you ever said that.' He slowly weaved his way back to the table and muttered to his friends with sideways glances toward the bar.

Half an hour later Jim had locked the doors for the night and doused the lights. Carrying a crate of empty bottles out into the darkened backyard, the sudden scuff of a boot sounded nearby, and he turned to catch the reflected light of a bottle swinging toward his head. He was no brawler, but he'd been in a few scraps in the bush. He was young, fit and agile, and had learned a few things from his Uncle Michael, who in his day had done some tent-boxing on the Ballarat goldfields. Instinctively, he ducked the bottle and drove a powerful uppercut into a dark shadow; connecting with a soft underbelly. He straightened and delivered a left cross to an exposed jaw, and the body groaned and crumpled to the ground. Under the cold light of a street lamp, Jim recognised the pock-marked face of the man who had complained about the Royal's clientele. As he dragged his unconscious attacker out into Perouse Road, Jim thought, *'Guilty as charged, under the 'Royal Hotel Act.'*

A few days later, Inspector McManus from Randwick Police Station shouldered his way through the doors of The Royal. A career policeman, McManus had risen through the ranks from a lowly constable in the Foot Police, and cut his teeth in the shady back-streets of Surry Hills and Woolloomooloo, where you step lightly and watch your back. He was a barrel-chested, red-haired Irishman, tough and uncompromising when it counted. He spied Jim at the bar and made his way over.

'Morning, Jim,'

'Morning, Inspector, can I shout you a dram?'

'Just a short one; I'm on duty, you see.'

'Yes, of course.' Jim poured McManus a shot of his preferred Irish whisky as the inspector leant on the bar and cast his eyes about, settling his gaze briefly on the pair of Aboriginal men who had been at the pub that night.

'Now, Jim, my Superintendent asked me to remind you of the regulations regarding serving alcohol to Aboriginals. You wouldn't be contravening the law now, would you?'

Jim maintained a straight face. 'Certainly not, Inspector. As you can see, everyone here is behaving themselves, just like white men.'

McManus allowed himself a smile and drained his glass. 'Just as I thought. Top of the morning to you and the family, Jim.'

'And to you and yours, Inspector.'

Chapter 3

A Nation Rises

Sydney Morning Herald
Tuesday 1 January 1901
COMMONWEALTH DAY
THE GREAT INAUGURAL PROCESSION
A Brilliant Pageant Expected

If the weather to-day proves fine, the preparations which have been in progress for several weeks past for the purpose of inaugurating the Australian Commonwealth are certain to result in a popular demonstration unparalleled in the southern hemisphere.
Various circumstances conspire towards this end.

Allied to the fact that the people of
Australia are on the threshold of entering
upon an indissoluble union is the
knowledge that we are not only
celebrating the passing away of one year
and the arrival of another but are
witnesses of the demise of one century
and the birth of a new one.
It is true that the arrival of the new year is
always regarded as a festal occasion on
which popular rejoicing comes
prominently to the surface, but in this
instance the rejoicings of the people are
tinctured by a deep feeling of patriotism.
It has been awakened by the knowledge
that the people of Australia are entering
into a bond of union which has all the
elements of brotherly affection and trust.
At the time of writing, it is impossible to
say for certain what the state of the
weather will be when the great
procession starts on its journey this
morning from the Domain to Centennial
Park. Even if it is unfavourable it is
certain that the great heart of the people
will be moved by the momentous
ceremony about to take place.

On the night of December 31, 1900, in ballrooms, back verandas, pubs and on street corners, Sydney celebrated the demise of another year. In Vaucluse and Potts Point they sipped champagne. In Ashfield they drank Hock or Claret. In the Haymarket they tossed back glasses of baiju, and in The Rocks, well, they drank whatever was cheap. And along with seeing the year off, they may have had an inkling that the country was saying goodbye to its adolescence. When sunrise lit Sydney Heads the next day, the city would no longer be part of an English colony, but part of a nation in its own right - a legitimate player on the world stage. That day would witness the greatest spectacle Sydney had seen since the First Fleet sailed up the sparkling harbour in 1788. Over half a million Sydneysiders would witness the Federation procession of 1901.

They shrugged off their New Year's hangovers, spilling from trains, trams and horse-drawn carts, or just walked from wherever they lived. They lined footpaths, hung over balconies, leaned from windows and balanced precariously on rooftops. The procession would muster in the Domain, do a circuit of inner-city streets and climb the Oxford Street hill to Centennial Park, where over 100,000 people would witness the swearing-in of Australia's first Governor-General, Lord Hopetoun, and the first Prime Minister, Sir Edmund Barton.

The route was overflowing with streamers, Union Jack flags, flowers and bunting, plus ten 'Federation Arches' depicting the new nation's pillars of wool, wheat and coal. Inexplicably, Australia did not yet have a flag of its own - its national banner would be born from a competition in April that year, with a prize of 200 pounds, and be hoisted for the first time in September. One design depicted of a group of indigenous animals playing cricket, and although popular, didn't make the final cut—an outcome for which future generations would be eternally grateful.

The Thornton family was no exception to the wave of excitement, and closed the Royal for a half-day. They caught the tram down to Centennial Park's Randwick Gate and walked along the Grand Drive to the parade grounds near Paddington. Jim carried young Danny on his shoulders past the Moreton Bay fig trees lining the street, playing 'chicken' with low branches as he stooped to avoid them at the last second, to the youngster's squeals of delight. John marched in military-style with a stick as his pretend rifle, in anticipation of seeing the 2000 or more uniformed troops that would be part of the procession. Cath had arranged to meet 'Eddie' Edmonstone at the park and was concentrating on how she'd find her among 100,000 people; and James and

Sarah brought up the rear, enjoying the buzz of expectation.

The morning was bright–Sydney's customary morning nor' easter blew freshness into a new and exciting day. As the Thorntons neared the parade ground, marching bands a 1000-strong children's choir drifted on the air. Around them, people of all ages walked with a spring in their step; eyes alive with the promise of a bright future.

They turned off the Grand Drive and followed the crowd across the grass and up a short slope, and as they breasted the hill, a panorama of colour, sound and movement opened up. The parade grounds formed a massive amphitheatre, dominated at its centre by a huge white-domed pavilion constructed for the occasion. Thousands of spectators milled about in a surge of hats and umbrellas against the sun while the procession snaked down from the Paddington Gate like a multi-coloured dragon. The Thorntons headed toward the centre of the grounds for a closer look.

Decorated horse-drawn 'allegorical cars', or 'floats' as they were later called, were the first to attract their attention. Each Australian state and several countries were represented. One float featured the 'Sons and Daughters of Temperance'-fervent men and women decrying the demon drink and advocating total abstinence. Their banner shouted: 'Forsake Alcohol - That Fruitful Source of Care, Misery, Drunkenness and Immodesty'. They were campaigning for reduced opening hours for Sydney pubs, and were steadily gaining the ear of State government and the voting public. The float that immediately followed the temperance movement may have been a coincidence, or perhaps an act of sabotage. It was the Italian float, featuring a band of smiling musicians and two women in Roman dress enjoying goblets of wine. James let go a hearty laugh. 'At least our side had the final say.'

The Trade Union movement marched by; their banners portraying the seamen, miners, stonemasons, tailoresses, shearers and others who were the backbone of Australia's burgeoning industries. The crowd gave a loud cheer as a cohort of Australian stockmen, lean men with chiselled jaws, rode languidly in the saddle. The Royal Queen's Guard was a stark contrast - riding stiff-backed with red plumes bouncing to the trot of their mounts, silver helmets flashing like lightning bolts in the morning sun. A platoon of Australian Light Horse, newly returned from South Africa, wore slouch hats - many with hollowed eyes and grim faces carved by the violence of the Second Boer War. Marching bands from Australia, England, Canada and the United States passed by, playing stirring marches; 'The British Grenadiers', 'Men of Harlech' and 'The Garb of Old Gaul'.

Cath had miraculously found Eddie in the crowd, and the two 14-year-olds joined the Thornton family. They'd been somewhat unladylike, running through the crowd, laughing and shouting to each other. Their elegant hats were askew, and strands of Cath's hair had rebelled against their confinement; blowing about in the breeze. Sarah watched the girls enjoying each other's company, recognising in Eddie the mark of a maverick; a bright-eyed and attractive girl with a bright gleam of intelligence and a hint of 20th century rebellion about her. Sarah had that uneasy feeling shared by all parents who realise their apron strings would soon no longer hold their children.

The procession's tail was approaching as each band reached its appointed position and concluded the music with a flourish of drums, while floats and military ranks came to a halt in orderly lines. James looked toward the end of the dragon's tail as cheering rose anew and hats were thrown into the air. The source of the tumult was the soon-to-be Governor-General, Lord Hopetoun and his wife Lady Hopetoun, rounding the bend and waving to the crowds from an open horse-drawn carriage.

The ceremony inside the central pavilion was out of ear-shot for most of the crowd, but all knew that Lord Hopetoun was being sworn in as Australia's first Governor-General, and would then proclaim the Commonwealth of Australia, and swear in its first Prime Minister, Sir Edmund Barton and his ministry. Queen Victoria had asked her Secretary of State for the Colonies to pass on this message through Sir Edmund:

TELEGRAM

THE QUEEN COMMANDS ME TO EXPRESS THROUGH YOU TO THE PEOPLE OF AUSTRALIA HER MAJESTY'S HEARTFELT INTEREST IN THE INAUGURATION OF THE COMMONWEALTH, AND HER EARNEST WISH THAT UNDER DIVINE PROVIDENCE IT MAY ENSURE THE INCREASED PROSPERITY AND WELL-BEING OF HER LOYAL AND BELOVED SUBJECTS IN AUSTRALIA.

After the swearing-in was over and the official papers signed, The Prime Minister appeared from the shadows and waved his hat to the crowd, and a fusillade of 21 cannons opened up; each with a deafening volley and a curling puff of white smoke. Shouts of awe rippled across the crowd until the echoes of the last explosion faded from the low hills, and an almighty roar went up from the crowd. Australia had been born.

It would be just over two weeks later in London, on January 17, that the queen's health would take a severe turn for the worse. When she awoke that morning, her personal physician, Dr. Reid, noticed that the left side of her face had sagged, and her speech had become slightly slurred. She had suffered a minor stroke, and more would follow. Early in the morning of January 19, she seemed to rally. She asked Dr. Reid if she was better, to which he assured her she was, but she quickly slipped from consciousness again. She was dying. Her children and grandchildren were summoned, and at 6:30 p.m. on January 22, Queen Victoria died aged 81, surrounded by her family.

~ ~ ~

Black clouds rolled over Sydney on a Sunday night in May 1902. At first the rain was coy and flirtatious; just a tantalising spot here and there, but it quickly gained confidence, and soon, fat blobs hit the pavement like breaking eggs as the torrent opened up. It was a sound that Sydneysiders had almost forgotten; the drought that began in 1895 had drained the Darling River and halved the number of livestock across the country. Farmers had lost everything–most of them walked off the land without even bothering to shut the gate. But after seven years, the rains had come at last, and Sydney breathed a sigh of relief.

James and Sarah were in the kitchen washing dishes. Rain on the Royal's tin roof sounded like stones, and its unmistakable smell, a musky mixture of vegetation, steaming road tar and damp earth, wafted in through the window.

James put a cup on the dish-rack. 'This'll lot will tell us if the roof leaks.'

Sarah paused with her tea-towel. 'And whether the drains work. Remember the last drought back home?'

'I sure do, in 1870, and the big finale was that damn bushfire coming through the farm like a steam train. By God, Sarah, we've been lucky. We've got four good kids, we've been in Sydney two years and the pub's doing well, and we have each other.' He lay his hand over her arm and smiled. 'By the way, how do you put up with an old bastard like me?'

She patted his hand and gave him a condescending smile. 'Simple love; I just ignore you.'

James pulled the rubber plug from the sink, sending sudsy water spiralling down the drain with a low gurgle.

'You know, that tramline's a godsend. It couldn't have been better if I'd planned it myself.'

The old steam trams took their last journey that year when the tramline linking the city with Coogee was electrified. The alternative route came right past the Royal in Perouse Street, then turned down St. Paul's Street to Coogee Beach. Pub regulars would stop off for a couple of beers on the way home, then hop another tram for the rest of the journey, or walk home in Randwick.

Sarah wiped her hands on the tea towel; stacking glasses in the cupboard. 'You know love, when we first got here, I was so worried that we wouldn't make ends meet, but as it's turned out, I wonder why I ever had doubts.'

James took her hands in his. 'It's your dour Scottish upbringing, my girl; Your Jock's daughter, through and through. We're like a pair of explorers, you and me; I charge around in circles like a blue-arsed fly, and you watch out for the wombat holes. That's why we've succeeded - you pull me back when I go off on some half-arsed scheme.'

She grinned. 'Yes, but sometimes it's like talking to a brick wall.'

James grinned. 'Jim's done a great job running the bar and keeping the place looking good. When I get too old to run this place, it'll be entirely his show; and then there's John and Danny after him.'

'And Cath?' Sarah asked.

James leant back in his chair. 'If she wants to, but somehow I can't see that happening; she's too smart to be a publican like her old man. And things are changing; there's more for a woman to do now besides being barefoot and pregnant. I think she'll want to go to university.'

Sarah nodded. 'You're right. She has the brains, but it's a man's world out there.'

James drained his glass. 'Yep, but that girl has a steel rod up her back; she'll come out on top, you wait and see.'

~ ~ ~

The Edmonstone family home loomed above Elizabeth Bay like a Grenadier Guard. The two-storey Georgian house was rigidly symmetrical, with 12-pained windows encased in stone, two double chimneys and a central entry portico with a circular stone arch. Cath thought it looked rather foreboding, like a police station or a courthouse. Eddie said it reminded her of Darlinghurst Jail, telling Cath that she'd devised a foolproof plan of escape when the time was right.

The girls lay on the floor of Eddie's bedroom in shafts of sunlight through billowing curtains. Outside, horses clipped along MacLeay Street, where the cries of paper boys and street hawkers floated up to the window. They were flicking through the *'David Jones Summer of 1902 Shopping Catalogue'*, their black-stockinged legs kicking rhythmically back and forth as they examined sketches of the latest fashions.

Eddie read a caption: *'House of Chantelle: Coral Silk Afternoon Dress, Sweet, simple and sophisticated.'* She wrinkled her nose. 'She looks like a wedding cake. Is that an albatross on her head?'

'Ladies keep their shape in a Royal Worcester Corset. Medium cotton, elastic, bone, metal. All sizes.' Cath giggled. 'Just what I wanted–trussed up in bone and metal, barely breathing; like a strangled sparrow.'

'Impress your guests with this beautiful white and black lace dinner gown. One-piece, cream lace with black Chantilly lace swags on bodice & lower hem, princess lines, scoop neck, short sleeves, bodice with jet & turquoise beads & jet ovals.' Eddie paused on this one. 'That one's not half bad, but I don't have the coconuts to fill it out.' Cath wore a puzzled look. 'Coconuts?' Eddie rolled her eyes. 'Yes, silly! You know, bubbies! Cupid's kettle drums! BREASTS, you

half-wit!' The two collapsed into howls of laughter; forgetting all about the catalogue.

Their laughter subsided into chuckles, and in the congenial silence that followed, Eddie lay on her back in a shaft of sunlight, gazing idly at the rose pattern snaking along the cornices. Her winsome face became pensive and she let out a long, dramatic sigh. 'My God, Cath, do you realise that next year we'll sit the "Leaving Certificate", and will finally be rid of St Vincent's?'

Cath propped her chin on a hand. 'I know; it's scary, isn't it? What are you going to do when you leave school, Ed?'

Eddie grimaced in mock agony. 'My father wants me to be a "proper lady", and "settle down", which translated means finding a rich husband, having lots of babies, and being boring. But what's the point of learning about history and science and all those other things, if you're going to become a vegetable?'

Cath studied her friend's countenance with curiosity. 'And what do *you* want?'

Eddie smiled and lowered her voice. 'I want to be an actress.'

'Gee, that sounds wonderful! You'd be so good on the stage.'

'Do you really think so? I read about films all the time; the glamorous actresses in their beautiful gowns, and the handsome men. They're making films in California now. That's where I'd like to go. What about you?'

Cath's eyes flittered self-consciously. 'Promise you won't laugh?'

'Cross my heart and spit in your eye.'

'I'm going to be a doctor.'

Eddie smiled. 'You know what? I thought you'd say that.'

'You did? Why?'

'Because you always get the best marks in science; and because, like me, you're not going to just sweep floors, cook, and have babies.' She punched Cath playfully on the shoulder. 'You and I are going to break all the rules. We're going to have a wonderful, exciting life–and bugger the consequences!'

Approaching her 15th birthday, Cath was a striking girl. She had her grandmother's chestnut hair, her eyes sparkled ice-blue, and her smile was a summer sunrise. Her life as a publican's daughter was her first university. As a girl polishing glasses in the pub's kitchen, she'd eavesdropped on the tales of sea-captains, drovers, paupers and prophets. It also exposed her to the darker side of life--the battlers, bludgers and blackguards, who helped forge her personal values and sharpen her perseverance to succeed where they had failed. Her drive and intellect would be invaluable in her quest for success, and she'd need every advantage in the male-dominated world of medicine.

~   ~   ~

A school of garfish floated in a cloud of silver off Sydney Heads; their zigzag ballet perfectly synchronised. Two hundred metres away, a pod of bottlenose dolphins caught their echo and cut through the water like an arrow. The hunters surrounded the school; attacking with timing and precision until they'd eaten their fill, then beat their flukes southward toward Coogee beach. Within minutes they'd echo-located three young boys skylarking among the waves, and broke the surface in a majestic leap before darting away to the open sea.

John Thornton and his two mates dove under the waves on the lip of a sandbar about fifty metres off the beach. John broke through the curve of a collapsing breaker and caught the last glimpse of the dolphins' farewell ballet.

'Geez! Did ya see that?' He called excitedly to the others, pointing out to sea.

Bill surfaced with hair plastered over his eyes, 'See what?'

'Three dolphins just jumped out there!'

'Yeah, they do that all the time, stupid.'

'Not three at once, they don't.'

'You're seeing things. The heat's got ya.'

'I'm telling you there were three; all at once, like a circus or something.'

Charlie turned to catch a swell. 'Come on; race you back to the beach.'

The boys launched themselves into a wave that slowed and died as they crossed a channel near the sand; and the three waded forward; giggling and elbowing each other aside. They gained purchase on the sandy bottom and sprinted up the shore, collapsing in a riot of laughter.

They lay on the warm sand, panting from the race as drops of saltwater on their eyelashes caught the sun. Twelve-year-old John had grown into a lean young man with his mother's good looks; bright blue eyes, a mop of dark hair and a firm jawline. Bill Bradley, the joker of the trio, was tough and stocky, with sandy hair and a winning smile. Charlie Schumacher, tall, with ginger hair and a mass of freckles, was a tearaway kid who was always in trouble.

Coogee Beach lay in shimmering heat under blue cobalt. Swimmers in neck-to-knee costumes glided over the swells as they rolled to the shore. The beach stretched away in a wide crescent where groups of men and women in fashionable Edwardian street clothes chatted together, enjoying the sea air. Men wore suits and ties; only a few had removed their coats in deference to the heat. Women shading beneath lacy white parasols wore long flowing dresses and close fitting, high-necked blouses. Children darted in and out of the throng, giggling and chasing one another through the surf.

John and his mates had become inseparable since meeting at St Mary's Cathedral High School. While Randwick and Coogee were slowly becoming urbanised, there were still plenty of trees to climb, knees to skin, rocks to throw and dirt roads to wander down. A couple of creeks ran down from the surrounding hills, meandering through the marshes bordering Coogee Beach-a perfect place for a boy to give full rein to a healthy imagination. A tree-covered bank would host Robin Hood's battle with Little John; a sandy clearing was the perfect place to dig for buried treasure, and a winding track was the ideal location for bushrangers to bail up a Cobb & Co coach.

Fishing the creeks became something of a passion for the boys when they learned that a local fishmonger would pay a penny for every freshly caught eel-and a bamboo pole, a length of string and a piece of rotting meat was all they needed. The method was simple; dangle the meat in the water and watch for the tell-tale flick of the eel's tail as it investigated the tantalising smell. Wait until its jaws closed over the bait, then pull like buggery on the bamboo pole. With any luck, the eel, reluctant to let go, would be dragged onto the muddy bank, and one of the boys would land an almighty blow with a stout tree-branch; and hey presto, they were a penny richer.

Little did the trio realise that they weren't the only ones in the neighbourhood to have embarked on a commercial fishing career. One Saturday afternoon a group of three young lads from Randwick High School parted the reeds and strode into view. Their leader, a tall, wiry boy in canvas dungarees and a battered felt hat, spoke first.

'You bloody Catholics're trespassing on private property.'

There was a well-known rivalry between schoolboys from opposing faiths in Sydney; a prejudice no doubt acquired from their parents in a day when religious intolerance was both severe and vocal. Charlie Schumacher didn't waste time reacting to the insult.

'Oh yeah? So, you public school blokes own Coogee, do ya?'

'That's right, and we own those eels too, so hand the bloody things over or we'll just have to take 'em off ya.'

John felt danger tingle in his gut. He tensed as Charlie stood to his full height and swaggered toward his antagonist. 'Now, that's not manners, old son. We caught these eels without your bloody help, and we'll sell 'em without your bloody help, too, so you lot can piss off.'

And without warning it was 'on for young and old.'

The interloper swung an unexpected punch into Charlie's stomach; doubling him over, and his two mates came at John and Bill Bradley, fists raised.

Bill, being one of five brothers, was no stranger to a 'blue', and without waiting for an invitation, hurled himself at one of the other boys, driving his shoulder in and bringing him down heavily in the long grass.

John saw a 'haymaker' coming at his face and weaved backwards out of range; shooting out a straight left and connecting to a nose.

In keeping with his ginger hair, Charlie was the owner of a volatile temper. He'd recovered from his body-blow, and letting out a blood-curdling wail, threw himself at his assailant; both of them landing with a thud.

The brawl became a melee of flying fists, curses and clouds of dust; a foot in the gut here, a handful of hair there, and over there, a kick in the nuts. John's opponent had crumpled to the ground, holding a broken nose and bereft of any further fight. Bill had pummelled his attacker into submission, and Charlie had the leader in a headlock, threatening to ram him into a nearby iron-bark tree. From underneath Charlie's armpit came the muffled but well-recognised surrender: 'Give! Give!'

The invaders had had enough, and struggling slowly to their feet, limped back from the muddy creek bank in the direction whence they came. Their leader turned. 'You blokes haven't seen the last of us; just you bloody wait!'

Charlie wiped the blood from his mouth and smiled, 'We'll be right here if you want another go, old son!'

That day would live forever in the memories of the three boys, and be told, re-told, and embellished many times in the years to follow. It would however be only twelve years later that they would be involved in a battle that was to be devastating on a global scale.

Chapter 4

Love and Other Sparks

Sydney Morning Herald
Saturday 9 July 1904
**SWITCHING ON THE LIGHTS
SYDNEY ELECTRICALLY ILLUMINATED.
THE LADY MAYORESS TURNS THE KEY.**

Shortly after 5 o'clock last evening, the
Lady Mayoress of Sydney turned a gold
key at the new power house, Pyrmont,
and a few minutes later, a number of
great arc lights and small globes were
illuminating the rain soddened city.
The Lord Mayor set the machinery in
motion, and the Lady Mayoress turned
the switch-key. There was no sudden
burst of light. Only two small globes had
been fixed, and a minute after the key
had been turned, they became gradually
illuminated.

The Lady Mayoress said, 'I have much pleasure in switching on the electric light for the city of Sydney. I trust it will be a boon to the citizens and an encouragement to the enterprise of the City Council.'

Umbrellas blossomed like black roses as people scurried through the rain. Secretaries held onto their hats for the dash across Castlereagh Street to catch a cab; the drivers hunched over in the downpour. Paper-boys hid their early editions under canvas cloaks as they called out headlines in their exclusive dialect. 'Paaaayyyyperrr! Getcha Sydney Mornin' Herald! The city gets Eeeeleeeectricity! The switch comes on tonight!'

For over fifty years Sydneysiders had moved through city streets with gas lamps projecting a feeble halo of light. A city's dark crevices can harbour danger; a shadow here, a faint boot scuff there, and Sydney's citizens were strong in their support for electric lighting. The state capital had been slow to adopt electricity - as early as 1891 the towns of Young, Penrith, Moss Vale and Broken Hill had set up their own supply systems. More embarrassingly, Redfern, so close to the municipality of Sydney, had already built its own powerhouse.

The transition to electricity as the city's principal power source was to be a slow process, mired in a controversy largely brought about by the Australian Gas Light Company itself. Under siege by the competition and at the end of its monopoly, the AGL began a campaign of misinformation, claiming that electricity leaked through the ground and played havoc with one's intestines. Suddenly, the price of rubber-soled shoes skyrocketed as Sydney's populace sought to protect themselves from the deadly threat of electric power.

Each Sydney gas lamp produced about 40 candlepower of light—some said that gaslight was so dim you had to strike a match to see if it was lit. But on this night, July 8, 1904, 343 electric streetlights, each shining at 2000 candlepower, would light up the city like New Year's fireworks from Circular Quay to Redfern Railway Station, and from Hyde Park to Darling Harbour. Sydney was about to shine.

~ ~ ~

A couple of miles away from the city centre, 9-year-old Danny Thornton leant elbows on the upstairs balcony of the Randwick Royal; eyes fixed on the huddle of buildings where the lights were to appear. He often came up to this spot to watch the parade of life play out on the streets below. The four years he'd spent in Sydney had seen a remarkable improvement in his health - his asthma had disappeared, and swimming at Coogee had developed his once-narrow chest.

He was the image of his father, with sandy-brown hair dropping over his forehead, expressive grey-blue eyes and a strong build reflecting his newly gained health. Despite the physical similarities, his personality contrasted with James's. While his father was 'a bit of a dreamer', and prone to emotional decisions, Danny pondered matters before reacting. He was well considered and logical, and the owner of a sharp wit.

He was drawn to the birth of Sydney's lights by his fascination with history and the excitement of new horizons. In the distance, bruised clouds drifted through a leaden sky, trailing a grey mist of rain, and underneath the canopy, Sydney brooded like a dark Camelot.

~   ~   ~

At precisely 5pm that Friday evening, under a winter sky already darkened with rain clouds, the city burst with a soundless explosion of light. Pedestrians crossing Hyde Park sprinted to the shelter of trees from a suspected lightning strike, and possums darted back into the leaf canopy, wondering where the night had gone. The lamps in Bridge Street had been moved to the centre of the ample thoroughfare, and when they erupted into life, disoriented pedestrians wandered aimlessly in a street they had no recollection of. In Darling Harbour, ladies of the night edged away from the harsh glare and calmly re-applied their makeup.

~ ~ ~

Danny was thinking something had gone wrong when a burst of light pierced the clouds like an enchanted sword. A flock of white cockatoos rose from Hyde Park, and the city suddenly glowed in a pearly lustre. A broad smile spread across his face at the promise of a future as bright as Sydney's new electric halo.

~ ~ ~

Jim Thornton swung down from the tram in Elizabeth Street on a humid afternoon in March 1907. Bloated clouds to the south promised a thunderstorm, and the wind was freshening. Dressed in a grey suit and straw boater, the 27-year-old strode down Liverpool street, cigarette dangling from his mouth as he weaved through a sea of pedestrians. His rangy frame and broad shoulders held the suggestion of a boxer, but the handsome, unmarked face and straight nose put that notion to rest - it was sheer hard work at the Royal that kept him lithe and strong.

He rounded the corner of Goulburn Street to the entrance of '*Anthony Hordern and Sons New Palace Emporium*'. Stretching across half a city block, the five-storey department store, in the words of its proprietor, sold 'everything from a needle to an anchor'. An imposing marble entrance was flanked by tall windows displaying mannequins in the latest fashion, and many up-to-the-minute items of furniture, glassware, and appliances were on display. Above the archway, carved into the marble, was the Hordern family motto: '*While I Live, I'll Grow*', with the company's oak tree logo. A uniformed doorman tipped his cap in greeting as Jim entered through glass doors. In a couple of weeks, it would be his mother's birthday - Sarah was fond of jewellery, but seldom bought any for herself, and he was on a mission for a gift to mark her 54 years.

An extensive array of merchandise greeted him as he navigated wide aisles flanked by young women in uniform. Ladies' cosmetics of every shape and colour lined the shelves as customers stared into mirrors, vigorously applying dabs of Ponds Cold Cream or Kiehl's Musk Essence Oil. Above the shelves, the signage spoke encouraging words: '*Feel Young Again*', and '*All Products for Popular Young Ladies*'.

Confectionary counters sparkled with a rainbow display of cellophane and silver paper, proffering the popular European brands Lindt and Neuhaus. Near the elevator he passed the smoking department, where 'Bond Street', 'Benson & Hedges' and 'Capstan' cigarettes depicted scenes of elegant drawing-rooms; while Cavendish and Brightleaf pipe tobacco displayed a range of meerschaum pipes. The signage spoke: *'Strong Men Smoke Capstan'*, and *'Cavendish For Your Pipe, And Nothing Less.'*

He pressed the button and within a few seconds the car glided to a stop. A uniformed operator slid back the scissor-gate, releasing shoppers clutching their purchases and chatting to one another. 'Which floor for you, sir?' 'Fourth, thanks mate.' The gate slid shut with a metallic clunk and the elderly driver rotated a lever to glide upwards. The walls contained oak panels with brass trimming; each bearing a metallic bas-relief of the Hordern oak tree. The driver wore a dark blue suit with matching peaked cap, giving him a military appearance. The floor was announced at each stop: 'First floor, ladies and gentlemen; men's and women's apparel, travel goods, tailor shop and shoe-shine. Watch your step.'

He exited on the fourth floor to the women's jewellery department, where rows of glass-topped counters displaying rings, bracelets, necklaces, earrings and pendants stretched across the floor. His mother was fond of pendant earrings, but beyond that, his knowledge of women's jewellery was about as extensive as his expertise in thermodynamics. Suddenly he felt out of his depth, and looking around for a sales assistant, he gasped involuntarily at the most beautiful woman he'd ever seen.

She was tall, with slender arms clasped loosely in front of her, scanning the floor for customers. Her honey-coloured hair, swept up from her neck, caught the light like sunrise on sandstone, and she wore the hint of a smile as if sharing a secret. But it was her large, hazel eyes that most enchanted him. They burned with intensity under sleepy lids and seemed to say 'I can see into your soul'; and at that very moment they did just that, as she locked with Jim's gaze and impaled him like a butterfly on a pin.

His legs seemed to move of their own accord, and suddenly he was standing across the counter from her. She smiled and his heart waved a white flag of surrender.

'Can I be of help, sir?' Jim took control of his slack bottom jaw and summoned breath to speak. 'Aaah….yes, thanks….I'm looking for a gift……earrings for my…..mother, miss….'

'Hargreaves,', she replied. 'Elizabeth Hargreaves. Do you have any preference for style?'

Jim knew he was sounding like a village idiot, and shook himself out of his trance. 'Well, she usually wears the ones that dangle.'

Elizabeth's smile widened. 'That's a fortunate coincidence; we have a sale on a range of pendant earrings. If you like, I can show you some examples.'

She produced dozens of black velvet trays with a mesmerising array of sparkling jewellery in silver, gold and platinum; set with diamonds, rubies, sapphires and pearls in a never-ending parade of styles and prices. Jim's head swam with a confusion of options, many of which were well out of his price-bracket, and while he listened to Elizabeth's comments and suggestions, he suddenly realised that the matter of buying a gift had been completely overtaken by his infatuation with this beautiful Hordern sales assistant. He'd taken good notice of the fact that she wore no wedding or engagement ring, and at one point he thought he caught her glancing at *his* left hand.

Jim wasn't a schemer, but in matters of love, the art of cunning is often a useful ally; or in John Lyly's words of 1579, 'All is fair in love and war.' He had to see this woman again, and if he made his purchase today, he'd have no excuse to come back. To stall for time, he nodded and smiled at her sales presentation.

'Thank you for your help, Miss Hargreaves.' He said as she returned the last earring display to its case. 'I really can't decide between the sapphire teardrop and the hexagonal ruby. Would you mind if I came back again?'

Her smile was taking no prisoners as she replied with a spark of mischief in her eyes. 'Why not buy both pairs–one for your mother, and one for your sweetheart?'

Jim was taken aback by her comment, and laughed nervously, but didn't let the chance go by. 'Well, I'd have to find a sweetheart first.' He offered his hand. 'Until next time?'

She shook his hand. 'Until then. Mr.….?'

'Thornton. Jim Thornton.'

He exited the doors of Hordern's as the 'southerly buster' arrived. Rain fell in sheets and thunder roared like a field gun. Pedestrians struggled with umbrellas turned inside-out from the wind. He lingered for a while under the awning, breathing deep of the fresh, rainy air; his mind a whirl. He'd never been a 'ladies' man'. Being rather shy with first encounters, he preferred to hang back and get his bearings. He'd had a couple of dalliances with women since arriving in Sydney seven years before, but none had led to anything lasting.

But this was different. It was as if the world was visible through another lens; a lens which, despite his logical and organised mind, had unleashed a myriad of emotions washing over him like a beach shore break. As he stood amid the storm, his first thought was 'When can I see her again?'

~ ~ ~

A Bondi tram rattled along Old South Head Road on a warm Saturday afternoon carrying weary commuters home from work. Jim stared absently from the window, wishing he was somewhere else, for today he would meet Elizabeth's parents.

He'd returned to Hordern's Emporium the next day, determined to speak to her again, but as the lift reached the fourth floor, his courage disappeared like a bandicoot down a hole, and suddenly he was 7 years old again, playing one of the three wise men in a school Christmas play. As the baby Jesus shone in his crib surrounded by Mary and Joseph (and a stuffed donkey from 'Blair's Taxidermy' on Anson Street), his mind had gone blank with fear. What were his lines again?

He was to lead the other two 'wise men' onto the stage carrying a cigar box disguised as a golden casket, and declaring boldly: *'We are three wise men from the north, and bear gold, frankincense and myrrh for the baby Jesus'*, but what left his quavering young voice was: *'We are three wide men from up north. We've got gold and Frankenstein, and fur for the baby Jesus.'* It was the end of a short and undignified stage career, and like a recurring nightmare, the memory flooded back to him in times of stress.

It was on his second sortie to Hordern's that he purchased Sarah's sapphire teardrop earrings and invited Elizabeth for a coffee in the rooftop dining room. She was vivacious and intelligent, with a lively sense of humour, and Jim's reserved nature eventually turned to bravado as he took the plunge and invited her out to the pictures. Elizabeth smiled. 'I'd be delighted.' Then, pausing for a moment, added: 'One minor matter, Jim; my parents are rather protective; would you be willing to meet them first? I promise they won't bite.'

He stepped down from the tram in search of number 227. The evening sun filtered through a row of fig trees, and a sea breeze cooled him down after the heat of the tram. The houses he passed were a time capsule of Old South Head Road's long history. A few humble bush bungalows hearkened from a time when a mere dirt track led out to Macquarie Lighthouse. One or two old farmhouses, their land long ago carved up for building blocks, held on stubbornly to a bygone century, while the more contemporary dwellings wore the fresh paint of Sydney's quickening pulse since Federation.

Number 227 was a white, single-storey bungalow settled comfortably amid low hedges and a well-kept lawn. A tall willow stood to one side; its branches sweeping back and forth in the breeze. A deep veranda ran across the front and down one side under iron lattice work. Three chimneys rose from a slate roof, and bay windows flanked a generous timber stairway leading to the front door. It was a comfortable house that beckoned the visitor; unless of course the visitor was one Jim Thornton, who felt like a fawn entering the wolf's den.

He knocked, and footsteps approached from inside. The door opened to a slightly built man in his late 40s; his expressive, hazel eyes fixing Jim with a smile beneath a wide forehead and sandy hair. He was a good six inches shorter than Jim, who immediately recognised the same sleepy eyelids that riveted him when he first saw Elizabeth.

He held out a hand in greeting.

'George Hargreaves. You must be Jim Thornton.'

Jim shook his hand. 'Yes. I'm pleased to meet you.'

George opened the door wide. 'Please come in.'

He entered a comfortable sitting room where Elizabeth and her mother rose from their chairs in greeting. Mrs. Hargreaves was tall, with dark, wavy hair. She wore a full dress in deep blue. Elizabeth clasped Jim's hands with a reassuring smile. 'Jim, this is my mum, Matilda.' She shook Jim's extended hand and replied. 'Welcome to our home, Jim.'

After the introductions and a round of tea, where Jim told the Hargreaves of his background in the Central West, the ladies cleared plates while George steered him out onto the side veranda where a bottle of beer, condensation rolling down its sides, waited beside two glasses on a low table between wicker armchairs. George poured their drinks and Jim took a long pull from his glass. It was as welcome as a cloudburst on a dry day.

Hargreaves's eyes held a certain sharpness. 'Jim, I'll get straight to the point. You seem like a nice young lad. Elizabeth's my eldest daughter, and this is the first time she's brought a young man into our home, so she thinks very highly of you.' Jim smiled at this, and Hargreaves continued. 'Elizabeth means the world to us, of course, and we'd be devastated if she was hurt by a relationship that went sour. I hope you won't give us cause to regret that she met you, because a Hargreaves does not forgive, nor forget.'

Jim paused for a moment to stare at the amber bubbles rising from his glass, reflecting on what he'd heard. He returned Hargreaves' stare with his own; his nervousness suddenly falling away. 'Mr. Hargreaves, I appreciate your directness. I've only known Elizabeth a short time, but I've never felt this way about anyone else before, and I doubt I ever will again.'

He put his glass on the table. 'I was lucky enough to grow up in a loving family with a strong set of values and a fundamental philosophy - to treat others the way you would want to be treated. The Thorntons are a family of strong men and women who live by their word, and my word to you is that I'll never give you cause to regret. I don't know what the future holds for Elizabeth and I, but I know that it will be a future in which I will always be true to my values. That's all I can say.'

The sharpness in Hargreaves's eyes had all but disappeared.

~ ~ ~

They boarded a tram and reached the city as a deep-purple evening sky surrendered to a three-quarter moon - walking arm-in-arm in flippant banter up George Street to the floodlit facade of the 'Empire Cinema'. The latest American silent comedy, 'How Brown Saw the Baseball

Game' was playing. They laughed and gasped in delight as trick photography portrayed how the intoxicated Mr. Brown saw the game in reverse, and in the darkened cinema, Jim's hand strayed across the arm of his seat to meet Elizabeth's in a gentle caress.

A late-night coffee in Rowe Street and a sleepy ride back to Bondi on the last tram saw them at Elizabeth's front gate. Old South Head Road was deserted - possums scampered through moonlit branches high in the willow tree. She looked up into Jim's eyes and chuckled. 'My father is a beast sometimes, but he was smiling when we left. What on earth did you say to him?' Jim plucked a sprig of willow-leaf, placing it in her hair. She looked like a Celtic priestess. 'I just told him the truth.' And with that, they shared a kiss that neither would ever forget.

The last tram had been put to bed at Waverley depot, and the moon was well past its zenith. Old South Head Road slumbered through the early hours of Sunday as Jim began the long walk back to Randwick; his feet failing to touch the ground.

~ ~ ~

Sydney Morning Herald
21 October 1907
THE ORDER OF THE BATH.
DEMONSTRATIONS OF PROTEST.
SCENE ON THE OCEAN BEACHES.

Some thousands of spectators visited
Sydney ocean beaches yesterday
morning to see what the surf-bathers'
next move would be in regard to the new
draft ordinances. The swimmers
themselves had organised a protest of a
humorous character, and carried it out in
detail, and without giving offence.

The draft ordinances to govern surf
bathing have been denounced on all
sides during the past week. The
spectators probably outnumbered
bathers by four to one at each beach, and
photographers were conspicuous.

A sea eagle launched herself from a tall eucalypt at
Watson's Bay, banking southward in search of prey.
Swooping low, she skimmed turquoise waters speckled
with waving kelp, hunting turtle, fish and penguin, but
her low pass as far as Ben Buckler Point proved fruitless.
She beat up higher into the sun and turned over Gordons
Bay, but again, nothing. Picking up a thermal over
Wedding Cake Island, she banked and turned her dark
eyes toward Coogee Beach.

The fairy penguin gave herself away with a flipper flashing in the sunlight, and from a height of 200 yards the eagle went into a dive - razor sharp talons curled for the kill. She came out of the sun, hitting the bird at 50 mph and lifting off from the water with her catch secured. She turned northward, back to her hungry chicks.

As the eagle's drama played out, John Thornton and his mates Bill and Charlie body-surfed off a sand bar at low tide. The boys had matured to young men since their days fishing the creeks of Coogee. They'd sat the 'Leaving Certificate' at St Mary's the year before and were now proud 'working men'. John was throwing beer kegs in the cellar of the Royal, Bill was apprenticed to his father as a butcher, and Charlie 'shovelled horse shit', as he put it, as a stableman at Randwick Racecourse.

The three scrambled from the water and dropped to the sand, watching the surf roll in. Bill shook his wet hair violently back and forth; spraying the others with beads of seawater. John punched his mate playfully on the arm. 'Hey! Cut that out! What are you, a bloody dog?' Charlie quipped; 'Nah, he's not a dog. Dogs're intelligent, and they've got bigger balls than old Billy-boy.'

Bill lobbed a handful of sand. 'Yeah? Drop your costume, old son, and we'll see whose balls are bigger.'

John broke in. 'Hey–speaking of costumes, did you hear about the demonstration tomorrow?'

Bill was puzzled. 'What demonstration?'

'An old bloke at the pub told me. The Council's trying to make men wear a special regulation swimsuit–with a skirt on it!'

Charlie laughed. 'Bullshit–that cove's havin' a lend of you, Johnny.'

'No, it's fair dinkum! He showed me the minutes from the Council meeting. He reckons there'll be hundreds here tomorrow.'

John was right. A few weeks earlier, the Mayor of Waverley, Alderman R. G. Watkins, had struck a blow for conservatism as he made an impromptu inspection of clothing standards at Bondi beach, and issued a blistering damnation: *'What we saw was disgusting. Some of these surf bathers are nothing but exhibitionists, putting on small trunks. They are in worse manner than if they were nude. But they won't continue doing it at Bondi Beach, not so long as I am mayor."*

Following the mayor's outrage, Waverly Council promptly issued an edict, aimed squarely at male bathers, for the type of bathing costumes allowable on all their beaches:

'A combination, consisting of a guernsey with trouser legs and reaching from near the elbow to the bend of the knee, together with a skirt not unsightly but simply attached to the garment and covering the figure below the hips to the knee.'

To add insult to injury, loitering on the beach was prohibited, and all communication between bathers and the public forbidden.

An attempt to have men wear dresses on the beach, or anywhere else, was always going to be about as popular as a fart in an elevator, and news of Waverley Council's Draconian edict travelled faster than lightning on roller skates. The newly formed Surf Bathing Association of New South Wales reacted promptly; planning an impromptu demonstration to parody the new regulations on Sunday 20 October at Bondi, Coogee and Manly.

~   ~   ~

John and Danny stirred from sleep as bells pealed from the 'Sacred Heart' church, calling the faithful to Sunday mass. Despite their Irish Catholic heritage, the Thorntons tried not to annoy God too much; especially since Sunday was their only day off. They reasoned that He was a very busy man too, and probably wouldn't notice their recalcitrance. Besides, since He rested on the seventh day, He wouldn't hold it against them if they did too; and anyway, Sarah always said enough prayers for the lot of them.

John rolled drowsily out of bed and dressed. Twelve-year-old Danny sat up, knuckling his eyes and blinking against sunlight pooling across the sheets.

'Where are you going, Johnny?'

'Gotta clean up in the cellar first, and get down to the beach before eleven o'clock.'

'What's going on down there? He gave a grin. 'Have you got a girlfriend?'

John threw a pillow at his brother. 'No, stupid. There's a demonstration today.'

'What's a demonstration?'

'It's like when you disagree with the rules and want to change a decision.'

'Like in Rugby when the ref gives a penalty to the other side?'

'Yeah, kind of.'

'Can I come?'

'Not this time, mate.'

'Why not?'

'Because you'd have to wear a dress.'

Danny watched his brother disappear out the door, hoping he wouldn't be as crazy as his brother when he was 17.

Coogee Beach shone in the sun as men of all ages, shapes and sizes turned up in the most outrageous clothing that a Sydney beach had ever seen. A large crowd of spectators leant elbows along the promenade railing, anticipating the spectacle to come. Although John had been the ringleader in this venture, a nagging doubt remained that the whole thing would be a hoax, as Charlie had thought, so at the last minute he'd thrown an old overcoat over his costume, just in case - but as he neared the beach, his doubts vanished as a young man passed by, wearing red 'long johns' under what appeared to be a Roman centurion skirt. John weaved through the crowd, searching for his mates, and stopped dead in his tracks when Charlie appeared.

He wore a pair of old blue overalls stained with horse manure, and around his hips dangled a large pink lampshade with a red frill, held up by a pair of suspenders slung over his shoulders. On his head a woman's calico bonnet in a fetching hue of yellow, tied up under his chin in a massive bow of green silk ribbon. As a rakish touch, a 'roll your own' cigarette dangled from the corner of his mouth. John convulsed with laughter as Charlie walked up with a wide grin on his face. 'Just as well you were right about this Johnny, or I would have been arrested by now.'

They heard a shout and turned to see Bill Bradley; a picture of radiance in a loosely laced corset above a pair of white 'grandma' bloomers reaching down to his hairy knees. He wore no hat, but a mass of pink curlers covered his dark hair. He wore a sheepish smirk and pointed to his hair. 'My mum did this. She reckons the mayor's an arse-hole.' The three erupted into laughter as Charlie regarded John with a sceptical look. 'All right sunshine, what's under the coat?' With a self-conscious grin, John shrugged off the overcoat to reveal one of Miss Minnie's magnificent Japanese kimonos in sky blue, with a daring slit up each side. He could have stepped from an Osaka whore house.

The beach was alive with colour and laughter like a burlesque show gone horribly wrong as five hundred demonstrators took up a ragged formation behind a large banner shouting *'Watkins Ordinance is a Dead Duck'*, and as if to underscore the slogan, a deceased seagull, which was given a wide berth by a downwind crowd, dangled from one upright. One conspicuous member of the throng wore his sister's old white wedding dress, its train washing in and out on the shore break. A little further down the ranks, a young, muscular man sported a grass skirt, with garish make-up, a large floppy sun-hat and carrying a rather stylish handbag over one arm. At the back of the crowd, one lone man wore a beer-barrel suspended from ropes over his shoulders.

The crowd was enjoying the spectacle, nudging one other and laughing as they pointed at the more outlandish sights. Not all the spectators were supportive, however; one man shouted out angrily: 'Go home you bloody hooligans, or I'll call the police!!' A loud retort fired back immediately: 'Too late, old son, where already in attendance!', as two off duty constables, wearing their uniforms garnished with white bloomers, strolled by. A burst of laughter and applause rose from the crowd.

One protester began calling out: 'Will we wear skirts?' And after a couple of repeat calls, in ones and two's, then in ten's and twenty's, voices answered back: 'Not on yer bloody life', and soon there were thousands of voices shouting the response. The marchers completed their lap of Coogee Beach and a roar went up as they broke ranks and ran for the surf. John, Bill and Charlie followed suit as five hundred costumed men cavorted in the waves with a steadily growing flotsam of wigs, corsets, tablecloths, bath mats and bonnets bobbing happily in the surf.

The *Sydney Morning Herald* had decried Waverley Council's Draconian regulations as *'an instance of the official mind run mad'*, and the public agreed. It wasn't long before the matter was quietly dropped, and although there was still a strong conservative movement across Sydney against anything seen as immoral (known as the 'Wowser' element), sanity had prevailed. The trio of John Thornton, Bill Bradley and Charlie Schumacher, and the rest of Sydney, had not only seen a peaceful demonstration bring about change; they had also seen 'beach culture' become key to the way Australians define themselves.

Chapter 5

Of Medicine, Marriage, and Maritime

The sun dangled in a faded blue sky on a humid Sunday evening in February 1908. Coogee beach had been crowded, but the streets soon emptied after the last sand-encrusted day-trippers boarded the tram for home. Upstairs at the Royal, James dissected a couple of roast chickens for dinner. The entire family was there and a pile of baked vegetables was disappearing by the forkful.

That afternoon James had opened the Royal's back door to the usual group of regulars who enjoyed a quiet, and illegal, drink or two on Sunday-a custom followed by most suburban publicans on favourable terms with the local constabulary. Jim and Elizabeth had picnicked under a fig tree in the Botanic Gardens, watching ferries plough through the harbour chop to Manly. Their courtship was under scrutiny by both families, and Sarah, though trying hard not to meddle, was already planning a wedding. John and Danny made liberal portions of chicken disappear under swirling cutlery-their appetites sharpened from a day at the beach. Twenty-year-old Cath, normally well-armed with barbs of sardonic wit, was unusually quiet, and the family understood why.

James grabbed a spoon and tapped his glass to quiet the rabble. 'Your attention please, everyone. As we know, tomorrow will be a special day for the Thornton family, when Cath enrols at Sydney University to study medicine.' Applause followed, and Cath smiled demurely with a nod and a wave as her father continued. 'As far as I'm aware, and I'd bet the Royal on this, Cath is the first Thornton in history to gain entry to university.' Danny piped up, 'Yeah, the rest of us are too smart for that.' Cath threw a napkin at her little brother. 'Cath,', continued James, 'We wish you every success in your studies. We're proud of you, love.'

It had been a long road for her, but having fixed a goal in her mind, there was no turning back. In her final year at St. Vincent's, Sister Alphonse, her science teacher, had taken Cath under her wing and coached her on as much physics, chemistry and biology as she could ingest. As Alphonse had confided to Cath at the end of a gruelling session one afternoon, 'Catherine, you must capitalise on the opportunities that women of my generation never had. We'll celebrate your achievements as though they were ours.' Come year-end, Cath graduated 'dux' of the school.

Her next hurdle was Sydney University's matriculation exams-notoriously tough, with a high failure rate. Painfully aware she needed practical experience, she badgered David Pilkington, the local Randwick chemist, for a job as an assistant and general dog's body, and once hired, bombarded him with incessant questions on chemistry, anatomy and cellular biology. Pilkington took the blows in good humour, knowing that the young woman would make a difference to the world.

She failed the exams two years running; but late in 1907, after three years of hard slog, she finally succeeded. But that was just the curtain-raiser to an even greater challenge-a medical profession steeped in conservatism and misogyny, blind to the 20th century's developing view on a woman's place in society.

~   ~   ~

The next morning she dressed conservatively to give herself a serious, 'bookish' air. She chose a charcoal-grey skirt and white cotton blouse, with a dark, wide-brimmed straw hat. She looked into her bedroom mirror: *'Suitably dowdy and shapeless—I could easily be a Quaker in this outfit.*' A tram trip up George Street past the newly completed Central Railway Station saw Sydney University looming in middle distance. Its imposing Gothic Revival buildings dated from the gold rush. Built of Pyrmont stone and cedar from the Tweed River, it recalled the great English universities of Oxford and Cambridge; frowning over the city like a humourless headmaster. A gravel road led up the hill to high stone walls befitting the battlements of an English castle, and a central archway beckoned inside to its cloisters. '*I wonder if it has a drawbridge, and a moat full of crocodiles?*' She thought.

Stepping down from the tram amid a crowd of students, she glanced up at the formidable walls, her initial sense of excitement suddenly dampened by a malevolent voice telling her she wasn't good enough. But she recalled a day eight years before, when she stood at the gates of St. Vincent's, intimidated by her first day of high school; and with the knowledge she had conquered those fears, summoned her courage and pressed forward.

She discovered there was no moat, nor crocodiles, and followed a knot of new students heading to the enrolment offices. She entered a high-ceilinged hall, and spying a door marked 'Faculty of Medicine', went in. Students stood in knots of conversation in a room entirely populated by men. At the front, a tall, stern-looking middle-aged man wearing a grey suit was behind a lectern. Despite her underlying nervousness, her natural extroversion drove her to initiate contact, and she approached a young man standing off to the side.

'Hello, I'm Cath Thornton. Are you enrolling today?'

He was about her age and height, with curly ginger hair and a slight frame, wearing thick wire spectacles that magnified the size of his brown eyes. He seemed startled at being approached, and shook her hand with rapid pumps.

'Yes. How do you do? I'm Peter; Peter Hannigan.'

She glanced about the room. 'It's quite a formidable place, don't you think?'

Peter nodded. 'I'm from Armidale. Everything in Sydney is formidable to me.'

'I know what you mean. I'm from Orange, but I've been here eight years. It's strange at first, but it's home to me now. One eventually gets used to the city.'

The ring of a bell interrupted them, and the room fell silent. 'Please take your seats, gentlemen, we're about to begin.' Peter glanced at Cath, aware of the faux pas, but she pretended not to notice. Chairs scraped the floor, and the man continued. 'My name is Professor Charles

Hammersmith, head of Sydney University's medical faculty, and I'm pleased to welcome you here.' As he continued, Cath noticed his eyes wandering in her direction. He was obviously aware he'd ignored the only woman in the room; but no acknowledgement followed.

The next two hours were a blur of information and form-filling, and her satchel was soon crammed with pamphlets, timetables and folders; her head reeling with half-remembered details. After the formalities, over tea and coffee she wandered to a small group of young men, presided over by a fellow student that she would soon come to know as Hugh Barrington–a graduate of the exclusive Kings School. He was tall and well-dressed, with a lick of dark hair falling over his forehead and small eyes that darted about as he spoke. He possessed an air of 'born to rule'; common among young men of wealth and privilege.

Barrington was holding court: 'My father is an eminent surgeon, so it was natural for me to follow in his footsteps. I intend to specialise in thoracic surgery after graduation.'

He glanced at Cath with a polite smile. 'I see we have a woman in our midst. What branch of medicine are you interested in, my dear?'

Her eyes darted around the group. 'Well, with the ink still wet on my enrolment form, it's a little early to say; but obstetrics interests me.'

Barrington tossed back his hair and smirked. 'Yes, but I understand that maids and midwives have the lion's share of that field.' A couple of chuckles sounded as he continued. 'It's a smaller specialisation; good for women though, as they find the physical work of a doctor much too demanding.'

Cath bristled at the insult; but remaining calm, fixed Barrington with a stare. 'Oh, so you ascribe to the view that women are the weaker sex?'

Barrington smiled. 'Well, miss……..'

'Thornton. Cath Thornton.'

'Miss Thornton; women are very emotional creatures.' He smiled at her again. 'Beautiful, but emotional, and not built to bear the stresses of the medical profession.'

She smiled… 'Mr……..'

He bowed slightly. 'Hugh Barrington, at your service.'

'Mr Barrington, are you familiar with a woman named "Zenobia?"

His brows knitted. 'No, I can't say that I am.'

'A Syrian Empress who conquered Egypt; defeating an army of 50,000 Roman soldiers. Perhaps you've heard of Mary Wollstonecraft, the women's activist who risked the guillotine in the French Revolution, or Joan of Arc?'

Attention was now on Cath as the group followed the verbal duel, and Barrington broke in. 'Joan of Arc heard voices, my dear; she was as mad as a March hare.'

'Mad enough to lead an army to defeat the English in the battle of Orleans in 1429.' She paused. 'Mr. Barrington, would you say that women who conquer empires, risk their heads on a chopping block and fight alongside men in hand-to-hand combat cannot bear stress?'

Barrington was forced into a corner and his calm reassurance of moments before quickly collapsed. His eyes flicked about the group with embarrassment. He mumbled, 'Well, those are just historical examples.'

'Yes, they are, but isn't it said that history has a habit of repeating itself?' Cath didn't wait for an answer, but went for the coup de gras. 'Mr. Barrington, hopefully your study of medicine will bring you to the realisation that opinions based on prejudice, and without solid data, are worthless.' Cath turned on her heel and walked from the room.

~   ~   ~

A pair of kookaburras perched on the spire of the 'Sacred Heart' Church in Avoca Street on a warm Saturday in November 1909. Afternoon sun lit their brown and blue feathers as they erupted into shrieking laughter.

Far below in the church's nave amid pews smelling of bee's wax, John Thornton elbowed his big brother with an aside. 'Hear that, Jimmy? Even the kookaburras reckon getting married is a bit of a joke.' He leant closer. 'It's not too late, you know. How about I create a diversion and you can beat it out the side door?' Jim stifled a grin. 'How about you just let us grown-ups get on with it, mate?' 15-year-old Danny, on Jim's other side, chipped in. 'Who said you were a grownup?'

Father Cameron materialised from the sacristy door while two altar boys with Brilliantined hair rose from their pews. A murmur rippled across the congregation- the bride was about to arrive. The three brothers moved to the head of the aisle as the church doors opened - silhouetting the bridal party in afternoon sunlight. The first notes of Mendelssohn's '*Wedding March*' sounded from the organ as all heads turned their way.

Bridesmaids led the party down the aisle in perfect time with the music, followed at a discreet distance by

Elizabeth, on her father's arm. In a long-flowing cream wedding gown, with the light shining onto her honey-coloured hair, she looked radiant. Her mind was a confusion of love, joy, pride, and not a little fear. She was acutely aware this moment was a defining point in her life-a landmark that would never come again; and she was torn between having it last forever, and just getting it the hell over with. Her eyes fixed on Jim at the end of the aisle, and the thought that he was the man she would spend the rest of her life with both warmed and terrified her.

The vision of his future wife gliding down the aisle was burned indelibly in Jim's memory. He wondered how lucky a man could be, and held no fear. No last-minute dash for freedom was on his agenda. This was for keeps. The party reached the head of the aisle and George gave Elizabeth's arm to Jim with a nod and a wink while James and Sarah looked on; each lost in their own thoughts.

As luck would have it, best man John hadn't forgotten to slip the wedding rings into his waistcoat, the bride and groom recited their vows without flaw, and no-one spoke up with 'any reason this man and woman should not be wed in holy matrimony.' The groom kissed the bride, the bridesmaids giggled, and Sarah dug into her purse for a dry hankie. High above Avoca Street, atop the church spire, the kookaburras gave another raucous laugh and launched toward a stand of gum trees at Randwick racecourse.

'The 'Sacred Heart' and the 'Royal' were built within a year of each other and conveniently separated by a mere 200 metres; and as the newly married couple and their entourage walked back up the aisle and out the front door, they turned left and headed for the Royal; followed at a respectful pace by the crowd of guests and family. It wasn't every day that Randwick witnessed a bride and groom and over 100 people strolling 'en masse' up Avoca Street and across High Cross Park. Passing vehicles tooted their horns and commuters leaned from tram windows, giving a whistle and cheer as they passed by. Up ahead, the grand old Royal waited in repose with its windows reflecting the setting sun; its doors open and welcoming.

The pub's dining tables were draped with starched linen, gleaming cutlery and wine goblets shining under chandelier light. Guests filtered through from the street and quickly filled the foyer with laughter as waiters relayed with trays of beer and champagne. The two senior Thornton brothers, Michael and John, now both in their 70s, had taken the train down from Orange, and brother James touched glasses with them both.

Michael swept his eyes around the Royal's interior. 'This pub's a bit of a change from the old 'Wellington Inn', mate.'

James smiled. 'Yep, when I was 15, the Wellington was a palace to me, but this puts it in the shade. But you know what? When it's all said and done, it's just a family home that has a pub downstairs.'

John pointed to the fireplace in the bar where the ancient 'nulla-nulla' hung above the mantlepiece. 'I see you're well prepared for a 'blue'.'

James grinned. 'Yes mate, and down in the cellar is a keg with both your names inscribed; see that you finish it tonight.'

Brother John's mind wandered back to his own wedding in 1862 at the family property in Orange, when he married Bridget, who had passed away only a year before. It had been a country wedding in a ring of gum trees under the stars; with prime spit-roast Gundungurra beef, old Irish music, kids running amok and people having a grand time. He wished Bridget could be beside him again tonight.

Jim and Elizabeth meandered through the gathering, accepting congratulations from friends and family. Sarah watched from the edge of the crowd; pride and happiness swelling in her breast as her mind travelled back 29 years to when Jim first came into the world under the care of midwife Edna Brown, now sadly passed away. He'd grown into a fine man, and one she was sure would make a fine husband.

The guests enjoyed a roast lamb dinner from the Royal's kitchen, and after the speeches, the band struck up; drawing the guests up to dance the tango, turkey trot and the hesitation waltz. The night was warm-an evening breeze carried the sea's tang through open windows.

Beer and wine flowed freely, and the night became a party. Miss Minnie, wearing her best kimono, demonstrated a new craze dance, the 'Cakewalk', with former 'Royal' owner Jo Hoskins, herself in a three-piece, deep grey suit. The Major, having consumed more than his usual amount of sherry, was loudly hailing the lounge as a 'damn fine club' to anyone who would listen. At one point, Father Cameron raised his eyes to heaven and formally blessed the pub and its guests - even the Protestants.

John and Danny surveyed the scene from their table; laughing at the good-natured antics of the guests. John was relieved that he'd gotten through his best man speech without getting tongue-tied, and had discovered that he didn't mind public speaking at all. Danny wondered what the attraction was for alcohol, if it made people take leave of their senses. For both boys, now 19 and 14, the concept of marriage and children was a far-off galaxy. The world waited at their feet, full of mystery and untold promise, and each had planned in their own way to take hold of life and ride it hard to a glorious future.

It was late in the evening when Inspector McManus begged a turn at the piano and played a new song that was becoming popular; 'Shine on Harvest Moon.' The babble from the guests quietened as the big man sang in a fine tenor voice:

'I can't see why a boy should sigh when by his side

Is the girl he loves so true,

All he has to say is 'Won't you be my bride,

For I love you?'

'I can't see why I'm telling you this secret,

When I know that you can guess,

Harvest moon will smile,

Shine on all the while,

If the little girl should answer "yes.'

'So shine on, shine on harvest moon

Up in the sky

I ain't had no lovin'

Since January, February, June or July.'

'Snow time, ain't no time to stay

Outdoors and spoon;

So shine on, shine on harvest moon

For me and my gal.'

Amid the applause, and as if on cue, Jim and Elizabeth appeared, dressed in their 'going away' outfits; Jim in a new suit of dark blue worsted, and Elizabeth in a fine tartan dress with matching tailored jacket, topped with a jaunty beret. The Renault taxi-cab stood waiting outside in Cuthill Street as the couple farewelled the guests. Tonight, they were off to the Hotel Australia in Castlereagh Street, and tomorrow they'd board the train to Medlow Bath in the Blue Mountains for a week at the 'Hydro-Majestic' Hotel. The uniformed driver held the door open, and as Elizabeth bent to enter the cab, her eyes caught her father's, holding a solemn look as he watched his 'little girl' leave him, in some ways, forever. She hesitated and blew him a kiss that meant more to George than life itself.

When the last champagne had been drunk, the last guest had weaved out the door, and with the laughter, music and love still ringing in their ears, James and Sarah sat in deep lounges enjoying a quiet nightcap; collars loosened and shoes removed.

James sipped his wine and chuckled. 'That's the first time I've ever seen a priest bless a pub.'

Sarah laughed. 'It's probably a sin; but with any luck, tomorrow the good Father will have no recollection of it.'

James leaned back in his chair. 'George Hargreaves told me about the first time he met Jim, and how he warned our boy in no uncertain terms not to cause him or Elizabeth any grief. Do you know what Jim said to him?

Sarah sat forward in interest. 'No, what did he say?'

'That the Thorntons were people of their word, and that George could trust him to be just that. George told me he's proud to have such a son-in-law, and that you and I are lucky.'

Sarah raised her glass to her husband with a smile. 'We didn't find our luck, sweetheart–we made our own.'

~   ~   ~

The sea reflected glazed sun as 16-year-old Danny Thornton squinted out past the break. A sudden gust of wind whipped sand against his legs as he surveyed the conditions for his surf patrol in December 1911. One of a small crew of volunteer lifesavers, he was 'belt-man' for the day, and there was none better at Coogee beach to swim out through the break on the end of a rope.

One wouldn't guess this young man to be the five-year-old who'd stepped from the train in 1900 with weak lungs and unused muscles; gasping for breath from a life-threatening asthma condition. His broad shoulders, narrow waist and deep chest were testament to years of physical training, and his dark good looks made quite a few young women hope they'd be rescued one day. He'd just completed his final year of high school at St Mary's, and had started work as an apprentice watchmaker at 'Prouds' Jewellers in Pitt Street.

As is often the case with the youngest child, his older siblings had overshadowed Danny. Jim, at 31, managed the pub now that their father was taking a back seat. Danny and Jim were similar in personality - quiet, thoughtful, imaginative and practical. Cath, 24, in her third year at university, was outgoing, smart and fiercely determined, and John, 22, was a born socialiser and risk-taker. He'd found a career at the Royal and loved the pub business. The Thornton children were all different, but they were close; there was nothing they wouldn't do for each other. The asthma had gotten Danny off to a slow start, but the experience had tapped a deep inner resilience that could overcome any obstacle put in his way, and this would serve him well in the years to come.

His love affair with the sea began when he was nine, with swimming lessons at Wylie's Baths. Sarah had rightly assumed that exercise would improve her son's breathing, and had invested her hopes in Wylie's as though it contained the miracle waters of Lourdes. Danny had only ever seen the sea in story books, but from the first time he plunged into the cool, salty water and felt the warm sun on his shoulders, he had found his element. The soft eddies caressing his skin as he stroked through the water became a soothing balm; and as he became stronger, he enjoyed nothing more than a long, hard swim, and that 'spent' feeling at the finish, when mind and body tingled with life.

He'd been body surfing at Coogee for years - he knew the sea's moods and the power of its waves. Instinct told him when to rise over the lip before it curled over into an avalanche, or dive deep beneath the crushing weight of white-water from a 'dumper'. He could spot a rip, its direction and strength, and keep his head in a dangerous situation. His membership of the Coogee Life Saving Brigade had refined his natural self-discipline and sense of teamwork-he knew all the knots, drills and signals of beach safety and rescue work. He was a volunteer, but his attitude was professional.

The conditions that day were not ideal. A four to five-foot surf was breaking in deep water about 50 metres out, but the south-east wind was kicking up a chop, making the waves sloppy and unpredictable. The current had churned a deep channel close to shore–swells collided with each other and swept back out in a boisterous rip. He planted the bathing flags beyond the danger zone, keeping swimmers close. At this early hour, only about a dozen people cavorted in the waves, enjoying the early sun. He blew his whistle and signalled the flags' position, and the crowd waded slowly back into the safe area.

The patrol crew monitored the conditions as the day progressed. The wind lifted in strength around midday and the waves were peaking their froth a little higher. The crowd had also grown, and the lifesavers continued to blow their whistles above the sound of crashing surf to keep them between the flags. Danny was at the water's edge when something caught his attention further out. He narrowed his eyes and scanned the spot, but white-water obscured his line of sight. Then suddenly, there he was-a young boy, a long way out-arm held vertically to signal distress. He had strayed from the flags and was caught in the rip.

He spun on his heels for a sprint to raise the alarm, but his mates had already caught the signal and were on the move toward him with the surf-reel. The team went into action in a drill they'd rehearsed many times. Team captain Matthew Staunton directed traffic as Danny secured the cork-filled vest and belt, and sprinted down to the water's edge. Four team-members had already fallen in behind him; lifting the rope above their heads as the lead man set the pace for line payout. Danny hit the water like a torpedo; hurdling the shore break and diving beneath waves in a bee-line to the struggling boy, now drifting out beyond the break.

The rope became heavier with each stroke as he propelled himself through the waves and more line was paid out. The team on the beach watched him like a hawk; keeping a steady pace. A knot of onlookers gathered as word of the rescue got around; and a couple of lifesavers kept them clear of the action.

Danny had covered more than half the distance to his target, and could now see the boy clearly. He was about 12, and drifting further out to sea, trying frantically to swim toward Danny against the rip-a futile attempt that would only drain his strength. Danny increased his stroke rate to close the gap.

He drew up to the boy, and the rope slackened as the team stopped paying out. Panic filled the boy's eyes, and he made a violent grab for Danny's neck, and in an oft-practiced manoeuvre, Danny spun around to grab the boy under the arms from behind.

'What's your name?'

'Help me, please!'

'What's your bloody name?'

'H, H, Henry,'

'Alright Henry, you're going to be fine. I've got you now and we're just going to relax while my mates pull us in like a couple of prize flatheads, you understand?'

The boy appeared to calm. 'Yes, yes, I do.'

'Alright. Just breathe easy, and we'll have you back on the beach in no time.'

Before signalling 'all secure' to the beach team, he gauged the time between sets, to get back through the break-line and avoid being caught in heavy white-water. He scanned the swells and rode over a couple before he sensed the lull, then gave the signal, and the rope began tugging the pair back toward safety. He maintained his backward hold on the boy with one eye on the swells as they moved swiftly shoreward; then, without warning, he caught sight of a threatening wave building up 'out the back', and his guts turned a somersault.

It was big; maybe 8 to 10 feet. A rogue swell, probably a freak combination of two swells into one, and it was coming fast. Immediately Danny felt a hard pull on the rope as the rescue team caught sight of it and were doubling their efforts to get him in. He manoeuvred his hold on the boy so he wouldn't see the wall of water behind them. 'Henry, we're not far now. There's a wave behind us that might break close, so when I tell you, take a deep breath and hold on. Don't worry, I've got a good hold on you and you'll be fine, you understand?' The boy merely nodded this time, but Danny could feel his entire body tense with fear.

The beast is rising to its full height as it spits spray into the wind with contempt; the sea hushing for the oncoming avalanche. It's going to break right on top of them, and the rope stops its pull as the team waits anxiously on shore. Danny speaks calmly. 'Henry, take a deep breath on 3; 1, 2, 3!' Their world becomes black as the beast pushes them down deep. Danny's grip on the boy loosens for a millisecond under an avalanche of pressure, but he holds on grimly. After what seems like minutes, he feels the tail of the beast pass above them, and pushes up to the light.

They broke the surface; sucking in grateful gasps of air as the rope renewed its pull. Danny looked towards the shore and thanked God he had such a skilled team on his side. They sprinted into the water and took Henry from him while Danny strode wearily up the beach and removed the belt that had just saved a life. Staunton sat on the sand beside him and ruffled his sodden hair. 'Great wave, mate–why didn't you catch it? Could've saved us the trouble of hauling you in.'

Chapter 6

The Trumpet Calls

The Old Orthodox Church rang its bells across Sarajevo, calling the faithful to worship, as it had since 1539. But on this bright Sunday morning, June 28, 1914, to Gavrilo Princip the bells tolled for freedom as the Serbian Black Hand Society struck a killing blow against Austrian tyranny. He felt for the bulk of the Belgian 32 calibre pistol in his coat pocket and thumbed the safety off. Down the street, the Latin Bridge over the Miljacka River had earlier thronged with onlookers hoping to glimpse the royal motorcade, but now, after an earlier failed bomb attack, the streets were deserted-eerily quiet. He leaned against the window of Schiller's Delicatessen; eyes trained on the intersection where the Archduke's limousine would pass. Traffic was light-police prowled Appel Quay's surrounding streets, but none had shown interest in the young man with the battered felt hat and dark eyes.

Growling engines heralded a motorcade approaching. The leading car of grim-faced security officers turned right into Franz Joseph street, and Princip's heart skipped a beat as it passed, just metres away from him. His body tensed with adrenaline-palms sweating and pulse quickening as the second vehicle carrying the Mayor and Chief of Police took the turn; the two officials muttering quiet words as they glided past.

Princip's target was the third vehicle, carrying Archduke Franz Ferdinand, heir to the throne of Austria-Hungary, and his wife Sophie, Duchess of Hohenberg. The 1911 Phaeton convertible rounded the corner as the driver dropped to low gear, and to Princip's astonishment, braked slowly to a halt only a few steps away.

There's confusion in the car and voices are being raised about a wrong turn as Princip moves trance-like toward the vehicle, drawing his pistol and taking aim at the couple in the back seat. Sophie's eyes widen in terror. Ferdinand follows his wife's gaze-turning toward Princip while the assassin mounts the running board and opens fire at point blank range. The Archduke dances like a marionette as the 32 slug slams into his neck; severing the jugular and spraying the car with crimson. Sophie screams and Princip fires a round into her abdomen. She slumps forward like a rag doll across her husband's legs. Princip turns the pistol toward himself and his world collapses into darkness.

The assassination reverberated across the world, igniting an avalanche of long-held grudges and nationalist fervour among European powers Austria-Hungary, Germany, Russia and France. There were scores to settle and territories to seize, and after demand and counter-demand, the tide of war rose to its peak. Austria-Hungary and Germany faced up against France and Russia; and it wasn't long before Britain threw its hat into the ring and joined the France/Russia alliance. By association, Australia was also committed to war.

~ ~ ~

The Sydney Morning Herald
Thursday, August
6, 1914.
WAR
DECLARED.

Great Britain's position in relation to Germany has now been clearly defined. Since the neutrality of Belgium has been violated by the latter Power, Britain is at war and that is now the condition into **which the Empire has been flung.**

> For good or ill, we are engaged with the
> mother country in fighting for liberty and
> peace. It is no war of aggression upon
> which Britons have entered, but one in
> defence of small nations threatened with
> humiliation and absorption, if not with
> extinction; and above and beyond
> everything, our armies will fight for
> British honour.

The nation was barely a teenager - only 13 years old. We were fiercely loyal to the British Empire and deeply mistrusting of foreigners. The legend of the tough outback bloke with the stoic, resourceful woman by his side was burned into our minds. We were also untried on the international stage, and this was to be our chance to show the world what Aussies are made of. So, despite being young, or perhaps because of it, when the mother country called, we were quick to respond.

Across the country, in every smoky city and dusty outback town, young men stopped what they were doing and raised their eyes to the Union Jack. In the bush, they slung a kit bag over their shoulder and hopped a train to the nearest recruiting station, with friends and family cheering them on. In the cities, they besieged the Town Hall, Police Station or army barracks to join up. In Sydney, within two weeks of war being declared, over

10,000 men had applied to enlist, and over the course of hostilities, almost half a million would wear a uniform.

For these fresh-faced men and boys with their dreams of gallantry, the horror of war would soon become all too apparent; but for the moment it was a grand adventure. Join up with your mates, see the world, give the dreaded 'Hun' a black eye, and get paid six bob a day. There was a fever to get 'in the thick of it' and grab part of the glory. Many believed that the war would be over by Christmas, and were keen not to miss the boat.

~ ~ ~

The Sydney Morning Herald
August 13, Thursday, August 13, 1914

There was another rush to enrol at Victoria Barracks yesterday, and several hundred men handed in their names for service in the expeditionary force. Already over 4,200 volunteers have enrolled at the barracks, besides the Frontiersmen and militia, who have volunteered through their own regimental or other organisations. Those who had already enlisted were paraded on the barrack square yesterday for medical examination.

> Nearly a thousand have
> passed through the doctors' hands
> already, and the medical officers will be
> working at full pressure now every day.

In mid-August 1914, a couple of home-made beef pies were rapidly disappearing at the kitchen table. The entire family was there, including Jim and Elizabeth with their newborn son Michael fast asleep in the bassinet. The escalating European war dominated the conversation.

As war blazed across the newspapers, James had listened to the locals as they elbowed the bar with a schooner in one hand and a cigarette in the other, spouting every item of gossip, rumour and conspiracy theory about the imminent conflict. The pub was a microcosm of the martial fervour sweeping across Sydney like a Spring tide, and recruitment posters hastily daubed on telephone poles told the same story: 'Is Your Home Worth Fighting For?' 'Boys! Come Over Here–You're Wanted', and 'Australians Arise! Heed the Call!'

James was at heart an Irishman; at his father's knee he'd learned of Cromwell's seizure of Irish lands in the 17th century, and the Crown's disregard for a starving populace during the Great Famine of the mid-1840s. He feared his sons would be caught up in the fervour of the

British Empire, and enlist on a whim-a decision that could cost them their lives-and tonight, he and Sarah intended to get their intentions out in the open and dissuade them from a hasty decision.

Cath, in her sixth year of university, was not holding back with her views. 'This war is about empires; it's as simple as that. Austria-Hungary wants to keep theirs, and Germany wants to build one. For years, Germany has been gearing up for war, and they believe this is their chance to dominate Europe. They have to be stopped.' John nodded. 'Germany's a threat to Australia too; they've got their eye on the rest of New Guinea, right at our back door. We have to do our bit.'

James drained his teacup. 'I hear what you say, and I don't disagree about Germany, but think about how insane it all is - some crazy bugger pulls a trigger in Serbia, and before we know it, there's a war on that could kill thousands in the long run. In my 71 years I've seen other wars–the Boer Wars for example; the men that didn't come home; the men that came home but were never the same again; the families that were destroyed. Mark my words - the decision to go to war is made by men who'll never witness a shot being fired; but the price of war is paid by the men who had no say in it.'

John pushed his plate away in frustration. 'Dad, if we just sit back and watch the Germans take over smaller countries that can't defend themselves, it won't be long until we'll be the next to go down. We have to stand up and be counted.' Silence fell upon the room as all heads turned toward James, knowing that these were the words he was dreading. He looked across the table to Sarah and saw the fear in her eyes. 'So, I gather you'll sign up like everybody else?' John glanced around the table at his family. 'Yes. I'm enlisting in the AIF.'

James was silent for a moment as he weighed his words. 'Son, I know how you feel. Every bloke your age is saying the same thing. But think about your future. You're 24. You've got the world at your feet, and your mother and I are afraid you'll throw your life away.' Light reflected softly from tears welling in Sarah's eyes. 'Don't do it, love; don't waste your life.' John dropped his napkin to the table. 'You two don't seem to understand. Australia can't just sit back and watch while these thugs walk over the rest of Europe. We're already at war, and everyone's got a responsibility to do his bit. I will not stay home while my mates are joining up.' He rose from his chair and walked from the room.

James made to follow his son, but stopped himself, knowing the discussion wasn't over yet. He looked across the table to Jim and Elizabeth. 'What about you, Jimmy?

There are plenty of blokes like you in their thirties signing up.' Jim squeezed Elizabeth's hand as he spoke. 'We've talked about it, Dad, and I think John's right in what he says, but I think you're right as well. Liz and I have had some heated arguments about it, and her parents have weighed in on the subject as well. But after all that, with young Michael not long arrived, and knowing the Royal will not run itself if I go, I've decided not to join up.'

James sighed gratefully and smiled. 'You've done the right thing. Your son will grow up with a father, and I didn't fancy running this place on my own again.' The kettle's whistle broke the silence, and Danny turned off the gas. 'You haven't asked me yet, Dad.' James and Sarah exchanged looks again. 'Danny, you're 19. The government doesn't want boys your age–that's why you need my permission before you can enlist. You've heard what I've said, so you don't need to ask–I won't sign the paper.'

~ ~ ~

The next morning, John swung down from a tram in Oxford Street at the gates of Victoria Barracks in Paddington. Its sandstone walls, convict-built a century before, were streaked in shades of mottled grey by a million grimy hands and generations of city rain and smoke. A soldier at the guard house gave him directions to the recruitment building in a bored voice, already heard by thousands.

He found a mess-hall where a small crowd of civilians milled about at the whim of the army recruiting machine. They were a motley mob - young and not-so-young, some with the sharp, grey faces of city life, others with the raw, weather-beaten look of blokes from the bush; paspalum seeds still in their hair. The room undulated with ragged conversation and the occasional guffaw from a bawdy joke as officials directed traffic through medical examinations.

A bored clerk at a rickety wooden table handed him a foolscap form and pen. 'Fill this in, mate, and bring it back here–*with* the pen, or you'll go to the end of the queue until you return it.' The form read, *'Australian Imperial Force–Attestation Paper of Persons Enlisted for Service Abroad,'*. John diligently worked through the form until reaching the bottom where the attestation stated:

I,………………………………………, do solemnly declare that the above answers made by me to the above questions are true, and I am willing, and voluntarily agree to serve in the Military Forces of the Commonwealth of Australia within or beyond the limits of the Commonwealth.'

He hovered the pen above the signature line as he recalled the previous night's discussion; the silence pervading the family dinner, the pained look on his parents' faces and their words of anguish:

.........'you could be throwing your life away.'

.........'Don't do it love; don't waste your life.'

At 24, John was a man of deep passion and a streak of recklessness, but such was the strength of his upbringing and the deep love of his parents, he hesitated for several moments, suddenly unsure of what to do. *'This is for keeps'*, he thought. *'There's no turning back.'* His mind whirled as he took a deep breath and signed the form.

They herded him through successive medical checks. Medicos peered down his throat, listened to his heart, checked his hair for lice and his penis for venereal disease (otherwise known as a 'short arms inspection'). He was finally pronounced medically fit, and at the end of the assembly line he took the oath beside several other men:

'I, John Thornton, swear that I will well and truly serve our Sovereign Lord the King in the Australian

Imperial Force until the end of the War, and a further period of four months thereafter unless sooner lawfully discharged, dismissed, or removed therefrom; and that I will resist His Majesty's enemies and cause His Majesty's peace to be kept and maintained; and that I will in all matters appertaining to my service, faithfully discharge my duty according to law.'

He exited the Barracks into Oxford Street like Alice falling back through the looking glass. Thoughts of heroism filled his imagination, and he walked a little taller toward the tram stop. The army loomed before him in a mammoth blank canvas, and fate was the artist. And like Alice, he hovered between two worlds. A tram squealed to a halt, and he swung aboard, while close by, an unseen figure stood watching under a shop awning. Danny saw his brother glide by on the tram, then crossed Oxford Street to the Barracks. Today he would magically turn 21.

The next morning a knock sounded on James's office door and Danny came in. He looked up from his paperwork and caught the serious look on his son's face. 'What's on your mind, Danny?' Danny avoided his father's eyes and remained silent as he placed his enlistment papers on the desk. James read the heading with his son's name on the form and thrust back into his chair; slamming his hand down hard, as Danny flinched at the sound. 'What in God's name have you done? Have you gone bloody mad? Are you trying to get yourself killed?'

Danny's face coloured with emotion. 'Dad, I'm nineteen. I've finished my apprenticeship and I can make my own way in the world now. I've joined up, and that's that.'

James raised his voice. 'No! That is not that at all! You've lied about your age–even signed that bloody form stating the details are correct. All I have to do is notify the army and you're out on your ear, and that's what I'm going to do. If you want to get yourself killed, you'll have to wait another couple of years.'

Danny's rage was palpable. 'I'm not waiting! I'll just hop a train somewhere else and enlist again under another name. You can't stop me!'

'I'll bloody-well stop you, all right! Someone's got to knock some bloody sense into you!'

Danny turned for the door. 'I'm shooting through. You won't find me!' He snatched up his papers, walked out and slammed the door.

Sarah had heard the commotion on her way down the corridor as Danny stormed past her, stormy-faced and without so much as a sideways look. She leaned into the office doorway. 'What was that about?' James sat with his head in his hands. 'The silly bugger upped his age and enlisted yesterday.' Sarah bent forward as if kicked her in her stomach; arms wrapped round herself. She slumped into a seat. 'Oh my God'. James reached across and grasped his wife's hand. 'I never thought he'd do it. He's normally such a thinker; I assumed he'd step back and wait, and by the time he got to 21 it would be over.' He shook his head. 'He said if I tried to stop him, he'd just go somewhere else and enlist again with a different name.'

The two sat immersed in their own thoughts. To Sarah, the thought of her two boys going to war halfway across the world filled her with dread. She'd spent her entire life with a dark premonition lurking in the back of her mind like a demon; an unspoken threat of disaster and ill-fortune that she'd tried to ignore. She'd depended on her husband's confidence like a talisman. Now the demon was on her shoulder.

James felt he'd failed. He'd prided himself on his ability to forge his family's future and their safety, and now, events had shown how ineffectual he really was. He knew in his heart that Danny couldn't be stopped, short of locking him in the cellar, and all he and Sarah could do was pray their boys would come home again after this senseless war.

They talked long into the evening, sharing their thoughts and fears; and as the shadows lengthened like dark fingers across the office floor, and the north-east wind from Coogee beach strengthened, somewhere in the night's dark they heaved their sighs and held tight to their hopes that tomorrow would be better.

~   ~   ~

Monday, October 19, 1914. The bull-shark prowls alongside the hull of the 'Euripides' as if inspecting its riveting. He's big; over two metres, and weighs about 300 kilos; his dorsal area blending perfectly with the ship's camouflage grey. He glides to the stern under three huge propellers, and catching the vibrations of a stingray in the mud below, disappears into the murky water toward his prey.

The *'Euripides'* was a 15,000-ton passenger liner of the Aberdeen White Star Line, launched in London on 29 January 1914 and requisitioned by the Commonwealth to carry troops from the 1st AIF. As the bull-shark enjoyed his lunch, the timbers of Woolloomooloo finger wharf drummed to the sound of the AIF 3rd and 4th battalions marching four abreast to the gangway stairs. This was no parade-ground spectacle; there were no brass bands or cheering crowds. It was more a light hearted stroll by a bunch of blokes bound for adventure.

Someone in the formation began singing a tune that had gained popularity in recent years; and the refrain was picked up as more voices joined in, like a stone spreading ripples on a pond; echoing across Woolloomooloo Bay until a thousand throats held the tune:

Once a jolly swagman camped by a billabong

Under the shade of a coolabah tree,

And he sang as he watched and waited till his billy boiled,

'You'll come a-waltzing Matilda with me.'

Waltzing Matilda, Waltzing Matilda,

You'll come a Waltzing Matilda with me

And he sang and he watched as he waited till his billy boiled

'You'll come a-waltzing Matilda, with me.'

Their eyes were bright and their heads held high. They were farmers and fishmongers, engineers and estate agents, lawyers and locksmiths. They were married and single, womanisers and widowers, adventurers and adulterers. Few of them had ever been to sea; many had never ventured far from the towns and cities where they were born - but they were to be the first Australian troops to sail halfway across the world to join the 'Great War', as the French would soon call it. The voyage was a closely guarded secret; and sadly, it was a voyage from which many would never return - and those who did would never be the same.

Each soldier carried a calico kitbag over his shoulder, holding a greatcoat, spare shirt and underwear, toiletries, and a few personal effects. If a bystander watched closely, they may have noticed an odd bulge in one or two kitbags, and even imagined they'd seen a slight movement inside. But it may not have been imagination. More than a few 'diggers' smuggled pet kangaroos, possums, and even the occasional koala aboard troop ships, as a reminder of home. At best, these animals were to become platoon mascots; at worst, they would sicken and die on the voyage.

John and Danny Thornton marched side by side in slouch hat, khaki belted jacket and breeches, woollen puttees and tan leather ankle boots. The 4th battalion's distinctive horizontal white and green patch was missing from their shoulders, and would not be issued until early 1915; such was the hurried formation of these first units. They had been inducted into the army several weeks before, and undergone rudimentary training at Sydney Showground. At the end of the voyage the training would continue at an undisclosed location; most believed it would be somewhere on the English moors.

The brothers had been assigned to the 4th due to their enlistment within an hour of each other. James had made peace with Danny in the realisation that the young men of Australia would follow their passion despite counsel from their elders. And after all, he decided, these men belonged to a different era. They teetered on the edge of a new world, and whether that world was better or worse than the old, was not for James to say. His job was to love his family, give guidance, and allow his sons to take that world to a future that he was not to be part of. He just hoped his boys would come home again.

The troops climbed the gangway of the *'Euripides'* to the 170-metre upper deck that pulsed with frenetic activity. The ship's fore-and-aft derricks swung cargo up from the wharf like a pair of storks delivering babies. Huge wooden crates stamped with the Commonwealth coat of arms disappeared into the shadowed hold at a feverish rate. A horse flew sedately overhead in a leather harness suspended from the derrick's boom, while dropping fresh manure. When a consignment hit the deck, narrowly missing one digger, he called out: 'Lunch is served, gentlemen!'

The column of soldiers moved like a long, khaki snake down a labyrinth of narrow companionways into the bowels of the ship; and as they descended, the temperature rose, and the air became oppressive. They came to a large mess-hall where rows of canvas hammocks hung from the ceiling. John slung his kitbag into a vacant space as a hand from behind clapped on his shoulder. 'That's my spot, arsehole!' He swung round at the familiar voice of Bill Bradley, his old school mate from St Mary's–they laughed and shook hands.

Bill gave John's shoulder a playful punch. 'Well, fancy seeing you here, mate! I thought you'd be up on the first-class deck.'

John smiled. 'No such luck; at least until I make Colonel. 'Didn't know you'd joined up. What battalion?'

'Fourth. And you?'

'The same. What about Charlie Schumacher? Seen him lately?'

Bill's smile faded. 'He tried to enlist, but when they saw his name, they said he was German, and didn't want him in the AIF. Turns out the whole bloody family was hauled off to internment camp out at Liverpool. "Enemy Aliens", they called them.

John shook his head in disgust. 'But he's bloody Dutch!'

'Turns out his mother's German, and that was enough to lock 'em up.'

~　~　~

The sun spread over Sydney Harbour in the morning stillness, casting a warm glow on Mrs. Macquarie's Chair, where 100 years before, the Governor's wife sat watching British tall ships sail into the harbour. A few hundred yards to the south, the funnel of the *'Euripides'* issued a plume of grey smoke as its boilers gathered steam for the voyage to Albany, Western Australia on Tuesday, October 20, 1914.

On board, the men of the 3rd and 4th battalions had been roused early from their bunks for an hour of callisthenics, and were in the mess-hall devouring breakfast. Danny had stumbled into his brother as he tumbled from his berth into the companionway, and they'd grabbed a spot on the same bench with their tin pannikins of bread and porridge. The word had gotten around that the *'Euripides'* would sail that day, and on deck that morning they'd noticed the gangway being hauled up.

In keeping with Australia's war footing, a dark cloak of government secrecy surrounded all troop movements, and transport ship A14 (aka *'Euripides'*) was no exception. No newspapers carried the story of Sydney's first departing AIF troopship; but the masterminds of Australia's military intelligence hadn't counted on one highly efficient unit that had eyes and ears across the city–the bar of the Randwick Royal, where those 'in the know' shared the contraband news of the departure.

James, Jim, and Cath got off the tram in William Street for the walk down to the wharf, and to their surprise, a steady stream of like-minded people was doing likewise. Sarah had remained at home; this was the day she'd dreaded ever since the boys had joined up, and it was more than she could bear to watch them sail away; perhaps forever.

As the Thorntons walked down Brougham street to the harbour, A14's superstructure loomed above Woolloomooloo's rusted iron roofs. At the wharf, the ship's deck was lined with khaki as diggers leaned over the gunwales from bow to stern, waving their hats to the crowd below. A cascade of coloured streamers was being hurled upwards from the dock, and the diggers vied with one another to catch the paper coils and tie them to the ship's rail.

For many, the scene was far from joyous - the faces of those left behind were brushed with emotion. Here was a young, curly-haired wife with a lost look in her eyes, searching the faces for her husband. There was a father, battered hat in hand, staring grimly up to his only son. Over there was a thin young mother nursing her baby as tears streamed down her face; her shoulders heaving with sobs. As John Milton wrote in 1655, 'They also serve who only stand and wait.'

A14 sounded a long blast on her horn as the brothers searched for their family on the wharf. Danny shouted, 'There they are!' John followed his glance. 'Mum's not there,' and Danny nodded. 'Too much for her nerves, I reckon.' Down on the wharf, the Thorntons had seen them, and began waving back frantically as the ship sounded a second blast–it wouldn't be long now. James felt a lump in his throat as his eyes shone pearlescent. Cath waved a handkerchief like a flag of surrender to the fear in her heart. Jim felt a fierce tug of guilt as he watched his two brothers and thought of their bravery. Was he staying at home because of family loyalty and love, or was it fear?

A third and final blast of the siren signalled departure as mooring lines were unwound and cast from bollards into the sea; freeing A14 from her bondage as the ship's triple propellers boiled white-water. Out on the street, a taxi pulled to a screeching halt and Sarah emerged at the run as the enormous ship pulled away from the wharf. From the ship's deck, the lone figure hurrying down the planking caught John's eye, and he yelled at the top of his voice: 'Mum!' Danny followed his gaze as Sarah heard her son's voice and halted; her eyes riveted on the two young men she ached for. She waved frantically as tears flowed from her pale blue eyes and her heart dissolved into sorrow. She stood on the dock, a solitary soul within a crowd, hugging herself in grief until A14 rounded the northern tip of Garden Island and disappeared from sight.

~ ~ ~

Jack Renshaw shovelled coal into boiler No. 3 with a fluidity that belied his stocky physique - years of stoking had whittled down his every movement to bare necessity. High above on the ship's bridge, Captain of the 'Euripides', Andrew Douglas, peered through binoculars at Michaelmas and Breaksea Islands lying like a pair of guard dogs at the entrance to King George Sound. He set a course change; ringing down 'half ahead' on the telegraph. In the engine room the command was acknowledged, and Renshaw took a well-earned 'breather'.

The passage down the east coast of New South Wales and across the Great Australian Bight had been uneventful for A14; the ship was blacked out after sunset, but there were no reports of German raiders. The first hurdle the troops had faced was seasickness; they had no sooner steamed through Sydney Heads and turned to starboard when the rolling swell took its toll. Hundreds were affected, laying ill on the deck wherever there was space until the swells moderated. That achieved, the rest of the six-day journey was a blur of inoculations, lectures and potato peeling, while the men debated their destination and when they'd be 'getting into the action'.

A14 cruised at 'dead slow ahead' through a curtain of grey rain as Douglas took regular depth readings. The Sound was a roughly circular bay about 5 miles in diameter, open to the sea from the east, with the town of Albany lying to the west at Shoal Bay. Along the north and south perimeters, low granite hills speckled with tussock-grass spread their protective arms against harsh winds; and 1,300 miles to the south, the vast Southern Ocean met cliffs of Antarctica ice rising in white majesty. King George Sound was remote - about as far from 'the action' as one could get.

As A14 proceeded, lines of hulking grey steamers loomed from a pewter mist. There were about 20 large vessels, but more would arrive in the days to follow as troop ships and cruisers gathered. To the men on the deck of A14, the import and scale of their journey was becoming apparent.

The troops had been ordered 'on parade' for their arrival, and 2000 men assembled on A14's superstructure. 'Euripides' was the largest transport of the flotilla, and she glided over the water with the dignity of a monarch past the line of anchored ships, as thousands of troops yelled their welcome–cheering and hurling hats in a show of support. The men aboard A14, mostly Sydney boys, were sorely tempted to join the party, but to their credit, maintained strict discipline under the steely eyes of their NCO's.

Euripides approached a significant ship of the line, '*A3 Orvieto*', aka 'The General's Vessel', carrying Scotsman Major General William Throsby Bridges, commander of the 1st AIF. Within 50 metres of A3, the military band on board A14 primed their instruments and struck up 'Scotland the Brave' in tribute to their commanding officer as the assembled troops snapped off a salute with perfect timing. The eerie, evocative wail of the pipes stirred men's souls, and a thunder of cheering echoed back from the hills. A14 slowed to its place in the line and gave a long horn-blast as it dropped anchor to the floor of King George Sound.

~ ~ ~

Over the coming days more troopships dropped anchor, and as the fleet grew, the sense of anticipation was palpable. It became abundantly clear to the troops they were part of something momentous. Day by day, ships lined up to take on water and coal in Shoal Bay, and lighters whizzed among towering hulls like pilot fish, carrying high-ranking officers with an air of urgency.

After several days of delay, however, a degree of tedium descended on the men despite the distraction of signals lectures and lifeboat drills; and they looked for any escape from the monotony. One afternoon, the Thornton brothers headed along a passageway toward the lecture room, where a Vickers Gun training session was scheduled.

John ducked under a bundle of cables and glanced at his brother. 'Another bloody lecture. I'm not sure I'll be able to stay awake.'

Danny chuckled. 'That's not entirely fair, mate– what about the one on 'care and maintenance of your feet in the trenches?' Or 'How to detect the presence of gangrene?' I found them quite riveting.'

'Yeah, my point exactly. This one may not be so bad, and if it is, there'll be a loaded Vickers Gun on hand if we need it.'

They entered the lecture room. Rows of steel chairs were arranged around a small platform where a Vickers Gun squatted menacingly on its tripod. A barrel-bodied British Army Captain with a silver walrus moustache and monocle stood to the side, his uniform so well pressed it looked carved from stone. The room was full of men chatting, trading jokes and generally horsing about. The brothers took their seats as the Captain cleared his throat loudly and began in a clipped, upper-class British accent. John groaned inwardly and looked at his watch.

'Thank you, Gentlemen, a bit of shoosh if you please, and we'll get underway.'

The noise subsided as the captain gestured toward the weapon. 'Gentlemen, this is a Vickers Machine Gun. It fires 500 rounds of 303 ammunition each minute at a muzzle velocity of 2,440 feet per second over 4,000 yards. If one ever points in your direction, I would suggest you try your best to appear as inconspicuous as possible.' Quiet chuckles rippled around the audience.

The Captain waited for quiet, and continued with a deadpan face. 'The Vickers Gun is carried in separate parts and assembled by a gun team; otherwise known as the "suicide squad". The gun team comprises 6 to 8 infantrymen. One fires the gun, which of course is the whole point of the exercise, one feeds the ammunition belt, and the rest carry equipment and spare parts. Teamwork is therefore essential, and it also gives the enemy someone else to shoot at besides yourself.' Chuckles became scattered laughter.

'Once the team has assembled the gun, and before opening fire, it's recommended that you ensure the barrel is pointing in the right direction. If you're aiming at uniforms that are remarkably similar yours, and you understand the swearing that you hear, I recommend a 180-degree course alteration. Having commenced firing, the support team is advised not to remain standing, but to take a seat at their earliest convenience, because if the enemy is in range, so are you.' The men were enjoying themselves now, particularly as the Captain seemed not to know what the joke was.

'The rate of fire of the Vickers Gun is equivalent to about 40 riflemen, meaning six men can do the work of 40, so some of you may be in danger of becoming unemployed at some point. That being the case, I advise seeking an occupation with greater longevity than one that requires you to be shot at by others.'

'The gun itself weighs 30 pounds; the tripod you see here is about 40 pounds, a full ammunition box weighs 22 pounds, and a full container of water is about 27 pounds, which is why you need another four or five men to carry everything, while simultaneously being shot at. If you _are_ carrying some of this heavy equipment in the heat of battle, and feel a sudden sharp pain in your groin area, you've either become the proud father of a newborn hernia, or you've been shot in the gonads.'

'The Vickers has a water-cooled barrel that requires changing every hour, like a shitty baby. If you find that the barrel of the Vickers Gun is glowing red, and you've used up all your water, you may wish to ask the enemy to stop firing back, while you fetch some more; or perhaps if you ask nicely, you could pop over and borrow some of theirs.'

The lecture continued for another half-hour in the same vein and led to a standing ovation from the men. The Captain maintained his serious demeanour and made an ever-so-slight bow as the room was cleared for the next group of unsuspecting soldiers.

Chapter 7

Calm Before the Storm

The Sydney Morning Herald
Tuesday, 8 December 1914
THE TRANSPORTS.
A GREAT FLEET.
DEPARTURE FROM ALBANY.
AN IMPRESSIVE SPECTACLE.
*BY A. B. ('Banjo') PATERSON, THE
HERALD'S SPECIAL
COMMISSIONER WITH THE AUSTRALIAN
TROOPS.*

Sunday, November 1, was a red-letter
day in the history of Australia, for on that
day our big fleet of transports put out
from Albany for the long trip across half
the world. The ships arrived at Albany in
ones and twos and threes, till at last all
the fleet was gathered.

They anchored in the roadstead outside the inner harbour of Albany. There they swung at anchor for five clear days while water and coal were taken in by the vessels that required them.

Each day there was a report that we were to sail on the following day, but day after day passed, and no move was made by any of the ships. At last, on Saturday, October 31, word passed round in the mysterious way in which word does pass round at sea that the transports would leave next morning.

READY TO SAIL.

Grey dawn sees pretty well everybody astir, and all eyes keep turning to the flag-ship of the transports. A red sun rises behind a long island away out to seaward. Not a sound, nor any movement of any living thing comes from the crowning hills on either side of the waterway. It is as if they were watching the transports getting ready for sea. From these, too, comes no noise at all that can be heard from one ship to another. The watcher on the deck of the inshore vessels sees the

three long rows of ships lying silent as painted ships at their anchors. The only sign of life is the column of smoke pouring from each funnel, and this alone it is that tells us that

Australia's greatest maritime venture is
about to put out to sea. Each ship seems
to stand out double her natural size,
every spar and rope showing clearly
outlined against the rosy
sky. The sea is dull, still grey, without a
ripple. A vague electric restlessness is in
the air.
What are those coming out of the inner
harbour? Two grim, gliding leviathans,
going Majestically out to sea to take their
places as guardians of the fleet. There is
something uncanny in the absolute
silence with which everything is done.
They glide past the frowning cliffs, whose
feet are awash with the sea, through the
long lines of waiting transports, and are
soon lost to sight, steaming right out into
the eye of the sun.
THE DEPARTURE.
Then there is a stir at the stern, a gliding,
oily rush of water, which tells us that the
screw is turning at last. At least a
thousand pairs of field glasses are
centred on her anchor chain.
Link by link it comes in-board, and the
leader of the fleet is under way.
Noiselessly the great ship gathers speed
and moves ahead through the waiting
fleet; and, as she goes out, the vessels
that are to follow her in line get silently
under way and wall in line behind her.

Suddenly, we too realise that we are
under way. So silently does the anchor
come in, so
smoothly do the turbine engines work,
that only the sailors on board know that
we are
moving, till the rocky headlands begin to
glide past us and we pass the waiting
ships of our own fleet. As we pass each
one it gets up its anchor and glides after
us.

A GREAT STRING OF SHIPS.

From the leading ship of our line, we saw
a great string of ships steaming along in
our
rear, the one just behind us keeping
always her distance, the white foam
always at her
bows, her great frame lifting and sinking
rhythmically to the swell. Day and night,
she is
always there, just behind us, until the
pursuit becomes a sort of haunting thing.
One looks
aft sometimes to see if by any chance she
may have relaxed her pursuit for an
instant, but
the great bow and the towering
deckhouses and bridge are always there
just behind us;
and behind her always trails the long line
of ships.

A PILLAR OF SMOKE.

Away ahead of the whole fleet, just in
sight, on the edge of the horizon, is a
pillar of
smoke—a cruiser is clearing the way for
us, setting the pace, giving the direction,
and
keeping a watchful eye out for enemies.
Far away to starboard, just visible on the
sky-line,
is another pillar of smoke keeping guard.
So, we move across the ocean like a large
regatta of great steamships, always the
same order being inflexibly kept. It is
sometimes hard to believe that 120 miles
have been covered since one saw them
last, they seem to be so exactly in the
same place. And always behind us are
the great towering leviathans of
merchantmen, each loaded with men,
horses, and war material. It is the most
wonderful sight that an Australian ever
saw.

The flotilla sketched tight lines of foam across the ocean as it cut northward in strict formation. Thirty-eight transports sailed under the protection of cruisers HMS *Minotaur*, HMAS *Melbourne*, HMAS *Sydney* and the Japanese *Ibuki*. On the day they departed, Russia declared war on the Ottoman Empire; and four days later, France and Britain followed suit. The inclusion of the Ottomans in the hostilities opened up a potential new theatre of war, and given their north-westerly course, conjecture was the 30,000 men aboard the flotilla would access the Mediterranean via the Suez Canal; but nothing was certain.

Such a large concentration of men and ships presented a tantalising target to enemy raiders, and the German light cruiser SMS *Emden* was the most feared of all. She was in the area, hunting across the shipping lanes between Singapore, Colombo and Aden–directly in the flotilla's path. Her captain, Karl von Muller, had captured or sunk 25 Allied steamers, a Russian cruiser and a French destroyer in just two months. Radio messages among allied ships were transmitted in code to foil the *Emden*, but a code could always be broken.

Muller was cunning–he struck hard and fast, then disappeared just as quickly into the vast expanse of the sea; so, when on November 9, HMAS *Sydney* picked up a report of an unidentified warship off the Cocos Islands, the big cruiser abruptly altered course; peeling off from the flotilla at top speed to hunt what they hoped would be the *Emden*.

The *Sydney* covered the 52 nautical miles in short order and was closing in on Cocos when the *Emden* was identified at a range of 9,500 yards. Muller lost no time in taking the fight up to *Sydney* and ordered *Emden's* cannons to open fire. The *Sydney* shuddered like a boxer in a clinch as she took a couple of blows to her superstructure, and a dance of death ensued as the *Emden* tried to lure *Sydney* into torpedo range. The men on *Sydney's* bridge scoured the surface for the feared bubbling wake coming their way, but their evasive tactics paid off as she turned broadside and brought her bigger guns to bear in a roar of thunder; taking out *Emden's* wireless unit, killing a gun-crew and disabling her steering gear. Further hits detonated ammunition; igniting a deadly fire aboard, and Muller knew the *Emden* was done for. He beached the ship to save his crew and jettisoned code books to thwart the enemy. The once-deadly raider was no more.

Emden's survivors were brought aboard. Some had sustained severe burns and were not expected to survive, but those who did were treated well, and *Emden's* officers were accorded recognition of rank in their incarceration. Captain Muller himself was transferred to the flotilla flagship, the *Orvieto*, and would later be asked by an Australian Army Lieutenant what he would have done if he had sighted the convoy on his way to the Cocos Islands:

'I was 52 miles away from you that night. If I had got up to you, I should have run alongside her (pointing to a cruiser nearby) and fired a torpedo. Then, in the confusion, I should have got in among the transports. I would have sunk half of them, I think, before your escort came up. I should have been sunk in the end, I expect. I always expected that.'

It was clear that good fortune had smiled on the armada of transports; and things could easily have been entirely different, but for the sake of a couple of hours' sailing time.

~ ~ ~

The night sky paled to dawn as the flotilla steamed northward up the west coast of Ceylon on Sunday, 15 November 1914; and soon the sun peeked over a sea of glass, bringing with it the promise of another humid day. On the bridge of *A14 Euripides,* Captain Douglas caught the triple flash of Colombo's lighthouse fifteen miles off the starboard bow, as a signal from the flagship ordered 'All Vessels Half Ahead'. They'd made good time in the long haul up from Albany, and after the news of the *Emden's* demise, breathed easier knowing that no other raiders were in the area.

Danny leaned against the ship's forward derrick-mast, watching the town of Colombo gather shape in the distance. A light north-easterly breeze sprang up, bringing with it the scent of Ceylon. It wasn't the smell he was familiar with; on-shore winds from the Australian coast carried a dry air tinged with eucalyptus, or the freshness of a clean southerly after a heat wave. The aroma of Ceylon was deeper; a heady fragrance of dark, mossy earth, and the alluring tang of spice.

Almost a month had passed since he'd steamed from Sydney Harbour aboard the *Euripides* with winds of change blowing at his back. He'd written home twice, but was sure his letters would be gibberish after the censors did their work. The thing was, he was so _alive_ now that he was ashamed to admit he'd not given home much thought. It was the present and the future, the possibilities, the unknown, and yes, even the risk, that excited him.

The *Euripides* cut northward through a vibrant blue sea fringed with palms; and in the distance, mountains brushed with every imaginable shade of green rose in a milky haze. Rickshaws, carts, bullock wagons and the occasional motor car weaved along the coast. Along the beachfront, low bungalows peeked between flowering trees until and a wider strip of foreshore revealed the colonnaded Galle Face Hotel, where a spirited polo match was in progress.

The line of steamers adjusted pace to 'Dead Slow Ahead' as the pilot boat took charge. One by one they rounded the breakwater near the mouth of the Kelani River; entering the harbour like ducks in a row. The day's normal shipboard monotony of mopping mess halls, lectures and gear inspections had been cancelled, and the men were granted shore-leave, albeit under NCO supervision, strict timeframes and the threat of swift retribution for any misbehaviour. A hem of khaki bordered the decks as soldiers peered over the ship's rail to the shore, eager to be on dry land after so long at sea.

John and Bill Bradley emerged from a hatchway with Private Doug Nutt, better known as 'Nutty', from the 4th Battalion. He was six foot three, with curly, flaming red hair and a freckled face framing twinkling blue eyes. A boy from the bush somewhere near Young, New South Wales, Nutty had never stirred from his home town until boarding a train to enlist in Sydney a few months before.

Bill snatched off his cap and wiped the perspiration from his brow. 'Jesus, it's hot here. No wonder the locals are small fellas–they've all melted.'

Danny laughed. 'Hey Nutty, is this as hot as Young?'

'Nah mate, in Young, it's so hot, the farmers feed their chickens ice cubes so they don't lay hard-boiled eggs.'

John pointed over the side of the ship. 'Hey you blokes–come and have a look at this.'

Outrigger canoes jammed together into a floating market, surrounding the ship like bees around a hive. Hawkers called up, offering figurines of carved wood, brass and copper, precious stones, fruit, bags of rice, laundry services–even pet lizards. Each boat had its own territory of green water, and each seller his own throaty offer of a bargain. Their dark skin glistened with the perspiration of the morning and the frenzy of commerce.

A few young boys put on a show, diving for pennies. They'd watch the coin winking sunlight as it spun down from the ship's rail and slipped into green water with an oily slurp, then spear in after it, their shapes blurring quickly from sight. A minute or more would pass before the surface was broken by a boy with a big smile and a coin between pearly teeth.

Two enterprising lads grabbed a loose rope and climbed to the deck like monkeys; cajoling the men for pennies for a dive from the ship's rail, over forty feet above the water. The young diver stood outside the bulwarks; elbows hooked back over the rail while his partner caught coins in a canvas sack. At a signal from his mate, he launched himself out, dropping like a stone into a patch of green in a classic dive. The brown body disappeared in a fountain of white-water as the hushed crowd leaned over, watching in silence until a rippling figure appeared, and the boy surfaced to the troops' cheers.

The Thornton brothers and their two mates made good their escape from the cramped companionways of the *Euripides* and hopped a fisherman's canoe to freedom; albeit until 10pm that night. As they paddled clear of the anchored transports, Colombo's waterfront pulsed in sound and colour - seagulls squawking over fishing boats, a cargo of tea off to London, shiny bodies under sacks of rice, honking horns and piercing whistles, the smell of fish, petroleum, sweat and melting tar. They climbed barnacled wharf steps; pleased to be on dry land once more.

Behind the waterfront, street stalls leaned against each another like loose palings in an old fence. A choir of hawkers called out in staccato Sinhala under the aroma of

spice - yellow turmeric, earthy nutmeg, pungent ginger
and the heady aroma of cloves. Rainbows of hand-woven
cloth spilt from bamboo baskets; and carved elephants,
milky moonstones and garish wooden masks vied for
attention. A few soldiers, cigarettes dangling from lower
lips, haggled over a figurine or a string of coloured beads;
others weaved unsteadily along the road, searching
Ceylon for their land legs.

The lads paused for a few purchases; speaking in
sign language as they struggled to convert rupees to
Australian shillings. Nutty attracted attention; towering
over the locals as they giggled and whispered: *'ratu
yodhaya desa balanna!'* ('Look at the red giant!'). The lads
were stunned by the beauty of Ceylonese women; some
with milk-coffee skin, some dark as polished teak, all
with eyes of endless depth, swaying in close-fitting saris
with the rhythm of desire and the poise of a gazelle. John
was so smitten with one young maiden, he stopped to
stare, and narrowly avoided being run down by an ox.

The four left the noise of the markets and headed
west along Abdul Cader Road into the 'Fort' area; home
to Colombo's old colonial buildings of local granite. The
arched and colonnaded General Post Office, the elegant
Grand Oriental Hotel and the Old Lighthouse in Queen
Street all stood proudly along wide, manicured
boulevards under the shade of mimosas. Traffic was

light-bullock carts, rickshaws and a sprinkling of motor cars passed by in sedate colonial order.

In the Gordon Gardens they followed the sound of a Pungi flute to a snake-charmer; his cobra rising from a woven basket. Bill hung back from the show, his eyes fixed on the reptile swaying rhythmically to the music. Danny wore a wry grin. 'What's the matter, mate? Scared of snakes?' Bill kept his eyes riveted on the reptile. 'Let's just say that me and snakes have an understanding. I don't get down on the ground and crawl about with them, and they don't come into the bar and drink with me.' He snapped himself out of a trance. 'Now come on you blokes, that's enough bloody sightseeing. Why don't we leave the bloody snake alone and piss off to a bar somewhere?'

That 'somewhere' was to be the 'Mount Lavinia Hotel', six miles to the south, and before long the four were motoring down the coast in a 1913 Wolseley Open Tourer, hired from the Grand Oriental Hotel, complete with driver. The four soldiers eased back into the buttoned black leather upholstery as a kaleidoscope of rural Ceylon wove its spell.

An ox ambled along the roadside under dappled shade. Ducks crossed a lane in single file, herded by a young boy in baggy shorts. A woman swayed beneath a basket of rambutans. Boys smiled and waved from the gate of a Buddhist temple. Danny leant on the window sash of the Wolseley and breathed deeply of warm spice; falling hopelessly in love with Asia. He felt strangely at home, as if he'd been there before, perhaps in another life. There was wonder, excitement, curiosity and intrigue of the unknown in his soul.

They turned off the Galle Road, and as they rounded a bend, the hotel loomed before them. Built in 1806 as the residence of British Governor Sir Tom Maitland (known as 'King Tom'), the white, two-storey colonnaded building epitomised British colonial grace; dominating a headland above sea-cliffs. During his tenure, Maitland fell in love with a beautiful mestizo dancer, Lovina Aponsuwa. They became lovers, and Maitland had a secret tunnel dug between Lovina's village and his cellar. He named the house after Lovina, and when failing health forced his departure from Ceylon, granted her a large parcel of land.

They turned up a gravel drive past fountains and manicured gardens to a covered portico where a doorman in white uniform and turban stood to attention. The driver pulled to a halt and the four young men got out. Bill took in the tall arched windows and Doric columns, and gave a whistle. 'Not a bad location for a beer and a spot of lunch, I'd say.' Danny nodded. 'Yep, it'll do. Let's have a look around.' They trotted up the steps as the doorman gave a greeting and swung open the doors.

The foyer rose to high ceilings over a polished teakwood floor. Fans rotated lazily as white-capped hotel staff moved baggage trolleys about with brisk efficiency. A scattering of guests and well-to-do Ceylonese congregated around the reception desk; the men in white linen suits and the women in flowing silks. At the rear of the foyer, large French doors opened to a terrace, and in the distance, the sea sparkled like diamonds in the sun. Nutty shrugged his shoulders. 'Nowhere near as good as the "Commercial" in Young, but I suppose it'll do.'

They found the bar in a dining room with an expansive view of the sea. It was almost lunchtime and waiters in long white aprons moved briskly about, tending to guests. As they climbed onto stools, a distinguished-looking Ceylonese man approached them. He was about 40, with black hair tinged grey at the temples, dark, piercing eyes and a look of quiet confidence. 'Good afternoon, gentlemen, allow me to introduce myself. I'm Robert Vander Wall, owner of the Lavinia. By the uniforms, I assume you're from Australia?'

John shook his hand. 'John Thornton. This is my brother Danny, and our mates—Doug and Bill. We're off the troopships in the harbour, taking a look around Colombo, and thought we'd have a drink and some lunch.'

'Welcome to Ceylon, gentlemen; we seldom have visitors from Australia. We saw the fleet sail past this morning; I'm sure you must be glad to be back on dry land again.'

Nutty replied, 'You're right there, sport. After a month at sea, we've been staggering around Colombo like drunks at closing time, so we thought we might as well have a few beers to give us an excuse. You got any beer in Ceylon?'

'That we do, sir–I recommend Ceylon Brewery Stout.'

'Make that four.'

Drinking certainly gives one an appetite, and the lads were ravenous after weeks of army rations. Dispensing with the menu, which they couldn't understand anyway, they simply ordered 'Ceylon food', leaving it to the kitchen to decide the details. By the grace of too many stouts and the expertise of the kitchen, they were to enjoy some of the best food on the planet - lamprais, string hoppers with kiri hodi and coconut sambal, prawn curry and chicken biriyani. Bill was so busy enjoying the food, he mistook a red chilli for a capsicum. No sooner had he begun chewing when fire exploded in his head, prompting the downing of a pint of stout in record time. It was thirty minutes before he could speak.

They consumed a prodigious amount of stout that afternoon, reminiscing about 'back home', swapping lewd jokes with Vander Wall and making lifelong friends of the waiters. Danny would later vaguely recall inviting the entire staff to the Randwick Royal for lunch the following day.

~   ~   ~

It was dark along the winding road back to Colombo. There was silence but for the purr of the Wolseley's motor as Danny immersed himself in the night. Village kerosene-lights filtered through the banyans as they glided past. The aroma of cooked rice and spiced meats hung in thick air, and the street was a stage where villagers appeared in the headlights like actors in a spotlight. Sarong-clad men in dusty sandals squatted and smoked. Slender women in sarees traded village gossip. Children sifted through the shadows like elves playing night games. Street-carts rattled by, offering lamb and fish dosa, cucumber and yoghurt raita and Kottu. Nocturnal creatures emerged from the shadows- fruit bats flapped leathery wings overhead, a wood owl scratched leaf litter for lizards and a stray dog loped down a laneway; eyes glowing amber in the dark. In the distance, the lights of Colombo glowed brighter as they approach.

They pulled to a halt at the entrance to the Grand Oriental; tumbling out onto Church Street in varying degrees of unsteadiness. John checked his watch, swaying under lamplight. 'It's only 9 o'clock gen'lmen, what say we partake of a cleansing beverage? They found themselves in the hotel bar, drinking potent Ceylon arrack, which they learned was made from coconut flowers. Nutty took a gulp from his glass. 'Jesus, if this stuff's made of flowers, I'll take half a dozen bunches.'

Their memory of that night would always remain hazy, and exaggerated over the passing years, but most would recall rickshaw races along York Street, a midnight skinny dip in Beira Lake, and Nutty climbing a coconut tree to eat the flowers. Somehow, they found their way back to the waterfront and hired a canoe to *A14*. It was well past the designated curfew of 10pm, and they risked a stint in the brig if they were caught.

As they stumbled up the gangway giggling and shushing each other in stage whispers, Sergeant Roger Roberts from the 4th Battalion leant on the ship's rail, watching; his cigarette glowing in the dark. The four young soldiers' drunken staggers reminded him of himself back in 1885, when he weaved from the Occidental Hotel at Wynyard Square and boarded a Woolloomooloo steamer bound for the Sudan with the New South Wales infantry. *'These young blokes don't know what they're in for.'* He thought, as images of the war returned to haunt him–the bodies, the flies, the fear, the smell. They would see the same or worse, he thought, and perhaps never return from this war. *'I'd better go easy on the buggers.'*

Danny was the first to reach the upper deck of *A14* as Roberts's flashlight cut through the darkness. 'Halt! Who goes there!'

Danny squinted against the sudden glare. 'Privates Thornton, Bradley and Nutt, sir. We've been, um, somewhat delayed.'

'Delayed by the drink, by the smell of you. Answer me these questions,' and be quick about it. Did you kill anyone?

No, Sir.'

'Did you injure, steal from, or assault any locals?'

'No, Sir.'

'Did you have sex?'

'Unfortunately, no, Sir.'

Roberts allowed himself a grin behind the flashlight's glare.

'Advance and be recognised. Now fuck off below, and consider yourselves lucky.' He watched them with a wry smile as they stole silently down the companionway to their bunks.

~ ~ ~

A camel train emerged from the shadow of the Menkaure pyramid into shimmering heat. The lead rider swayed with the rhythm of his mount, face hidden beneath his 'kufiyya' as the wind whipped across the sand. Without compass or map, he'd led the caravan across the vast desert, guided only by the night sky and the flight of fan-tailed ravens. His camel strode gracefully forward; proud and aloof.

In the distance a sea of white tents sprawled across western Giza; their pointed roofs seeming to mock the ancient pyramids with their impudence. A company of soldiers marched in strict formation, 303 rifle-barrels glinting in the sun. The leader muttered to himself: 'The Australian soldiers march about like ants in the heat of day. They have the brains of a goat. 'Majnun!' ('crazy!'). He altered course to the markets of southern Cairo.

The flotilla had crossed the Indian Ocean and traversed the Suez Canal without incident, arriving at Port Alexandria on December 3, 1914; and within two days the troops had arrived at Mena Camp, about 7 miles south-west of Cairo. They were to spend the next four months being drilled into an efficient fighting machine; but just where their battles were to take place was still a matter of debate–some held that Western Europe was their destination, while others voted for the escalating conflict with Turkey in the Mediterranean. Regardless of the outcome, the troops underwent their training with zeal and wry humour.

Mena Camp stretched across the sand in an orderly grid a few hundred yards from the pyramids; and at its peak would house over 25,000 troops. Within days, roughly made signposts appeared at street corners: 'Pitt Street', 'Hyde Park', 'Bondi Beach' or 'This Way to the War'. Impromptu Rugby or 'Aussie Rules' games sprang up on a field of packed sand with little observation of the rules of fair play–some would call it 'Rafferty's Rules'. Each morning reveille would sound at 6.15am, sending soldiers tumbling from their cots, farting and coughing with their first cigarette of the day as they emptied sand from boots. At the ablution troughs, they'd throw brackish water over themselves and devour a breakfast of powdered eggs and tepid tea.

The training was rigorous; jolting the men to the realisation that they were at last being prepared for the heat of battle. The days turned to weeks in a blur of small arms drill, unarmed combat, trench warfare techniques and mock battles. Each day they marched, dug, paraded, sweated and swore; and by the ten pm 'lights out' they slumped into their cots fully clothed; too exhausted to care.

After six straight days of hard work, they were ready for some entertainment on their one 'day off', and Cairo, with its bazaars, cafes and brothels, was more than willing to provide them the opportunity to spend their accumulated pay. The Australians were the highest paid allied troops in the world at the time; it was a constant complaint of the British that wherever the Aussies were, prices took a leap. The vast majority had never travelled beyond the coasts of Australia, and the wonders of the pyramids, the ancient Sphinx and the museums of Cairo were high on the list. Cairo's brothels also did a roaring trade, and more than a few troops were willing to risk the dangers of venereal disease to sample the merchandise.

~ ~ ~

Sweat stung Danny's eyes. It was hot for March– pushing 30 degrees Celsius and not a puff of wind. His calf muscles groaned with each step through the fickle sand, and his pack was a leaden weight. A movement in the distance caught his attention; a camel and rider were crossing the desert away to the south. *'These crazy Arabs rug themselves up in dressing gowns in the blazing sun. Bloody crazy. 'Wish I was on a camel though.'*

The platoon had marched from Mena in the afternoon, heading southward on an overnight bivouac; and although the sun had dipped lower, its venom remained potent. The Sahara undulated away to eternity beneath a bleached sky; each sand dune was etched with wind-ripples up to its razor-sharp peak. Random patches of hard, pebbled ground appeared from nowhere, making the going easier for a while, but the sand soon returned to remind them who was boss.

The line momentarily lost momentum as Danny passed a soldier who'd collapsed; apparently semi-conscious and breathing rapid, shallow breaths. The Lieutenant's voice rang out, 'As you were men! Retain formation!' A pair of stretcher-bearers appeared and tended to the fallen man. *'Heat stroke'*, thought Danny, and continued up the face of the next dune.

Further up the line, John breasted a low ridge to the sight of the Djoser Pyramid glowing ochre-red in the sunset. Checking his watch, he guessed the ancient structure would be their destination. The platoon finally reached the 62-metre-high tiered monolith as dying light played shadows over its immense stone blocks. Edges once sharp as a scimitar had been blunted by 46 centuries of wind and sun. *'If only its walls could speak, what stories would they tell?'* He thought. At the command to 'fall out', the men dropped their packs and collapsed to the sand. The temperature dropped and a light breeze cooled them through sweaty tunics. Canteens were filled and a few men climbed the stone terraces as the sun disappeared over the Nile Valley.

Danny leant against an ancient tomb wall, wondering at the huge pyramid; reflecting to deep time and the wars it had seen. *'The tribal wars of the ancient Pharaohs, the Persian conquest, and Alexander the Great. Then it was the Macedonians' turn, then the Romans, the Turks, and the British. And now, here we are on our way to another war, threatening to be bigger than anything the world has seen. And I hope to God I come back in one piece.'* He absent-mindedly tossed a pebble at a lizard, sending it scurrying under a stone.

Night came swiftly. Clouds scudded across a pale moon and a skittish wind kicked up snatches of sand. The Djoser loomed above the platoon like a sleeping giant as the troops huddled together, greatcoat collars turned up against the cold after a meal of bully beef and hard tack biscuits. One corporal in Danny's group broke into their banter:

'You know why they put bully beef into square tins?'

Another soldier replied, 'No, why's that, Jack?'

'Because it makes it harder to shove it up the cook's arse.'

A ripple of laughter skittered across the group, and Nutty chimed in. 'My uncle Harry once went to a fancy restaurant at Claridge's Hotel in London, where they guaranteed to serve every famous national dish in the world, or they'd pay the customer 100 pounds.' The men nudged each other; Nutty was becoming well known for his yarns. 'Well, Harry was a bit short of a quid, so he ordered Kangaroo balls on toast. The waiter took down his order without raising an eyebrow, but after a few minutes, came back with an embarrassed look on his face. He slips uncle Harry 100 quid under the table, and he says, 'Please don't tell anyone about this sir, it would be bad for business,' and Harry says, 'I suppose kangaroo's balls are pretty rare in London.' And the waiter says. 'Oh no sir, you don't understand— we've run out of bread.'

It was late. Dark shapes lay on the sand. Cigarette-ends glowed like fireflies amid a chorus of snores and snatches of low conversation. John lay wrapped in his greatcoat, staring at the ruins of a mortuary temple, its stone walls defying time. His thoughts strayed to Charlie Schumacher, locked behind barbed wire in Sydney. They were good mates; went through high school together, got into fights, surfed at Coogee, laughed a lot. And now, suddenly, he was an enemy. German families were being spat at in the streets–all because of what happened on the other side of the world. *'It seems to me that wars are fought between blokes that could have been mates in another time, just like Charlie and me. Makes no sense, but that's our job–shoot the other bloke before he shoots you.'*

Bill Bradley was sound asleep, riding a river of dreams. He was running across an open field toward the enemy. He could see their helmets, but not their faces. His Lee-Enfield 303 rifle was hot from firing, and he was alone; running alone at the enemy, and their helmets were ringing with the ricochet of his bullets. Then he was in a parade–he was a hero and girls were waving to him. Pretty girls. 'General Bradley!' They called; waving and smiling. Bill smiled back at them, fingers jiggling in a dream-wave from the sand beside the Djoser.

Danny stared up at a night sky with a million points of blinking starlight. He thought about the endless bayonet drills they'd undergone. How to thrust. How to parry. The vertical stroke with the rifle-butt. The 'smash' following the vertical stroke. The downward slash. All well-rehearsed and perfected, but could he ram a blade through someone's guts? It was easy to stab a post covered with hessian, but could he watch the blood gush from a man's body, and the light die from his eyes? He didn't know. He honestly didn't know.

Nutty smoked a Woodbine and scanned the horizon. To the north, the lights of Cairo glowed in a low halo. From the east, there was a faint aroma of the marshy wetlands lining the Nile. His thoughts turned to home and the family he left to go to war. For a naïve 22-year-old it had been a decision made in the excitement of the moment, spurred on by the patriotic fervour of his mates. And while it wasn't a decision he regretted, his heart yearned for home. *I'm the funny bloke. The clown; always with the jokes and the tall stories. Everybody laughs, and every night I lie awake and miss Mum, Dad, Katie, my sister. Miss my home.'*

~   ~   ~

5 April 1915
Cath Thornton
c/- Randwick Royal Hotel

2 Perouse Rd.
Randwick
NSW
Australia

Dear Sis,

Greetings from the Mediterranean. We're on the move again after four months in the desert near Cairo. Egypt was a welcome change from being on the ship, and we did some hard training, but we were glad to be rid of the sand and flies, and all the blokes are itching to see action, wherever that will be.

John and I are both good, although I had a bout of dysentery and John was crook with flu for a while. We got to see the pyramids and the Sphinx and made a few visits to Cairo, which is a beautiful city with good beer and awful tea.

We marched out of camp at 4.30am a few days ago and got on a train that smelt like camel dung, and got to Alexandria at 3 in the morning after not much sleep. We worked all day loading stores and equipment on board the 'Lake Michigan' troop ship and finally left port at midnight. The boys and I just slept on deck we were that tired.

This morning we paraded on deck and the CO told us we're sailing to the island of Lemnos in Greece. Why we're going to Greece I haven't a clue, but that's the army for you. Some blokes reckon we might be headed for Turkey.

Hope university is going well, and you haven't killed anyone yet. Give everyone our love.

Danny.

Chapter 8

Into Hell

At 2.30am on Sunday the 25th of April 1915, a convoy of warships steamed eastward across the Aegean in battle formation. On the deck of the *'Lake Michigan'*, Danny dreamed of Coogee Beach. He was swimming through a gentle swell - the throbbing of the ship's turbines became the rhythm of his stroke as he glided through the water. The sun was warm on his back.

The battalion had reached Lemnos earlier that month, and the men were immediately thrust into training for the Turkish invasion; climbing in full pack through the hills above Moudros Bay toward an enemy they were yet to meet. The small Greek island, only sixty miles to the west of Turkey, was the allied base for the landings, where reinforcements would muster and the sick and injured would return for treatment and recuperation. After several false starts the day had come -

they boarded the 'Lake Michigan' at 11pm on April 24, bound for Gallipoli. The 4th Battalion was finally about to get 'into the thick of it'.

Something bumped Danny's leg. In his dream he felt the rough skin of a shark and he woke with a start to John's grinning face in the half light. 'Wakey wakey brother! Hands off snakey! The army's calling you!' Across *'Lake Michigan's'* decks, soldiers roused from sleep and stumbled below for a breakfast of beef stew and bread. For most, it would be their last meal eaten in safety for months. For some, it would be their last meal.

Each soldier must deal with the lull before battle as best they can. Some are raucous; indiscriminately firing jokes about like a Vickers gun. Some are silent; their heads buried in a book or whispering a prayer. Some get the shakes, some are catatonic, and some are completely unfazed. For those about to taste battle for the first time, like most of the fourth battalion, inexperience can be a blessing or a curse–it can mask the horrors to come, but when reality hits, it can overwhelm. The officers and senior NCO's of the 1st AIF were well aware of this, and moved among their charges, uttering words of support and confidence, checking bayonets were sharp and water bottles filled.

Danny ate mechanically, paying little attention to the chatter. The knot in his stomach that began as he walked up the ship's gangway refused to leave. He was swept along by events beyond his control - his only lifeline was his training and his duty as a soldier, and his one great fear was he wouldn't have the courage to carry it out. *'What will I do when the firing starts? Will I run forward with my mates, or just cower in a corner of the boat?'*

The battalion commander issued a message to his troops that morning: *'Men, you are about to go into action. Your training has made you fit for it, and I have the greatest confidence in your courage and resolution. Just one word– keep a cool head and listen to the fire orders of your officers. When you shoot, let every bullet find its mark; when you use the bayonet, see that you stick it in. Good luck.'*

He wondered again over his resolve to plunge a bayonet into a man's body, and he shuddered. *'Perhaps if it's "kill or be killed", it'll be easier.'* He thought. Death lurked in the dark corners of his mind, but he allowed it no light. Every soldier is self-inoculated with the unshakable belief that he will survive–it's what keeps him sane.

At 4am the convoy had steamed to within 800 yards of the Turkish coast as the troops mustered on deck to board the landing boats. The crack of small arms fire from the coast sounded like tentative spits of rain, answered promptly by Turkish machine gun fire flashing in the dark. The rain suddenly became a storm as the AIF's 3rd Brigade were the first to wade ashore on a deserted beach soon to become known as 'ANZAC Cove'.

The battalion was well-drilled in the disembarkation procedure. They would board the *'Lake Michigan's'* lifeboats and be lowered by davits to the sea, where steam pinnaces would secure a line and tow them to within 150 yards of the coast; setting them adrift to row themselves ashore. Each pinnace was armed with a Vickers gun that would provide answering fire to the Turkish defences. The men themselves were merely passengers–they would be in no position to return fire from the rocking, crowded boats. They'd take whatever cover they could until reaching the shore.

Dawn's first glimmer silhouetted the Turkish hills. The battle was louder now - return fire from the ANZAC troops intensified as more boats landed. An on-shore wind blew smoke laced with cordite across the deck as the troops on board the *'Lake Michigan'* gave a cheer - 'Abdul' was getting a black eye. John turned to Danny, his face lit by shellfire, eyes wide with excitement. He grabbed Danny's arm. 'This is it, Danny!'

The troops took cover below the ship's rail, and each man steeled himself for what was to come. A few quips about 'cracker night' were heard, followed by ragged laughter. Smoking had been banned since the previous day, lest a flared match be seen by spotter planes; and now, the same telltale match could invite a bullet from a shore-based sniper - the Turkish army's German-made M1903 Mauser rifle could kill a man at 650 yards. As the sun rose in a misty beacon through the smoke of battle, the ship slowed and the men began moving in double file to their allocated boats. As the guns raged, the odd joke could still be heard:

'Nice day for a boat ride.'

'Oh shit–sorry, forgot my wallet–be back in a tick.'

'Yeah, no worries mate–I'll mind your spot.'

The sky was lighter as Danny boarded a boat crammed with 40 comrades. The davits let go, and the hull hit the water with a thud, bobbing in wait for the tow. They sat hunched over, gripping their rifles as the pinnace came alongside with a surge of bow-wave to secure the line. A sailor stood in the bow cockpit manning the Vickers gun; eyes wide, jaw set firm and knuckles white on the trigger housing. Around the boat, men took cover; eyes darting back and forth, adrenaline pumping. The jokes had ceased.

The towline twanged taut, and they sped shoreward under a rain of fire. Bullets buzzed overhead like angry wasps; thudding into the hull as men ducked under the gunwale's fickle cover. A bullet slammed into one man, spinning him backwards into the water. Another was hit in the face, spraying the boat with crimson pulp. The pinnace's Vickers gun spat back in angry staccato; boiling seawater steaming from its barrel. The armada of landing boats weaved through the chop at full speed, scarring the sea with curves of frantic wake water. A shell exploded aboard one of the boats with a deafening roar, killing dozens.

The sun is now bright above rugged hilltops—the beach is only 200 yards away and enemy fire is intense. The cliffs rise almost vertically; perhaps 200 feet high. Danny can see soldiers scaling like ants up through scrub toward the summit. Enemy fire flashes from the ridges and more men in the boats are dropping; eyes glazed with the patina of death. The towline is released and the pinnace pulls away in a shallow arc to starboard. The skipper opens the throttle wide and retreats out to sea. The man on the Vickers gun is dead; one arm hangs limply over the stock; its barrel aimed upward to a sky smudged with smoke.

They try to row toward the shore, but oars clash and skate over the water in their clumsy fever of survival. The Lieutenant screams out a stroke rate and they start to make progress. There are bodies in the water—one still holds a rifle to his chest in a claw-like grip. A couple of blokes near Danny take hits, slumping together in death like a pair of sleeping drunks. He can see the sandy bottom through the green depths and the Lieutenant yells, 'Over the side!'

Danny rolls over the gunwale and drops into the water. For a moment, the murderous sound of battle is silenced as his head dips under the surface, but he finds purchase on the sand and pushes upward to the sunlight. The sea is cool on his face and he shakes the water from his eyes. He holds his rifle high and pushes off the sand toward the shore, less than 50 metres away. He looks around for John but can't see him. Bullets zip into the water everywhere. The yells of the living and the agonised cries of the dying form a hideous duet. The water is getting shallower—his pack is sodden and he's in waist-deep water now, gathering momentum as the sea slowly releases him from its grip.

He reaches the shore. Bullets kick up sand and bodies lie on the beach like ink blots; some are dead, others are screaming and calling for help, but he can't stop. Many have abandoned their wet, heavy packs and they lie on the beach like stranded turtles. The Lieutenant is running alongside Danny and then he's gone; taking a bullet to the chest and falling dead to the sand. The beach is only 50 feet wide and he sprints forward, zigzagging toward hills rising like castle battlements.

Danny dropped to one knee and worked at the bolt of his rifle to free it from sand. The magazine engaged, and catching the flash from a Turkish muzzle, he sighted on his target and squeezed the trigger. The Lee Enfield bucked against his shoulder and he worked the bolt and fired again. He had begun to fight, and the knot in his stomach had vanished.

He joined his comrades and weaved through sand dunes and clumps of gorse toward the cliffs. Amid the deafening pulse of battle, someone passed on a rumour that they'd landed on the wrong beach, adding, 'Perhaps if we let Abdul know we've made an honest mistake, they'll stop shooting at us.' A sergeant bleeding from a head wound joined the rush upwards. 'C'mon you blokes–there's a war to fight up on top. Fix bayonets and keep low. Bring yer packs if yer still got 'em, and follow me up to the party.'

The track climbed almost vertically through rosemary bush and stunted tree-roots poking from the sand. Machine gun fire became louder with each step - a man in front took a bullet in the thigh and fell spread-eagled into the undergrowth. Danny wondered at how a living, vibrant man could become a shapeless dead thing the next. After a while he stopped taking notice–he was already adapting to the horror. Stretcher bearers passed down the track carrying wounded to the beach. One man appeared, crawling along with half a leg blown off. 'Other blokes are worse off than me' he said, 'Anyway, I don't think I'll last more than an hour.' Danny watched him descend to the beach, wondering at his resilience.

They breasted the top and immediately descended into a steep ravine recently christened 'Shrapnel Gully', that held troops in reserve. At the command to 'stand down', Danny dropped his pack and collapsed to the ground. The chaos of the landing crowded his mind in a maelstrom; the noise, the fear, the blood, the screams, the bodies, and above all, the exhilaration of survival–of being alive when so many around him were dead. He had risen to the moment despite his self-doubt, and had not been found wanting. Around him were the twisted bodies of Turks caught in the assault. *'Strange.'* He thought, *'Dead men all look the same, regardless of what side they're on.'*

Around him, all was confusion. The men who had undergone their baptism of fire now looked for leadership. His platoon had lost its CO on the beach, fighting units were intermingled, the command structure was unclear and battle plans were fluid. The entire Anzac invading force was spread across a two-mile front created by 16,000 brave men who pushed back the Turkish army with guts and determination. One undeniable fact though was certain; if the line didn't hold, the Anzacs would be pushed back to the sea, where no evacuation plan was in place. They'd be slaughtered on the beach.

Nutty leant against a tree; his face grimy with dirt and sweat. A crimson patch of blood surrounded a jagged rip in the shoulder of his uniform. Danny slumped down beside him and they nodded a greeting.

'What happened to your shoulder?'

'Piece of shrapnel got me. I thought it was a mozzie bite–we've got big ones in Young, ya know,'

Danny grinned. 'Don't you ever stop joking?'

'Who's jokin'?'

Danny braved the question: 'Have you seen John or Bill?'

'No, mate–I think they got off before us–they could be anywhere by now.'

As the sun passed its zenith on day one of the Gallipoli campaign, Anzac Cove had been cleared of all but intermittent sniper fire, and a battle headquarters of sorts had taken shape. Field hospital tents appeared, and barges had unloaded much-needed ammunition and other supplies. By the next day, the Commander of the campaign, British General William Birdwood, along with the commanders of the Australian and New Zealand Forces, would establish his headquarters in a gully overlooking the cove, but at this precarious point in the campaign, all attention was focussed on establishing and holding the front line.

~   ~   ~

Major General William Bridges was in deep thought; gnawing on the arm of his spectacles as he conferred with his battalion commanders. He was on the horns of a dilemma. As head of the Australian forces, he controlled a thin line of defence against the Turks, who had already begun to reinforce their numbers. The first day's tally of Anzac dead, wounded and missing was put at 2,000, and reinforcements were not even on the horizon. Bridges was holding the 4th Battalion in reserve to plug the gaps, but they were all he had, and he meant to use them wisely.

Half a mile from Shrapnel Gully lay '400 Plateau' - a relatively flat area of scrubland amid a maze of sharp ridges and steep ravines. It was the obvious spot for the Turks to break through, attack the Anzacs from the rear and cut supply lines. The 2nd and 3rd Brigades were struggling to hold the line, facing constant artillery fire and bayonet charges. The field telephone was running hot with calls to reinforce the plateau, and when the urgency of the situation was confirmed by one of

Bridges' senior advisors, he ordered the 4th to advance into the thick of battle.

~   ~   ~

Afternoon shadows crept through the undergrowth as they reached the defence line on 400 Plateau. Danny was deployed as part of a scratched-together 'A Company' - 200 men under Major Matthew Hunter, a shopkeeper from Ashfield and veteran of the Second Boer War. The trenches snaked away to the left for about 500 yards, and to the right along Bolton's ridge for some 600 yards, until cliffs dropped to 'Brighton Beach'. They had been dug in haste between attack and counterattack during the day—and though stacked with sandbags, were only just deep enough for a man to stand upright.

The men of the 3rd Brigade stood down, hollow-eyed from incessant battle and lack of sleep. As they passed to the rear, a few of them nodded weary greetings to the relieving force:

'Welcome to Gallipoli Heights, mate—worst real estate this side of Lemnos.'

'Keep yer arse down, boys. Abdul can't shoot for shit, but sometimes he gets lucky.'

'Keep me spot warm, would ya? And no pissing in me tea mug while I'm gone.'

Danny cautiously mounted the firing step and took his bearings. The Turkish line was only 70 yards away - there was movement behind the barbed wire and sandbags. Out in 'no-man's-land', bodies from both sides were strewn about, but it appeared the Turks had taken greater losses. To his right, only 30 yards away, the ground dropped away into a steep ravine, christened 'Cooee Gully' by the Anzacs. The gully was a weak spot - it was feared a small attacking force could move undetected to the lip, leaving only a 30-yard charge to the Anzac line.

The maze of deep ravines and sharp ridges above ANZAC Cove had made a co-ordinated advance almost impossible, fragmenting the front line to the point where in some stretches the Turkish lines were uncomfortably close. British reconnaissance of the peninsula's terrain had been perfunctory, and a major blunder had been discovered when field artillery couldn't be hauled up the rugged cliffs. Without artillery, the ANZACS would be fighting with one hand tied behind their backs, and on 400 Plateau, the Turks had been shelling them continuously; taking a mounting toll of dead and wounded.

Major Hunter was moving along the trenches, chatting to his men. He was in his mid-40's, a little taller than Danny; perhaps 6 feet, with greying hair and deep brown eyes. Danny had seen quite a few senior officers over the previous six months, and regarded them as falling broadly into two types. As far as he was concerned, most of the British were Eton-types; born to rule, dismissive of anyone below their rank, and inclined to be careless with other men's lives. The Australians had some of those, but most of them were from the second type–more down to earth, which was just as well, as the average Australian soldier didn't care much for being ordered about; particularly by 'Pommies'. By the style of him, Hunter looked to be in the second type. He paused and regarded Danny with a knowing eye.

Danny saluted and Hunter shook his hand.

'You look a little young to be on a mountain in Turkey, private….?'

'Thornton, sir. Danny Thornton, 4th Battalion.'

'From New South Wales?'

'Yes sir, Randwick, to be exact.'

'Randwick, I know it well. You wouldn't be from the Thornton family at the Royal Hotel, would you?'

Danny was startled. 'Well actually sir, James Thornton, the publican, is my father.'

Hunter smiled and jerked his thumb back over a shoulder. 'And your brother John is 100 yards down the line that way.'

Danny laughed, suddenly hugely relieved. 'I was hoping he'd made it through the day. Sir, could you please say g'day from me if you see him again?'

Hunter placed a hand on Danny's shoulder. 'Of course, Private–consider it done.'

~   ~   ~

A cold-night mist crept along the trench floor, clinging to Danny like a damp sponge. The smell of Abdul's cooking drifted across no-man's-land, and he could hear them chatting in Arabic as they ate. The battlefield had been quiet, other than a few speculative rounds fired by both sides. Low snatches of conversation drifted down the Anzac line as NCO's patrolled their sections, keeping the men alert. From down the line he heard Nutty's familiar voice, followed by a chorus of chuckles. *'He's telling another of his jokes. That bloke should be on the stage,'* he thought. *'The next Cobb & Co stage out of town.'*

'A-Company' had formed two 100-men units, sharing a 24-hour guard. Those on relief were bivouacked behind the lines, throwing down a meal of bully beef or grabbing much needed sleep wherever they dropped. Those on the front-line scanned the battleground for any sign of imminent attack. It reminded Danny of patrolling Coogee Beach - watching for rips or potential rescues. *'You learn to spot things out of the ordinary.'* He thought. *'A raised arm, a sudden panicked yell or a stretch of current that surges with unusual strength. It's the same here–a faint sound, a rustling of canvas or muffled knock of metal. The hairs on your neck stand up and your stomach turns a somersault.'*

~   ~   ~

At 12.30am on Monday 26 April, Lieutenant Ahmet Kaya led a platoon of 50 Turkish soldiers down the escarpment of Pine Ridge, away from their own lines. Among their number was a gun crew carrying an MG09 Maxim machine gun. Kaya was a career army officer from a military family. His father had served in the Crimea, and his grandfather fought the Greeks at the battle of Navarino in 1827. He was a patriot; imbued with the passion of a strong Turkish nation. He didn't trust Germany. *'They might be allies for now,'* he thought, *'but they're barbarians, bent on domination.'* He was devoted to ridding his country of every foreign interference–especially the damned Australians.

They came to a ravine that narrowed to a track between steep walls running northward for 800 yards. On their right, the escarpment rose some 80 feet to their own lines, and atop the ridge to their left were the Anzac trenches. They were like hares burrowing through a secret passageway, leading to the ravine known to the Australians as 'Cooee Gully'.

Kaya slowed the pace–silence was critical. *The cold night air in these hills carries sound like the 'Salat al-fajr' prayer at sunrise.'* He thought. *'There'll be time enough to make a noise when it counts the most–driving the infidels from our country.'*

~ ~ ~

Danny checked his watch–12.30am. He'd been on active duty for almost 24 hours, but it seemed like a year–the launching of the boats, the rain of fire in their assault on the beach, the terror of wading through deep water, scrambling up the hills, and now, an endless night with the threat of attack sitting on his shoulder like a grinning gargoyle. He was tired–dog tired and not a little hungry, but it would be hours before he'd be relieved.

He thought about the four mates who dined in style that evening at the Mount Lavinia Hotel in Colombo–John, Nutty, Bill and himself. *'Was that five months ago?'*

Back then, war was only a vague thought–like threads of a half-forgotten dream in the light of day. But now, here he was, half-asleep on the end of a 303 with thousands of Turks a stone's throw away; itching to put a bullet in his brain. *What happened to Bill? He's the only one not accounted for….*

~   ~   ~

At 1.00am Lieutenant Kaya halted the platoon as the gully closed into a single 50-foot fissure; the hares had attained their first objective. The plan was in three phases. The Maxim gun crew would scale the ravine and dig out an emplacement from the scrub, just below the top–low enough to provide cover for the gun crew but high enough for the barrel to spit death at the invaders.

Once the gun was in place, the rest of the platoon would climb to the top, fanning out on each side of the Maxim for about 50 yards. At the lieutenant's signal the Maxim would open up on the Anzac line, only 30 yards away. The platoon would then attack in a concentrated bayonet charge; opening a hole for the Turkish lines behind them to advance and overwhelm the Anzacs and drive them back to the beach. Casualties were expected to be high. He fully expected to die tonight, and was unafraid. 'Victory will surely follow our deaths, "*inshallah.*'

~ ~ ~

Lieutenant Colonel Gerald McVie hunched over a map with his senior officers. As commander of the 4th Battalion, his focus was to give his men every chance to hold Plateau 400. He stabbed at the map with a stubby index finger and glanced around the group.

'Gentlemen, without artillery, we've one arm tied behind our backs–the bloody Turks can just sit back and lob shells over us without retaliation–or so they think. There's been a suggestion to utilise cannon fire from one of the battleships in Anzac Cove. The Brits tell us their guns can elevate only 13.5 degrees, which means their arc of fire will be long, but they assure us they can land shells on Abdul without blowing our blokes up. We've been given the go-ahead from the top, and a communications line out to HMS Triumph is operational. She's an old ship, but she has the firepower we need. We must be her eyes–call the co-ordinates and pinpoint the elevation of the hits, but I believe it can be done.'

~ ~ ~

It was slow going for the Turkish gun crew to clamber up the steep ravine loaded with a Maxim gun and ammunition, but by 1.45am it was assembled and ready. The all-clear signal was given, and Lieutenant

Kaya gave the order for his men to take their positions at the top.

~ ~ ~

Danny knuckle-rubbed his eyes and yawned. Something caught his ear, off to the right–a metallic clicking sound. It didn't seem to come from the Anzac line. He whispered to the soldier on his right.

'Hey, Rus–you hear that?'

'Mate, I'm so bloody tired I wouldn't hear a howitzer shell if it hit me up the arse.'

Danny listened again, but the noise was gone. Maybe he was imagining things–getting spooked.

~ ~ ~

2am. Lieutenant Kaya lay flat against the lip of the ravine; staring through the scrub across 30 yards of open ground to the Anzac trenches. He could see their cigarettes glowing in the dark. His platoon was in place, ready to advance after the Maxim did its job. He reached down, and drawing his Mauser semi-automatic pistol, gave the order to open fire.

The Maxim began its deadly chatter, raking the Anzac trenches with fire. A Vickers crew was the first to be taken out–they fell dead over their sandbags, steam curling from their bullet wounds in the cold night air. Along the line all was pandemonium as NCO's screamed orders to fix bayonets in anticipation of a charge. A second Vickers crew returned fire, but the enemy's cover proved effective, and the Maxim continued its deadly bark from the edge of the ravine. Kaya knew he could only rely on the gun's impact for a short time until the Anzacs took effective cover. He gave the order for his platoon to charge, and a long line of Turks rose up with bayonets fixed. They came at the Anzac line firing from the hip, screaming *'Allah Akbar'*.

Danny rapid fires his.303 at the charging line and Turks are falling, but they're covering ground quickly and hurling themselves into the trenches. Bodies crash down in the half light–he lowers his rifle to the 'guard' position as one Turk appears - eyes wide, mouth open in a scream of Arabic as he lunges forward. Deadly blades clash against each other and Danny parries a blow; but the man is quick and lunges forward again.

His fighting is instinctive from endless drilling-it's stripped his nerve fibres to bare wires that know nothing but survival. He senses the gleam of light passing over a blade; the sudden shift of his opponent's stance; the sharp intake of breath before a deadly lunge. All these signals are received and interpreted in milliseconds as his mind commands his body to live.

Danny bats the blade away and slams the butt of his rifle hard and fast into the Turk's temple, then buries his bayonet deep down into the man's chest–he can feel it scrape over ribs. He withdraws the blade and steps back, his eyes flicking about like a wild animal, ready for the next attack.

Lieutenant Kaya leaps into the trench and fires his Mauser point blank into Rus's chest - the young digger looks down at the gaping hole and drops dead to the ground. Danny aims at the Turk and squeezes the 303's trigger but nothing happens–the bolt's jammed. Kaya raises his pistol to fire and Danny dives at the man in desperation, feeling a red-hot pain in his left shoulder as he cannons into the Turk and they come down heavily to the ground, covered in mud. Danny's left arm is useless. He pins Kaya's pistol hand to the dirt while Kaya smashes his fist repeatedly into the younger man's face, sensing victory. Danny is weakening and Kaya's pistol arm is working loose. Danny throws his head back and brings his forehead down across the bridge of Kaya's nose like a human hammer. Blood fountains and Kaya's eyes are wild with pain and a new expression–fear. Danny hits him again. And again. And again, until everything fades.

~   ~   ~

Lieutenant Colonel Gerald McVie huddled over a collapsible table in a makeshift field HQ; pressing the field phone firmly to his ear to muffle the noise of battle. The line to HMS Triumph crackled like crushed cellophane.

'Captain', 'I need urgent support,'

The tinny reply came through his headphones. 'Aye Gerald, we're standing by for your shelling co-ordinates.'

McVie rattled off the Turkish line's position. 'I also need you to shine a light on this mess. Are you able to focus searchlights up here as well?'

'Of course. We have your location. It can be done right away.'

'Roger that. Open fire on the bastards Captain, and light up Plateau 400 like a Christmas tree.'

~　~　~

'A' Company's rear guard hurled themselves back into the front line to defend against the Turkish charge. Screams cut through the night as men fought hand to hand in the darkness. A Turk was sliced shoulder to groin by a bayonet; his intestines slipping to the ground in a thick dribble. A bomb exploded in the middle of a knot of Anzacs; shrapnel blossoming like deadly fireworks. A digger snapped off a round from his 303, point blank into a Turk's chest, blowing him apart.

On the other side of no-man's-land a bugle sounded and hundreds of Turkish throats invoked Allah as they rose from the trenches like a barbarian horde. They moved in a dark wave across the killing ground, bayonets fixed, roaring death. A young Anzac private turned at the bugle's sound to see a dark wave of humanity rushing toward him across the killing ground, and knew they were hopelessly outnumbered. As he raised his 303, ready to die fighting, he thought of his mother, and whispered goodbye.

~   ~   ~

HMS Triumph's ten-inch guns locked into place at maximum elevation; their muzzles pointing away to the Turkish coast like fingers of doom. High in the ship's superstructure a mechanical computer calculated trigonometric firing instructions, transmitting them to the waiting gun crew. The gun's 500-pound shells were loaded from the projectile hoist and the breech chamber was secured. The gun crew signalled ready. At the same moment the ship's searchlights aimed landward using identical co-ordinates. From the ship's bridge came the order to fire.

Shafts of white light split the darkness like a cleaver, blinding the charging Turks as they lost direction and cannoned into each other like billiard balls. A split second later, an almighty roar erupted out to sea as a shell screamed overhead through the night sky at over 2,500 feet per second; exploding in the Turkish lines with surgical precision. A red ball of flame fissured the darkness, silhouetting destruction and death.

The artillery support heartened the Anzacs, and sensing the tide of battle was about to turn, they fought back with renewed strength. The enemy was soon repelled from the trenches, and with a blood-curdling battle cry the Anzacs were up over the top and running head-on through the scrub with the searchlights at their backs. Pandemonium reigned on no-man's-land, with the Turkish attack in disarray. The diggers shouldered their 303's, worked the bolt and fired. Worked the bolt and fired. Worked the bolt and fired. Enemy soldiers were falling everywhere; their faces confused and terrified at the ferocity of the counterattack until the command to retreat resounded along their line. The Turkish forces had been decimated in a matter of minutes, and as the enemy turned back toward their own lines, the diggers continued to fire.

~   ~   ~

Dawn paled the eastern sky as stretcher-bearers moved through the morning mist, searching for wounded and collecting ID tags from the dead. Death didn't discriminate by uniform, and neither did the men who cared for the survivors. Men who had fought and killed each other only a few hours before were stretchered away together for triage and evacuation to Lemnos. Such is the futility of war.

The battle had been short and furious. Artillery fire from HMS Triumph was halted when the Anzacs charged from their trenches, but the initial shelling had done the required damage–the attack had been repelled and the Anzac line remained unbroken. Abdul would now be reluctant to mount a night-time assault, and could never again be certain that further naval shelling would not be called into play.

One of the stretcher-bearers found two bodies intertwined at the bottom of a trench, frozen in the midst of a struggle. The man underneath wore the insignia of a Turkish officer, still grasping a pistol in his left hand. He stooped down to the digger who was face down, partially on top of the Turk, and gently rolled him over. It was a young private. His face was covered in blood and gore and a shoulder wound seeped dark blood. His eyelids flickered for an instant. 'Bobby! Live one over here!' Called the man to his mate, as he felt for the young

Private's pulse–it was slow and weak. He glanced over at the uncovered Turk, and gasped–he was dead; his face completely caved in, in as if someone had beaten him to death with a hammer.

Chapter 9

"O" Ward

Stokeland House nestled in a ring of Norfolk pines above Hermit Bay in Sydney Harbour's elite suburb of Vaucluse. Built in the 1850s, the two-storey Italianate mansion commanded broad views sweeping westward to Shark Island and Bradley's Head. Cath stood at the front gate, admiring the view. *'Nice neighbourhood.'* She thought. *'If you could afford it.'*

It was May 1915-her final year of medicine at Sydney University. With fierce determination she'd dived into the mysteries of cellular biology, chemistry, physics, and physiology–and that was just the first year's syllabus. Anatomy, biochemistry, mathematics, embryology and more were to follow, and she took them on like an Olympic hurdler–one jump at a time. And like a hurdler with a painful calf muscle, she'd battled the 'handicap' of being a woman.

In an anatomy lecture involving a naked male cadaver, her professor suggested she should avert her eyes while the sheet was drawn back. During an amputation, he advised her to keep smelling salts handy in case she swooned. Resisting the temptation to explain where he could insert his vial of smelling salts, she replied: *'Professor, I grew up in the country, and lived above a pub with three brothers, so I know what a penis looks like. I've helped deliver babies and watched cows being butchered. I've survived droughts and bushfires, witnessed a few pub brawls and stopped a couple, so I'll tell you what—you keep your smelling salts - I think you'll be needing them more than me.'*

She doggedly chipped away at the stone walls of misogyny and gained the grudging respect of many male students, and some of her professors; working twice as hard as most. A requirement of her final year was practical experience at a suitable medical facility, and despite applications to every hospital in the city, she'd been unsuccessful, while her male colleagues were besieged with offers. Her one offer had come from Stokeland House—a convalescent home for ageing, well-heeled women.

A maid answered the door and showed her to a reception hall flooded with sunlight from tall windows. A corridor led away on each side where nurses in starched uniforms scurried back and forth. Presently, a middle-aged man in a navy-blue suit descended the main stairway from the first floor. He was of average height with auburn hair thinning at the temples, wire spectacles and a pair of mutton-chop whiskers. His eyes were close together, accentuating his rounded face and broad nose, reminding Cath of the 'man in the moon'. She rose and shook his outstretched hand.

'Doctor Hugo Sainsbury–Superintendent of Stokeland House. Miss Thornton, is it not?'

'Yes. I'm very pleased to meet you.'

'Likewise, I'm sure. Please follow me–my office is just down the way.'

Sainsbury led her down the carpeted corridor. A few nurses passed by, nodding deferentially to Sainsbury and casting inquiring looks toward Cath. They entered a well-furnished office with wide bay-windows overlooking the harbour. Sainsbury sat behind an imposing mahogany desk.

'Now, Miss Thornton…..'

'Oh, please, call me Cath.'

Sainsbury blinked at her, owl-like and humourless behind his spectacles. 'Miss Thornton, here at Stokeland, we observe the formalities. I shall refer to you by your surname, if you don't mind, and you may call me 'Sir Hugo'.

She groaned inwardly. 'Very well… Sir Hugo.'

'Thank you. Now, I've looked over your academic results and read your professors' reports. You've made satisfactory progress in your studies and are to take your final examinations at the conclusion of this academic year, is that correct?'

'Yes, that's right.'

'And what field of medicine might you pursue with further study?'

'I haven't quite decided, but I've been considering general surgery.'

'Surgery! Well, that's a long hard road, Miss Thornton.'

'Long hard roads are no stranger to me, Sir Hugo.'

He eyed Cath with a puzzled look, as if she was a suspect urine sample. 'Getting back to the matter at hand - your six weeks here will be spent under the guidance of Matron Dewhurst, whom I shall introduce to you in due course. Matron will be your superior, and you will take your instructions from her.'

Having expected the opportunity to work closely with a doctor, Cath was disappointed, but maintained her composure. 'May I ask what my duties will be?'

He waved a dismissive hand. 'I'm leaving that to Matron. Your opportunity will be to learn the science of convalescent care and the particular challenges it holds.'

She bit her tongue and reminded herself that Stokeland House was her one and only option. 'Yes, of course.'

A knock sounded, and a woman entered. She wore the elaborate headdress of a hospital matron, reminding Cath of an Egyptian Pharaoh. She was a large and dumpy, in her late 40s, with flinty eyes and dark hair pulled back severely from an unsmiling face. Her countenance portrayed a woman who expected nothing from life, and hadn't been disappointed.

'Matron Dewhurst–Miss Catherine Thornton.' Cath shook a firm hand devoid of warmth, and beyond a half-formed smile, the matron remained silent as Sainsbury continued. 'Matron will show you around the facility and brief you on her expectations. We shall expect you for duty tomorrow at 7.30 am sharp. Good day, Miss Thornton.' He busied himself with a pile of papers as Cath rose to leave.

Cath followed Dewhurst down the corridor. Its cream-coloured walls were hung with original paintings - she recognised the work of Rupert Bunny, John Longstaff and James Ashton. *'Not bad wallpaper—they'd be worth thousands.'* Dewhurst slipped into a well-worn monologue. 'The ground floor contains patients' rooms. In the southern wing there's also a kitchen and dining room, plus a library, craft area and common room for communal singing and the like.'

They crossed the reception hall to the common rooms. The craft room was furnished with floral upholstered armchairs and lace curtains. A group of elderly women sat at a large table, sketching a vase of roses. They looked up briefly and continued with their art. Notes from Chopin's Mazurka in A Minor sounded from the music room where a patient played piano to a small audience. They returned up the hall to an un-numbered door. 'My office—please come in.'

The small room was devoid of windows and sparsely furnished with a small desk and filing cabinet. Cath thought she'd start off on the right foot. 'I much appreciate the offer of placement at Stokeland, Matron.'

Dewhurst remained emotionless. 'It's a requirement of our license that we take students each year.'

'Oh, I see.' She forced herself to brighten. 'I'm interested to know what my duties will be.'

'You'll undertake the duties of a junior nurse - we have assigned you to work with one of my senior girls.'

Cath was taken aback. 'Oh….. I was hoping to be involved in more complex matters such as diagnosis and treatment.'

'Sir Hugo is far too busy to involve you in his detailed work, Miss Thornton.' She cast a practiced eye over Cath's figure. 'I'm sure we'll have a uniform your size - you can change into it tomorrow when you arrive. Please wear sensible shoes.'

As she followed Dewhurst back to the reception hall, Cath glanced up the staircase. 'By the way, Matron, you haven't mentioned the first floor–what is up there?'

Dewhurst turned with an icy stare. 'The first floor contains "O" Ward, for Sir Hugo's private patients. It's a restricted area–accessible only by Sir Hugo and myself'. She held open the door. 'Until tomorrow, Miss Thornton.'

As the tram rattled down New South Head Road, she mulled over her visit. From the outside, Stokeland House was a grand old building that pleased the eye and beckoned the visitor forward, but her experience once inside had been quite the opposite. Sir Hugo was a pompous ass, and Matron Dewhurst a sour prune of a woman.

There was also a lack of exuberance in the nursing staff. They paced the corridors, in and out of doors without so much as a smile, and while they showed deference to Sainsbury and Dewhurst, there was no connection, no sincerity. It was the same with the patients–she saw no warm greeting or casual conversation with either Sir Hugo or the matron. She assumed that the coldness of the two had somehow rubbed off on the rest, like a virus. *'Oh, well.'* She thought. *'Only six weeks to get through and I'll be rid of the place.'*

~ ~ ~

On her arrival the next morning she was greeted by a woman about her own age in nurse's uniform. 'Cath? Hello, I'm Madeleine Russell, senior nurse. Matron has asked me to chaperone you.'

Cath shook her hand. 'Hello Madeleine–thank you; I hope I won't be in your way.'

'Not at all-I understand you'll qualify as a doctor soon-you must be very pleased.'

Cath laughed. 'I'll be pleased when the exams are over, that's for certain.'

'Let's get you into uniform and we'll get started on our rounds.'

She led Cath to a storeroom where laundered uniforms hung from a rack. Cath chose one her size and reappeared minutes later in a white full-length dress, white cap and red cape about the shoulders. She felt like Florence Nightingale.

Madeleine smiled. 'Perfect–it fits you well. Shall we go?'

Cath had expected a repetitive process of basic health checks–blood pressure, pulse, etc. She certainly didn't expect any medical revelations. However, she was to find that Madeleine Russell's world was much more than that. A visit with Mrs. Frazer in 'G12' taught her the body's normal ageing process can sometimes misrepresent ailment as disease, leading to over-medication. A conversation with Mrs. Gladstone in 'G22' highlighted that an old woman can over-react to a seemingly mild amount of sedation. And in 'G32' she realised the benefits of listening to patients and their emotional as well as physical needs. She marvelled at the transformation of Mrs. Littlewood, who had been admitted in a semi-comatose state, disoriented and barely able to communicate. With little more than increased human contact, a regulated diet and gentle exercise, within a week she'd become active, completely lucid and engaged in Stokeland's craft group.

In her university studies, ageing was discussed in the context of the loss of faculties, failure of organs, heart disease and stroke-in other words, the symptoms of declining health leading to death. Nothing was said about the ageing as a distinct group of patients presenting a unique and often conflicting medical challenge. In 1915, 'Geriatrics' was a word uttered by a small group of researchers whose voice was not yet loud enough to penetrate the hearing of the medical establishment, and Cath realised the immense body of knowledge held by a small number of nurses like Madeleine. She harkened back to Sir Hugo's words, '*Your opportunity will be to learn the science of convalescent care and the particular challenges that it holds.*' Clearly there was more to gain from Stokeland House than she had thought.

Her first two weeks went by in a blur. Much to Cath's delight, Dewhurst had delegated her supervisory duties to Madeleine, and the matron would only be seen briefly, thin lipped and unsmiling in some other part of the building, or climbing the stairs to "O" Ward. Despite her developing relationship with Madeleine, the feeling of disquiet she experienced on her first visit to Stokeland

House continued. Something about the place wasn't right, and she puzzled over why.

~ ~ ~

Frances Mitterrand looked more like a child than an elderly woman as she lay in a drugged haze in "O" Ward. Born in 1840 from a French father and a Martinican mother on the tropical island of Martinique, as a young woman she'd migrated with her family to Sydney where they worked a market garden south of the Cook's River. She married in 1867, but to her eternal sorrow, was never blessed with children; and to fill the void, she devoted herself to charity work. Her husband Joseph passed away in 1895, leaving her a substantial estate, and she had lived a solitary existence until being admitted to Stokeland House after a stroke robbed her of speech.

Her room in "O" Ward overlooking Hermit Bay was large, but it was curtained, locked and barred. In her occasional moments of consciousness, vague figures stood over her, speaking in hushed voices. She imagined she was dying. Sometimes she'd rise from a fog while a uniformed figure fed her broth, and she'd drift away again. Other times she'd wake, shivering with an incessant craving for another injection until the doctor murmured to her and took away the pain.

~ ~ ~

Cath and Madeleine sipped coffee in the dining room after their shift. Madeleine watched as the next team of nurses moved along the corridor to prepare for another eight hours of gruelling work. She glanced at Cath.

'If you don't mind me asking, what made you become a doctor?'

Cath paused in thought for an instant. 'You know, I sometimes ask myself the same question, especially before those damn exams–I don't really know the answer, other than I was good at science, and I suppose I wanted to prove something to myself.'

'What's that?'

'That I could do it, that I could succeed in a man's world.'

'That's important? I mean, about a man's world?'

'Yes–I tire of people telling me I can't do this and can't do that.'

Madeleine took another sip of coffee. 'Strange, but that never really occurred to me. I became a nurse because I just like helping people.'

Cath was pensive. She'd watched Madeleine interact with the patients, and how the elderly ladies would brighten when she entered the ward. Cath's studies had focussed entirely on the 'hard' sciences, and it now seemed to her that little thought had been given to the psychological effect that doctors could have on their patients. It made her realise that as far as the medical establishment was concerned, if it wasn't in a chapter of 'Gray's Anatomy' or somewhere in the Periodic Table of Elements, it didn't warrant consideration. She hoped to learn more from Madeleine.

'I've been meaning to ask you something about Stokeland House.'

'Yes, of course.'

'There's something about this place that I can't put my finger on.' A puzzled look crossed Cath's face. 'It has no…..'

'Soul?'

'Yes–that's it. It's like a machine that ticks over, but it's cold.'

Madeleine looked away, pensive. 'I suppose I take it for granted now, but I know what you mean. Sir Hugo drives us like a team of bullocks–all whip and wallop. He's a humourless man who gets his results through fear–and Matron's the same. The thing that keeps me here are the patients themselves–most of them are lovely old people who just need someone to talk to and take care of them. Luckily, Sir Hugo stays out of our way. Most of the time he's upstairs in "O" Ward.

'What goes on up there?'

'We don't really know, but they tell us it's where he treats his private patients–he and the matron are up and down the stairs all the time, but no-one else is allowed up there. There's a locked gate at the top of the stairs.' She shrugged. 'Anyway, we have enough to do down here to keep us busy.'

~ ~ ~

Cath yawned and switched off the desk lamp. It was 3am and her shift would soon be over. The trams had long since stopped for the night - she'd have to walk up to Old South Head Road and hope for a passing taxi. Stokeland House stood silent; it's normally bustling corridors were dark and empty. Outside, a strong southerly rattled the windows and crowned Hermit Bay with white caps. It was time for her final round, and as she reached for her keys, a faint noise came from upstairs. Was it a whimper, or just the wind moaning through the pines? She started for the staircase.

The first floor was in darkness and she peered through the gloom, taking each step carefully. The sound came again, and she stopped to listen. No, it wasn't the wind. She approached the top few steps and a rustling of soft fabric came to her. A faint glimmer showed from a white robe. A body lay at the top of the stairs. She looked closer. It was an old woman. Her dull, glazed eyes shone in the half-light from a window.

The entrance to the first floor was barred by a tall iron gate set into the wall. She tried the handle–it was locked. The woman was clearly distressed; she whimpered like a newborn kitten as her eyes wandered vaguely about in the gloom. Cath had to get to her. She gripped the bars and hoisted herself up to the top of the gate. Teetering for a moment, she straddled the iron and dropped to the floor with a thud that seemed to resound throughout the house. She scooped the old woman up in her arms and headed toward a dim light showing through an open door.

Cath carried her to the bed and laid her gently against the pillows. The woman was clearly distressed and disoriented. She checked her vital signs–her pulse was low, pupils dilated, breathing slow but regular. Nothing in the room seemed out of the ordinary. A sign above the bed read "Frances Mitterrand."

'Mrs. Mitterrand.' The old woman's eyes fluttered opened.

'Mrs. Mitterrand, can you speak?' A tear dropped from an eye as she slowly shook her head.

Cath noticed a medicine cabinet on the wall. It was locked, but the contents showed through the glass. Several bottles of chloral hydrate lined the shelf, but little else. She checked a waste bin on the floor–three more empty bottles. Someone was making sure Mrs. Mitterrand was heavily sedated. She crossed to the window and parted the curtains. The windows were barred.

She returned to the bed. The old woman had lapsed into sleep, and she re-checked the vitals - all seemed unchanged. She was about to leave when she noticed a scrap of paper in the woman's fist–she was sure it wasn't there before, and the stub of a pencil lay on the sheets. Two words were scrawled: 'HELP ME'.

Cath exited to the corridor and quickly checked the other rooms–all were empty. Mrs. Mitterrand was the sole patient in "O" Ward. She stood in the darkness, thinking. *A sole patient on one floor, heavily sedated, finds the strength to get herself down the corridor to the stairs, but she's trapped. She's under heavy sedation and can't speak. Perhaps she's been sedated for good reason; there may have been self-harm involved. But why lock her away up here, and why aren't there any other 'private patients'?* She climbed back over the iron gate and returned down the stairs.

~ ~ ~

The waiting room was small and stuffy–just a table, two chairs and a naked lightbulb–not exactly welcoming, but not surprising, seeing she was in the headquarters of Sydney's Criminal Investigation Branch in Phillip Street, just around the corner from Hyde Park. For the third time since arriving, Cath rose to leave. She was over-reacting; Mrs. Mitterrand was probably just a confused old woman. But why hadn't she told Sir Hugo what she'd found? *'I know why.'* She thought. *'Because I don't trust him.'*

The door opened and a young man appeared. He was slimly built and in his 30s, with jet black hair and dark almond eyes. His suit was well-tailored; his collar loosened in deference to the warmth of a warm Autumn day. He offered his hand. 'Cath Thornton? Detective Tom Wong. You wish to report an incident?'

'Yes. I mean, I have something to report, but no actual crime–at this stage.'

The detective took a seat opposite her and flipped open a notebook. 'Why don't you start at the beginning, Miss Thornton?'

She took a deep breath and related the events of the previous night while Wong listened to her dispassionately.

'So, you work at Stokeland House as a nurse?'

'Well yes, but only for six weeks–it's my final year of medicine.'

Wong's eyebrows raised. 'A woman doctor. Unusual.'

'Unusual, but not unheard of. I'm not the first.'

'Nor will you be the last. Times are changing. Now, Miss Thornton, you're saying that because you found empty narcotic bottles in a hospital room, that there's some wrongdoing?'

Cath took on a defensive tone. 'What about the note?'

'The words *"help me"* on a piece of paper don't constitute evidence of a crime.'

'Detective, the entire floor is empty save for an old woman in a barred room who's obviously been over-sedated, and I would add, it appears she's been kept there against her will. And why would the rest of the staff be forbidden to go up there? I'm telling you, Sir Hugo Sainsbury and Matron Dewhurst are keeping her there against her will for a reason–it's just that I don't know what that reason is.'

Wong leaned back in his chair, pensive for a moment. 'Miss Thornton, we get our fair share of hysterical people coming in here, convinced their next-door neighbour is an axe murderer, or the stewards fixed the last race at Randwick; but I'll admit you're not hysterical, and your questions are logical. I'll tell you what–I'll do some background checks on your two medicos at Stokeland House and see what I come up with. If there's a reason to take it further, I'll contact you.'

Cath rose from her chair. 'That's all I can ask for, Detective Wong. Thank you. What should I do in the meantime?

'Just carry on with your work as normal.'

After she left, Wong remained in the room, replaying the conversation over in his mind. He gave it an eighty percent chance that this was nothing more than some misunderstanding over hospital protocols, but for two reasons he was going to continue with it–first, his intuition was telling him the woman's concerns may just be warranted, and second, she was very easy on the eye, and he wouldn't mind seeing her again.

~ ~ ~

Wong headed up Phillip Street, skirting Hyde Park to Queen's Square and the NSW Registry of Births, Deaths and Marriages. After showing his Police ID, a records clerk led him to the archives room where document boxes dating back to 1788 were piled high on dusty shelves. The clerk was a thin young man with a pale face and thick glasses. 'How can I help you, detective?'

'I'm looking for records on a Clara Dewhurst, Sir Hugo Sainsbury and Mrs. Frances Mitterrand.'

'Dates of Birth?'

'I don't know.'

'Australian?'

'I believe Mitterrand would be French. The others are probably Australian.'

The clerk sighed as he scanned the shelves stretching away down the room. He pushed a lock of unruly hair from his forehead and got to work.

~ ~ ~

A chill wind swirled leaves along Glebe Point Road on a blustery afternoon. Horse-drawn wagons and a couple of smoking lorries crowded the street in their quest to satisfy the city's craving for commerce. From down the hill in Blackwattle Bay, timber barges sounded horns in their scuffle for wharf space.

Wong was headed for the Ancient Briton Hotel, an old haunt from his days as a constable on the beat. The pub had been standing longer than anyone could remember - it was a favoured watering hole for local factory workers–a common man's pub where you could buy a good feed, a cold beer and for Wong, information. Billy Radford was a fixture at the Briton–a little man with darting eyes, a photographic memory and more connections than the GPO switchboard. Sometime petty criminal, sometime police informant, it was said that if Billy didn't know you, you weren't worth knowing. He was old, but no-one knew exactly how old–the guesses ranged from 75 to 'one foot in the grave'. Wong found him in a corner next to a noisy bar–a good place for conversation without a hope of being overheard. He bought two beers and joined the old man.

'G'day Tom.'

'G'day Billy–how's tricks?'

'Can't complain–nobody wants to hear it anyway.' He sipped on his beer and glanced around quickly. 'You wanted information on this bloke Sainsbury?'

'That's right. What've you got?'

Billy lit a cigarette and inhaled deeply, exhaling a grey cloud. 'The doctor, right?'

'That's right–runs a place called…'

'Stokeland House–a rich woman's last stop before eternity.'

'That's him.'

'Who wants to know?'

Wong took a pound note from his pocket. 'Someone with more of these.'

Billy smiled thinly and palmed the money. 'You want the dirt?'

'The dirtier the better.'

The little man's eyes darted about again, then rested on the detective. 'Sainsbury likes to gamble big–the ponies, rugby, the boxing, two flies crawling up a wall–he doesn't give a rat's arse as long as the odds are long. He's been in the red with a few of the loan sharks in town. Been roughed up once or twice for late payments. He walks a fine line. And there's something else.'

Wong waved another pound note before the old man.

'Sir Hugo is as much a knight of the realm as I'm Prime Minister.'

Wong's eyes widened ever so slightly. 'He's a fake?'

'Fake as a sixpenny watch.'

~ ~ ~

Cath listened to Mrs. Hawthorne's breathing through her stethoscope. She heard 'stridor'—a high pitched, almost musical sound. She'd ruled out croup or whooping cough, as no other symptoms were present, and suspected it may be aspiration, an abnormality in the vocal cords, and made a note on the file. As she completed her check-up, a nurse knocked and entered. 'Sir Hugo would like a word with you as soon as you can.'

On her way to Sainsbury's office, she wondered why she'd been summoned. The incident on the first floor was still nagging at her - she was anxious to hear progress from Detective Wong, but there'd been no word. Could Sainsbury have gotten wind of her visit to the CIB? She knocked on his door and went in.

He was bent over a document and glanced toward her. 'Please take a seat, Miss Thornton–I'll be just a minute.' She glanced out the window. The sun was keeping its distance behind dark clouds as a squall lashed the harbour. A ferry ploughed to Manly through the swell; its funnel-smoke whipped away by the wind.

Sainsbury capped his fountain pen, holding a grave expression. 'Miss Thornton, a few nights ago one of our patients couldn't sleep, and at about 3am went to borrow a book from the library. She says she saw a nurse going up the stairs to the first floor–do you know anything about this?' Cath was instantly on the alert, and her mind raced. Did Sainsbury already know it was her, and was trying to catch her out? She decided to play it straight.

'Yes, Sir Hugo, it was me. I was about to do my last rounds when I heard a noise from upstairs, and went to investigate.'

Sainsbury remained emotionless. 'What kind of noise?'

'A moaning sound. I wasn't sure if it was the wind or not.'

'And what did you see?'

'Nothing–it was pitch dark, and the noise had stopped, so I returned downstairs.'

Sainsbury leaned back in his chair. 'You are aware, Miss Thornton, that the first floor is a restricted area?'

'Yes, Sir Hugo–but I was concerned that one of our patients may have wandered up there and become disoriented.'

Sainsbury remained silent and continued to stare at Cath for what seemed like a lifetime. 'Very well, Miss Thornton. You may go.'

~   ~   ~

Wong sat back in his chair, hands clasped behind his head, gazing up at the ceiling. He'd pounded the pavement and pored over old government records for days. It was like sifting through a mountain of sand to find a penny–but the wheat had finally begun to separate from the chaff. He considered the various bits of information.

'Frances Mitterrand - a 75-year-old widow who took a stroke that robbed her of speech. She was admitted to Stokeland House early this year. She's wealthy–owns big chunks of land across Sydney, and she has no family. There appears to be no connection between her and Sainsbury, so if he's doing her harm, it's nothing to do with history.'

A surprise piece of information on Dewhurst had surfaced. It turned out she was widowed, and the clerk of records tracked down her maiden name–it was Sainsbury. *'And Clara Dewhurst is Hugo Sainsbury's sister–nice and cosy.'*

'Stokeland House operates under 'Stokeland Trust'. Its trustees are Sir Hugo Sainsbury and Clara Dewhurst.'

'Sainsbury has a big appetite for gambling, and we have an old woman with plenty of money and nobody to leave it to, who's isolated and under sedation in Sainsbury's care - this is smelling like four-day-old fish. Let's suppose for a moment that a kindly doctor gets the trust of an old lady, introduces her to the joys of chloral hydrate and keeps her doped until she's hooked, then persuades her to leave her estate to Stokeland House. Once the deed is signed, he puts her to sleep permanently, and hey presto, the Sainsbury kids are rich. It's a long shot, but worth a look.'

Later that morning Wong visited the archives room in Queen's Square. If his suspicions about Sainsbury were to be proven correct, he needed to know if there were deaths at Stokeland House over recent years, and whether any bequests had been directed to the Trust. With the help of the ever-patient records clerk, he came up with four death certificates:

1. Gladys Kennedy–Date of Death–27 March 1913, aged 81. Cause of Death–Cardiac Arrest.

2. Violet Simpson–Date of Death–2 June 1914, aged 79. Cause of Death–Lung Cancer.

3. Millicent Fanshaw–Date of Death–20 December 1914, aged 77. Cause of Death–Pneumonia.

4. Allison De Mestre–Date of Death–February 1915, aged 89. Cause of Death - Cardiac Arrest.

Sir Hugo Sainsbury had signed all four death certificates. It was only a short walk to the Supreme Court in St. James Road to check on probate details of the four women, and Wong immediately hit pay dirt. Two of the women, Fanshaw and De Mestre, had died without surviving relatives, and left their entire estates to Stokeland Trust.

~ ~ ~

Wong exited the State Coroner's office and quickened his pace up George Street toward Burney's Coffee Palace. His discussion with the Coroner had been fruitful, but frustrating. He had confirmed that if the two women had been murdered, chloral hydrate could be detected in their bodies for up to six months, particularly if administered in large doses. A post-mortem examination could give him the proof he needed, but a court order for the exhumations could take weeks–and in the meantime, unless Wong's hunch was entirely wrong, Frances Mitterrand remained in danger.

He swung open the door to Burney's and scanned the tables. Cath was sitting by a window overlooking the Town Hall. He paused for a moment and admired the way her hair caught the light, and his stomach turned a somersault.

'Sorry I'm late Miss Thornton–I was caught up at a meeting.'

Cath sipped her coffee. 'I understand–and please call me Cath–only Sir Hugo calls me "Miss Thornton", and it gives me the shudders.'

Wong smiled. 'Very well, Cath. I have an update on our enquiries, but first, have you seen or heard anything on Mrs. Mitterrand?'

'I've been watching activity up and down the stairs. Food goes up, and plates come back. There's no file on her in the ground floor office, so it's hard to be sure what's really going on up there.'

'That sounds like good news, nonetheless-at least we know she's alive. Things have escalated. We have circumstantial evidence against Sainsbury, pointing to criminal activity, but I'm not at liberty to go into detail yet.'

Cath slapped a fist into her palm. 'I knew there was something going on–I could feel it. If only we could get that woman out of the place.'

Wong was as concerned about Mitterrand as Cath, but his hands were tied. There wasn't enough evidence to substantiate a search of 'O' Ward. 'I'm sorry, Cath, but we have no case until we get the proof we need. He scribbled on a slip of paper. 'Here's my home phone number. If you see or hear of anything suspicious, ring me, no matter what time of day.'

~   ~   ~

Cath stared at the stairs disappearing up into darkness. She checked her watch–11pm. Stokeland House was as quiet as a tomb, just like the night Mrs. Mitterrand called to her. *Was that only a week ago? It seems like a month.'* She was restless. A powerful sense of frustration hovered over her. Never one to back away from a challenge, she felt an overwhelming urge to get Mitterrand away from Stokeland House. *'What if she's up there now, choking on her own vomit, or just quietly slipping away into a coma? Is she still alive?* Madeleine's words came back to her: *'I became a nurse because I just like helping people.'*

She thought about options–*phone Detective Wong? What for? He's moribund with legalities. Do nothing? Not likely. Get Mitterrand to safety? Yes. It has to be done–but I'm not going to climb over that damn gate with her over my shoulder.'* She headed to Sainsbury's office–there had to be keys. She hurried up the corridor and tried his door–it was unlocked, and she rifled through drawers until her fingers found a key ring–one must surely fit the first-floor gate. She glanced out the window to Hermit Bay. A full moon drifted through clouds pushed by a northerly breeze. The harbour glowed softly pearlescent, and she longed for the calmness it promised. She headed for the stairs.

The first floor was silent, and the iron gate rose upward like the doors to a dark castle. She fumbled with the keys. Tried one–no. Tried a second–no, damn it. Tried a third and a metallic tumbling granted her wish– the gate swung ajar.

She edged down the walls in the darkness, opening the door to Mitterrand's room where thin moonlight outlined a shape in the bed. She turned on the bedside lamp and gasped. Mitterrand's face was ashen. What were once fine lines of age were now deep furrows eroded by suffering. Her mouth gaped open in a silent scream, breath rasping. She was bound to the bed by rope at her wrists and ankles, and her tiny body seemed to wither before Cath's eyes.

She glanced toward the bedside table at a buff-yellow legal document rolled and tied with purple ribbon. She read the heading that protruded"….terrand Last Will and Testam…." Answers bombarded her consciousness as pieces fell into place like an arcane jigsaw puzzle. She fumbled into her tunic pocket and snatched the scrap of paper with Wong's phone number; retreating out the corridor to a nurse's station. As she dialled the number, overhead lights blinded her like a bolt of lightning.

~   ~   ~

The phone chimed into life in Wong's Darlinghurst flat. He padded down the hall and picked up the receiver: 'Hello?'…'Hello?'

~   ~   ~

Sainsbury stood menacingly in the glaring light; the barrel of a Smith & Wesson automatic pointed at Cath's heart. Gone was the 'Man in the Moon' face–she was looking at a cold-blooded killer.

'You've gone one step too far, Miss Thornton. It's a pity you had to be such an impulsive young thing.'

~ ~ ~

Wong's grip tightened on the handset as he listened.

~ ~ ~

Stark terror gripped Cath's every fibre. She'd heard Wong answer–the line was open. She had to alert the detective. 'Sir Hugo–I had to check on Mrs. Mitterrand–I was afraid for her safety.'

~ ~ ~

Wong slammed the phone down and sprinted out the door; vaulting down the stairs three at a time and bursting out the back door to his 1913 Triumph TT motorcycle. He kicked it into life and roared down Victoria Street into New South Head Road.

~ ~ ~

Sainsbury chuckled mirthlessly and shook his head. 'It's too late for more of your fairy tales Miss Thornton–who were you calling?'

'No-one–I was just seeing if it was connected.'

Sainsbury's eyes hardened. 'You're lying.'

~ ~ ~

The Triumph screamed at full throttle through Rushcutters Bay and up the hill to Edgecliff. A car swung out from Ocean Street and Wong swerved at 50mph through the intersection with inches to spare, fishtailing down the bends to Double Bay.

~ ~ ~

Sainsbury took a step closer. 'You know I can't let you live, Miss Thornton. You know far too much for your own good.'

As he spoke, further down the corridor a door swung silently open and Matron Dewhurst appeared. She moved silently toward Cath from behind.

~ ~ ~

Wong checked his watch as the Triumph raced through Rose Bay. It was 11.35pm, and he'd covered over half the distance–about 3 minutes more and he'd be there–if he didn't kill himself in the process. He kicked the Triumph back a gear, flying past the Royal Sydney Golf Club and up through the 'S' bends past Kambala School, its tall chimneys looming over a dark harbour.

~ ~ ~

Dewhurst grabbed her from behind–one powerful arm trapped her shoulders while the other hand clamped a cloth over her face. The chloroform was stifling; she couldn't move. Her struggles weakened and her world misted over.

~   ~   ~

Wong gunned the Triumph into Vaucluse Road past Hermit Point, veering left into Carrara Road. Up ahead the shadow of Stokeland House showed above the pine grove. He killed the Triumph's motor and glided down the slope to a stop.

The house showed only one light downstairs, and the first floor was in darkness. Sainsbury's voice had been menacing–Cath had been discovered on the first floor, so whoever was up there was probably waiting in the dark. And what had happened to Cath? He felt for the comfortable weight of the Webley revolver in his shoulder holster. It was 11.45pm - he needed to get inside that house–right now.

He hugged shadows, circling to the back of the house. The third window he tried was unlocked. He slid over the sill and dropped like a cat to the library's carpeted floor; senses taut as piano wire for any movement or sound. He edged into the corridor and moved to the brightly lit entrance hall. He would be a target in the light, but there was only one way up. He drew the Webley and climbed the stairs into darkness.

~ ~ ~

Cath's head ached and her mouth was dry as ashes. She was in the dark, gagged and tied with rope in some kind of closet. Fear gripped her heart like a vice. Survival. Fight back. The fear turned to anger as she remembered Sainsbury's face; he would not let her live, but she wasn't going quietly. Where was Tom Wong? Did they get him too? A thought invaded her muddled mind, and she remembered the nursing scissors in her tunic pocket. She had to get her bound hands into the right position.

~ ~ ~

Wong reached the first floor to dim light glowing from a room halfway down the corridor; its door slightly ajar. He edged along a wall and looked carefully inside. An elderly woman lay strapped to a bed, apparently conscious and staring at the ceiling–Frances Mitterrand? There was no movement; no sound but her raspy breathing. *'Still alive, at least.'* He thought. *'This is a suicide gamble. A half-seen room and a killer, possibly armed, inside somewhere.'* He took another furtive look and Mitterrand saw him. Her eyes widened and darted to an unseen part of the room, then back at Wong, then a second time, then a third. *'She's pointing at Sainsbury with her eyes–clever old girl. At least I know where the bastard is.'* He nodded to the old woman, and she seemed to understand. He drew a deep breath. *'Here goes.'*

Wong launches himself into the room in a low dive and a bullet splinters the swinging door. He rolls and comes up on one knee with the Webley levelled in both hands at a man in the corner, and another slug zips past his ear. He pulls off a round in the same instant and the man spins about in a crazed pirouette, dropping to the floor–his chest blossoming crimson. Wong trains the Webley on the man and moves across the room, kicking the pistol out of reach. Gunsmoke wafts upward in a languid cloud and a primal scream pierces the darkness as a woman lunges from a curtain with a carving knife; her teeth bared like a she-wolf. He turns to bring the Webley to bear, but in that microsecond, he knows that she'll get to him first. But from a corner of his eye a shadow streaks from nowhere and the woman with the blade suddenly collapses at his feet; blood spurting from her head.

Cate's eyes blaze with adrenaline. She holds the broom handle high in a double grip as the Matron's blood runs down over her white knuckles. Dewhurst lays motionless, and Wong feels her pulse–still alive. He turns to Cath and lowers her shaking arms. 'It's over now, It's all over.'

~   ~   ~

A week later Cath was in the CIB meeting room once more. It seemed that her destiny was to sit and wait for Tom Wong. The incident at Stokeland House seemed like a nightmare to her now, but she knew it had been real–she wasn't sleeping, and had developed a fear of dark places. Mrs. Mitterrand had survived her ordeal; she and the other patients at Stokeland House had been moved to other facilities. The house remained closed pending an investigation into the Trust.

The door swung open and Wong took a seat across the table. 'How are you?'

'I'm getting better. And you?'

'I'm fine, thanks to you and Mrs. Mitterrand.'

Cath sighed. 'She's a tough old bird–she held them off for a long time–I don't think they got her signature on that will.'

'No, they didn't–she knew it was the only thing keeping her alive.'

Cath shuddered. 'It would have been a death sentence for both of us if you hadn't been there. I wonder why they didn't kill me when they had the chance?'

'I suspect they knew you'd called someone and decided to wait for me to show up. Perhaps they thought they could have used you as a bargaining tool.'

'And where's the Matron?'

'She's been remanded in custody and will be tried for murder, pending the exhumations.' Wong softened as he saw the lack of sleep in Cath's eyes. 'Cath–if you hadn't gotten free and followed me down the corridor, I'd be dead by now.'

She smiled wanly. 'I suppose we're even.'

Wong wanted to say more to this incredible woman, but held back.

Chapter 10

Life is Short

Sounds came to him like whispers through cotton wool. The darkness receded and his fingers scraped on fabric. Soft light nudged his brain and his eyes fluttered open as the pain invaded. A face loomed above him. An angel?

'Danny. Danny Thornton.'

A nurse's face came into focus. 'Yes.' His mouth was dry.

He tried to raise himself up. 'Don't move, Danny– you have multiple stitches and a shoulder wound.'

'Where am I?'

'You're on Lemnos - the Field Army Hospital. You were evacuated from Anzac Cove three days ago–do you remember?'

'No…….. I was in a trench. They came at us with bayonets……'

'Lie still, Danny. I'm going to give you something to make you sleep.'

The needle-jab was quick and the merciful darkness returned.

~   ~   ~

He convalesced on Lemnos for three weeks. He'd taken a bullet in the shoulder and had a broken nose, a fractured jaw, severe bruising and multiple lacerations from his struggle with Lieutenant Kaya. Scraps of memory came to him like crime-scene photographs, bringing with them the shock that he'd run one man through with a bayonet and beaten another to death. His survival was sobered by the knowledge that he'd destroyed two lives–such was the primitive force of self-preservation.

When he'd gained strength, he ventured long walks through the hills of Lemnos. The steep granite-strewn slopes revived his muscles, and he breathed deeply of wild sage and oregano. Goats would pause gimlet-eyed as he passed; skittering away if he came too close. Occasionally a farmer gave him a wave and a toothless smile. The sun smiled as he gazed over the blue

Mediterranean, a plucky breeze at his back. He thought of John and his mates back at Gallipoli, and knew it wouldn't be long until he'd land again on Anzac Beach.

~ ~ ~

From Destroyer Hill to Pine Ridge, trenches gouged the landscape like scars from a cat-o'-nine-tails. It might have been a mining town, with its piles of earth, shovels clanging on rock and the aroma of cooking fires. But look closer and the bloated bodies in no-man's-land and the stench of death told a different story.

The trenches along Bolton's Ridge were deeper and better fortified than when Danny was stretchered off to Lemnos. Sections were covered with logs and cramped dugouts served for rudimentary officers' quarters. Communication wires looped along ramparts like humourless garden-party bunting; initials were carved into posts in a plea for immortality. Soldiers with vacant eyes ghosted back and forth past blood-stained stretchers stacked for the next battle.

Abdul's artillery was silent; only the occasional crack of rifle fire from both sides kept up appearances. As lookouts manned the fire step, the rest were engaged in their own affairs–a game of two-up, reading, or writing letters. Danny's new posting overlooked Cooee Gully at

'Silt Spur', about 150 yards south of his original position, and on the other side of the gully, also about 150 yards away, the Turkish lines on 'Sniper's Ridge' were plainly visible at a slightly higher elevation - '*it would pay to keep your head low around here*', he thought.

He heard John's voice and a flood of relief washed over him, knowing that his brother was alive. He was stirring a pot of bully beef stew over a fireplace as Danny approached.

'That stuff smells like shit.' John turned and a smile broke across his grubby face like a sunbeam.

'G'day mate–glad to see you're still in one piece.' The brothers shook hands as John looked him up and down.

'Must be good tucker on Lemnos–you've put on weight–and you smell like you've had a bath.'

'Yeah, but don't worry, I'll be as filthy as you in no time at all.'

John gestured at the fresh scars on his brother's face. 'What happened? Where were you hit?'

Danny glanced away, suddenly embarrassed by his appearance. 'My gun jammed when they came over the top, and I copped a bullet in the shoulder.'

'So, where'd you get the train tracks from?'

'Playing Rugby with the nurses–they're a hard lot over there. Have you seen Bill?'

John's face fell. 'He's dead, mate. We were talking with a group of blokes, and I just turned away to get a mug of tea when a shell burst. Threw me a few feet away. When I came to, there were just pieces.'

~ ~ ~

The Gallipoli conflict had descended into a war of attrition. The front lines formed from the first push on April 25th had remained largely unchanged, and bitter experience had shown that neither side would likely break through. The Turks would keep the Anzac forces hemmed in behind their own lines, and the Anzacs would hold their ground and increase it if possible, until someone said otherwise.

Allied military planners were unaware that Gallipoli's terrain was scarred by deep ravines, and had predicted the assault would overcome the Turks quickly and sweep eastward to take Constantinople in a matter of days. Trench warfare was not anticipated, and as a result the diggers were poorly equipped with throwing bombs– in short, they had none. The Turks used manufactured bombs about the size of a cricket ball, easy to throw, with a fuse lit with steel and flint. The ever-resourceful Anzacs were forced to make their own with discarded food tins filled with nails, razor blades and anything else they could find. Dubbed 'jam-tin bombs', they were clumsy to throw, unpredictable, and had a home-made fuse lit with a match. One digger commented that the tins they used were now only slightly more deadly than the food they once held.

Bayonet charges over open ground had proven costly for both sides, and it wasn't long before the conflict had entered an extra dimension–underground. The process of 'sapping' involved tunnelling forward under no-man's-land to create a new trench from which a charge could be mounted. Sometimes, a 'sap' would be dug underneath enemy lines and detonated with explosives. The Turks were also digging their own saps toward the Anzacs; making it doubly dangerous– engineers sometimes heard muted conversations in Arabic from an adjacent tunnel.

Snipers were a constant threat. The Turks were familiar with the rabbit warren of trenches and deep ravines used by the men, and from such vantage points as 'Baby 700', 'Dead Man's Ridge' and 'Sniper's Ridge', they took a cruel and consistent toll; particularly in the afternoon, with the sun behind them. Showing one's head was ill-advised, but Lance Corporal William Beech of the 2nd Battalion had come up with an ingenious solution to the problem with a contraption dubbed the 'Periscope Rifle.'

Essentially a 303 rifle with planks of timber attached to the stock and incorporating two mirrors, it faintly resembled a cricket bat, and enabled the firer to sight down the barrel without the need to poke his head up. When the first periscope rifle arrived in the trenches, the man who carried it up the path remarked to puzzled onlookers, 'I'm tired of fightin' the Turks - I'm goin' to play them cricket.' It proved to be an odd-looking, but very effective weapon.

Burying the dead soon became a problem. Those killed behind the lines were interred by burial parties whenever time could be found, but as the body count rose, space was at a premium in the rugged terrain, and often a shovel would uncover a previously buried corpse. The graves themselves were shallow and hastily dug, and when the rain came, bodies were exposed by the runoff; giving rise to the comment, 'Even a dead digger's hard to keep down.' Those who died in no-man's-land remained where they were–it was too dangerous to venture out– and as the summer brought higher temperatures, the stench of rotting corpses became unbearable to the point where an armistice was called for both sides to retrieve their dead. The corpses gave rise to millions of flies, leading to an outbreak of dysentery that was to plague the great majority of troops.

Daily food rations were prescribed as 450 grams of canned corned (Bully) beef (better known as 'tinned dog'), a similar amount of Army biscuits, 113 grams of bacon, cheese and a serving of peas, beans or dried potatoes. Tea was supplied, plus jam (dubbed 'fly bog') and sugar. Infrequent and unreliable supply however meant that many items became scarce. Army biscuits, nicknamed the 'concrete macaroon', were reputed to be 'one of the most durable materials used in the war', and could break teeth unless softened in tea or ground up to make porridge.

Water was scarce in the dry climate–it was shipped into Anzac Cove in barrels and hauled up the cliffs. Once at the top it was a long and dangerous hike to cart water to the front lines, usually by donkey or horse, or by hand. One digger who carried five gallons of water in a kerosene tin some half a mile to the front lines was nearing the end of his journey when a shell exploded behind him. Miraculously, the deadly shrapnel missed him entirely, but three pieces tore through the tin; emptying it instantly. When a mate remarked on his good luck, he replied. 'Good luck my arse–now I 'ave to go back for another one.'

~   ~   ~

The Mediterranean stretched into distance; dipping over the earth's curve in a blue haze. The water was clearer than glass–tiny fish swam in formation, reflecting sunlight in a luminous ballet. Behind Danny, the scarred cliffs of Anzac Cove rose to a charnel house, but he dared not look, lest the sea's spell be broken.

He swam with his platoon mates after many days 'standing to' in the firing line up on Bolton's Ridge. The water was bracingly cool, and the salt cut away the filth and stink of war. The cove was mercifully free of barges for a change, but on the beach, stacks of every kind of supply–biscuits, disinfectant, beef, sugar, clothing, carts, spare wheels, engineer's stores, great beams and rails–assaulted the eye between the headlands of Arıburnu in the north and Hell Spit in the south.

He swam to John. 'Bloody nice in, don't you think?'

'I'll say–hasn't been any shelling yet, either.'

The beach was always under threat of sniper fire or a shell lobbed over by 'Beachy Bill'–a Turkish artillery battery about 2.5 miles to the south at Gabe Tepe. Occasionally a digger would be killed while swimming, but such was the attraction of the water, particularly during the heat of summer, that the men ignored the danger–and besides, it was a lot safer than being up on the front line.

As if on cue, a rifle round zipped into the water a few yards from them. After a second or two, another followed–there was a sniper somewhere, and he was getting his range. Private Samuel Harper shook the water from his black, curly hair and grabbed Danny's arm. 'I know where he is, Danny–I just saw the flash when he fired–come on, let's get him.'

The two waded ashore and pulled on their breeches. 'Which way, Sam?'

'Maclagan's Ridge–up on the headland. Follow me, but don't run, or he'll know he's been spotted.'

They grabbed their rifles and scaled the cliffs through well-worn trails and swung east along the ridge; Danny following Sam's ebony back through the scrub. Sam was a rarity at Gallipoli–one of the few Aboriginal soldiers who had enlisted successfully. Recruiting orders allowed indigenous Australians to enlist only if their skin was considered 'white enough', but some recruiting officers ignored the rules, reasoning that a soldier was a soldier, regardless of colour. When asked how he 'got in', Sam would say that he'd threatened to spear the officer if he wasn't accepted, and that seemed to do the trick.

They reached the Hell Spit headland. An offshore wind buffeted through the grass, chilling Danny in his wet breeches while swimmers down in the cove rose over the swell like flotsam. Sam crouched, edging forward to peer over the steep slope through a jumble of rock and scrub. The glint of gunmetal caught his eye, and he beckoned Danny forward; whispering. 'There he is. The bugger's got an Aussie uniform on.' There was much speculation on how Turkish snipers infiltrated Anzac lines to prey on swimmers in the cove, and this was their answer–they re-cycled dead Australians' uniforms.

Sam shouldered his 303. 'This bloke'll be one less Turk to worry about.' He sighted and gently squeezed the trigger as the sniper's back exploded into red; his body slumping forward, rifle pointing to the sky. They scrambled down to the body. Droplets of blood and gore hung from the bushes; glinting in the sunlight like Christmas tree baubles. The man's face was calm, as if he'd fallen asleep. He was heavily bearded and as thin as a rake–clearly the Turks were suffering as much as the Anzacs in this grinding war.

Down in the cove the men continued to enjoy the water, unaware of the drama that had just unfolded. John was trudging up the sand when a breakfast feed of bully beef, hastened on by a hint of dysentery, made its presence felt, and he quickened his pace to the latrine.

The convenience straddled a narrow ravine in the centre of the cove–just a couple of long timber planks where diggers sat with breeches around their ankles, like budgies pooping from a perch.

John edged out along the plank to a vacant spot and dropped his pants. Several men gave him a casual nod; each occupied with his own personal agenda. Without warning, the sound of incoming artillery from 'Beachy Bill' cut through the air, spitting and hissing like a cobra as it soared in a low trajectory at 250 feet per second toward the cove. The diggers knew the sound well–some could predict to within a few feet where a shell would explode. Those perched on the plank, given their vulnerable position and severe lack of mobility, were especially attentive, and became quite pale when the telltale bursts of yellow smoke signalled the release of shrapnel directly overhead.

Bare arses dived for cover in all directions. A wave of laughter spread cross the cove as a dozen or so men beat a hurried retreat while pulling up their breeches in a macabre hopping motion, like a semi-nude sack-race. Those on the plank were not as lucky; several of them choosing, wisely, to drop into the pile of excrement below. John attempted to flee, but lost his footing on the plank and joined the others at the bottom. As the laughter subsided, the casualty count luckily resulted in only a few arses with bits of shrapnel, and one Private John Thornton, with a twisted ankle, severely injured pride and smelling like, well, like shit.

It is said that that the following words were inspired by the bombing of Anzac's latrine:

There's a certain bloody nuisance called 'Beachy,'

Whose shells are exceedingly screechy;

Especially when we sit, for a peaceful shit.

But we're keeping the score,

And we're after your gore–So look out, 'Beachy Bill,' when we meet ye.

~   ~   ~

On a moonless night in July 1915 at the eastern end of Sniper's Ridge, a Turkish unit worked at covering trenches with pine logs. On the other side of no-man's-land the diggers pinpointed their low conversation and took the occasional speculative shot. The Turks used trees felled from a nearby grove, and by August there would be just one left–the 'Lone Pine'. This was the most fortified section of the Turkish line due to the proximity of the opposing forces, and perhaps also because unbeknown to the Anzacs, the Turks' regimental headquarters lay directly behind, in a gully called 'The Cup'.

~ ~ ~

A team of soldiers swung picks while sappers shored up the tunnel roof behind them. It wouldn't do to have a cave-in; the Turks would easily spot it and the jig would be up. Danny stopped digging and peered back along a line of faltering candles. They'd run out of the army-issue variety a week ago, and some genius had invented the ANZAC variety - a wick of cotton threads dipped in bacon fat. They'd come a long way since the engineers had pointed at a dab of whitewash in the dirt and said 'dig'. Danny turned to Harry Chapman labouring beside him. The carpenter from Kensington's lean torso was covered in dirt; his singlet ringed with sweat. 'You know, Harry', Danny began, 'It's not so bad down here. It's cool, there're no flies, and nobody shoots at you.'

Harry brushed a clod of earth from sandy hair. 'Yeah, and the price you pay is working like a navvy all bloody day.'

'You reckon there'll be a push?'

'Yep, no question. I haven't seen this much sapping before–they say it's going to be a big one.'

Harry was right. The British were planning a major offensive at Suvla to the north of Anzac Cove, and the attack on Lone Pine was to be a diversion. The epicentre would be 'The Pimple', a bulge in the Anzac line where combatants were only 80 yards apart. Communication tunnels would push out under no-man's-land at right angles to the Anzac line for about 30 yards; linked by a parallel trench from which they'd charge the Turks, and hopefully, break through.

The attack on 'Lone Pine' was set for August 6 and the troops were keen to break through the Turkish defences after months of stalemate. The days leading up to the attack were spent making jam-tin bombs, sharpening bayonets and cleaning rifles. One afternoon, John, Danny and Nutty shared a dugout. They'd been issued white calico patches to be sewn on the back of their tunics, to aid identification during battle.

Nutty squinted cross-eyed as he tried to thread a needle. 'Jesus, I come half way across the world, survive months of combat training, and here I am sitting on my arse in a sewing circle.'

John grinned. 'Mate–I've got a couple of holes in my socks–could you darn them for me?'

'Yeah darling, I'll darn 'em for you, then I'll stuff 'em down your bloody cake-hole.'

Danny admired his handiwork. 'This will make a nice target for the Turks to shoot at.'

John replied. 'You'd have to be retreating, mate, and there'll be none of that going on.'

~ ~ ~

Two thousand men stood in the forward ANZAC trench like Qin's Terracotta Army as their artillery hammered the Turkish lines. It was 5.15pm on August 6, 1915 and the sun hid in a cloud bank, as if too was taking cover. In another fifteen minutes the bombardment would cease and they'd go over the top to attack across the heights of Chunuk Bair on a front of 200 yards. The Turks would absorb the shelling and defend their territory to the last man. The diggers stood grim-faced, staring up to an evening sky that might well be their last. Some snuck a last look at a faded sepia photograph. Others whispered a prayer and made the sign of the cross. As zero hour approached, they shook hands and turned toward the parapets.

The silence in the shelling's aftermath is shattered by battle yells as diggers charge over Lone Pine's killing ground. There's a queue to climb the parapets—there are four in front of Danny, then three, then two, then one, and he climbs up to a firestorm. He sprints, sidestepping barbed wire like a rugby winger as Turkish barrels spit death. He's covered 30 yards and men are dropping around him. Some continue to fire while their blood oozes into the soil; others lie staring with dead eyes.

They reach the Turkish line and to their horror the trenches are covered with logs while the Turks fire up at point blank range through loopholes. The diggers are ramming bayonets down through the gaps in frustration - others are desperately trying to lever the timber up to get inside. Another wave of troops swerves past, and Danny follows. Resistance is lighter at the rear and he drops into an open trench. Turks attack from the flanks and he fires his 303 from the hip. The trench widens and the two sides clash with bayonets, fists, feet, and anything they can find. A bomb sizzles through the air and lands at his feet. He hurls it back where it came from.

~ ~ ~

John drops through a hole in the logs and follows his mates into the dark. A Turk peers round a bend and he shoots him in the head. Another lunges out and he bayonets him through the stomach, twisting the blade free. There's an intersecting trench and men are fighting hand to hand. He hears a shuffle behind gets off a round into a Turk's stomach. A man screams up ahead and a Turkish bayonet comes out through his back, blossoming blood right in the centre of his white calico patch. He's limp, hanging on the end of the blade like a dead lizard.

Fierce fighting continues throughout the night, and by the next morning they'd heaved scores of dead bodies out onto the ramparts to provide cover. Danny stands on more bodies at the bottom of the trench–they're soft underfoot and already smelling as he fires at Turks in a nearby gully. Bombs sail through the air in a deadly arc, their fuses spinning like Catherine wheels in the half-light of dawn. One lands a few yards away and a man picks it up too late– it blows his hands off. A bugle sounds from somewhere and Danny tenses for a counter-attack. Around him, the screams and groans of the dying fill his ears.

He lights a jam-tin bomb and hurls it like a fast bowler and the explosion is peppered with screams–'got a couple at least'; he thinks. The digger next to him has blood all over him from shrapnel wounds, but he's still going strong. Danny has a gash in his forearm from a Turkish bayonet but the bleeding has stopped–hurts like buggery though. He spots a Turkish machine-gun crew advancing across open ground toward a bomb crater. He jams another magazine into his 303. and says to his mate–'Nick! Over to the right.' And they both open up on the Turks and stop them in their tracks. He turns to say something when a bomb spins toward him and he's blown off his feet.

John drags a case of ammunition along the trench floor–they ran out long ago, and this is well overdue. He throws open the lid and the men grab boxes like they're stolen apples. There's a sharp bend in the trench up ahead and they can hear Turkish whispering. He crouches, waiting with bayonet fixed, and the Captain gives the sign as they move up to the opening. The lead digger lights a jam tin bomb, letting it burn down dangerously close, and lobs it around the corner. The explosion numbs the senses and John leaps into the tunnel. He glances to his left as a shell explodes overhead.

~ ~ ~

Nurse Mary Connolly moved among the wounded like a bee in a field of dying daisies; setting down beside stretchers to read a ticket tied to a toe or a finger, making life and death decisions–this one was too far gone; this one could wait–then moving on to the next. The hospital tents in Anzac Cove smelt of blood and rang with the moans of shattered men. She placed faith in her hands– grim experience had taught her the difference between the simple cold of night and the creeping chill of death. She paused by Danny; unconscious and seeping blood. She read the ticket and took a glance at his prone form; calling for a stretcher-bearer.

~   ~   ~

British hospital ship HMHS *'Gascon'* steamed southward across the Aegean, passing the lights of Andros to starboard. In a forward operating theatre, Navy Surgeon Captain Arthur Shepherd bent over Danny's inert figure, surveying the damage to his right leg while a theatre nurse looked on.

'What a bloody mess. His right foot's mangled–most of it must be back in Turkey. Tibia and fibula shattered almost to the knee.' Shepherd glanced up at Danny's face and shook his head slowly. 'He's practically a child. Nurse?'

'Yes, doctor?'

'Saw, if you please.'

~   ~   ~

The ship's throbbing turbines come to him through the depths of darkness. He was back on the 'Lake Michigan'. He'd fallen asleep and was dreaming of Coogee. Any second now, John will wake him–Gallipoli must have been a dream. He opens his eyes, but he's not where he thought he was. Is he awake at all? He turns his head and there are people in beds lined up all around him. The bayonet wound—Lone Pine—he lifts his right arm and there's a bandage on it.

He sighs…..

Something's not right.

And instantly he knows.

He moves his legs, and he knows.

He let out a soft cry of anguish as the realization hit him. He moved his right leg again, and it was almost weightless. His foot tingled, but it wasn't there. His first thought was, *'How will I go on surf patrol with one leg?* He wouldn't–*couldn't* - lift the covers and look. A nurse appeared from nowhere; her face saying it all. She glanced at the name on the chart.

'Danny–I'm nurse Richardson. Please don't try to get up.'

'How much of my leg is left?'

She grasped his hand. 'You have about four inches past your knee, Danny. Your leg was badly damaged by shrapnel fragments. I'm very sorry.'

He rubbed a hand across his eyes. 'What else? Am I going to live?'

Her smile held compassion and fortitude. 'Yes, of course. In a few days we'll be in London and you'll be transferred to a hospital. They can do wonders now with prosthetics.'

'What's prosthetics?'

Her smile faded. 'An artificial leg–don't worry - you'll be walking again in no time at all.'

~ ~ ~

For two days he stared at flaking paint on the ceiling, lost in thought and lulled by the gentle roll of the ship as it steamed westward across the Mediterranean. They were blacked out at night against the threat of torpedoes. Nurses glided by like angels with kerosene lamps, tending to their patients; holding a trembling hand, mopping a brow, wiping away a stray tear.

Around him were men injured and diseased beyond the medical capability of Lemnos or Alexandria–limbs missing, faces half blown off, severe infections, shell-shock, rotting teeth and chronic dysentery, to name a few. For most of them, Danny included, their war was over, but many would face a lifetime of deprivation, poverty, pain, discrimination and depression. Their families would suffer from the loss of a breadwinner and the mental instability caused by war. Many families would simply disintegrate. Single men would be rebuffed by their fiancées. Men with jobs would lose them. Men without eyes would live in darkness. Men with demons born from war would carry them to their grave.

Danny replayed his past over and over like a badly scratched gramophone record; looking back at his naïve 19-year-old self with his dreams of valour. How he had changed–he knew all too well now that valour wasn't a knight in shining armour–it was a filthy, lice-ridden digger dragging his wounded mate back through the mud of no-man's-land under fire. And what lay ahead for him? The life of a cripple? People looking away as he hobbled along the street? Girls would toss him a few thin words of pity, then look for a normal man. He was still a virgin–how would he ever 'be' with a woman, looking like a freak? He laughed bitterly at his middle name– 'Lucky'. *'Not so fucking lucky anymore, am I?'*

He was tossed on waves of despair and anger and told himself his father was right–he'd been a fool to sign up. At night the horrors of war would infiltrate his mind like a virus, and he'd wake up screaming in a pool of sweat. He thought of John and wondered what had happened on Lone Pine–did his brother survive? Did the Anzacs hold their ground?

On the third day, nurse Richardson returned to his bedside.

'Feel like a walk around the deck?'

He looked askance at the crutches she held. 'With those?'

'Yes–you're well enough now, and we don't want those muscles to atrophy. Shall we?'

Danny sighed and swung his body to the edge of the bed. He wore hospital-issue pyjamas–one empty leg trailed behind, and Richardson produced a safety pin. 'Let's get that tidied up.'

She slipped the crutches under his armpits. 'Now, ease forward, take the weight on your leg and I'll help you up.'

He shuffled forward and touched the floor with his foot as she hoisted him to the vertical. For an instant he teetered out of balance as his mind tried to move a non-existent leg into place.

'Steady Danny–that will happen for a while until you get used to it. Now, you've seen people with crutches before–two ends on the floor, then lean on the crutches and swing your foot a little forward.'

His brain was befuddled. He shifted his weight; immediately over-balancing as Richardson grabbed him at the last second. He spat out a soft curse.

'Get me back to the bed.'

'Now Danny, you just need to……'

'GET ME BACK TO THE BED!'

He would have two more attempts before taking his first unassisted steps. His leg stump shot nerve pain up through his knee and thigh, and he was sure he could feel a tingling from the calf muscle that lay at the bottom of a trench somewhere on Lone Pine. His arms ached with the unaccustomed strain of his own weight; his armpits numb with loss of circulation. But walk he did, first a few steps, then a quarter of the outside deck, then half. The sea air was like nectar to him, and soon the *'Gascon'* passed the Rock of Gibraltar rising from the water like a breaching humpback as they turned to starboard for the English Channel.

~ ~ ~

The *'Gascon'* steamed into the Thames estuary on a cool afternoon in mid-August 1915 and cruised upriver to where Victoria Docks occupied a stretch of water at London's industrial back door. Tugboats nudged the ship into a finger wharf in blustery wind as Danny took in the scene before disembarking. Rail yards, warehouses and factories belching smoke surrounded the dock. Trucks lumbered by with tarpaulins flapping. Barges weaved among cargo ships with derricks splayed like wheel spokes. A coal hulk floated listlessly in a forgotten backwater, performing its final service before yielding to the scrap-dealer's blow torch.

He hobbled down the gangway to the wharf on crutches, where a knot of people searched for their loved ones among the damaged and deformed. He wore his uniform–the only clothes he owned. It had been laundered and disinfected on the ship, but the bloodstains of Gallipoli still brooded in faint crimson patches.

A group of twenty or so amputees climbed awkwardly into the back of a Medical Corps lorry that rumbled through London's docklands, crunching gears and farting black smoke. A British soldier beside Danny with stumps for hands gave him a nudge. 'Hey, sport– could ya light us up a smoke? They're in me jacket pocket.' Danny fished one out.

'Thanks.' He exhaled a cloud of blue smoke and glanced down at Danny's leg. 'Ya won't be doin' the quick step for a while, I suppose.'

Danny shrugged. 'Think I'll start with the waltz first. Looks like you've had a game of "catch and pass" with Johnny Turk.'

The man took another drag from his cigarette. 'Yeah–I lost. They tell me Queen Mary's Hospital is the place to go to if you want a new leg or a pair of hands.'

'Is that where we're off to?'

'That it is, mate.'

The lorry pulled to a halt outside the hospital with a squeal of brakes. Built in the 18th century, it was an impressive three-storey mansion with tall leadlight windows, two curved pavilions and arched colonnades. The complex was turned into a hospital only two months before. The new arrivals were shown through the facilities - patients' dormitories, cafeteria, gymnasium, rehabilitation centre and indoor swimming pool. After months of trench warfare, it was an alien world to these men; conditioned as they were to shell-fire, filth and flies, inadequate food, insufficient sleep and the constant threat of death. One would think that they would welcome such unexpected luxury; but a mind conditioned to deprivation must adapt at its own pace. Their rehabilitation was to be a long road; mentally and physically. Danny was no exception - the whirlwind of emotions that swept over him on the *'Gascon'* would be his constant companion for some time to come–perhaps forever.

~ ~ ~

No matter how he tried to deny it, the ghost of his right leg wouldn't go away. Each time he gripped the parallel bars and made to step forward, a phantom tingling would stop him in mid stride.

The end of the parallel bars was only a few yards away, but to Danny, it might as well have been Sydney. Nurse Emma Parkinson stood at his elbow. 'This is normal, Danny. Your mind wants to believe that your leg's still there.'

'I can't blame it for that.'

'Well, the more you think that way, the longer you'll take to get moving. Now, do you want to walk again or don't you?'

Parkinson was Australian–one of hundreds of nurses who volunteered their services to the Empire during the carnage of Gallipoli and France; some even paying their own way to come half-way across the world. Her open, serene face and hazel eyes, and her no-nonsense, sometimes outspoken attitude had grabbed Danny's attention from the outset. He was in his first week of rehabilitation, and progress had been slow; but being a force to be reckoned with, Parkinson was undeterred.

'One more time. Let your mind go blank—most men have no problem with that. Let's try again.'

He gripped the bars once more and concentrated on the polished wooden foot beneath him; the veins in his forearms bulging with his own weight. The alien appendage reminded him of a Dutch clog, and an idea came to him. *'My real foot is inside this wooden clog—I'm wearing a wooden clog.'* He held the image in his mind for a few moments and slowly moved his new leg forward one complete stride.

'Excellent–what were you thinking about just then, when you took that step?'

'That it was the only way I was going to shut you up.'

'Well, that's where you're wrong–if I shut up, you'll just get lazy on me.'

He laughed. 'Yeah, I suppose so.'

His sessions with Emma became a ray of light in an otherwise grey existence. They shared their typically Australian sense of directness and wry humour. She was insightful. She realised the enormity of the challenge faced by her patients, and was careful to guide them, both in their physical rehabilitation and their ability to cope emotionally. He wondered at his attraction to her– was it because of his vulnerability, or was it deeper than that? She was quite good looking, and sometimes he caught a glance from her that seemed to hold something more than professional care.

His new leg was manufactured in the hospital's basement workshop and fitted within days of his arrival, and weeks of rehabilitation followed as August gave way to September, and the London days became cooler. His initial steps were the foundation for more challenges– climbing steps, catching, throwing and kicking a ball, obstacle stepping, climbing a ramp, and kneeling. He'd line up in weak sunshine on the hospital lawn with his fellow amputees, practising lunges like a troupe of grotesque ballerinas. All the things that his mind and body had taken for granted for so many years had to be re-learned. Many times, he tried and failed; many times, he wanted to give up, but then he'd recall a five-year-old boy from Orange who couldn't run and play with the others for longer than five minutes. That little boy kept telling him he would succeed.

By October he had mastered the tasks that would return the mobility destroyed at Lone Pine. Somehow, the lump of hardwood strapped to his thigh slowly became part of his body; it was as if his mind had forgotten that there once was living bone and tissue below his knee. His youth and level of fitness were a great asset, even after four months at Gallipoli had taken their toll, and in the gymnasium and rehab room, he was constantly reminded that there were others with amputations more severe than his own. Some had no legs at all, some no arms–theirs would be a road much longer and harder, and while many would struggle to find work, his trade of watchmaker would hopefully continue unaffected when he finally got home.

One afternoon the Chief Surgeon, Doctor Ralston, paid him a visit in the reading room as he read chapter 7 of Wilkie Collins's 'The Moonstone'. Ralston was in his mid-50's, grizzled and bespectacled, with a warm, personable manner. He carried a thick manila folder under his arm.

'A word if I may, Danny?'

'Of course, doctor, what's up?'

'I've been reviewing your rehab reports. You've done extremely well.'

'Thanks–I'm getting pretty comfortable with the leg now.'

'Excellent. I'm recommending you complete your treatment in a couple of weeks–we'll put the paperwork through the system, and your repatriation back to Australia will be arranged.'

Danny paused for a moment. 'I'm going home?'

'Yes–a four or five-week sea voyage.' Ralston smiled. 'The sea air will do you good.'

~   ~   ~

There was a 17th century pub about a half-mile from the hospital–the 'King's Head'. In the short history of Queen Mary's, it had become something of a rite of passage that leg amputees would prove their readiness for 'graduation', by walking from the hospital to the pub, downing four pints of ale, then walking back–without falling over. While not being officially condoned, the management turned a blind eye to the practice as long as one or two of the medical staff were on hand to supervise.

On the occasion of his 'graduation', Danny and three other amputees were accompanied by two men with new arms, who sought to prove their own worth by downing a beer without crushing the glass in their mechanical hands. That afternoon the King's Head patrons were entertained by demonstrations of physical prowess from the patients, while the resident bookmaker gave odds on whether the group would pass the graduation test, or just pass out. One entrepreneurial patient with a glass eye charged a shilling to see him remove it.

After a couple more than their required pints of ale, the four amputees made their way back to Queen Mary's. Under no circumstances could their condition have been described as 'legless'; after all, when they arrived at the hospital, instead of the required eight, the quartet of soldiers had possessed only three. Now, eight sturdy legs carried them home, and no-one fell over. Mind you, there was much laughing and leaning on one other.

A few days later, Danny received his papers to board the steamship *'Osterley'* for his passage to Sydney. He was to depart in 24 hours, on October 18. The news startled him–while the prospect of going home and reuniting with the family filled him with anticipation, he felt a tug of reluctance. Queen Mary's had been a refuge in a storm of uncertainty, and he'd miss the support he'd received from a dedicated group of carers.

That afternoon, an orderly placed a small suitcase on his bed. 'Private Thornton–Queen Mary's wishes you a "bon voyage"–we've arranged a few things for your trip back home.'

Danny opened the case–it contained a new suit, two shirts, a pair of shoes, socks, underwear, pyjamas and toiletries. In a wallet were several pounds in cash. 'My goodness - thank you–this is wonderful–I was hoping not to have to wear my old uniform for the entire trip. By the way–where's nurse Parkinson? I'd like to say goodbye.'

The orderly shook his head. 'Sorry squire, she's off for a couple of days–if you like, I'll let her know you asked after her.'

~ ~ ~

The *'Osterley'* rode at anchor at the Royal Docks; grey smoke curling upward from its twin funnels. The sea was steel-grey under brooding cloud as Danny pulled his coat tighter against the cold and watched the last of the passengers board. Uniformed porters steered baggage trolleys through the crowd with the skill of a race car driver, and the air hummed with the babble of voices, squawking gulls and tinny announcements over the Tannoy. Here and there a khaki uniform would appear– soldiers like himself in varying states of damage were being shipped back home.

His mind wandered back to the ships that had carried him across so many ocean miles, and changed him forever. Almost exactly a year before, he'd climbed up the gangway of the *'Euripdes'* in Woolloomooloo as a wide-eyed 19-year-old, besotted with adventure and the 'glory' of war. Then the *'Lake Michigan'* took him to Gallipoli as a young soldier with his guts churning at the thought of death. Next it was the *'Gascon',* with the terror of an amputation and the realisation that he was now only half a man. And now, the *'Osterley'* was to take him full circle, and he wasn't the same person any more. It scared him he wouldn't fit back in when he got home–his world was no longer the same–perhaps never would be. A small voice in his head whispered: *'You can take the man out of Gallipoli, but you can't take Gallipoli out of the man.'*

He shared a cramped cabin on a lower deck with three other Australian soldiers: Cedric Balfour had lost a leg in France, Harold Carmichael's arm was crushed at sea, and Phil Mulholland had his face mutilated by shrapnel at Gallipoli. Mulholland's injuries were horrific. Shrapnel had torn through his face–destroying his nose and half his lower jaw. He'd lain in no-man's-land for 12 hours before his mates dragged him back in the dark. They treated him at Erskine Hospital in Glasgow, where a small team of pioneering surgeons collaborated to repair what they could of the damage, but a facial mask was the only way to save him from a life hiding from the world. A plaster cast of his face was made, and the details sculpted into clay. From there they made a prosthetic mask using thin galvanised copper, painted to match his skin tone. The resulting piece was fashioned with a moustache of human hair and fitted with undetectable silk fibres. Mulholland had eventually shown him photographs of what lay beneath the mask, and Danny had cause to consider what could have been his own fate.

And what of nurse Parkinson? He felt her absence keenly; but was that just the thought of leaving the security of Queen Mary's? He'd never even asked her where she lived, back in Australia–perhaps she'd never go back home. *'She'll probably marry some rich Pommy and that'll be the end of it.'* He thought. *'Oh well, "Que sera sera"–whatever will be, will be.'*

Chapter 11

Making and Breaking

On Monday morning, October 25, 1915 the postman blew his whistle and pushed a wad of envelopes through a slot in the Royal's door. James padded down the stairs, checking his watch as he gathered the mail from the floor. *'8.15 already–Jim'll be in the cellar tapping kegs by now.'* He thought, as he shuffled the mail. One envelope grabbed his attention–a letter from Danny, postmarked London. *'What the hell?'* Resisting the urge to tear it open, he trotted quickly back up the stairs.

'Sarah!–a letter from Danny–it's from London!' Word from John and Danny had been scant over the past year–a postcard from Colombo, another from Egypt, but nothing since. They knew the 4th Battalion had been in action at Gallipoli, but the lack of news had distressed the family. They'd spent many a sleepless night worrying whether the boys were alright; not daring to entertain the dreadful possibility of them being wounded or killed–it was as if the very thought of it would somehow make it happen.

James smoothed the thin paper on the table top:

August 18, 1915.
Mr. and Mrs. James Thornton,
Royal Hotel,
2 Perouse Rd.
Randwick
NSW
Australia

Dear Mum and Dad,

Sorry for not writing sooner, but things have been pretty eventful lately.

I'm in Queen Mary's Hospital in London–I evacuated out of Gallipoli a couple of weeks ago and it's taken a while to get sorted.

I'd like to say everything's alright, but it's not. I'm not dying or anything, but I got on the wrong side of a Turkish bomb, and they had to amputate my right leg below the knee–it was pretty smashed up by shrapnel.

The hospital specialises in artificial limbs, and they tailor-made me one, which was fitted about a week ago. I'm still getting used to it–they give me plenty of attention here with exercises and learning how to walk properly. Some other blokes here are much worse off than me.

I hope you have heard from John. Last time I saw him, we were both going into action.

Please don't worry about me–I won't be fighting anymore, and I'm doing alright. I expect to be on a ship home in a month or two.

Your loving son,

Danny.

A moan escaped from Sarah. James just stared at the letter, hoping that somehow the words would re-arrange themselves. His teardrop hit the paper, turning the ink to cerulean watercolour. 'Oh Jesus–the poor little bugger– how must he feel, trying to cope with this on his own?'

Sarah broke into sobs, and they hugged each other. She thought of her little boy who'd beaten the life-threatening scourge of asthma only to have this happen to him. No-one was ever meant to endure such a thing as losing a limb–especially a teenager who had a whole life yet to live. For the first time in her life, she hated the world.

They broke the news to Cath and Jim that afternoon, and the next day James sent a telegram to Queen Mary's for news of Danny's whereabouts. A curt return wire advised only that they had discharged his son, and details of shipping departures were classified as 'Top Secret'.

~ ~ ~

Tuesday afternoon, 23 November 1915. The *'Osterley'* steamed north up the Sydney coastline at 'half ahead'; its bow-wave hosting a pod of dolphins curving through white-water. Danny leant on the port rail in the teeth of a brisk north-easterly wind billowing dresses and snatching hats. The voyage had been uneventful save for a near miss with a cargo vessel in the Suez Canal. The ship's roll was a challenge with his new leg - he'd developed a one-sided 'pop up' motion that he feared would make his handicap more apparent. Physically, he was healed, but emotionally, turmoil brewed.

The rugged sandstone cliffs of 'The Gap' dozed in shadow as the ship rounded South Head and steered hard to port, entering the calm waters of Sydney Harbour. Passengers lined the rails, taking in the view as they passed Bradley's Head and slowed to Garden Island where tugs nudged the liner into Woolloomooloo Bay. Heavy ropes lassoed iron bollards as she eased into port.

Homecoming - a year after he'd marched up the same wharf with a kit bag and a 303. This time there were no crowds, no streamers, no singing 'Waltzing Matilda'. He had expected none of that, but something else was missing–he didn't *feel* like he was home. He was supposed to be triumphant, like some chisel-faced hero in a penny-dreadful novel. Instead, he was a confused teenager who jumped when a car backfired. Jumbled emotions of home skated through his mind, muted by echoes of Turkish machine gun fire. He straddled two worlds, but belonged to neither, and it troubled him. He hailed a taxi to Randwick.

City streets rolled by the window like a canvas backdrop in a Mack Sennett two-reel comedy. Little had changed except for more uniforms and shorter dresses. He mused over how one part of the world could be bathed in blood while another wiled away a sunny afternoon. The taxi crossed Coogee Bay Road and he glimpsed a sea turning ultramarine blue as the sun set. His mind projected flashes of childhood–another world.

He stood on the footpath with suitcase in hand, staring across the street at the Royal as the taxi pulled away down Perouse Road. The pub was busy - city workers lounged beside windows open to an evening sea breeze, enjoying a beer on their way home. He wore his new suit, rather than the uniform. '*No need to attract* attention', he'd thought, '*and a wooden leg looks pretty silly in puttees anyway.*' He entered through the bar and up the stairway, taking the steps with care–it wouldn't do to break his neck on the first day home.

Sarah and James are in the kitchen–he's reading the 'Telegraph' while she prepares dinner. Footfalls sound down the hallway. 'Cath's home.' James says, turning to greet his daughter - and Danny stands in the doorway like an apparition. The boy has become a man. He has lines across his brow that weren't there before, and he needs a haircut. His mouth wears a smile, but his eyes hold back–they've seen too much.

The frypan hit the floor with a clatter as Sarah hugged her son as if he'd disappear if she let go. James hugged them both, and the three stood there for a moment like a Bernini sculpture, their tears of joy, sadness and love combining as one.

James pumped Danny's hand. 'Welcome home, son. We tried to find out where you were, but they wouldn't tell us anything.'

Danny smiled thinly. 'Yeah, the Army's good at that.'

Sarah dared not look down at his leg. 'You're as thin as a rake–we'll have to fatten you up.'

'I could do with some of your cooking, mum–I dreamed about it in Gallipoli.'

James broached the subject. 'We got your letter a few weeks ago. How's the leg?'

Danny looked down absently at his new appendage like it was a wilful puppy needing further training. 'I can get around pretty well now–got a bit of a hop in my walk because there's no ankle joint, and it gets heavy after a few hours, but it could be worse–there were some blokes with no legs, some without arms.'

Sarah hugged him again. 'Oh God, love, I wish I could take all those memories of yours and throw them into the ocean.'

'Me too, Mum….. me too.'

While conversation flowed freely at the dinner table that night, any mention of the war was avoided like a stream flowing round a boulder. Jim and Elizabeth had a daughter now; Helen, aged 7 months, and young Michael had turned two. Cath had just sat her final exams at University and was expecting to graduate in March. Her drama at Stokeland House had passed into family folklore, and was related in some detail, much to her embarrassment and Danny's delight.

'You actually clobbered her with a broom handle?' He asked his sister with eyes wide.

'It seemed like a good idea at the time.'

'We could have done with you at Lone Pine.'

The reference to Gallipoli wasn't lost, but no-one pushed the subject as Danny continued.

'Who's this Detective Wong? He's Chinese?'

Cath hadn't heard from Wong since their meeting a few months before–but she'd thought of him often. 'I think so–but he doesn't look Oriental.'

James stood to help clear the dishes. 'What're your plans Danny? Are you going back to Prouds? George has held your job open.'

Danny shrugged. 'Yeah, I probably will, but not right away, Dad–I just need some time to settle back in.'

'Of course–that'd be wise.'

~   ~   ~

August 22, 1915
Mr. and Mrs. James Thornton,
Royal Hotel,
2 Perouse Rd.
Randwick
NSW

Australia.

Dear Mr. and Mrs. Thornton,

It is with deep regret and that I inform you of the death of your son, Private John Michael Thornton, of the AIF 4th Battalion, killed in action on August 7, 1915.

John succumbed to enemy fire as he fought alongside his battalion mates in the battle of Lone Pine. I had the pleasure of knowing John personally. He was a fine soldier and well-liked by all. He died a brave man in the service of his country.

On behalf of the AIF and the fourth Battalion, I offer you and your family our deepest sympathies.

Yours Sincerely,
Major Matthew Hunter,
"A" Company,
4th Battalion,
AIF, Gallipoli.

The letter arrived six days after Danny's return, and grief fell upon the Thornton family like a suffocating fog. Sarah's heart, already bruised by Danny's amputation, broke in two. It scared James to see her staring out the bedroom window as if John would come walking down the street any minute– *'It was all a mistake, Mum–they got the name wrong - it was someone else that died'*. James descended into a deep pit of despair.

He was empty inside, and the face of his dead son would come to him at odd times during the day, making him wonder whether John was calling to him from beyond the grave.

Something snapped inside Danny like dry kindling as the brute violence of Gallipoli returned anew. As clear as an icicle, he would hear John's 9-year-old voice, *'I have to take care of my little brother, and if he's going to Sydney, so am I.'* And the tears would flow unabated. He took long walks along Coogee's rugged coastline to Gordon's Bay, Clovelly, Bronte and the cliffs of Tamarama, hoping that somehow the briny air and rough sandstone would grind away the pain; but the sea, which for so long had been his refuge, refused to listen.

~   ~   ~

A cheap novel lay on the frozen ground, its dog-eared pages fanned back and forth by a bitter wind. A battered bully beef tin fell from a niche in an earthen wall; bouncing down an abandoned trench. All that remained of 40,000 troops were faded echoes and a few 'drip rifles' spitting .303 rounds into the air to fool the Turks.

It was dawn on December 20, 1915 and the last of the diggers had withdrawn from Anzac beach a few hours before, leaving piles of equipment and stores, and the graves of over 8,000 Australians. In time, an engraved plaque would appear above Anzac Cove-a monument to the fallen from the Turkish government:

'Those heroes that shed their blood and lost their lives ...

You are now lying in the soil of a friendly country.

Therefore, rest in peace.

There is no difference between the Johnnies

And the Mehmets to us where they lie side by side,

Here in this country of ours.

You, the mothers, who sent their sons from far away countries ...

Wipe away your tears.

Your sons are now lying in our bosom and are in peace.

After having lost their lives on this land, they have become our sons as well.'

~ ~ ~

The Great Hall's stained-glass windows caught the sun, throwing colour across the stone floor. Murmurs drifted among the audience in anticipation of the graduation ceremony. It was a proud day for James and

Sarah, who'd followed their daughter's tenacious progress over the previous eight years - sharing her trials, her successes, failures, and the occasional tantrum. James eyed the portraits of past chancellors lining the walls– austere mutton-chopped men, staring down gimlet-eyed on the unworthy. *'These blokes don't look like they enjoyed their jobs very much.'* He thought. *'They should have loosened up with a couple of beers now and then.'*

A hush descended as the Chancellor stepped onto the podium, shuffling papers. 'Good afternoon ladies and gentlemen, and welcome to the Sydney University Medical School graduation ceremony of 1916. During these turbulent times, when unprecedented numbers of our young men are falling in battle, there was never a more urgent need for qualified medical professionals. The advancement of medical science continues to demand that our doctors are at the forefront of the latest scientific advances. It is with these thoughts that I am pleased to present to you today the men and women who will take the proud legacy of Sydney University's Medical School into the future.'

There were 18 graduates, announced in alphabetical order. Early in the batting order was Cath's old nemesis and sparring partner, Hugh Barrington–a 'King's School' old boy and son of the eminent surgeon Professor Walter Sterling Barrington. Master Barrington paced regally down the red carpet, nose raised slightly higher than cruising altitude, and his acceptance of the purple-bound scroll reflected more entitlement than enrapture. Further down the list was young Peter Hannigan, the wide-eyed boy from Armidale who Cath had chatted to on enrolment day, eight years before.

Cath's role in the Stokeland murders had appeared in the Herald, and despite her abhorrence of the limelight, she had captured a degree of popular admiration as the 'plucky woman who saved the detective's life that night.' So, when the Chancellor finally reached the interesting part of the alphabet, and announced 'Miss Catherine Thornton', the family balked as the audience rose for a standing ovation. Cath turned crimson as she walked down the red carpet in cap and gown, and the Chancellor seemed even more embarrassed. The Thorntons rose to their feet and applauded with the crowd, and James would later swear blind he saw one of the old fogies on the wall roll his eyes in disgust.

Later that day there was a gathering at the Royal to celebrate Cath's graduation. Guests included The Major, now in his mid-80's, Miss Minnie Fitzroy of the naked first floor art studio, George and Matilda Hargreaves, David Pilkington, the chemist and Cath's onetime hapless boss, 'Eddie' Edmonstone, budding actor, Police

Inspector James McManus and Sister Alphonse–Cath's old tutor and mentor from St Vincent's. It was a warm March evening–the pub's doors were open to catch the breeze wafting in from High Cross Park.

Cath and Eddie had kept in touch over the years - remembering one another's birthdays with a phone call or a card. Eddie's pursuit of an acting career, although mortifying for her parents, had brought her some success in live theatre, with the occasional supporting role earning a mention in the playbills under her actual name - 'Charlotte Edmonstone', which she felt sounded much posher than 'Eddie'.

The two hugged.

'Congratulations Cath–I knew you'd make it.'

'Thanks, Ed. I'm just glad it's over and I can relax for a while before I try to find a job somewhere. I heard you were appearing in "Naughty Marietta" at the Grand Opera House–a star is born!'

'More like a crashing meteor. I'm playing "Lizette, A Casquette Girl". It impressed Mum and Dad–they thought a French character had bragging value with the neighbours, until I told them a "Casquette Girl" was a mail-order bride.'

A barman tapped Cath on the shoulder.

'Excuse me Cath–there's a call for you.'

'Oh, thanks Jack–I'll take it upstairs.' She turned to Eddie. 'Sorry Ed–I'll be back in a minute.'

She trotted up the stairs to the hallway and lifted the receiver.

'Hello?'

'Cath? It's Tom–Tom Wong from the CIB.'

She hesitated for an instant–she hadn't heard from him in months. 'Tom! How are you?'

'I'm good–just fine. And you?'

'Yes, of course–I'm really well.'

'I wanted to congratulate you on your graduation.'

'How did you know?'

'You forget–I'm a detective–we have ways.'

She laughed. 'Thank you–that's very sweet.'

'You don't forget someone who saved your life.'

'No…. No, you don't.'

There was a brief silence over the line other than faint voices and the far-off clicking of switchboards.

Wong's voice was hesitant. 'Cath, I was ah… wondering whether you might like to go out one night, perhaps dinner or something? That is, if you aren't already attached, or anything.'

'Why, yes, of course, I'd like that–the only thing I've been attached to lately are medical books.'

'Wonderful. Shall we say next Saturday? We could meet at Burney's at 7?'

'Of course–until then.'

She returned downstairs smiling, and spied Danny standing at the edge of the party, looking a little lost.

'Hello little brother–thanks for coming today.'

He smiled. 'I wouldn't have missed it for the world–still can't believe you're a doctor now.'

'It feels a little strange to me too–I'm terrified some patient will ask me a question and I won't be able to answer it without looking up "Gray's Anatomy". She paused, unsure of whether to broach the subject of Gallipoli. 'I suppose you've had your fill of doctors after what you've been through.'

He looked off into space for a moment, seeing something no-one else could. 'You know, I'd wake up not knowing where the hell I was, or how I got there. Blokes screaming, blokes dying. The smell of antiseptic makes me sick now. Sometimes I think the doctors and nurses had it worse than we did.'

She hugged him and saw fear in his eyes.

~ ~ ~

Tom arrived early at Burney's and grabbed a table for two. George street's clamour faded as the doors swung closed behind him. The old coffee-house was looking its best. Leadlight windows and polished timber breathed elegance, and soft lighting murmured warmth and conviviality. The aroma of roasted coffee beans pervaded, but if something stronger was more one's style, its wine list would fit the bill.

The clientele was egalitarian - men in suits browsed evening newspapers over an espresso, taking time out between the office and a tram ride home. Hair-swept young women caressed macchiato cups with polished fingernails. Studious types with lank hair and frayed collars smoked while they pored over seditious pamphlets. Patrons meeting colleagues or sweethearts came and went.

Cath arrived, and they shook hands.

'It's good to see you again.'

'And you, Tom—it's been a while since we were last here.'

'How have you been?'

She raised her eyes to the ceiling in mock supplication. 'Insanely busy, focussing on my finals. It's as if a lead weight's lifted from my shoulders–what about you?'

'A string of ordinary cases since the Stokeland affair, none of them as dramatic….. or as rewarding.'

She hoped the inference was intentional, but made no remark. A waiter materialised and took their order.

'Are you working on anything exciting now?'

'Not really-an embezzlement and a couple of missing persons in Chinatown. The boss always gives me those cases.'

'You speak Chinese?'

'Cantonese–my family's from Hong Kong, but I was born here.'

'Forgive me for being nosey–I'm always fascinated by the Far East–I've thought about practising medicine there someday.'

He smiled. 'You're not being nosey. You should go–a lot of British live there.'

She sipped her coffee. 'You know, if I went, I think I'd rather see how the locals live, rather than the British. How did you come to be in the police force?'

He was silent for a moment, watching Sydney's evening street performance through the window. He followed the unconscious habit of policemen everywhere–checking faces, watching movements. 'It's a long story. My grandfather was a Hong Kong policeman, and my father was the first Chinese to join the New South Wales Police. Like me, he didn't look very oriental–his grandmother was British. Dad thought the name 'Wong' would go against him, so he joined under the name of 'Walsh'. He was eventually found out, but kept his job anyway–he was in the CIB by then, and when I was old enough, I joined the force too.'

'Is your father still a policeman?'

'No, he's retired now.' He grinned.' But he still gives me unsolicited advice on police work. So, tell me–what's it like to be a doctor?'

She shrugged her shoulders. 'I haven't had time to find out yet–my first priority is getting a hospital residency.'

'Sydney?'

'Sydney would be my choice.' She crossed the fingers of both hands. 'In fact, I have an interview there in a few days, but I'm not fussy–I've applied to the Prince of Wales, South Sydney, Royal Prince Alfred, even Liverpool, but so far, no luck.'

He gave a thin smile. 'Would that have anything to do with being a woman?'

'I try not to think about that. I'm going to wear them down with persistence.' She smiled. 'It's what I'm good at.'

~   ~   ~

After coffee they exited Burney's as the Queen Victoria Building's domes glowed in the fading sunset like copper planets. Traffic had deserted the streets with the end of the working day, and with the coming of night, men in suits and women with billowing sleeves meandered along the footpath, stopping randomly at shop windows. Couples headed like moths to brightly lit theatres, and young men in military uniform swung through pub doors in varying degrees of imbalance. On a corner lamppost, a tattered recruitment poster flapped in the wake of passing trams.

They turned up the rise of Rowe Street, the haunt of Sydney's bohemian push. Its glass-fronted shops offered an array of diversions; bookshops with downstairs rooms where one could buy 'daring' postcards, musty bric-à-brac emporiums offering planchettes, glyphoscope cameras and stuffed elephants' feet, and art galleries thick with the smell of oil paint.

Shop owners were closing doors for the day as Tom guided her to a small café with a painted wooden sign proclaiming *'café Jean-Claude'*. Inside, candlelit tables crouched beneath a cloud of aromatic Gauloises cigarette smoke, and an old man in a striped shirt played Corsican folk songs on a violin. A stocky, middle-aged man with dark oily hair and a dishcloth over one shoulder approached them with a smile and bow.

'Monsieur Tom. Bienvenu.'

They shook hands, smiling. 'Hello Jean-Claude. May I introduce Miss Cath Thornton?' He bowed from the waist and kissed Cath's hand. 'Enchantee, Mademoiselle.' He motioned to a table for two. 'S'il vous plaît.'

Cath surveyed the café. There was no Edwardian formality here–no pretence, no stroking of the moustache, no clicking of fingers to summon the 'garcon'. People were absorbed in the moment, with no need to impress. Tables were barely elbow distance apart and the animated conversation, mostly French, combined in one low babble like a wave receding from a rocky shoreline. Jean-Claude moved about the tables, scattering witticisms among his customers with the skill of a vaudeville comedian while the tiny kitchen clattered and sizzled with tantalising aromas and clouds of steam.

She smiled at Tom. 'I like this place–it's so…..'

'Different?'

'Yes. It's like the kitchen at home–just a comfortable place for good food, without the 'show'. Do you know Jean-Claude well?'

'You could say that. I met him during an investigation. A fellow came in here one night, just as they were closing up. He pulled a gun and demanded the contents of the cash register. Jean-Claude refused, and there was a struggle. Our amiable host is an exponent of 'Savate'–a French boxing style–he disarmed the thief and taught him a lesson - it was a month before he could leave hospital to appear in court.'

'I'll avoid upsetting him tonight.'

Tom grinned. 'Don't be concerned–he almost never hits anyone in his own cafe. Are you hungry?'

'Frankly, I'm starving. We should ask for a menu.'

'Don't bother–Jean-Claude's wife Collette cooks one dish each night–everyone gets the same until it runs out.' He pointed to a blackboard on the wall. 'And tonight it's "Agneau Corse"–roast Corsican lamb with rosemary, potatoes and garlic.'

'That sounds superb.'

The food didn't disappoint, nor did the dusty bottle of Corsican Shiraz Jean-Claude produced from the cellar. Conversation ebbed and flowed - the perils of being a policeman, the unshakeable Mrs. Mitterrand, motor bikes and medicine, to name a few. It was when they broached the subject of the war that Cath became suddenly withdrawn, and the smile that had played about her lips all evening suddenly disappeared as she told Tom of the death of John and Danny's amputation.

'Oh, Cath–I'm so sorry–I didn't realise……..'

She placed her hand on his. 'No, please, it's alright. I'm getting better at dealing with it now.' She sighed resignedly. 'John's gone, and he's left a void in our hearts, but we can't bring him back. Right now, I'm worried about Danny. He's simmering like a volcano. She sighed. 'God, Tom - he's only 20 year's old. He should be having the time of his life, but the light's gone from his eyes, and he looks lost, sometimes confused, sometimes fearful, sometimes angry. It's not surprising, after what he's been through–I just wish I could help him.'

Tom squeezed her hand tenderly. 'Your brother's been through hell and back. I've seen a few coppers who've lived through some terrible things–mangled bodies, train wrecks, suicides, grieving families. They don't talk about it much, but they're affected by it–we all are. My dad was on a case before I was born–multiple murders. They called it the 'Doctor Hacksaw' case. He would relate to what Danny's feeling.'

She sipped her wine. 'One thing I plan to do, now I'm qualified, is to look into any research being done on his condition–God knows, this thing is happening to a lot of young men now.'

With that interchange their relationship had suddenly moved to a deeper level, like a cave explorer entering a subterranean vault. There was a connection between them–conversation flowed easily, meandering from one topic to the next in unhurried enjoyment of one another's company.

They exited the cafe as the GPO clock tolled 10pm, and theatre-goers milled along Pitt Street. The Randwick tram trundled by-they boarded and rattled up Oxford Street.

Tom called above the clamour. 'My stop is just up ahead at Taylor Square–I hope you had a good time tonight.'

'Yes, I did. Thank you. Lovely food and lovely company–just what I needed. And thanks for your concern for Danny.'

'My pleasure entirely. Would you like to do it again? I know some great places to eat down in Chinatown.'

She smiled brightly. 'I'd love to.'

~   ~   ~

The maple trees in Macquarie Street were tinged with autumn-yellow as Cath trotted up the steps of Sydney Hospital on a bright April morning. She was early for her interview with Medical Superintendent Doctor Herbert McIntosh and took a seat in the corridor. She had dressed conservatively–a navy-blue, waisted dress and brocaded bodice, matching cape and a simple wool beret'. *Somewhere between Marie Curie and Marie Doro'*, she said to herself in the mirror that morning.

She was ushered into McIntosh's office by a humourless secretary and sat opposite the man she hoped would be her boss. He was shortish and in his early fifties, with wiry grey hair thinning at the temples, limpid-blue, baggy eyes and a rather unkempt moustache, reminiscent of the poet and story-teller, Henry Lawson.

'Good morning, Miss Thornton - congratulations on your graduation.'

'Thank you.'

'As you know, we offer a limited number of placements each year–our budgets are always under pressure–so gaining admission is quite competitive.'

'Yes, of course.'

He tapped a fountain pen on the ink-blotter, like an orchestra conductor calling for attention. 'I had heard of you, of course, in the media–that nasty business in Vaucluse last year.'

'Here we go again.' She thought. 'Yes–something that I'd rather put behind me, I'm sure you understand.'

He beat a tactical retreat. 'Yes, um, quite. So, looking at your academic record–your studies extended an extra year–I see some subjects required repeating.'

'Yes–like most people, I found some areas more difficult than others, but my final results were well above average.'

'Yes. And tell me, what are your expectations for a placement at Sydney Hospital?'

She'd pondered the question many times, and her thoughts had always strayed to Madeleine Russell, the nurse who had taught her, unknowingly, that medicine is not just about science, symptoms and diagnosis–but also people and emotions, and ultimately, service to others.

Her years of learning had also provided self-insight–she'd realised that she unconsciously hid her feelings under a pile of medical books, and defined success purely as being better than men. But experience had taught her that was a narrow road to travel. Where once she'd been a crusader with fire in her eyes and one hand at the hilt of her sword, she was now more a pilgrim seeking insight, and the sword, although still sharp, was a last resort.

'I'd like to give my academic learning a firm foundation by practising medicine in the real world, not behind university walls. I want to be challenged in the broadest sense–mentally, physically, emotionally–that's what develops and matures one, I believe.' McIntosh was pensive for a moment, and his tapping had ceased. 'Yes, quite so. Miss Thornton, I'm going to ask you a question that may sound provocative, but I have good reason to ask it. Why should I offer this placement to a woman?'

Cath was taken aback at his directness, and took a deep breath. 'Doctor McIntosh, I don't think you *should* offer it to a woman. I think you should offer it to the best applicant–and 'best' doesn't necessarily mean the person with the highest marks at university, or the best social connections. It doesn't mean the person who thinks they are *entitled* to the job, nor the person who thinks they *deserve* the job. It means the person who has the knowledge, the strength of character and the dedication to contribute as much to this hospital as this hospital contributes to them.'

~ ~ ~

The interview was a marathon event–two hours of scrutiny and rapid-fire questions that had her reeling like a boxer on the ropes, but each time, she fended off the body blows and came back with a couple of left jabs of her own, evidently to the satisfaction of her inquisitor. At the end of the final round, McIntosh shook her hand.

'Thank you, Miss Thornton. We'll be in touch.'

As McIntosh's secretary escorted her to the door, Hugh Barrington, the professor's son and Sydney 'upper cruster', was walking down the corridor.

'Good Morning Cath.'

'Hello Hugh. Fancy seeing you here.'

He passed a hand through his mop of hair with an air of affectation. 'Yes, quite.'

The secretary waved him through the office door. 'This way, Mr. Barrington–Doctor McIntosh will be just a few minutes.'

Barrington tipped his hat to Cath. 'My father set up the interview–he and McIntosh are old classmates.' And with a cheesy grin, he brushed by her and the door closed.

Her heart sank, and she thought. *'You can't beat the old school tie.'*

~ ~ ~

10 April 1916
Dr. Catherine Thornton
2 Perouse Rd.
Randwick
NSW
Australia.

Dear Dr. Thornton,

I am pleased to inform you that your application for medical residency at Sydney Hospital has been successful.

Dr. McIntosh would be pleased if you would meet with him at 9am on Monday 17 April at his Macquarie St. office to discuss the details of your residency, including a starting date that would be mutually agreeable.

Yours Truly,
Mrs. Dulcie Johnstone
Secretary to Dr. McIntosh.

~ ~ ~

The beer garden was once the access for the Royal's clandestine Sunday drinkers, but when James put an end to illicit trading in 1908, he saw no reason to keep it cluttered with old beer kegs, particularly not on warm sunny days when a cold beer in the open air was becoming popular - and a few wrought-iron chairs, potted palms and beach umbrellas was all it took.

One April Saturday afternoon he sat with Danny over a beer. On the other side of the fence trams rumbled down Perouse Road on their way to Maroubra. James worried about his son's emotional well-being–he hadn't returned to his old job at Prouds, and he seemed distant - lost in his own thoughts. James would often hear him at night from down the hallway, crying out in his sleep; reminding him of the days when Danny would get an asthma attack and wake the whole house. And he'd been drinking more–a familiar sign of emotional turmoil.

Danny finished his beer and signalled for another. 'Dad, I um, wanted to talk to you.'

'Yes, mate–what's on your mind?'

He let out a deflated sigh like a three-am party balloon. 'I'm not good, Dad–not good at all.'

'What's the matter, Danny?'

'I can't settle in–I don't know where I am anymore. I'm home, but I can't stop thinking about the war, about John. I get nightmares, headaches. A car backfires and I almost shit myself. Sometimes I want to hit someone– anyone, and sometimes I cry for no reason. He eyed the licks of froth inching back down his empty schooner-glass. 'And I'm hitting the piss a bit, too. What's wrong with me, Dad?'

James placed a hand on his son's shoulder. 'We've all noticed that you're not yourself, and we're worried for you. Cath has a word for it–"Shell Shock"–something that they don't really understand yet. I'm no doctor, but I've given it a lot of thought.'

'And?'

James leaned back in his chair. 'Nobody's seen a war like this before, Danny–not on such a scale, nor the huge number of casualties. We've been very clever, inventing more efficient ways to kill each other–machine guns, bombs, mortars, mustard gas, bigger canons. And look at where you've been - you've spent months in a trench where each breath could be your last - your nerves have been stretched tighter than catgut. You've seen blokes blown apart. You've been wounded twice and you've lost a leg.' James felt the anger rise. 'And what do they do? They knock up a wooden leg on a lathe, strap it on you and send you home with a new suit, expecting you to laugh it off and go back to civilian life like nothing ever happened–like the hero of some fucking story book.'

He looked away for a moment, calming himself. 'Danny, I think the change from Gallipoli to Randwick has been too sudden for you–and don't think for a minute you're the only one going through this–I'll bet most blokes who've come back are going through exactly the same thing you are, and they keep it bottled up in case they're called "weak" or "soft'. Everyone expects them to be the big, tough outback stockman–and that's a bloody fairy-tale.'

Danny's beer arrived. He stared idly at the rising amber bubbles, but didn't pick it up. 'You know Dad, you were right - I shouldn't have signed up. I should have listened to you–if I did, I'd still have two legs.' James sighed. 'You can't blame yourself, mate–a car could have bowled you over in Pitt Street–nobody knows what fate has in store for them–we just have to play the cards we're dealt. The important thing now is getting yourself better, dealing with the demons on your back.'

'What should I do?'

It was hard for James to say it. 'Son, if I was you, I'd get the hell away from here for a while–go where nobody knows you; where nobody expects anything from you.

Hop a train or hitch a ride to anywhere and let fortune take its course. Sometimes a wanderer finds answers to questions without looking. Your uncle Michael and uncle John did exactly that during the gold rush in 1855–got on their horses and rode down to Ballarat–didn't come back for six months.'

'Did they find what they were looking for?'

'They found more–a little gold and a lot of self-knowledge.'

~   ~   ~

It was to be a long time before Sarah forgave James - in fact, he was convinced she'd never forgive him at all, and he couldn't blame her–Danny had been home only five months, and now he was off again on his father's advice - in Sarah's words, 'on some odyssey that would have him tilting at windmills, as crazy as Don Quixote himself.' James didn't really know if Danny would find any answers, but he was convinced that the Royal Hotel would not give him any.

Danny ambled down to Randwick Racecourse one morning, shopping for a horse, and found a four-year-old bay mare of 16 hands for sale–a sleek, graceful animal. She cost a pricey 20 quid, but he had his army back-pay, and she was worth it. He'd done a bit of riding at Mena camp with the blokes from the Light Horse and had found he was a natural horseman. In the racing game, back when the mare was a skittish two-year-old, she was called 'Stout and Bold', but Danny christened her 'Balla', in honour of Ballarat, where his uncles had found answers in 1855.

On Friday morning, 21 April 1916, he climbed into the saddle and said goodbye to his family with the undertaking that he'd write home once a week. He was heading west, he said, over the Blue Mountains and into the plains–beyond that, he hadn't a bloody clue where he'd go. Sarah was transported back to Woolloomooloo wharf, 1914, with the *Euripides* pushing down the harbour and her two sons fading to specks in the distance. It seemed that at 63 she'd never have a calm and peaceful life–the happiness and contentment she'd yearned for was to be forever just out of reach. *'Life'*, she thought, *'has a habit of making other plans.'*

He rode down Randwick Road and across Moore Park, heading for Parramatta - planning to make Emu Plains at the foot of the Blue Mountains sometime that night. He carried a swag, a billy and a water canteen, and in his wallet was an old photo of him and John on Coogee beach. The morning was cool and bright - a light southerly whisked away the chimney-smog and the sun was at his back. Balla moved in an easy gait as motorised traffic gave him right of way up Cleveland Street. Passers-by gave him a nod or a wave when they noticed his slouch hat.

Somewhere in the crevices of his mind a faint voice told him he was moving in the right direction–that the road ahead held more promise than perfidy. He feared that if he looked back over Balla's haunches he'd think of his family - how he'd left them behind once more, and be tempted to turn around. He kicked Balla forward into a canter, and didn't look back.

Chapter 12

Tides of Change

James passed below the spires of St. Mary's Cathedral as dead leaves scratched along the pavement in a chill southerly wind. Across the road in Hyde Park, over the rattle and honk of passing traffic, he heard a familiar song:

'Now William, I'll prove if you really are true.

For you say that you love me—I don't think you do;

If really you love me, you must give up the wine,

For the lips that touch liquor shall never touch mine.'

He followed the sound to a shadowed stretch of grass where a group of women had assembled in an impromptu choir. The Women's Temperance Movement was on the march, their banners proclaiming: 'Money for Beer Doesn't Buy Shoes', 'Drink is the Devil's Crowbar', and 'Have Your Say for Early Closing

Hours'. The campaign to reduce alcohol consumption had been bolstered by an incident in January that had brought shame to the Australian army and put the New South Wales liquor industry under a glaring spotlight.

At the outset of the war, military training camps were built on the outskirts of Sydney at Liverpool and Casula. Bush was cleared and land levelled for parade grounds, and a sea of canvas tents sprang up like new mushrooms after autumn rain. Thousands of recruits were processed, outfitted and hastily trained before they were packed off to the battlegrounds of France and Turkey. The camps themselves were rudimentary, with overcrowding, spartan facilities and a punishing training regimen. At neighbouring Holsworthy, internment camps for enemy aliens were also established, which in 1915 were the scene of riots over rations and work duties; and it was said that the internees now enjoyed better conditions than the soldiers.

The enthusiasm of the 1st AIF volunteers was never in question, and thousands would eventually pay the ultimate price for their patriotism. But with their personal sacrifice also came an unspoken expectation of 'a fair go'. This, combined with an in-built reluctance to comply with authority, fomented unrest, and the recruits agitated for improved conditions–better sanitation, more flexible leave arrangements, and dubiously, a canteen that served alcohol. Unsurprisingly, their demands fell on deaf ears, and when, on the morning of February 14, 1916, the Casula soldiers were told their training regime would increase from 36 hours to over 40 hours a week, it became the straw that broke the camel's back.

They broke ranks and deserted the camp, declaring they were on strike until conditions improved. Around 3000 Casula men marched to the Liverpool camp, and a combined mob descended on the town, invading pubs and ransacking local shops, then hopping trains to the city. Behind a makeshift sign that proclaimed, 'STRIKE–WE WON'T DRILL 40 ½ HOURS', they marched down George Street, but the march soon became a 'pub crawl'–windows were smashed, fights broke out, and several German-affiliated businesses, such as Kleisdorff's tobacco shop in Hunter Street and the German Club in Phillip Street, were attacked.

The police were heavily outnumbered, and soldiers from Sydney Showgrounds arrived to help turn the mob back to Central Station, where most were herded onto west-bound trains. The unrest continued into the night as a hard core of protesters, fired with anger and grog, set fire to rubbish bins and hurled rocks at police. In the heat of the 'free-for-all', shots rang out, and in the light of the flames, a 20-year-old Light Horse recruit, Ernest William Keefe, lay dead.

Aside from the many military and civil court cases that followed, the incident provided the temperance movement with valuable ammunition. The soldiers' demands for a canteen serving liquor and their drunken spree through city streets was a perfect opportunity to decry the evils of alcohol. In 1916 pubs enjoyed liberal regulations–many opened from 6am to 11pm, Monday to Saturday, and the movement seized their opportunity; bringing pressure to bear on the NSW State Government for a referendum over pub opening hours. It wasn't long before the government bowed to public opinion and agreed to put the question to the people of New South Wales in a referendum, scheduled for the 10th of June 1916.

James watched on as the protesters ended their performance to polite applause from the small crowd, then hoisted their banners and continued down Macquarie Street to Parliament House, where he was sure they would break into song once more.

At the Royal later that night, the referendum was the dinner-table topic.

'So what exactly do we think will the question will be? Jim asked.

Sarah sipped her tea. 'The closing hour will be the question–and the wowsers are insisting on 6pm.'

James added, 'I'm not against reducing hours–most nights it's pretty quiet here after 9pm, but 6pm is going a bit too far.'

Elizabeth offered her opinion, 'And 11pm is also going too far–why would you need to drink in a pub at that hour?

Jim replied. 'Some nights you have to pour a few of them out the door.'

James considered for a moment. 'I'll tell you what'll happen if 6 o'clock closing comes in. Sly grog shops will open up all over Sydney. While the coppers watch the pubs turn out their lights, the drinking will go underground and there'll be an increase in organised crime. At least in a pub, drinking has rules, and anyone who makes trouble is quickly out on his ear, but in a sly grog shop, there are no rules, and alcohol will cause more trouble than it does now. What do you reckon, Cath?'

'I think the temperance people have a point. At work we see most of our emergency admissions come in late in the evening, and alcohol is usually involved–a drunk walks in front of a tram, a husband comes home from the pub and knocks his wife around, or young hooligans get drunk and fight each other in Woolloomooloo, but I've no doubt that sly grog will bring a greater criminal element into the system–and probably more violence on the streets.'

Jim grinned as he puffed on his pipe. 'Stop me if you've heard this one. There was a temperance meeting one night where the speaker was earbashing the audience on the evils of alcohol, and he gave a demonstration. He had two glasses of clear liquid on a table–one, he said, held water, and the other one was pure alcohol. He pulled a tin of worms out of his pocket and dropped one into the water, where it wriggled about happily. Then he put a second worm into the alcohol, and it instantly shrivelled up and died. "Ladies and gentlemen!" He shouted. "What is the moral of that?'

'There was silence for a minute until an old bloke up the back called out. "That if you drink alcohol, you won't get worms.'

Time would tell that the referendum would not only have a profound effect on the nature of hotels in New South Wales, but also cause a seismic shift in the social habits of many Australians.

~ ~ ~

Balla took the steep trek into the mountains at a steady pace, and soon Danny found himself in cool mountain air among towering blue gums. He'd spent the previous night at the 'Orient Hotel' in Emu Plains-a boxy building crouching ogre-like near the noisy railway, and spent the night tortured by a lumpy mattress. He was glad to be in the bush.

The road undulated through tree ferns bathed in soft light from the canopy. Lizards basking on the road's verge scurried into the undergrowth at the sound of Balla's hoofbeats. He heard echoes of a motor car's farts and gear-crunches five minutes before it arrived, and a goggled, scarfed dandy and his beau gave him a jaunty wave as they passed by in their Wolseley convertible.

In afternoon light on the outskirts of Wentworth Falls, he heard the unmistakable sound of a bullock team–clanking chains, the bark of a working dog, bullocks lowing, a whip cracking like a starting pistol. They had once been a common sight along this road, carting everything from wool and timber to furniture and people, down to Sydney. They'd carve up roads with hoofmarks and get bogged in the mud of Broadway as they swung left down George Street to the clippers at Circular Quay. As the railway pushed over the mountains, they retreated westward, making shorter runs, but they'd be seen on New South Wales bush tracks for a few years to come.

The team rounded a bend in a cloud of dust as the bullocky kept a languid pace beside his animals and a dog darted back and forth, nipping at heels. Twelve pairs of beasts were yoked to the wagon, carrying an assortment of machinery, bricks, railway sleepers, and inexplicably, a dozen or so toilet bowls encased in wooden packing crates. The bullocky controlled the team with his whip– not as a weapon, but as a conductor controls an orchestra. His signals were well learned by the bullocks - if the whip was held horizontally overhead, it meant slow the pace, or held in the left hand, to back up. The huge, intelligent animals watched for their cue.

Danny moved off the road to let them pass. The bullocky gave him a casual wave and signalled for the team to pull up as dust floated past him through shafts of sunlight.

'G'day young fella, Michael McShane's the name.' He was in his early fifties, with dark, lively eyes and a full grey beard, wearing brown dungarees, a muddy-grey shirt and faded tartan vest.

'G'day. Danny Thornton. How's it going?'

'Steady enough–how's the road down to the flats? Any hold-ups?'

A blocked road could mean hours of delay, and the possibility of no feed for the team at the end of the day's journey.

'All clear from Emu Plains when I came up this morning.'

McShane conjured up tobacco and paper from his vest, and shot a glance at Danny's slouch hat. 'Been in the "blue" have you?'

'Yes–Gallipoli.'

The bullocky let out a cloud of cigarette smoke and nodded. 'Mine was in Africa–the Boers. Hard bastards– they didn't die easy.' He fingernailed a stray piece of tobacco from his teeth. 'Is that where you lost the leg?'

Danny was taken aback. 'How'd you know?'

He pointed. 'You're left ankle's bent in the stirrup, but your right one's at a right angle - straight as polished hardwood.' Then he bent forward and pulled up a trouser leg to reveal a weathered replica of Danny's artificial limb. 'Look a bit familiar? He smiled. 'I've had this for seventeen years–a cannon ball sheared the bastard clean off one afternoon when I wasn't looking.'

Danny couldn't help but return the smile. 'Can I ask you a question?'

'Why not? I've been nosey enough.'

'How long does it take to get over it?'

The bullocky drew on the last of his cigarette and ground the butt under a boot-heel. His countenance held a combination of humour and bitterness. 'You don't get over it, mate–you just get on with it.' He let out a whistle, and the dog sprang into life. 'Be seein' you, young fella–go well.' The team rumbled past down the slope and turned another bend in the road, and the silence soon returned.

He stopped for the night at Toll's Hotel in Wentworth Falls - a two-storey pub among wattle trees, with deep-shaded verandas looking onto the street. After stabling Balla for the night he wandered into the bar where a few locals swapped yarns by a fire that filled the room with eucalyptus. He was happy just to sit and sip a cold beer, alone with his thoughts. He'd ridden out of Sydney with a vague feeling of dislocation, like a foot soldier deserting his post as the city gates slammed shut behind him. But there was something about the mountains that cleared the mind and whispered that while his journey might not give him answers, it may ask the right questions.

He was five years old when the family boarded the train to Sydney to free him from the chains of asthma, and he remembered little more of the journey than a blur

BREAKING LUCKY

of yellow sandstone, straggly bush, red iron roofs and train platforms speeding by the carriage window. He wanted to learn more about these mountains, and in slow conversation, the barman suggested he visit the 'Three Sisters' rock formation in Katoomba, overlooking the Jamison Valley. Sheepish at his own poetry, he'd described the Sisters as the 'soul of the mountains'. The words echoed in his mind, and in the stillness of sunrise the next day, he pulled his army greatcoat closer against the chill, and followed the road westward.

He turned off the main road past a cottage with a smoking chimney; the smell of bacon making his stomach growl. He passed a few modest brick dwellings, a low, welcoming guest house and an austere Masonic Hall. Following a sign to 'Echo Point', he came to a clearing where a sturdy timber railing overlooked a valley stretching away to the horizon.

Rugged cliffs lit with a tangerine sunrise dropped hundreds of feet to a blanket of trees covering the Jamison Valley. Danny was so stunned at the beauty stretching before him, he almost missed the famous Three Sisters standing shoulder to shoulder on a rock ledge, like teeth in a sandstone jaw.

The clearing was deserted except for an Aboriginal man leaning against the railing. He was in his thirties, tall and wiry with a full black beard, white shirtsleeves under a waistcoat, corded dungarees and bushman's boots. Danny thought of Sam Harper, the aboriginal digger at Anzac Cove, and wondered where he was at that moment. The man turned to catch Danny's look and ambled over. He glanced across at Balla, tied to a tree at the edge of the clearing.

'Nice-looking horse - looks like she's bred for the track.'

'That's right–she's a racer; a bit long in the tooth for that now, but she was a stayer in her day.'

'Looks that way. 'You from Sydney?'

'Yeah, Randwick–I bought her at the racecourse stables. You work with horses?'

The man shrugged. 'Done a bit here and there– some drovin', some racin' when I was a young bloke, but I was too tall for a jockey.'

Danny looked to the valley. 'It's the first time I've seen this view–it's beautiful. A bloke down at Wentworth Falls said the Three Sisters are the soul of the mountains.'

The man shook his head. 'Nah, mate–the soul of the mountains is the soul of the people. The Sisters are just rocks, but my people believe that once, those rocks were real sisters. Have you heard my people's story about the Sisters?'

Danny was intrigued. 'No. But I'd like to.'

His gaze meandered over the valley for a moment as he composed himself. 'In the Dreamtime, Tyawan was a Clever Man of my people - the Gundungurra people, and he had three beautiful daughters–Meenhi, Wimlah and Gunnedoo, who he loved deeply. Somewhere in the caves of these mountains, also lived the Bunyip - a huge beast that feasted on human flesh. When the people heard the Bunyip's terrible howl, they banded together in case of attack.'

'One day Tyawan went into the valley to hunt wallaby, but before he left, he hid his daughters behind a rock wall so the Bunyip couldn't get them. But while he was gone, an earthquake came and shook the rocks and trees, and woke the Bunyip from his sleep. The rock wall behind the three daughters crashed down and left them standing on that narrow ledge over there, high above the valley. The Bunyip was angry at being woken up. He roared and came over the rocks to where the sisters were, and crept slowly toward them. They howled in fear.'

'Tyawan looked up from the valley as the Bunyip tried to grab his daughters, and pointed his magic bone at them, turning them to stone so they'd be safe there until the Bunyip had gone, and then Tyawan would change them back again.'

The man's eyes widened with the emotion of a seasoned story-teller as his narration gained pace. 'But the Bunyip was very angry and chased Tyawan through the valley until he trapped him on top of "Korowal" over there.' He pointed to scarred clifftops rising through the mist like ancient city walls. 'Tyawan pointed his magic bone at himself and changed into a lyrebird, gliding down to the valley floor to escape the Bunyip. But somewhere, high above the ground, he dropped his magic bone, and ever since that day it's been lost. He still searches for it, scratching on the ground, feeding on insects and calling with great sadness to his three daughters. The three sisters stand here in silence, watching him from their ledge, hoping that one day their father will find his magic bone and set them free.'

Danny paused in thought. 'Do you think the sisters will ever be free?'

The man gave a wintry smile. 'The sisters are like the Gundungurra people–like all Aboriginal people. They will be free only when the land is returned to them.' His bitter smile was lit by the morning sun. 'We tell the stories from the Dreamtime to keep our culture strong, but we must also think about the future–we must have a Dreamtime, but we must plan for a Futuretime–only then will we survive.'

Danny replied. 'My grandfather came across these mountains over 70 years ago. A Gundungurra Man named Galu rescued his son from the bush, and he and my grandfather exchanged gifts - a silver religious medallion for a beautifully carved nulla-nulla, that I'm told has spiritual powers. My family still has the nulla-nulla as a treasured gift.'

The man smiled as the sun struck over the Three Sisters. 'Your grandfather was lucky–the name 'Galu' is the mark of a Smart Man, like Tyawan. Their meeting was no accident–just like our meeting here today.' His dark eyes searched Danny's face as if taking soundings. 'You have the look of a seeker, but whatever it is you're looking for; you won't find it in Katoomba.' He reached out and Danny felt a tingle as the man gently touched his temple. 'You'll find it in there.' And with that, he shook Danny's hand and disappeared into the bush.

Danny lingered on a bench-seat as the Gundungurra man's words echoed in his mind. He stared at the Three Sisters, now crowned in full sunlight. The Dreamtime story had painted them as captives of a force beyond their control–and that's exactly how he viewed himself–caught up in an unstoppable torrent that had tipped him into a pit of despair, just like the sisters' 'stone cages.' But were his cages unbreakable? Could he free himself?

~ ~ ~

Another day's ride took him to Mt. Victoria, and at dawn the next morning he followed the winding road down the mountains to rolling hills where rich pastureland stretched into the beyond. He rode north-west for most of the day until he reached Marrangaroo, where a sign pointed north to 'Gulgong - 90 Miles', and west to 'Bathurst - 35 miles.' He stroked Balla's neck. 'Which way, girl?' The mare shook her head, snorting with indifference. He glanced up to an afternoon sun already well past its zenith, and turned Balla's head westward.

As the sun ebbed below the horizon, he pulled off the road at a stream winding through a clump of she-oaks. Chill air signalled a cold night, and he soon had the billy steaming over a fire while he gnawed on dried beef from the Mt. Victoria General Store. The night closed in like a velvet cloak beyond the edge of the flame light–a distant pinprick of light from a farmhouse was the only sign of life other than the night-call of a Willie Wagtail. He turned in early and lay by the fire, watching bright orange sparks drift upward to a sky scattered with stars, and sleep soon overtook him.

~ ~ ~

He's flying like an albatross over the Gallipoli Peninsula, looking down at blossoming grey battle smoke and orange fire, and suddenly he's floating downward to the trenches, violating the landscape like an infected wound. He's on the ground now and can see the Turks' bayonets glinting in the sun as they prepare to go over the top. A bugle sounds and here they come, chanting 'Allah Akbar!'

He's frightened and wants to go home and he tries to run away but he's in molasses and can't move as the Turks come at him. They have blood coming out their eyes and their screams hurt his ears. He feels a bullet hit his leg and looks down, but it's alright because it's only made of wood. There's a Turk with a bayonet coming at him and it goes through his chest and out the other side. The Turk pulls it out and sticks it in again, and again, and again.....

He woke in mid-scream, drenched in sweat and panting like a marathon runner. The eastern horizon was lifting back the folds of night, and the bush appeared in dim silhouette. The disturbing dreams that began in London had stayed on like an unwelcome guest, despite his homecoming; and if anything, they were becoming more frequent. He sighed, knuckle-rubbed his eyes and stoked the fire back to life.

The Bathurst Times
Tuesday, April 25, 1916 ,
ANZAC DAY
HOW BATHURST WILL CELEBRATE IT

> The programme for the Anzac Day
> celebration is advertised this morning.
> After the morning church parade there
> will be an assemblage of troops with the
> Military Band on King's Parade. Later in
> the day will come the opening of the
> Recreation Hut and the presentation of
> colours to the departing troops. This
> should draw a large crowd to the camp.
> In the evening there will be a parade of
> troops to the railway station.

Rain-bloated clouds heaved up from the south as Danny saddled Balla and headed for Bathurst, 25 miles westward. The road wound between bushy hill-tops and green pastureland, past cattle grazing with their backs to a rising wind. The road seemed to belong to him–for long miles only a one-horse dray passed by, stacked to the gunnels with vegetables and driven by a square-framed farmer with his plentiful wife. They gave him a nod and a wave as they passed. The fields were all colours of green - autumn rain had closed the curtain on a dry, hot summer, and the land relaxed, comforted by plentiful dams reflecting the sky.

A flutter of movement snagged his attention as a Peregrine Falcon beat her wings high against the breeze, hovering above the fields in search of prey. *'She's looking for waterbirds around the dams',* Danny thought to himself, and as if on cue, she folded herself into a vertical dive.

Down on a billabong a cormorant hunts food, timing its dives to catch yabbies. The falcon reaches speeds of close to 200mph as she levels out, baring her talons at the last split second and hitting her prey; instantly breaking its neck. She secures the dead cormorant and lifts off to her nest high on a rocky outcrop.

A few miles down the road he rounded a bend to a farmhouse where a group of boys played cricket in the front yard. A barefoot youngster in dirty overalls flicked the six-stitcher in the air as he turned and ran in to deliver a 'yorker' to the batsman, who danced down the wicket and lofted it skyward. The ball arced down toward Danny-instinctively he shot out an arm and plucked it from the air as the boys leapt with a *'How's that?'*

One tousle-haired lad ran over with a beaming smile. 'Good catch, mister.' Glancing at Danny's slouch hat, his eyes widened. 'Are you a soldier?'

Danny smiled and tossed him the ball. 'I used to be.'

'Are you marching in the parade?'

'What parade?'

'The Anzac Day Parade.'

'What's Anzac Day?'

The boy looked askance. 'You're not a soldier, or you'd know about Gallipoli, and all that.'

'What's the parade for?'

'For the heroes of the war–the blokes that killed the Turks and made Australia famous.'

The significance of the date–April 25, suddenly hit Danny like a sucker punch. It was exactly a year since he'd charged across Anzac Cove under a hail of gunfire.

'The parade's in Bathurst, is it?'

'Yeah–my dad said the soldiers are 'gunna catch a train to Sydney, to join the war.'

'Are you going?'

The boy scowled. 'Nah–my Mum won't let me.'

Danny smiled as he nudged Balla into life. 'You'll have more fun playing cricket. See you later.' The boy looked on as Balla trotted away down the muddy road. A call sounded - 'Come on, Jimmy–it's your bowl', and he re-joined the game.

Memories of war escaped from the recesses of his mind like a cold draft under a cellar doorway. One corner of his brain told him to give Bathurst a wide berth–the other corner said 'you must go'.

The southerly blew itself out, and by late afternoon a dying sun was casting church-spire shadows across Bathurst. He found the railway line and followed it to the station–he was looking forward to a warm bed for the night, and he'd never seen a train station without a pub close at hand. And besides, the Bathurst soldiers–the new 'heroes of the war'–might be there. They held a strange fascination for him, as if he could go back in time and watch himself, back when he was normal.

He followed a side road past a railway bridge that spanned the Macquarie River, bucking with turbid water from the surrounding hills. Low cottages and shop-fronts lined the street like tattered books on a shelf. Awnings advertised 'Sunlight Soap', 'Griffiths Brothers Teas', and 'Rosella Tomato Sauce', while old men in knitted cardigans smoked pipes in wicker chairs. Children laughed, rolling hoops through puddles, and a red kelpie lifted a leg at a lamp post.

As he approached the town's edge he heard marching music, and presently a line of khaki uniforms rounded the corner. He pulled Balla to a halt. The faces were varied–some young, probably too young, like he had been, but many were older, and would have been rejected a year before, '*but*', he thought to himself, '*someone has to replace the dead*'.

He felt like a general reviewing his troops–'*this one has fear in his eyes. That one will be a trouble-maker*', but most were like he once was–a boy with dreams of glory. The troop came to a halt at the railway station where a black locomotive puffed and panted. The NCO ordered 'fall out', and the soldiers broke ranks to board the train. Family and friends had gathered to see them off–a girlfriend hugged her beau with tears in her eyes, a mother cried openly, a father shook hands grimly, and children stood wide-eyed and fearful, knowing only that their Daddy was leaving.

He remembered Woolloomooloo Wharf when his mother had stood waving a hankie forlornly at her two boys high on the deck of the '*Euripides*'. The excitement of adventure and a naïve optimism had blinded him to the reality of leaving home and family and the chaos that awaited him–and he saw exactly the same in these men. He'd seen enough, and silently wished the soldiers the best of luck as he turned Balla back onto the road.

Lengthening shadows ushered him to the Farmer's Arms Hotel—a squat, weatherboard building where the river wound through grazing land. He secured a room for the night and stabled Balla before taking a hot bath. The pub had weathered many years—ceilings that were once white had acquired a patina of umber from generations of open fires, and its hardwood floors sagged under the memory of a million boots. He wandered into the bar where a scattering of locals sat beneath clouds of cigarette smoke.

He ordered a beer and noticed a middle-aged man staring balefully in his direction, swaying from too many drinks. Danny looked away and focussed on his beer as the man called out.

'Hey you–Sunshine!'

Danny looked across at the man. He was middle-aged, tall and paunchy, with mousy-brown hair over bloodshot eyes and a nose that had taken a punch or two.

'Yeah–I'm talkin' to you, Sunshine. Where'd you blow in from?'

Danny sighed, 'Sydney.'

The man gave a mocking smile. 'Did they chase you out with a white feather, Sunshine?'

Danny's eyes remained fixed on his beer. 'I don't know what you're talking about.'

The drunk looked about him, chuckling at the other drinkers in an invitation to join in the game, but they ignored him. 'Where's your uniform, Sunshine? At the laundry, is it?'

The room had fallen silent as the barman watched them both.

The man lurched toward Danny as the barman spoke. 'Mick, you've said enough, now sit down and behave yourself.'

Mick chuckled again. 'Come now Jack, I'm just havin' a chat with me old mate Sunshine here. Hey Sunshine–lost your voice?'

'I don't need to explain myself to you.'

Mick thrust his face at Danny; it stank of stale beer and tobacco. 'Ya let others do your fightin', don't ya? Fuckin' coward.' He pushed Danny hard in the chest, knocking him backwards as beer spilled across the bar.

The man's punch is already on its way as something snaps inside Danny's head and he's back in the bottom of the trench and Lieutenant Kaya is coming at him, Mauser pistol levelled. The fist slams into Danny's temple, but he feels nothing. The man's eyes widen as Danny shoots out three lightning left jabs to Mick's face, snapping his head back and spraying droplets of blood over the floor. Danny uppercuts the man's chin and follows with a left cross as Mick pirouettes like an overweight ballerina and drops heavily to the floor. Danny grabs an empty bottle by the neck, smashes it on the bar and leaps toward Lieutenant Kaya as everything goes black.

~   ~   ~

Early sun cast iron-bar shadows on the wall. A puff of wind nudged a dead spider further along the window ledge above a sleeping figure. Danny woke with bleary eyes. Somewhere a currawong warbled and for a moment he was back on the Bathurst road, until a clanking of keys revealed a lined face under a faded blue police cap.

'Rise and shine, Danny Thornton.' The man splashed a mug of tea on a steel table bolted to the floor. 'Hope you like your tea black and bitter.'

Danny made to rise, but one hand was handcuffed to the cot. 'Where the hell am I?'

'Bathurst lockup - Sergeant Jim Hennessy, at your service.'

Danny grabbed the mug with his free hand and took a gulp. 'What happened?'

'The pub called us to a disturbance last night. Apparently, you tried to murder someone with a broken bottle. The barman hit you with a sockful of florins, and we picked up the mess.'

He had no recollection of the night before, other than the red mist that descended as the drunk threw a punch. He shuddered, knowing he'd lost control.

Hennessy continued. 'The man you fought with, Mick Thurgood. He's a violent drunk and petty thief, and up until the point you tried to kill him, the blokes were cheering you on.'

Danny dropped his gaze to the floor. 'I don't remember anything.'

'What started the fight?'

'He was goading me, talking about white feathers, calling me a coward, then he threw a punch.'

'You've just come back from the war, haven't you son?'

Danny clamped his jaws and looked away through the bars.

'We carried you in last night. You were unconscious, and we took your belt and shoe laces in case you tried to top yourself. You have a brand-new wooden leg, and a letter in your wallet says you've been medically discharged from the 4th Battalion, AIF–Gallipoli, correct?'

'That's right.'

The sergeant picked up his keys. 'You're twenty years old–I'm not going to ruin a young bloke's life with a jail sentence–especially after what you've been through. But you need to get your head right, son, and that's not my department–it's a job only you can do.'

'The publican's already forgotten last night, and Mick Thurgood's in no shape to argue after the hiding you gave him.' He unlocked the cuffs. 'Your horse is out the back, and your belongings are in the office. This never happened–now ride out of town and don't come back.'

~ ~ ~

The New South Wales referendum of 10 June 1916 delivered the temperance movement a decisive victory, enshrining six o'clock closing into law. The public bar, traditionally a place where one could drop in after work and linger over a quiet beer or two, was about to change.

Any shortage of valued commodities gives rise to panic - and in Sydney pubs, the two valued commodities were time and beer. In the last hour of trading, drinkers lined the bar three and four deep like pigs at a trough, knocking back as many beers as possible before the dreaded hour. At the call of 'last drinks, gentlemen', the scrum would surge forward in a frenzy of panic buying, and it was said that often, if one of the drinkers was 'caught short' with the call of nature, rather than give up his place in the queue, he'd urinate on the floor. Say 'hello' to the 'six o'clock swill'.

To the casual onlooker the public bar had suddenly become a pit of debauchery–a loud, smelly bastion of testosterone fuelled by too many beers in too short a time. When the doors finally shut, patrons would stagger home much the worse for wear. In time, the consumption of alcohol in New South Wales would increase, as would the incidence of domestic violence–but for now, the temperance movement congratulated itself for having saved the state from moral decay.

Pubs would also change physically, as walls were knocked down to cater for bigger crowds. Community rooms, lounges and recreation facilities like billiard rooms and dart boards were sacrificed. Carpets were ripped up and replaced with tiles that could be easily hosed down. Women who had frequented the 'Ladies' Lounge', now avoided the pub altogether, and what was once a community meeting place and an opportunity for recreation had regressed to a male-dominated drinking house.

Most pubs profited from the changes–the crowded bars did more business, and earlier closing meant fewer wages to pay. Suburban pubs like the Royal however suffered a down-turn in revenue - city workers who once rode the tram to Randwick for their evening beer now scurried from their workplace to the nearest pub and swilled there 'til six.

James resisted the temptation to disfigure the Royal with cold, efficient tiles and sawdust on the floor to mop up the slops. In his mind, early closing wouldn't last forever–and he was correct, but it would last a lot longer than anyone thought–it would not be repealed in New South Wales until 1955.

~ ~ ~

Cath hadn't really thought about being called 'Doctor'–nobody had ever called her that, except the family when they teased her - so it took some time for her to answer to the name. For the first few days at Sydney Hospital she'd scurry down corridors to the next ward, blissfully unaware that when a voice called 'doctor', it may well have been meant for her. It was only when a frustrated nurse shouted *'Doctor bloody Thornton!'* that the penny finally dropped.

She'd also never expected the deference that went with the title. Telephonists would connect a call from 'Doctor' Thornton with lightning efficiency - apologising profusely for even a few seconds' delay. Nurses would dutifully hang on her every word as they trotted ahead to open doors for her.

Cath been taught to give deference only when it was deserved, and to value deeds more than words or titles. As far as she was concerned, doctors weren't gods–they pulled their pants on one leg at a time, just like the rest of us. The same applied to giving 'VIP' patients special attention–her creed was that every patient deserved the best treatment she could give them.

Her first couple of months had been a steep learning curve with twists and turns under the scrutiny of Superintendent McIntosh. She'd found that hospitals had their own peculiar dialect, virtually incomprehensible to the outside world - and her mind reeled from jargon with little in common with the text books she'd pored over for years.

Her experience with the nurses of Stokeland House had given her a sense of teamwork that crossed doctor/nurse boundaries, and she sometimes helped to turn a patient over, changed a dressing or just sat for a moment to have a genuine conversation. While this gained her the respect of hospital staff, it took up valuable time, and she often wished she could just magically reappear at her next station instead of climbing stairs or waiting for the lift.

Early one morning in her third week, she'd no sooner thrown on her coat and slung the stethoscope round her neck when she ran into her old sparring partner, Hugh Barrington.

'Ah, Cath Thornton. Bert McIntosh told me you were working here.'

Barrington's familiar use of the Medical Superintendent's name was not lost on her. 'Hello Hugh, I gather we're *both* working here.'

'Yes–I'll be following you on the evening shift, starting tomorrow–I couldn't get here any sooner–social engagements and all that, you know.'

She gave a sardonic grin. 'Oh yes, Randwick's a gay, mad Ferris wheel this time of year too. I'm so glad you could squeeze us in.'

His Cheshire-cat grin faded ever so slightly. 'Yes, quite, I'll see you about the place. Ta-ta.'

As he strode past her down the corridor with his customary air of superiority, Cath thanked providence they were not to share the same shift.

~ ~ ~

Commuters hurried to work across the Sydney Domain under stately Moreton Bay figs as Cath surveyed the view from the hospital's first floor. She tore herself away from the veranda, and pulling on her surgical mask, entered the Respiratory Unit. She moved along the row of beds, nodding and chatting as she headed for bed 22. The patient was a 25-year-old man who'd been admitted two days before, suffering from a high fever, chronic sore throat and general debility.

'How are you today, Mr. Crawford?'

He lay on a nest of pillows, pale and drawn, with perspiration beading on his forehead. 'Not much better I'm afraid, doctor.'

'Let's take a look.'

The thermometer read 40 degrees Celsius–not dangerous, but not far from it, and his pulse was elevated–just on 110bpm.

She checked his chart. On the previous shift, Hugh Barrington had diagnosed a 'benign upper respiratory infection', and prescribed bed rest and a course of cinnamon and quinine tablets, but something told her he'd missed the mark. The chest x-ray was indecisive–there was some congestion, but in her mind, it wasn't consistent with the severity of the man's fever.

'Are you coughing a great deal?'

'No, doctor, not at all.'

That was another thing–the absence of a cough showed something else was going on. She suspected 'epiglottitis'–a swelling of the epiglottis, usually caused by a bacterial infection, and if left untreated, could cause a blocked airway. She ordered a thoracic x-ray and made a mental note to talk to Barrington about her concerns.

But events were to overtake her well-laid plans. Later that afternoon, a nurse burst through swinging doors. 'Doctor Thornton! Emergency in Respiratory!'

She sprints down the corridor, somehow knowing it's bed 22. Crawford's in the tripod position–hands on knees, bent over, straining for breath with deep, ragged gasps–his lips already turning blue.

Her mind goes into overdrive - she calculates he has about sixty seconds to live.

'Nurse–surgical instruments, and a tracheostomy tube–quickly.'

'But they're locked in the cabinet.'

'Break the bloody glass–NOW!'

She eases Crawford back on the bed, placing pillows under his heaving shoulders as he looks at her with the eyes of a dying man. She hears glass smash, and someone slaps a scalpel on her palm.

'Hold him down.'

Thirty seconds left, and Crawford's bulging eyes gape at the ceiling while his neck convulses with the effort of sucking in feeble molecules of air that won't keep him alive for long.

She runs her finger along his neck to the gap between the third and fourth tracheal rings and makes the incision. Blood pulses out like hot lava.

'Sponge!'

Twenty seconds left.

'Forceps!'

She clamps an artery, easing the blood flow.

Ten seconds left.

'Retractor,'

Sweat runs down her face and a nurse swabs it away. She inserts the instrument between the tracheal rings and twists them open. Air whistles through the tiny gap and down into the man's lungs like a force twelve gale.

'Tube!'

She feeds it into the trachea and binds it fast with surgical tape.

Time's up.

Cath slumps back and the nurses take over—mopping, binding, securing. She calls to them–'Take his vitals. Disinfect the wound–it'll need watching–I patched it like a bloody bicycle tube.' She's still panting with the effort–totally drained, physically and emotionally, and thinks to herself, 'I don't think I'll be specialising in surgery after all.'

~ ~ ~

The summon to McIntosh's office the next morning was no surprise to her. As she took a seat, the Superintendent sat tensely at his desk, his icy blue eyes steady under a furrowed brow.

'Thank you for being so prompt, Catherine. I'll get right to the point - I've had a report regarding a patient in respiratory, a Mr. Crawford, I believe. It shows that you performed emergency surgery yesterday in the open ward–a Tracheostomy. There was also a report of an instrument cabinet being broken into under your instructions. What do you have to say about this?'

'It sounds fairly accurate to me, except that you didn't mention Mr. Crawford was in the last phases of asphyxiation, and would have died, had I not acted.'

'What evidence did you have that the patient was in danger?'

'When I entered the ward he was in the tripod position and extremely agitated - moreover, he was drooling heavily, which I took to be evidence that he couldn't swallow, due to an impeded airway. These indications, plus the fact that his lips had turned blue, and he was convulsing with the effort to gain oxygen, convinced me he was in imminent danger of total asphyxiation.'

McIntosh was pensive as he glanced out the window to the GPO Clock tower rising above the city like a warning finger. 'I've interviewed the nurses who assisted you. They've been somewhat traumatised by the experience.'

'They're not alone in that, Dr. McIntosh. I'm a first-year intern - I've only ever read about the tracheostomy procedure in books. To be frank, I don't know how I got through it, but I'm convinced that the patient would have died.'

'And how is he now?'

'I checked in on him this morning. He's breathing normally. An x-ray was taken last night, and it appears the epiglottis is still badly infected, but he's a young man in otherwise good health—we're hoping he'll overcome the infection in due course.'

McIntosh sat back in his chair. 'I've instigated a full inquiry into the incident.' Her hackles rose, but she remained silent. 'But off the record, I believe you did what had to be done–and you did a damn good job. A few weeks ago, you sat in that same chair and told me you wanted to be challenged–mentally, physically, emotionally–I gather we have granted you your wish.'

Cath smiled. 'Yes–but I'd have preferred to work my way up to emergency surgery.'

He returned the smile for an instant, then his face became grim. 'There are doctors in this hospital who, if faced with the same situation, would have followed strict procedure to cover their own arses - but it would have cost a life.'

Chapter 13

Town and Country

A cold westerly wind sliced down Campbell Street as four figures moved under pools of streetlight. Up ahead, a row of Chinese lanterns swung wildly under a shop awning.

Jim turned to Tom. 'Is that the restaurant?'

'Yes, *The Teahouse of the August Moon.*'

Elizabeth hunched down inside her coat. 'This wind is freezing–I hope it's warm inside. What's the food like?'

Cath answered. 'It's delicious–and different.'

'I could eat a horse.' Jim quipped.

'Sorry Jim, if you want horse, I know a place around the corner.'

The tang of star anise, garlic and fresh coriander assaulted senses as they were shown to their table.

Waiters balancing steaming plates of food weaved through a maze of tables. It was a Saturday night in August 1916.

It's thought that Chinese cuisine had existed in Sydney almost from the beginning of European settlement. In the early 1800s Chinese sailors would occasionally jump ship, and vague references were made to street food stalls in The Rocks. They were apparently little more than rough stoves under canvas, and as trade from the Orient opened up, a small 'Chinatown' took root. By the 1870s the Chinese had migrated to the Haymarket where clan houses rubbed shoulders with godowns, and clouds of steam rose from eating houses, where rich merchants and poor market gardeners ate at the same table.

The investigation into Cath's emergency tracheostomy had confirmed Dr. McIntosh's assessment that it was a legitimate and timely reaction to an emergency, and her life had returned to normal at the hospital, and although no mention of Barrington's faulty diagnosis had been made, his demeanour had become a trifle less braggartly.

Jim and Elizabeth had scraped enough money together to buy a terrace house behind the horse stables in Dine Street, a short walk from the Royal, and tonight,

Sarah and James were babysitting their grandchildren, Michael, 3, and Helen, 18 months.

Jim flicked through the menu with a bewildered look. 'No steak and chips?'

Elizabeth sighed with a smile. 'Time to own up– we've never eaten Chinese food before.'

Cath replied. 'Until four months ago, neither had I– but Tom's an expert–he can do the ordering.'

Tom signalled to a waiter. 'The food here is Szechuan, from southern China. It has strong flavours, particularly garlic and chili, and Szechuan pepper.' He waved an arm across the room. 'As you can see, most customers are Chinese, and the place is almost full, so you know the food is good. But don't worry–they won't drown you in chilli–they usually hold back for gweilo.'

'What's gweilo?' Asked Jim with a puzzled look.

'Gweilo is their term for white people, like us.' Answered Cath.

Tom continued. 'When gweilo come to their restaurant, they are very proud, because you come to eat their food. They respect that, and know you'll tell your friends about it. And seeing it's August, like the name of the restaurant, they believe you will also bring them good luck. So tonight, you are honoured guests.'

Tom rattled off the order to the waiter as Chinese tea was served by an old woman with an enormous teapot. Tom bowed to her. 'Xie xie, shu mu' (thank you, aunty).

Jim scanned nearby tables. 'Ah, Tom, any chance of getting a beer?'

'Sure.' Tom translated, and the waiter hurried away. Elizabeth sipped tea from a porcelain cup. 'Cath told us you're a third-generation police officer - you must have an exciting life.'

Tom gave a shrug. 'Most police work is about dusty records and filling out forms–not that exciting. My grandfather was a policeman in Hong Kong–my family came out here during the gold rush, when my father was five. He became a detective in the Sydney CIB–he's retired now, and I joined the Foot Police when I was 21, so yes, three generations. We were lucky to come here before the 'White Australia Policy.'

Jim smiled thinly. 'I find that bloody ironic. This whole country is practically empty, and we won't let people in because they're supposedly the wrong colour - the Aboriginals were here before Jesus played fullback for Jerusalem, and they're definitely not white–so are we going to put them all on a boat and push them out through the Heads?'

Cath butted in. 'Few people know this, but my brother invented a famous act of parliament–he calls it the 'Royal Hotel Act'. She grinned. What does it say again, Jim?' As a waiter poured the beers, Jim replied. 'It says that at the Royal, we judge people by their behaviour, not by the colour of their skin; and as long as our customers behave themselves and respect others, we don't give a rat's arse where they come from, or what colour they are–please excuse my French, ladies.'

Tom raised his glass. 'That's an act of parliament worth drinking to.' They took the toast and Tom continued. 'But everyone is afraid of being invaded–it's natural to fear what you don't understand. The Mongols overran China in the 13th century and ruled for a hundred years. If the Chinese could have passed a law to get rid of them, they would have.'

Elizabeth had been listening intently. 'I'd like my father to be at this table right now. He has a black and white attitude to this issue, if you'll excuse the pun. He firmly believes the white race is superior, and rightly rules the world. He points to the British Empire as his proof.'

Cath added. 'He better check his history–the Romans ruled the known world for 500 years, and they were very much on the swarthy side of white, and the Egyptians ruled for 1500 years–and most of them were

African. The whole race debate comes down to the contribution of individuals.' She paused in thought. 'Something Tom didn't mention was that his grandfather died fighting alongside the diggers at the Eureka Stockade.' She turned to Tom. 'What was that quote from your grandmother?'

Cath's revelation momentarily embarrassed Tom. He always avoided bringing the issue to light, but was intensely proud of his grandfather's last words, as passed on by the men who carried his body back to the Wong's tent the morning after the battle in December 1854. He stared into his beer glass and recited the well-worn sentences:

'They said to my grandmother: *"We told him to leave the stockade. We told him it wasn't his fight…… You know what he said? He said, "If I'm good enough to swing a pick beside you blokes, I'm good enough to fight beside you as well.'*

There was an awkward silence before Jim spoke. 'Those are fine words, Tom. Here's to your grandfather.' As if on cue, two waiters materialised at the table, and Tom shook off his reverie. 'Ladies and gentlemen–our dinner has arrived'. He pointed to each dish:

'This is "Kung Pao Chicken" - stir-fried chicken, dried chili pepper and deep-fried peanuts - it's sweet, sour and spicy. Over here we have "Twice Cooked Pork". They boil the pork belly until it's almost cooked, then fry it with garlic sprouts and fresh peppers. The seasonings are Szechuan doubanjiang and dou-chi. And this one is "Crispy Beef"–dry fried beef with spices and seasonings, and lastly, "Szechuan Green Beans with Fried Rice". Enjoy!

Elizabeth took a careful forkful of Kung Pau Chicken. 'Oh, my heavens–it *does* have three flavours at once–sweet, sour and spicy–and the chicken is so tender.'

Jim swallowed a healthy spoon of the pork and immediately reached for his beer. 'Jesus–I think I just swallowed a fireball–someone order more beer while I sneak up on this from behind.'

The waiter spoke to Tom in Cantonese and they both laughed, and Jim asked, 'What did he say to you?' Tom chuckled. 'He said, "Your friends came in here as gweilo, but maybe they'll go back out the door a little Chinese.'

The meal continued as Jim and Elizabeth gradually adapted to the foreign flavours. Jim watched intently as Tom wielded his chopsticks like a surgeon with a scalpel. 'How the hell do you do that?' Tom grinned. 'You start at about 12 months of age, and you keep practising–by the way, what news from Danny?'

Jim replied. 'He's been writing to Mum and Dad now and then. The last I heard, he was somewhere near Goulburn, sweeping out shearing sheds or something. He said he was fine and would probably head over to the coast to get work on a dairy farm. Sounds like he might head back up to Sydney, but who knows–that boy could end up in New Guinea.'

Elizabeth shook her head. 'Didn't he just turn 21?'

Cath nodded. 'Yes–last month. We're all hoping he'll find what he's looking for out there, and kill his demons. I'd love to see him come home–this war is taking a terrible toll on the entire world.'

Jim momentarily turned pensive. 'Hey, Sis–did I tell you I got a white feather in the mail?'

Cath stared, aghast. 'Oh my God, what the hell is wrong with people? Do you know who sent it?'

'Not a clue–it doesn't really matter.'

Elizabeth spoke. 'Jim decided to enlist in the AIF a couple of months ago. We had a hell of a fight over it, but he was adamant.'

Jim cut in. 'And they knocked me back–apparently I've got a dodgy heart.'

Cath shot him a worried glance. 'You didn't tell me–what did they say?'

'They told me it was probably a dicky valve, and said I shouldn't over-exert myself–that it should be fine, but not for fighting a war.'

'If you'd like, I could arrange an examination.'

'Thanks Sis–I'll let you know, but I've been throwing beer kegs around most of my life, and I haven't keeled over yet.'

Elizabeth placed a hand on Jim's shoulder. 'I'm keeping an eye on him–he was disappointed, but I believe sometimes these things happen for a reason.'

Jim decided to cheer things up. 'Speaking of medical conditions, stop me if you've heard this one. A concerned mother once took her 16-year-old son to the doctor because his willy was still the same size as a 10-year-old's. The doctor examined the boy and prescribed plenty of hot buttered toast to boost growth. The next morning the boy sits down at the table and there's this huge pile of hot buttered toast. He reaches for a slice and his mother slaps him on the wrist and says. 'Leave your father's breakfast alone.'

The meal was a success, and after the chilli was extinguished with another round of beer, Jim tried his hand at using chopsticks, and deciding to go 'solo' after a basic lesson from Tom, accidentally catapulted one stick across to the next table, where it landed upright in a bowl of rice like a flag on a snowy mountaintop. After the appropriate apologies, they decided it was time to go; settling the bill and exiting into the cold night air. The four were heading to the nearest tram stop when a cry sounded from dim light across the street.

There's scuffling and sounds of anger, and Tom runs to it, shouting 'Police!' A body lies inert on the pavement while two youths struggle with an older man. Tom calls again – 'Police! Step away, NOW!' And one of the attackers lunges at him with a knife. Tom blurs in a sidestep, grabbing a wrist and slamming his forearm against an elbow joint that snaps like a tree branch as the man drops with a scream. The other youth breaks off in a sprint and Tom collars him; taking his legs away with a sweeping kick and bringing him down with a handful of hair and a painful arm lock.

Tom called across to a knot of people drawn to the noise. 'Someone phone the police. Cath–there's a woman hurt here.' He produced a pair of cuffs from his jacket and secured the youth's hands, dragging him back to where Cath was already tending to an injured woman. Jim stood guard on the first youth, but a broken arm had taken the fight out of him.

'How is she?'

'Slight concussion, cuts and abrasions, but she's alright.'

The older man sat panting on the pavement, cradling a handbag. 'They came out of nowhere and grabbed my wife's bag. They shoved her over.'

~ ~ ~

The tram grinded its motor up Elizabeth street toward Hyde Park as Cath tapped Tom on the arm.

What was that you did back there?

Tom shrugged and glanced out the window. 'My job.'

'No, I mean, where did you learn to fight like that?'

He smiled at her. 'Police work wasn't the only thing handed down from my grandfather.'

'Why didn't you use your gun?'

'Guns kill people–it wasn't necessary.'

'You're full of surprises, Tom Wong.'

~ ~ ~

Bleating sheep, harsh shouts, and boots scraping on timber mingled with the smell of lanolin, man-sweat and dung. A tin roof radiated heat onto shearers' backs as they bent to their task - their sinewy arms moving with a rhythm whittled down to bare necessity by years of back-breaking work. It was a long day manhandling 150-pound sheep from the catching pen, and energy was too valuable to waste.

Shearers were a nomadic mob - drifting down dusty roads, following the season from one shed to the next with their precious blades wrapped in oiled cloth. Their faces had changed - most young men had gone off to war, and the older hands–known as 'snaggers', had coaxed their tired bodies back into the harness for one more year.

Danny paced along the board, watching their progress - timing his move to retrieve the fleece just as they sheared the last leg. He moved in, crouching like a lock forward into a scrum - folding the fleece over and securing it with the leg-strips to carry it to the skirting table, where the 'Classer' made his inspection. With a dozen shearers lined up along the board, they kept him busy, and by the 9.30am 'smoko' he'd be ready for a spell.

Another boyish face on the board was Johnny Ealing, a strapping 27-year-old from Dubbo who'd had lost an eye in the Somme. His government-issue glass replacement had never really performed to standard–it had a mind of its own–gazing wistfully off into the distance one minute, then suddenly darting about like a confused compass, as if Johnny had dropped a ten quid note. He'd been a shearer before the war, but his lack of depth perception with a sharp blade had demanded a fresh approach. He'd studied a Dubbo barber's technique of pinching hair between fingers, and so far, there was no need for the 'tar boy'.

Danny had travelled over a hundred miles since the sergeant had unlocked his cell door, and he'd passed through many dusty towns - Caloola, Trunkey Creek, Binda, Crookwell, getting work where he could– hammering railway spikes, hosing out abattoirs, cleaning toilets. The district's grassy plains stretching off to infinity were a balm to his mind–there was no barbed wire, no piles of blood-stained sandbags - nothing was looming toward him with menace–he felt free.

Out here it was a two-day ride to anywhere. There was always a smile and a wave for a lone rider, and a natter over a front fence in the amber glow of sunset was a welcome distraction from the road. A pub's shady veranda promised a cold beer, news and gossip, a joke or two and the chance to find work; and staring into the night's campfire gave time for reflection. His nightmares were becoming scarcer, and the rage that possessed him that night in Bathurst had slunk off to a dark corner, at least for now.

~ ~ ~

The bar of Goulburn's 'Hibernian Hotel' was a pitching, bucking sea in the storm of the six o'clock swill. The shearers had downed tools at 4pm, as was customary for a Friday, and shared tepid bathwater before hopping the truck into town. It was only an hour to closing time, and they were making the most of it. Danny and Johnny Ealing shouted to each other over the noise.

'Happy days, Danny–we can sleep in tomorrow–it's Saturday.' The shearers' huts were rusty tin sheds with lumpy straw mattresses, and Danny, being a roustabout and at the bottom of the food chain, had the thinnest mattress in the creakiest shed.

Danny replied. 'What are we going to do after closing time? It's too bloody early to go back to the station.'

Johnny's glass eye wiggled as he performed his version of a wink. 'The old blokes'll probably go back with a few bottles, but I know somewhere to kick on–are you in?'

'Bloody oath.'

~ ~ ~

He expected a sly grog shop–perhaps a dingy shed at the end of a dark lane, but Johnny led him to a red brick building near the centre of town, with stairs leading down to a basement door presided over by a large tattooed Maori. Quiet words were exchanged, and the door opened to a scene befitting a Sydney gentleman's club. A cedarwood bar underlined by a brass foot-rail ran the length of a room where drinkers yarned and laughed under lazy tendrils of tobacco smoke. Chandeliers cast a muted light over bar staff, conjuring up drinks with the finesse of a Tivoli magician–it was clear that big money and important people were behind the Goulburn sly grog trade.

An arm raised in greeting from the far end of the bar and he followed Johnny to a trio of men, one of whom was spinning a yarn: 'So one night, this bloke walks into his local pub, looking a bit down in the mouth. The barman says, "What'll it be, Harry?" And Harry says, "Oh, just a beer." The barman pulls a beer and says, "You're not your usual cheery self." And Harry replies, "Well, the wife and I got into a terrible fight, and she said she wouldn't speak to me for a month. The barman says, "So what's wrong with that?" And Harry says, "The bloody month's up tonight.'

'Danny, this is my Uncle Bill–Bill the butcher.'

Bill was an older version of Johnny - thick set, with sandy hair and a ruddy complexion under eyebrows like rampant lantana. He thrust out a hand.

'Good to meet you, Danny.' He cocked his head toward the other two. 'This is Al and Phil.'

They ordered drinks. Danny's eyes wandered across the bar to the barmaid, and for an instant he thought it was Emma, the London nurse he'd never said goodbye to–either in mind or deed. She held that same expression in her hazel eyes–a glint of good humour and a blunt directness. To Danny, she wasn't exactly a spring chicken-perhaps in her early thirties, with a slim figure and dark wavy hair framing a porcelain face. He felt a stirring from within. *'She looks bloody good for an old girl.'* He thought as she caught his gaping stare with a smile playing about her lips. Danny blushed.

As the beers continued, in conversation it emerged that Bill Ealing's mate Al ran a jewellery and clock store in the main street, and he and Danny fell into deep discussion over the merits of the 'free-sprung English-made interchangeable chronograph watch movement', versus the 'lever movement with Class 'A' Kew certification', while the others rolled their eyes and continued telling bawdy jokes.

Danny returned from the bar with a round of drinks. 'What do you do for a living, Phil?'

'I'm an undertaker'. He was tall and well-built, as if he could have carried a fully loaded coffin under each arm. His nose was askew from some prior altercation; making him look more like a boxer than an undertaker.

'Really?'

'Yeah. I've been planting people six feet under for over 20 years–I reckon I've buried more secrets than a confessional.'

'You must have had some interesting experiences.'

He took a gulp of beer. 'Yeah, I reckon. I remember when I first started out–I was pretty green in those days, and this one month, there was an unusual number of deaths in the town, and the mortuary was crowded with stiffs. After I came back from a service, I realised that I'd mixed up the records and buried the wrong bloke.'

'Gee - did you tell anyone?'

'No, of course not–no need to upset the family any further, and besides, I wouldn't have gotten paid, so I kept mum about the whole thing–I refer to that experience as my one and only "grave mistake.'

After Bill the butcher recalled an apprentice who accidentally backed up into a meat grinder, and got a 'little behind' in his work, Danny told of a time a young man on the beach approached him.

'The bloke says to me" All you lifesaver fellows are popular with the ladies–do you have any advice on how to attract women?'

'I told him to buy a swimming costume that was a size smaller, then get a potato and put it down his trunks. Well, the bloke goes off and takes my advice - and he turns up at the beach the next day, parading past the ladies. Well, suddenly there's a disturbance on the beach and people are yelling at the bloke and throwing stuff at him. He runs up to me and says. "You told me I'd attract women, but they're yelling at me to get off the beach.'

I took one look and said, "Yeah, mate–you were supposed to put the potato down the front of your trunks.'

While all this was going on, Danny's gaze kept wandering to the barmaid, and when their eyes met, their minds connected like a semaphore. He was still a virgin–his age had leapt from 19 to 21 that day at Victoria Barracks back in 1914, and since then he'd been Army property until a few months ago. At Mena Camp it was common for soldiers to visit the brothels of Cairo, but the incidence of syphilis and gonorrhoea was high, not to mention the possibility of being sent back home in disgrace, so he abstained. Now, at 21 years of age he was far from home with hormones raging like a bull in a cow paddock. He wondered what the night would bring.

The disturbance erupted without warning a few minutes after 10pm. Danger burst into the room with the speed of a tidal wave as the door flew open with a flash of blue uniforms and shrill police whistles.

'Bugger!' Curses Bill the butcher as he scans the room for escape. 'Out the back, boys, or we're up shit creek.' Bodies fly in all directions and the coppers draw their batons as someone turns the lights out. A curse here and a howl of pain over there. A fist connects with a jaw and a truncheon rams into an ample belly. Curses, breaking glass, a thump and a crack, a grunt and a roar. A glint of handcuffs, a twinkle of breaking glass, the thud of a falling body. A hand grips Danny's wrist and yanks him backwards. 'Oh shit, it's a copper.' He thinks, but a woman's voice hisses in his ear. 'Keep low and follow me.'

She leads him behind the bar where a trapdoor lies open over a steep set of stairs. 'Down you go, and quickly. Wait for me at the bottom.' He descends into blackness as steps follow and the trapdoor slams shut. The sounds of mayhem fade, and the barmaid's unmistakable face flares in the light of a hurricane lamp–her hazel eyes bright with excitement.

'What's your name?'

'Danny.'

'I'm Rose.' She nodded to a row of beer barrels disappearing into the dark. 'There's a way up to the back lane down there. Come on.'

Danny climbed another set of narrow stairs, drawing back a rusty bolt and easing open a chink in the metal hatch. The lane was in shadow - a misty rain drifted in a gossamer cloak, but he could see no-one.

'All clear.' They emerged into a deserted lane where a stray cat pawed at scraps. Out in the street, men cursed as they were flung into paddy wagons. The rain had stopped and a half-moon dodged through clouds. They retreated from the pandemonium.

'Thanks for getting me out of there.'

She dusted off her dress. 'My pleasure–you look too young to go to jail. You're a shearer, aren't you?'

'No, just a roustabout at Gurrundah Station.'

'That's about 15 miles to the west–how're you going to get back there at this time of night?'

He shrugged. 'There was a truck, but the other blokes went back at 6. I suppose I'll walk.'

Rose folded her arms with a twinkle in her eye. 'And which way would west be, Danny?'

He looked up and down the street and shrugged again. 'I suppose I'll just wait for the sun to come up, then go the other way.' He grinned. 'Or you could take pity on me, and point.'

'I tell you what–I live near here.' She nodded up the street. 'About 15 minutes that way. It's on your way–you can keep walking for another five hours if you like, or sleep on the veranda and hitch a ride out to Gurrundah tomorrow morning. Your choice.'

~ ~ ~

The house was set back from the road, tucked behind Camelia bushes–their leaves reflecting moonlight. Inside, a hallway opened to a plainly furnished sitting room. Rose lit a fire while Danny glanced about self-consciously.

'Do you live here by yourself?'

She looked up from the first lick of flame and nodded. 'Ever since my husband shot through a couple of years ago.'

'I'm sorry.'

'Don't be–he liked to knock me around when he drank too much. The last I heard, he enlisted in the army–he could be anywhere by now, even dead.' She stared blankly into the fire for a moment, then continued. 'I'm starving–there's corned beef with bread and butter if you'd like some.'

They ate by the fire–a warm beer for him and a sherry for her. The flame light played soft shadows across her face, and her hazel eyes lustred like pearls. Every thought that passed through his mind was a journey through an unknown world–a journey he would only ever take once. His body stirred with a million nerve-endings–he was at once exalted and terrified. They talked of life in Goulburn, Danny's journey from Sydney, and Gallipoli–he danced around his return from the war, trying not to think about the wooden appendage beneath his chair.

The kiss arrived like a surprise guest as they were gathering dishes from the table, and their reserve melted away like ice in summer heat. Rose searched his eyes.

'How old are you, Danny?'

'Twenty-one.'

She smiled. 'This is your first time, am I right?'

'No, of course not.'

She searched his eyes with the ghost of a smile on her lips, waiting silently with her question hanging in the air.

'Well…..actually, yes, it is.' He dropped his gaze to the floor. 'And there's something else you should know.'

'Yes?'

'I have an artificial leg.'

She pressed herself against the heat of his swollen groin and smiled. 'It's not your leg I'm interested in.'

~   ~   ~

In later years, Danny would often recall that night with a smile and a quiet chuckle to himself. He would never see Rose again–they both knew that–but that night would always remain theirs, pure and perfect–a fire that would remain bright forever, and not die by the tyranny of familiarity, as many do.

She was a patient teacher, and he a willing pupil, and although no report card was ever completed, both were more than satisfied with the results–one could say a mutual 'A-plus'. And for Danny, there was something else. The thought that he was not quite 'right', or 'normal' any more had haunted him–as if the skin and shattered bone he'd left behind in Gallipoli had taken part of his self-worth with it. But when he unstrapped his wooden leg that night, crimson with embarrassment, all Rose said was 'good solid calf muscle you have there.' And for the first time, he laughed at his own handicap. From that moment he began to see himself in a different light–and it was this, more than anything else, that he treasured about a woman named Rose, who saved his arse from jail, and invited him to share her corned beef.

~   ~   ~

The shearing had run out at Gurrundah station. Icy wind moaned through the deserted tin shed, tumbling knots of old wool across the yard. The fleece had long since been bailed with hessian and carted off on rail trucks, and the shearers had left nothing behind but boot scuffs and cigarette butts. Danny tightened Balla's cinch straps and considered his options. He could head south and follow Johnny Ealing down to Tarago, by Lake Bathurst–God knows there were enough sheep down there to keep him busy for weeks. But he'd followed dusty tracks through the Central West for almost five months and the sea was calling him back. He drew his pay and rode back through town, pulling up at the cottage behind the camelias. He lingered there for just a moment, but part of him would remain there forever.

He rode northward on the Great South Road through forests of grey bark, red king parrots and screeching black cockatoos. A three-day ride in the misty Southern Highlands took him zig-zagging down the escarpment to the green pastures of the Illawarra. He'd heard about a local quarry hiring labourers, and rode into Kiama as the sun dipped behind Jamberoo Mountain.

As he turned Balla's head off a rutted country track into Terralong Street, the scent of pastures gave way to the sea's cooling breath, and in the distance, Kiama Lighthouse rose like a cautioning finger at the edge of the famous 'Blowhole'. Narrow train tracks ran down the street, and a shrill whistle moved him aside as a line of freight cars rumbled past.

He followed the tracks to 'Tory's Kiama Hotel', perched on a corner overlooking a small harbour bathed in afternoon shadow. *'This'll do,'* he thought. *'I won't get a pub any closer to the water than this.'* The building was girthed with a lace wrought-iron veranda and crowned with a triumphant third level with windows gazing out to sea. A cargo ship belched black smoke at the dock, taking on basalt from the nearby Bombo Headland Quarry– which with any luck would be his new place of work.

250 million years before Danny's ride down Terralong Street, the world's landmass was a single

supercontinent, and the fragment that would become Australia was a volcanic cauldron venting boiling basalt lava and ash for hundreds of miles. The continent fragmented and the lava was eroded under millennia of rain and wind, spreading the rich dark soil that Illawarra dairy farmers would eventually call their own. But it wasn't just the soil that would be sought after; the tough knots of basalt that survived intact would also have their uses.

Quarries had been in the area since the 1850s, and by 1916, mining hadn't changed apart from the power of steam. The transportation of basalt by ship to Sydney had become known as the 'Blue Diamond Trade', inspired by the blue-grey Kiama basalt and its hardness- and the dozens of small ships that carried the rock were known as the 'Stone Fleet'.

The next morning he walked the train line northward around the crescent of Bombo Beach, where the swells rode in from the Tasman like charging cavalry. The line rounded a bend and rose to the headland, and after a bespectacled clerk scribed his details in a dusty ledger, they issued him a slip of paper identifying him as 'Casual Employee No. 3217'. Handing him a shovel, they pointed to a wheelbarrow and told him to 'go and see Jack Clancy down by the crusher.'

The headland had been blasted, crushed and carted off for over thirty years, and what was once a vibrant, tree-covered peninsula bathing in blue water was now a stark lump of rock jutting from the sea like a Pitt Street kerbside. The mining process was simple. They detonated gelignite on the cliff-top, cleaving away huge chunks of stone that was broken up and fed into the gaping maw of a rock crusher. The resulting rubble was clawed up by steam shovels and whisked away along the railway line, while the cliffs retreated under the mine's inexorable march. In the eternal cycle of life and death, the lava that had once made a planet tremble would end its journey as 'blue metal' beneath railway tracks at some sleepy country train station.

Danny guessed that the tall, angular bloke with a smoke dangling from the corner of his mouth would be the foreman, Jack Clancy, and he was right. He received his entire job description with a nod of the head and thirteen words: 'Shovel them rocks inta the 'barra, and dump 'em on that heap, son.'

As he bent to his task, Danny took stock of the quarry. He'd expected a crowd of workers with hammer, rope and pulley, toiling like ancient Egyptian slaves in the shadow of emergent pyramids, but technology had reduced numbers considerably. Most men either operated machinery or saw to it that it continued to operate, while 'dog's bodies' like himself shovelled, swept or ran errands. There were a few actual stonemasons–raw men with arms like steel girders heaving hammer and chisel; fashioning bespoke pieces for the facade of a bank or a church.

The work was hard, but the dust was a nightmare; cloaking the headland in a grey veil. His eyes watered, his nose clogged, his mouth was gritty, his shoes inundated; and it wasn't long before he adopted the same facial expression as the rest of the men–eyes squinting and mouth firmly shut, like a boxer in the final round. Being on a headland made matters worse–in a blustery north easterly the grit sandblasted any exposed skin as if the ancient rock was fighting to the very death. He fashioned his handkerchief into a makeshift mask, but he'd be borrowing a tea-towel from the pub's kitchen that night.

Jack Clancy spelled him from the shovel and sent him to help the cook, whose domain was a low timber hut on brick piers at the entrance to the quarry, relatively free of the dust storm. Danny pushed open the door to the sound of clashing pots and pans, and curses muttered in a distinct Indian accent. The noise stopped as a turbaned head and dark eyes poked above the shelving.

'Lunch is not ready–go away until you hear the bell–then you may enter.'

The head disappeared.

'Ah, sorry, but the foreman said I should come and give you a hand.'

The head reappeared.

'Ah, that is different. Please come forward.'

Danny passed rows of trestle tables into a kitchen. The cook wore all white–cotton trousers, apron, shirt and turban, making his ebony skin vibrant under the lights. He was middle-aged, with soft eyes in a plentiful face radiating calm.

'What is your name?'

'Danny.'

I am very pleased to meet you, Danny. My name is 'Rayaan', which means 'fragrant herb' in Hindi. Evidently my parents knew I was to become a cook.'

'The food smells good.'

Rayaan sighed. 'It is devoid of spices, like the Taj Mahal hidden in fog–but it is what I am told to cook. You can start by peeling potatoes–in the large tub over there.'

Although being a kitchen hand was unexpected, he was glad to escape the dust, and spent the next couple of hours cutting onions, stirring pots and mopping floors, and at precisely 12.30PM a bell sounded the lunch break, and men were soon filing through the door. Rayaan handed him a ladle. 'I will dish out the stew, Danny. Please scoop out one ladle of mashed potato for each worker–no extra's, or we will run out.'

Quarrymen were renowned as being 'tough bastards'–you didn't last long at the job if you were afraid of hard work; and these men were about as hard as the basalt they worked with. Like the shearers at Gurrundah, they were mostly past enlistment age, but all of them looked like they could handle themselves in a 'blue'. Danny noticed one man edging down the queue. In his time in the army, he'd seen every type of soldier, from bank managers to murderers, and this one had trouble written all over him–the type who would slacken off at any opportunity, pinch anything that wasn't nailed down and dob in anyone if it suited him. He shuffled forward to Rayaan with a leer across his grubby face.

'Hey, Brownie–what kind of bloody muck are ya servin' today?'

Rayaan muttered without looking up. 'It is beef stew.'

'Smells more like cow shit–ya didn't touch it with ya darkie hands, did ya?'

Danny's hackles were up. He was yet to meet a digger who held racial prejudice after fighting alongside Aboriginals, Indians, Ceylonese, Gurkhas and Senegalese at Gallipoli–it was perhaps one of the few positives to come out of the war. 'You've got a foul mouth, mate–how about you show some respect for people?'

The queue went quiet as the man swivelled his gaze to Danny. 'How about ya shut *your* fuckin' mouth, sonny? I wasn't talkin' to you. Anyway–why aren't you in uniform? Are ya queer, or just a coward?'

Danny dropped his ladle and rounded the counter to face the man, who stood braced for a fight. Ignoring the posturing, he bent and pulled up his trouser-leg. 'You see this? It was a present, after the Turks blew my leg off at Gallipoli.' He straightened and pointed to Rayaan. 'This bloke here is from India, part of our British Empire. I've seen Indians carry wounded Australians on their backs under fire, and I've never met a digger who wouldn't gladly return the favour - because in the trenches, no-one gives a fuck what colour you are. And here you are, making fun of this man because it makes you feel superior–but every word from your mouth dishonours the soldiers that fight and die for the Empire every day.'

A murmur rippled along the queue, with a general nodding of heads. Danny took a step forward, nose-to-nose with the man, who looked about him, suddenly unsure of himself as Danny continued with a flinty stare. 'I've killed better men than you before breakfast, old son–so take your stew, shut your mouth and fuck off before I lose my temper–you wouldn't like that.'

~   ~   ~

The lunch break was over and the quarrymen filed back out the door. The abusive man had held his tongue and concentrated on his food–Danny's cutting retort had lost him whatever support he would have had from the others. It was bad form to abuse a wounded digger; especially one from Gallipoli, where a young nation had so recently found its pride.

Rayaan stacked a pile of clean dishes on the shelf as Danny wiped down the counters.

'Danny, I would like to thank you for what you said today. That man is rude and ill-mannered, and I have never seen him lost for words before.' A smile spread across his face.

Danny shrugged. 'People make a song and dance about the ANZAC's, as if we were the only ones at Gallipoli, but nobody talks about the others that were there, especially the Aboriginals. I just set him straight. You don't need to thank me–it was a pleasure to take the wind out of him. A month ago I would have just hit him, but I'm learning.' The image of a jagged beer bottle passed through his mind.

Rayaan became solemn. 'Forgive me for being forward, Danny, but I sense a great deal of turmoil inside you.'

Danny paused. There was a depth to this man that brought down his defences and evoked trust. 'Yeah–that's why I've been wandering for almost six months–trying to sort myself out.'

'And have you?'

'Like I said–I'm learning.'

'Do you mind if I tell you something that may help?'

'Not at all.'

Rayaan leant back against the kitchen sink. 'I have spent many years practising Buddhism–searching for inner peace, seeking enlightenment. In many ways, my journey does not differ from yours, but perhaps I can make your road a little smoother.'

He clasped his hands together and continued. 'The past is dead, Danny–it does not exist, except in our minds, and if we let it govern our thoughts, we cannot live fully in the present. Likewise, the future–it also does not exist, but if we worry about it, we also cannot live fully in the present. So, we must let the past go, and allow the future to be created by what we do now.'

Danny was a young man who sifted life through the filters of his reason, and this insight struck him like spider-lightning on a brooding Sydney afternoon. Had he actually created his own rage and terrifying nightmares by trying to re-live a past that was non-existent? Could he rid himself of his demons by changing the way he thought?

The possibility energised him, and momentarily deprived him of words. All he could manage was, 'Thank you Rayaan–I need to think that through. By the way, what will you do about that bloke if he keeps on with his foul mouth?'

Rayaan reached up to the top shelf and grasped a glass bottle filled with red powder. 'This is chilli powder, Danny–If he persists, I will add a generous helping to his next stew.'

'Will that stop him?'

Rayaan smiled. 'Perhaps yes, perhaps no, but he'll certainly be knowing what his arse is for.'

~ ~ ~

His career as a kitchen hand was abruptly cut short–word of his meal hut run-in had passed around, and he found himself back at the end of a shovel, masked with a 'Tory's' tea towel and whiplashed by basalt dust as steam shovels angled like praying mantises.

After two weeks of toil, Sydney was drawing him northward like the tug of a three-pound flathead on a beach rod. He collected his final pay and headed back to Tory's, stopping on the way to bid Rayaan farewell. It turned out that there was no need for the chilli powder–the abusive quarryman had curbed his language, and had even gained a degree of civility, aided by the not-so-subtle persuasion of his work mates. While returning along Bombo Beach, the sparkling sea convinced Danny to celebrate his freedom with an early morning swim the next day. He hadn't been in the water since Anzac Cove, and imagined it would be very pleasant to take a dip without being shot at.

The next morning he pulled on a pair of shorts and headed down to the beach while Kiama rolled over to steal another hour of sleep from Saturday. At the harbour a candy orange sunrise met rail cars dripping dew, and seagulls squawked and flapped over scraps on the concrete. He took his usual shortcut along Gipps Street and weaved down through the dunes. A playful northeast wind had risen early, pushing the swell against a curve of rocks. Removing his wooden appendage, he hopped to the water's edge.

The water was cold and clear. The shore break rebuffed him for an instant, but he re-gained his balance and was soon diving under waves that slapped him on the back like an old friend. He propelled through the break, beating his good leg dolphin-like into deeper water. The swell lifted him gently as he lay on his back and gazed up to a million miles of cobalt sky. It was good to be back in the water.

The cramp hits him like an iron vice–first the calf muscle, then the thigh as his good leg seizes up in crippling pain, and he has to get back to shore. He begins to swim, windmilling his arms to drag himself toward the shallows, but fatigue overtakes him and his body becomes an anchor. A wave breaks and he's pushed into blackness, but panic brings him thrashing back to the surface for a wafer of air. He goes under again and his lungs scream. He wills his arms to fight upwards to the light and breaks the surface as another wave punches him back into submission. His lungs give up the fight as an iron grip wrenches him into the light and drags him onto the sand.

'Are you alright, mate?' A vague face loomed above him as he rolled to his side and retched seawater and breakfast onto the sand. He sucked in a lungful of delicious air as the face came into focus. 'Yeah–I'm alright, thanks.'

'I saw a wooden leg on the sand and wondered who'd left it there. Then I saw you thrashing about.'

He wore a battered hat studded with fishhooks and sported a full grey beard. Danny sat up and looked out to a sea that had almost killed him.

'That'll teach me to knock off training for two years–I was lucky you came along.'

The man gave him a smile. 'I just waded in and grabbed you–the surf would have rolled you in anyway–can I help you up?'

'No, thanks mate–I think I'll just sit here for a while and get my breath back.'

The man retrieved his rod and basket from the sand. 'Righto–I'll just be up the beach a bit, trying my luck.'

The man tracked away across the sand as Danny gazed out to sea and tried to make sense of the previous five minutes. *'I underestimated what swimming with one leg would be like. I should have taken it slowly and not dived in like I was still on patrol.'*

A crystal bolt of reality struck his consciousness as he glanced down at his stump, and Rayaan's words came back to him: *'The past is dead, Danny—it does not exist, except in our minds, and if we let it govern our thoughts, we cannot live fully in the present.'* The eighteen inches of bone and gristle that had once been there was dead, and it wasn't coming back, but he'd spent almost a year of his life trying to do just that. And now the sea had taught him just how precious his life was–too precious to waste on ghosts.

He sat for a while, watching waves spend their energy on the shore and thinking about how close he had come to dying. *Could it be that a middle name like "Lucky" isn't so much of a joke anymore?* After what seemed like an eternity, he brushed away the sand from his wooden leg and strapped it on, and struggling to his feet, turned to leave. He glanced back absent-mindedly at the man who had pulled him from the water. He'd hooked a decent fish by the look of it, and was wrestling his catch into a net, totally absorbed in the moment. Danny headed back through the dunes.

Chapter 14

Trysts and Turns

Annandale elbowed its way between Leichhardt and Glebe to dip its toes into Rozelle Bay. Once a farm owned by Captain George Johnstone of the New South Wales 'Rum Corps', by 1916 it was home to an assortment of grand mansions, terrace houses and humble cottages cascading down to a working harbour. Cath and Tom ambled along Booth Street on a warm October afternoon. They'd been seeing each other for over six months, and while he'd met the Thornton family and become good friends with Jim and Elizabeth, she was about to meet the Wong's for the first time.

'So, what can I expect this afternoon?'

'Well, a Chinese family is different from an Australian one.'

'In what way?'

'They're nosey, and a little pushy.'

'So, what makes you think that's any different to Australian families?'

'Point taken–although my grandmother is a force to be reckoned with.'

'Tell me about her.'

'She's 91 - born in Canton in 1825. She married my grandfather in Hong Kong, and they sailed for the Australian gold fields in 1853. After he died at Eureka she retreated to Sydney, when my dad was five, and sold everything she owned to start a boarding house in the Haymarket. It was tough on her own–being a woman and Chinese, she's battled discrimination on both fronts for over fifty years, but built her fortune nonetheless.'

'She sounds like a remarkable woman.'

'She is–but a word of warning - she can be as blunt as a brick wall.'

Number 37 was a white, two-storey terrace house with a pair of stone 'temple dogs' guarding the front door. Tom's knock was answered by footsteps and the door opened to reveal an older version of himself. Henry Wong was of medium height with greying hair, brown eyes and a slim, compact physique that belied his 67 years. He shook his son's hand.

'Dad–this is Cath Thornton.'

'I'm pleased to meet you, Cath.'

She smiled. 'Thank you, Mr. Wong–it's good to be here.'

'Please call me Henry–come in.'

Tom's mother Victoria hugged her son in the light-filled hallway. In a navy-blue satin dress, with gently greying hair swept above a refined face, and dark, expressive eyes, she exuded a natural grace. 'Welcome, Catherine. I've been looking forward to meeting you.'

A cosy sitting room reflected the low gleam of rosewood and velvet cushions. A painted screen framed in ebony depicted warlords galloping across a vast plain, and aloeswood incense wafted on the air. Cath's attention drifted to a framed photograph on the wall, depicting a young Detective Henry Wong with a Caucasian man in front of a mammoth domed building. Henry caught her look of interest.

'That was in 1879. Are you familiar with the old "Garden Palace" building?'

'It sounds familiar–wasn't it in Macquarie Street, near the Botanic Gardens?'

'Yes–it was built for the Sydney International Exhibition, but burnt to the ground just a few years later.'

'That's you on the left?'

Henry smiled. 'Yes, I was a young, bright-eyed detective in those days.'

'Who's the other gentleman?'

'That's my old partner, Liam Kennedy. We'd just wound up a murder case that nearly killed us both.'

'The 'Doctor Hacksaw' affair?'

He was momentarily non-plussed. 'You've heard of it?'

'Yes–Tom mentioned it a while ago.'

Tom grinned. 'Always singing your praises, Dad.'

Victoria appeared in the doorway with a tray of crockery. 'Henry–can you bring the other tray from the kitchen?'

'I'll get it, Mum.' Answered Tom.

Victoria gestured Cath to a chair. 'Please make yourself comfortable. Mah Ma (mother) will join us shortly.'

Tom returned with the tea, coffee and slices of cake. 'We're in luck, Cath–Mum's made her famous sponge cake–we call it "Ma Lai Gao"–it melts in your mouth.'

Cups were filled and cake passed around with the clinking of spoons on china.

'You have a lovely home, Mrs. Wong.' Said Cath.

'Thank you. We bought it a year before Pearl was born–both our children grew up here, but it's just us and Henry's mother now–Henry retired two years ago, and I've handed the family business over to Pearl.'

'Oh? What type of business is it?'

'A Millinery shop in Pitt Street–"Chen's Millinery."'

Cath's eyes widened. 'Chen's? The best millinery outlet in Sydney–as a young girl I dreamed of owning a "Chen's" hat.'

'That's kind of you. My mother started it and I took it over when she passed away, over 40 years ago. Pearl couldn't be here today, but she wants to meet you–if you don't mind, I'll have her call you to arrange something.'

'That would be lovely.'

Tom added. 'She'll tell you how wonderful her brother is.'

Henry chuckled. 'More than likely, she'll tell you what a damn nuisance her brother is. Pearl and Tom haven't stopped arguing for the last thirty years.'

An elderly woman appeared in the doorway. Tom rose from his chair and bowed. 'Ah Tai' ('Grandmother'). She was a diminutive woman with snow-white hair pulled back into a severe bun. Her ninety-one years had sculpted a rounded face with fine spider-web lines framing eyes as clear as starlight. She crossed to Cath with the aid of a cane, and shook her hand.

'Hello,–my name is "Yu Yan", but please call me "Yvonne". I'm pleased to meet you.'

'It's a pleasure, Yvonne.'

She eased herself back into a chair as Victoria handed her a cup of tea. 'My grandson tells me you've graduated in medicine from Sydney University–that is quite an achievement for one so young.'

'Thank you–I believe there is a Chinese saying– 'Seize every opportunity - the Yangtse never flows backwards.' Tom threw her a surprised glance.

'Yvonne smiled. 'Yes–and they also say "Rejoice in youth, and have no regrets in old age" - have you travelled to China?'

'No, but I'd like to someday. Since meeting Tom I've become a devotee of the food–particularly Szechuan.'

'China is not a safe place these days–warlords fight one other like spoiled children over an empire in tatters–I fear there will be turmoil for a long time.' The old woman put her cup on the table. 'But I digress - and when a woman reaches my age, she doesn't waste the time she has left. This may seem an odd question, but are you familiar with the term "Chinoiserie"?'

'Yes–it's an artistic style that imitates Asian interior design and architecture.'

'Yes - it was very popular last century, and continues today as something of a fad. But these days, I believe there is another aspect of Chinoiserie that young women practice in the art of romance-those who think it "avant-garde" to flirt with Chinese men.'

Tom exchanged glances with his parents. Cath's eyes held a querulous look.

'These women like to be seen at clubs and private parties frequented by Sydney's privileged young Caucasian people, parading an Oriental man about like something on a charm bracelet, in the hope they will impress their friends. It's an entertaining distraction, but they soon tire of the game and abandon their plaything like yesterday's newspaper.' Her eyes hardened. 'I hope you're not fond of charm bracelets, Catherine.'

The only sound in the room was a ticking mantlepiece clock and the dull drone of street traffic from outside. Henry and Victoria stared at the floor. A dark shadow of anger crossed Tom's face. The old woman's russet-brown eyes were aimed at Cath like a loaded gun.

Tom made to rise. 'Ah Tai…..' but Cath stopped him short with a raised hand as she spoke to the old woman in an even tone; her eyes bright with emotion. 'Mrs. Wong, perhaps I should tell you more about myself. I don't come from privilege–I come from the bush. My parents are publicans, and they've worked hard all their lives to give their children the best they could. As for me, I don't have time for parties. I work long hours at Sydney Hospital, because I believe in caring for the sick and saving lives. I'm not interested in impressing people, or playing mindless games at parties. The women you describe sound to me like vapid little rich girls without the moral or mental firepower to ignite a match.' She paused for a moment to let her words sink in. If the old woman was affected by Cath's words, she wasn't showing it. 'Tom and I have earned each other's respect, Mrs Wong, and we have a strong bond–far stronger than any charm bracelet.'

She rose and turned to Tom's parents. 'Thank you both for inviting me today–I'm so pleased to have met you. Please excuse me, but I must be on my way.' She returned down the hall. Without a word, Tom bowed to his parents and followed her out the door.

He caught up with her on the street. 'Cath–wait.' She turned with tears of hurt and anguish in her eyes, and trembled as he held her.

'I'm sorry–I had no idea she'd be like that. It was unforgiveable.'

'I couldn't stay, Tom–your parents are lovely, but I couldn't take the venom coming from her.'

Tom replied. 'Neither could I. Chinese people place a great deal of importance in creating a favourable impression–some call it "maintaining face"–and my parents just lost a great deal of it–as have I. My grandmother insulted you, and she insulted her family as well.' Cath looked into his eyes. 'Tom, it's you I want to be with, not your grandmother–let's just walk away from this–forget it ever happened.'

Shadows stalked the rooftops of Annandale as the sun reflected its fire in wispy cloud. Two figures walked arm-in-arm up Booth Street with heavy hearts.

It was two days later when one of the Royal's bar-staff knocked on James's office door. 'Sorry to interrupt, boss, but a Chinese bloke downstairs wants a word with you–says his name's Henry Wong.'

James capped his pen with a puzzled look. 'Alright–I'll be down in a tick.' As he came down the stairs, James knew from the resemblance that it was Tom's father standing hat in hand. 'Mr Wong–I'm James Thornton–won't you come up and have a cup of tea?' They shook hands. 'Tea would be fine–thank you–just call me Henry.'

Sarah met them in the kitchen, and James made the introductions.

'I'm sorry for turning up unannounced, but I was in the neighbourhood on business.'

'Not at all–how do you take your tea?' Replied Sarah.

'Black, no sugar, thanks.' Blue flames licked the bottom of the kettle with a low whisper as Henry took a seat at the table and fidgeted with his hat. 'I ah, wondered if you knew that Tom brought Cath to meet our family a couple of days ago.'

James put a plate of biscuits on the table. 'No, she didn't mention it.'

'I see, well actually, that's why I'm here - to apologise for what happened.'

James's eyebrows lifted. 'Oh?'

He let out a sigh, raking a hand through greying hair. 'Yes–my mother said some things that gave offence–not only to Cath, but to the rest of the family.' He briefly related Yu Yan's outburst, and the young couple's untimely departure. 'It would be easy for me to excuse her behaviour as old age taking its toll, but her mind hasn't dulled–it's just become bitter.' His eyes flitted between James and Sarah. 'Cath seems a wonderful young woman–I don't want this incident to sour her view of my family.' He paused as his eyes drifted to the kitchen window framing Maroubra headland in the distance. 'You know, I've lived in Australia since I was five, with one foot in Hong Kong and the other in Sydney. Most Chinese frown on relationships outside their race, but I believe it's the best way for our culture to thrive. I wouldn't like this incident to push Tom and Cath apart.'

Sarah re-filled his cup with a gentle smile. 'No family is perfect, Henry–least of all ours. My father is famous for putting both feet in his mouth.' She winked at James. 'And the Thorntons are well known for going off half-cocked on quests of self-discovery. As for Cath and Tom, they're forging a relationship with two careers, two cultures and two strong personalities–that's unusual, and not easy. Tom's a nice young man, and Cath seems very happy–she's also a strong woman, and I don't believe this incident will damage their relationship–it may even strengthen it.'

~ ~ ~

A couple of nights later the hall phone rang above the clamour of the six o'clock swill from downstairs. Cath clasped the receiver to her ear. 'Hello?'

'It's Bob down in the bar, Cath–there's a call for you–a young lady.'

'Thanks Bob–I'll take it up here.'

The phone clicked over. 'Hello–Cath Thornton speaking.'

The voice was strong, with a broad Australian accent. 'Hello Cath–it's Pearl Wong from Chen's Millinery. Mum gave me your number.'

'Hello Pearl–yes, I remember. It's nice of you to call.'

'Sorry I didn't get to meet you the other day–I've been flat out at the shop–The Spring Carnival races are on at Randwick - all the old ducks want to outdo each other with a new hat - it's like a playground brawl.'

Cath chuckled. 'I can imagine.'

'Mum tells me you're a fan of my work–would you like to come to the shop tomorrow afternoon for coffee?'

'Yes, I would. It so happens I have tomorrow off from work–what time would suit?'

'How about 3? Afternoons are usually a bit quieter around here.'

'That's fine Pearl.'

'Excellent. Sorry Cath, I have to fly–see you tomorrow.'

~   ~   ~

Trees danced with a north easterly wind, throwing graceful shadows across Hyde Park. Cath was early for her meeting with Pearl, and got off the tram to walk the rest of the way to 'Chen's'. Rivers of people jostled their way down Pitt Street's cauldron of motion-men in suits and boaters, women in low heels, flowing dresses and wide-brimmed hats.

A tram clattered by; electric sparks sizzling from the overhead cable as its passengers dangled from hand-straps. A maze of electrical wires stretched in a tangled maze above the street, and Hansom cabs jousted for position with cars belching smoke. A paper boy in a flat-cap held the *'Herald's'* afternoon edition aloft in inky fingers. 'President Wilson gets back in! - Getcha Daily Telegraph here!'

She passed the Strand Arcade, its cast-iron finery cascading over five floors to chic cafes. A plume-hatted woman emerged with a clutch of shopping bags and a well-clipped poodle prancing on a leash. On the corner of King Street, 'Prouds' jewellery store reminded her of Danny, riding somewhere down on the Illawarra, looking for answers. At Martin Place, the new 12-storey 'Commonwealth Bank Building' was being unwrapped from scaffolding while the GPO scowled at the upstart who had dared to rise above an elder statesman.

Cath thought about Pearl. *'She sounded quite young on the phone, but then, some women did have much younger voices - still, Tom had just turned 30, and Pearl was older than him......... I wonder whether she knows about the other day at the Wong's? I'll bet Mrs. Wong told her—will this be an attempt at reconciliation? An olive branch? Perhaps an expensive "Chen's" hat as a peace offering?'* She smiled to herself. *'God help me, they **can** buy this girl.'*

Her reverie was broken by raucous laughter from patrons enjoying a Friday afternoon beer at the Angel Hotel, as a prelude to the coming weekend. *'They'll be well and truly oiled by closing time.'* She mused. Between passers-by she glimpsed the harbour spangling diamonds in the sun's reflection. A ferry's horn sounded faintly above the traffic.

Chen's Millinery snuggled under an elegantly striped awning between 'Wallace's Coffee Emporium' and 'A. J. Henshaw and Sons, Solicitors'. Its full-length glass windows were edged in polished brass and framed with Alexander palms. Cath caught glimpses of movement and colour from inside as she opened the door.

It was like stepping into a Paris boutique. Rows of cabinets lined a carpeted floor under chandeliers hanging from a duck-egg blue ceiling. Along the walls, polished shelves held an array of hats for every occasion, with flowers, feathers and netting in every colour-all 'Chen's' originals. A blue and yellow macaw parrot perched in a gilded cage, chatting to itself: 'Hats, Ladies! Hats, Ladies!' Sales attendants cooed and fussed over customers, while at the rear, a young Asian woman stood with hands clasped loosely before her, surveying the landscape.

Pearl looked as young as she'd sounded. Her jet-black hair was cut in a short, masculine style with a wispy fringe over thinly sculpted eyebrows. She wore a black, high-necked silk 'cheongsam' dress that accentuated her willowy figure. But the most striking feature was her almond-shaped eyes - dark, limpid pools in an alabaster face that held a whisper of innocence with a shout of defiance.

'Cath?'

'Yes–hello Pearl–it's good to meet you.'

'Likewise.'

Cath glanced around. 'I've passed this shop a thousand times, but I've never been inside–it's beautiful.'

Pearl's smile shone. 'Thank you–I've just redecorated. Why don't we chat in the office? It's up the back.' She led Cath up a narrow hallway and through an open door.

Light dribbled over red brickwork through a cobwebbed window. A large desk lay buried under swatches of fabric, bundles of netting, stubby pencils, reels of cotton and lengths of dried whale baleen tied with ribbon. A stack of art-paper sketches spilled onto the floor, and on the window ledge, bald plaster heads were lined up like laughing clowns in sideshow alley.

Pearl followed her gaze to framed photos of buxom, naked women lining the wall. The female form has always fascinated me–give me Aphrodite over Adonis, any day.'

Pearl cleared two tub chairs of assorted jetsam. 'Sorry about the mess, but I work better in chaos. Have a seat–coffee or tea?'

'Tea, thanks.'

A staff member who'd hovered at the door disappeared to fill the order.

'I was the tea-wallah when I started here at 15 years of age.'

'No preferential treatment?'

'On the contrary - Mum worked me like a dog–she thought it was good for my soul–and it was. She hung up her scissors a couple of years ago, but still pesters me on the phone every day.' She did a convincing imitation of Victoria. *"Pearl, did you check inventory? Pearl, watch that fabric supplier–he'd steal the pennies from a dead woman's eyes.'*

Cath laughed. 'I mentioned to your mother that I used to walk past here when I was young, and dreamed of having a "Chen's" hat someday.'

Pearl nodded. 'Yes–she told me.' She brightened as a thought came to her. 'I believe we have a mutual acquaintance–Minnie Fitzroy, the artist?'

This surprised Cath. 'Yes–the Royal's longest-serving guest, since 'The Major' passed away a few years back. You know her?'

'She's my best customer, and something of a mentor–she's been buying her hats here for as long as I can remember.' She gestured to a painting that Cath had missed. 'She painted that portrait of me for my 21st birthday'.

Cath studied the painting. The subject was definitely Pearl–the same high cheekbones and unfathomable eyes, with a hint of coquetry. 'Her work is excellent, isn't it?' She turned to Pearl with a grin. 'Mum tells the story of Minnie painting on the upstairs veranda of the Royal in the nude.'

Pearl chuckled. 'That doesn't surprise me–she's a free spirit, that one.'

'Didn't she spend time in Paris?' Asked Cath.

'Yes–she studied art there for a few years when she was young. She'd probably still be there if she hadn't gotten her heart broken–her girlfriend robbed her blind and left her for another woman. She never got over it–that's when she ended up in Sydney'.

The door pushed ajar as a tea tray appeared and cups were poured. Cath waited for the door to close. 'Did your mother tell you what happened when Tom and I visited your parents?'

Pearl's face hardened as she sipped her tea. 'Yes, she did. Cath, allow me to be frank - my grandmother's a damn bitch. I call her "The Dragon Lady"–the mind of a lizard, the skin of a crocodile, and a mouth that exhales words of fire–she'll burn you alive, if you let her.'

Cath laughed. 'Well, I hadn't thought of it that way, but I appreciate your candour–but….. doesn't your culture command respect for elders?'

'That's the good thing about being born in Australia–here, people don't get respect unless they've earned it. Of course, I go through the motions, say the right things, but only because of my parents. Tom's traditional that way too, but not me–convention doesn't sit well on my shoulder.'

Cath replied. 'He was outraged the other day–I don't think he's spoken with his family since.'

'No, he hasn't–he came 'round here the next day and bashed my ear about it.'

'He and I had a long talk, too–we're not letting this change anything.'

'I'm glad.' You know, Tom thinks the world of you, though he may not say it. People think of him as the tough copper who fights like a whirling dervish, but like most men, there's a little boy inside, afraid of being hurt.'

Cath nodded. 'I think most men are the same–they never really grow up. Tom's introduced me to an extra dimension of Sydney - other cultures, wonderful food, parts of the city I didn't know existed. It's a shame more people don't appreciate those things.'

Pearl smiled thinly. 'One day, perhaps they will– more people like you will change minds, and the Chinese community also needs to come out from the shadows. Tell me–what's it like being a doctor in the hallowed corridors of Sydney Hospital?'

'Not much different to working at "Chen's" by the sound of it–they work me like a dog too.'

Pearl laughed. 'In China, having a doctor in the family is a huge social advantage, but I don't believe there'd be any female doctors there–not yet, anyway.'

'Tom's told me a lot about Hong Kong - he's very proud of it, even though he hasn't been there yet. I'd like to travel there one day.'

'You must let me know if you're planning anything–I export to Hong Kong and have some good contacts there.

~ ~ ~

On the way home in the tram, Cath thought about Pearl. She was a forthright woman, that was for sure. Only an astute business person could run 'Chen's' and retain the loyalty of Sydney's well-heeled, but fickle, high society. And exporting to Hong Kong, with a couple of thousand British expatriates, not to mention wealthy Chinese - would be lucrative. She'd described her Surry Hills workshop, or 'engine room' as she called it–twelve seamstresses in a converted terrace house, making bespoke hat designs six days a week. Then there was her range of accessories imported from Paris and Milan - handbags, parasols, gloves, shawls, scarves and stockings– very impressive.

Her lesbianism didn't surprise Cath–it fitted perfectly with her unconventional personality. On the surface, same-sex relationships were frowned upon in Sydney's Edwardian, straight-laced society, but they'd existed from the earliest days of the colony, not only in 'women's factories' and male convict prisons, but equally in the so-called 'upper classes.' Queensland's first doctor, Lillian Cooper, and her partner Josephine Bedford were a well-known couple among the medical fraternity. Cath was ambivalent on such matters. Her philosophy was, *'What people do behind closed doors is entirely their own business.'*

'And what of Detective Tom Wong?' She thought. He was so many things–strong, extremely attractive, ethical, not to mention lethal. Emotionally, he was a cornucopia of hard and soft, light and dark; or in the Oriental sense, 'Yin and Yang.' Cath was drawn to him like Mercury to the sun; and she could feel her orbit spiralling towards his light.

~   ~   ~

Later that month James answered the hall phone, and it was Tom on the line. He was about to call Cath to the phone when Tom cut him short.

'Actually, James, I wanted to talk with you.'

'Oh? What can I do for you?'

'I'd like to have a confidential chat if you're free sometime tomorrow–somewhere other than the Royal.'

James's interest was aroused–*what could this be about? Police business? Illegal Sunday trading? He hadn't opened on Sundays for years.* 'I'll be in town tomorrow–I could drop by your office if you want.'

'That would be good–what about 11 o'clock?'

'That works for me.'

The NSW Police Headquarters at the corner of Phillip and Hunter Streets was a three-storied sandstone building a short walk from Parliament House. James entered the reception area where a uniformed sergeant sat at a polished timber desk. An air of seriousness pervaded. A stairway led to a gallery area where officers with manila files whisked back and forth or stood in earnest conversation. He gave his name to the Sergeant, and within a few minutes Tom emerged from a side door and shook his hand.

'Thanks for coming in, James–come this way.'

Tom led him through an open office area crammed with desks. Plain clothed police hunched over typewriters, squint-eyed from dangling cigarettes, or pored over piles of paper; stub pencils behind the ear. The room throbbed with sharp conversation and the occasional muttered curse. No-one took any notice as Tom motioned James to a chair in his small office and shut the door.

'Sorry to drag you into town on short notice.'

'Not at all–I've never been inside a Police Headquarters before–am I in the shit?'

Tom chuckled and shook his head. 'No, not at all.' He dropped his eyes for an instant, with a hint of embarrassment. 'I just needed to have a quiet chat. In fact, I have a question to ask you.'

'Alright–ask away.'

'Well, I ahh, it's like this–Oh, damn it–James, I'd like your permission to ask Cath to marry me.'

James paused for a moment to let the words sink in, and while the question itself was not wholly unexpected, what took him by surprise was the realisation that *his* Cath would now be someone else's Cath–something that many fathers never really get used to. And while he contemplated these thoughts, he realized Tom was becoming increasingly nervous at the lack of a reply.

He snapped himself out of reverie. 'Sorry Tom–I was lost in thought for a moment. The answer is yes, of course, you have my permission.'

Tom smiled and shook his hand again, then seriousness hardened his face. 'I know it's unusual for a Chinese and a white woman to marry, and I know many people are against it–from both sides. I just hope that you and Sarah don't think that way.'

James replied. 'You've heard of the 'Royal Hotel Act'?

'Yes, I have.'

'Well, that Act applies to the whole pub–not just the bar. It has jurisdiction upstairs as well. Tom, it doesn't matter to us where you come from, what language you speak or what colour you are. What matters is the man you are.'

And so, the next evening at 'Café Jean-Claude', under a cloud of Gauloises smoke and serenaded by violin music, Tom proposed to Cath……

And she said 'yes'.

~   ~   ~

A humpback whale drifted through blue water off northern Wollongong. She'd journeyed over a thousand miles from Hook Island in the warm Whitsundays and still had a long way to go. Her calf swam alongside, whispering to his mother as they touched pectoral fins in affection. She could hear male whale-song in the vicinity, but kept her song low to avoid the Orcas. It was time for air. She nudged the calf upward and they surfaced together, spraying rainbow breath as they curved back down to deep indigo.

Danny saw the white-water as the whales surfaced a mile out from Bald Hill lookout. A thousand feet below, ocean swells rolled steadily into Stanwell Park beach, and away to the south, green headlands pushed into the sea like gloved hands. A southerly wind buffeted the hill with updrafts, where 30 years before, Lawrence Hargrave rose from the ground under the power of his own experimental box kites.

He'd journeyed north from Kiama, skirting the shores of Lake Illawarra under a smudge of orange from the copper works. He was in no hurry–Sydney wasn't going anywhere and he had plenty to think about. Balla had sensed his languid mood, and paced a steady walk, following back roads through Towradgi, Corrimal and Bulli along the glittering Tasman Sea. When the sun dipped behind the escarpment, he'd pitch a tent in the sand dunes and watch the sea darken until it was ink lit with a rising moon, and the surf would whisper to him of life's sanctity, even with its sufferings.

From Bald Hill he rode north as waves dashed against the rocks far below. Honeyeaters flittered through the scrub, flashing yellow in their hunt for nectar. Occasionally a goanna would creep from the mallee like a dragon, its beady black eyes watching him pass. After a mile or so the road turned its back on the ocean to twist along a ridge above the Hacking River, and by late afternoon the main road at Sutherland announced its presence in a low hum. As the tree canopy thinned, the distant lights of Sydney rose in the dusk like a modern-day Camelot.

He camped under a crown of peppermint gums for his last night before joining the city's madding throng. He'd been a long time in the bush - his ears had been lulled by the morning cry of currawongs; his eyes soothed by soft hillsides and open grassland. But the city had other plans–sharp, brassy shouts, guarded looks, stacks belching smoke, bells, whistles and a screech of rubber on tar. *'Welcome to Sydney'*, he thought with a wry smile.

By mid-morning he'd reached the Georges River at Horse Rock Point and joined the queue for a one-shilling steam ferry passage across the 500 yards to Tom Ugly's Point. The line stretched up a grassy hill for some 50 yards, and there was much grumbling about government inaction to build a bridge - but it would be 1929 before that came to pass. By the time he rode Balla up the ramp on the other side, his stomach was growling, and as luck would have it, the 'Tradewinds Inn' stood just up the road from the wharf. He headed toward it.

He secured Balla to a railing post and took in the view. The inn sat comfortably on a rocky outcrop looking east over the Georges River. Flanked by large Norfolk pines, it was built in the old tradition–single-storied with a deep veranda that welcomed the ocean's tang. To the north, the river nudged its way into Kogarah Bay, where oyster-bed posts poked from the water like the foundations of some uncompleted mansion. A mile to the east, Sans Souci Peninsula and Taren Point eyeballed each other over 500 yards of water that had finally been conquered by a ferry service, and off in the distance, sailing skiffs glided across Botany Bay, stark white against sapphire blue.

He took the steps to the veranda and entered the bar where cooking smells rekindled his hunger. Windows were open to the river on three sides, their muslin curtains billowing like spinnakers in the nor'- easter. A couple of locals sat nursing beers in quiet conversation, and he took a stool at the bar where a middle-aged man was stacking glasses.

'G'day mate–what can I get you?'

Danny took up a dog-eared card from the bar, listing "Counter Lunch Meals–12 to 2PM". 'G'day–am I too early for lunch?'

'Not by the time it's cooked–what'll you have?'

He glanced down the list. 'The pie and mash looks good….. and a middy of new, thanks.'

As the barman took the order and reached for a glass, a raucous voice shattered the quiet. *'RRAAARRK!!!*

Middy o' new, thanks, mate! Middy o' new, thanks, mate! RRAAARRK!!! What Else? What Else?' Danny started at the noise, turning to see a large bird strutting down the bar and staring at him, gimlet-eyed.

It appeared to be a sulphur-crested cockatoo, but unlike any he'd seen before. Its scrawny grey skin was almost bereft of plumage, and the few feathers that had survived were stringy, sparse excuses poking out at odd angles like errant signposts. Its black, intelligent eyes blinked at Danny from baggy sockets that were wrinkled with the weight of years. Its outburst had drawn not so much as a flinch from the other patrons, nor the barman, and the bird stood steadfast, clearly regarding Danny as an interloper.

The barman plonked Danny's beer down and glanced at the parrot. 'Don't mind that old bastard–he's called 'Bosun'–part of the furniture.' The parrot continued to pin Danny with his stare as the barman continued. 'He's waiting for an answer.'

'What answer?'

'He asked you "What else". Just tell him "That's all", and he'll bugger off.'

Danny turned to the indignant bird. 'That's all.'

'The Bosun' blinked twice, turned his back on Danny, shit on the bar, then ambled back to his rattan cage with an expression of satisfaction.

'How old is he?' Asked Danny.

The barman wiped up the bird dung. 'As far as we know, he's about 96. He's had an interesting life….'

'Bosun's' story was folklore on Tom Ugly's Point; dating back to the early 19th century. Captain Henry Rawson was skipper and owner of the two-masted schooner "Maureen" out of Amsterdam in the 1830s. It was rumoured that Rawson had become amorously involved with the wife of a London peer, and under the threat of death the captain and his ship promptly disappeared. He resurfaced in the Dutch East Indies some years later, plying the trade routes from Calcutta to New Guinea and North Queensland, carrying spices, cotton, silks, and the occasional well-paying fugitive.

On a steamy Port Moresby night in 1840, Rawson won a high stakes poker game, and the purse included a talkative 20-year-old cockatoo. He christened the bird 'Bosun', and from that day on, for almost 40 years, the cockatoo perched on Rawson's shoulder aboard the "Maureen".

In the 1850s Rawson became good mates with policeman Fred Delaney in Cairns. Fred had helped the captain out with a ticklish situation involving the kidnapping of men from the Solomon Islands to work on Queensland's sugarcane plantations–known as the 'Blackbirding Trade'. Getting on in years, Rawson pledged to leave 'Bosun' to Delaney in his will. Years later, Delaney retired to Sydney, where he bought the 'Tradewinds' hotel in 1878.

A heart attack dropped Captain Rawson to the deck of the "Maureen" in 1880, somewhere between Surabaya and Makassar, and as he fell, 'Bosun' fluttered from his shoulder to the yardarm, crying, *'Get up, ya drunk! Get up, ya drunk!* They buried Rawson at sea, but it would be four years before the 'Maureen' could deliver its feathered cargo to Sydney. In 1882, the late captain's nephew knocked at the door of the 'Tradewinds' with a rattan cage housing a parrot that could swear in five languages, and 'Bosun' had been there ever since.

The cockatoo was known for its lack of manners and forceful language. One often-told story involved a visit to the area by Sydney's Lord Mayor, Sir James Winthrop, and his wife Lady Evelyn in 1899. The couple took tea on the veranda of the 'Tradewinds' one afternoon while 'Bosun' swung nearby in his cage, his beady eyes quietly observing. Lady Evelyn was afflicted by a rather large nose, and as she raised her cup to take a sip, 'Bosun' erupted. *'RRAAARRK!!! Get your bloody great beak out of that! RRAAARRK!!!'*

~   ~   ~

Danny downed the last of his pie and mash and went out to the veranda. The afternoon had warmed up and traffic ebbed and flowed on the road below. He judged it was about fifteen miles to Randwick–up the main road to Rockdale, then east through the marshlands of Botany Bay, over to Pagewood, Maroubra, then home. 'Home'........the word sounded somehow odd to him after six months of travelling to nowhere in particular for no special reason, other than escaping his ghosts. And had he? Half-digested thoughts blew around in his mind like dust-devils in an alleyway, but they were starting to fall into place.

As he swung into the saddle, a strident voice sounded from inside the bar. *'RRAAARRK!!! Look lively! Shove off, ya mug! shove off, ya mug! RRAAARRK!!!'*

~   ~   ~

The day had been a scorcher, and the Royal was an oven. Sarah wiped perspiration from her brow and shook the soap-saver through the hot water, clinking teacups and making rainbows in the suds. Her mind wandered.

'Where had the time gone?' Sixteen years before, they'd hopped off the train from Orange with a few suitcases and limitless hope. She was 47 then, with a Peter Pan husband and four kids that became three because of a senseless war. She brushed away a tear and swirled the dish mop over a plate flecked with gravy, leaning it in the dish-rack. 'And now I'm 63 and looking backward, like we all seem to do at this age.' She smiled. 'And my Peter Pan husband is 73, going on 5.'

Out of nowhere, images of Danny stormed her mind. They hadn't heard from him in weeks, and though she tried to put it out of her mind, the old sense of foreboding returned–was he alright? Where was he now? Something tugged at her consciousness, and she looked out the window at afternoon shadows edging over Perouse Road. In the distance, a figure on horseback quivered in the hot light, and she knew it was her son.

She hurried down the corridor, pausing for an instant at James's office as he looked up from paperwork. 'Danny's back!' He watched his wife disappearing down the stairway. 'Be careful, love! You'll break your bloody neck at that pace!' The screen door clashed back against timber as Danny rounded the laneway with a lop-sided smile under a battered slouch hat. Sarah felt a surge of emotion as he embraced her.

She held him at arm's length to get a good look–her eyes weren't as good as they used to be. His face was thin and angular, his body lean and hardened by months in the saddle. His eyes were clearer than when he'd come home from the war, and the haunted shadow no longer showed in his youthful face.

Her nose wrinkled. 'You smell like a stray cat–when did you last took a bath?'

He grinned. 'Dunno–what month is it?'

She slapped him playfully on the shoulder. 'Cheeky bugger. Here's your father.'

James came through the gate with a smile lighting his face. 'My son, the cowboy.' They shook hands warmly. 'Let's get you and that horse inside–although the way you smell, I think we'll take the horse upstairs, and leave you in the stable.'

While Danny took his time in the bath scrubbing away weeks of grime, Sarah threw his clothes in the copper with a double dose of Lux Flakes and a handful of Epsom salts. 'That should kill anything.' She thought, stirring the boiling water with a paddle. James leaned against the wringer, watching steam curl to the ceiling.

'He looks different, doesn't he?'

'Yes–do you remember when he came home from England? His eyes were always darting about, as if he was afraid.'

'I do. He looks calmer now–thin as a rake though–you'll have to fatten him up, love.'

'I know–and when he gets out of that bath, I want to know exactly what he's been up to for the last six months.'

As James poured the tea, Danny's eyes lingered on the table's time-eroded surface. 'I remember this table from when I was three years old.' He pointed to a faded incision on its surface. 'That's where John stuck his penknife between Cath's fingers for a dare–and got a clout over the ear for his trouble.' A round scorch mark grabbed his attention. 'And Mum, you stuck a boiling saucepan there one night when I had an asthma attack.' He turned to his father. 'You told us so many yarns around this table, Dad–you convinced us with that story about being a pirate, until Cath checked the "Encyclopedia Britannica", and figured you had to be a hundred and fifteen years old to have sailed the Spanish Main.'

James chuckled. 'Your mother and I believed you kids should enjoy a world of fantasy for as long as possible - the realities of being an adult come soon enough, and besides; I enjoy a good yarn myself.' He gathered his thoughts. 'Son, you look so much better. What've you been up to out there?'

Danny drains his tea and stares blankly at the empty cup, and he's back on the road under a wide sky with nowhere to go but where fate nudges him. The sun's warm on his shoulders and whip birds' calls cut through the air.

Sarah and James exchanged nervous looks until he shook himself back to the present. 'Dad, you once told me that a wanderer sometimes finds answers to questions without looking. When I rode away from here, I didn't know what to do or where to go–but I knew I couldn't stay. You were right - I had to find my own way–my own answers.'

'On the first day, up in the mountains, an old bullocky pulled up for a yarn, and you wouldn't believe it - he had a wooden leg–shot off in Africa. When I asked him how he handled it, he told me he just 'got on with it.' Danny shrugged. 'But that didn't help me much - with nightmares all the time, and my nerves playing up something shocking, how was I going to get on with it?'

'Then the very next day, I meet an aboriginal man from the Gundungurra tribe at the Three Sisters. He was a good bloke - I told him about Grandad's nulla-nulla. Just before he walked away, he looked at me like he could read my mind, and told me I'd find what I was looking for inside myself.' Danny smiled and shook his head. 'So I'm thinking, jeez, what's in the air up here? There's no shortage of blokes wandering around and giving me vague advice, but how the hell do I find answers inside my own head?'

He paused for a moment and ran a hand through a mop of hair, still damp from the bath. 'Then I almost killed a bloke one night.'

James started. 'You what?!'

Sara's face darkened. 'What happened?'

'It was in a pub in Bathurst - he was drunk and egging me on, calling me a coward - said I should be in the army, then he threw a punch. I can't remember after that, but the Sergeant told me I tried to cut him up with a broken bottle.'

James glanced at Sarah. 'What Sergeant? They arrested you?'

'No–he sent me on my way the next morning without charge–and told me not to come back.'

The table was silent for a few moments before he continued. 'Anyway, it was down in Kiama a few months later when I began to figure things out. I was labouring in the quarry, and this Indian bloke called "Rayaan" was the cook. He was a Buddhist - I'd seen them in Ceylon, walking along the road in their robes and shaved heads, always happy and smiling–nothing like Catholic priests and nuns. He told me that Buddhists live only in the present–as far as they're concerned, the past is dead, the future is unknown, and the present was all that mattered. That's when the penny dropped–I'd been dredging up the past; feeling sorry for myself and wishing I had two good legs again. I realised that I couldn't go back in time - I had to change the way I thought about things.'

Sarah sat forward. 'That's all very well for the Asian races, but our Catholic faith is the one true religion. Why, where would we be if…..' James clasped her hands, cutting her short. 'That sounds like good advice Danny, no matter what religion it comes from. I'm so glad you've come to terms with everything…….'

Danny interrupted. 'But that's not all of it, Dad. In Goulburn I met a girl, well, a woman actually.' Sarah's face paled at the words, and her lips pursed in disapproval. 'Her name was Rose, and she taught me an important lesson - that a man is defined by what he is and what he does; not by how he looks.' Sarah's lips pursed again, and James stifled a grin. 'Sounds like Rose knew what she was talking about.' Danny returned the smile. 'Yes, she did……….. Mum, Dad, I'm not saying everything's going to be rosy from now on. I still think about the war sometimes, and the things I've seen and done, but I'm not scared any more. I think I'm going to be alright.'

Outside the Royal, a black onyx sky glowed with starlight. The cogs of fate had clicked into place, and a young wanderer had found answers from strangers on a dusty road - was this an accident, or was fate guided by some unseen hand–Karma? Divine providence? Kismet? When Danny was a young boy, James told him that stars were the lights of heaven shining through tiny holes in a velvet curtain. Perhaps there's more to the world than that which we can see. Perhaps we just need to look to the stars, and listen to our heart…..

Chapter 15

All Things Must Pass

January 15, 1917. Michael Thornton knew he would die today, despite the doctor's bullish promise of another week, and Father Flynn's reluctance to don the purple stole for the last rites. You see, Michael had the 'third eye', or the 'fey', as they call it in Ireland. He heard the whisper of the supernatural, like his mother and grandmother, and God knows how many before them. The good Father had finally relented, and anointed him with the sacred oils, but only after Michael had threatened to return and haunt the old bastard if he didn't.

He wasn't afraid. He'd long ago accepted his part in the eternal cycle of renewal–we are born, we live, we die. Only life itself, in its infinite diversity, continues unmolested. And what lay on the other side of the dark curtain? Despite his Catholic upbringing, he didn't really know, but he was sure of one thing, and one thing only–that there's more to this universe than we can comprehend; and he was prepared for the ride.

His bed looked southward over his beloved 'Gundungurra' property, rolling to the foot of Mount Canobolas like a lumpy green carpet. The 'Old Man' shone brighter than a new penny in the morning sun, as if basking in the satisfaction that it had outlasted Michael Thornton junior, just as it had Michael Thornton senior. '*Such is the right of ancient mountains.*' He thought. He gazed idly at his old tartan slippers with the flattened heels, laying askew beside the wardrobe in mute expectation of further service; but he doubted whether he'd need footwear for his journey.

Mary slept soundly in the old rocker - a twist of her grey hair buffeted by the wind of her own exhausted breath. She'd sat with him throughout the night as he'd wrestled with the pain. He wouldn't wake her–she looked so peaceful, and they'd said their goodbyes. He'd never forgotten the day he first set eyes on the willowy girl with bewitching eyes skipping down the stairs of 'Byrnes Feed and Grain' with sunlight dancing in her hair. That was August 1856, and he'd loved her from that day forward. She'd borne him three fine children–a better wife there never existed, and for that matter, for him, a better life had never existed.

And with that thought, Michael Thornton Jr, aged 81, drew his last breath, and heard the song of angels.

~   ~   ~

'Jimmy!'

James turned to his brother's voice coming from the hall, but no-one was there; and the shiver down his spine told him Michael was gone. It was 8am, January 15, 1917, and he slumped back in his chair with memories of his big brother raining down like a summer thunderstorm: Michael hoisting him up on a horse for the first time. Michael teaching him to tie his shoelaces. Michael swapping salt for sugar in his tea and laughing like a hyena when he spat it out. And taking him swimming in the dam - scaring the hell out of him with crocodile stories.

Tears of laughter, love and loss welled in his eyes, and he let them come.

~   ~   ~

The locomotive's whistle echoed over rolling grassland as the train sped through the village of Spring Hill, eight miles from Orange. James gazed up to a blue sky flecked with bloated clouds hinting at rain. Sarah sat beside him, rocking gently with the rhythm of the carriage, her head buried in a book–'The Getting of Wisdom'. A dark shape against the cobalt snagged his attention–an aeroplane–he'd never seen one up close. The Bleriot XI monoplane circled Orange aerodrome in a graceful arc, its paper-covered wings seeming incapable of holding it up. The pilot sat hunched forward in an open cockpit, intent at the controls. James nudged Sarah, and she gasped in wonder until the machine dipped from sight.

Sun splashed over slate rooftops as the train gave another whistle blast and curved into the outskirts of the town. James wrestled their bags from the overhead rack as Sarah glanced out the window to the Wolaroi Grammar School tower rising above distant trees. They hadn't been back to Orange since making the pilgrimage to Sydney 17 years before, and she felt the past tug at her, like a caught thread in a woollen shawl. Dalton's Flour Mill glided by and the train eased into the platform, panting clouds of steam.

George Thornton sat idly in a sulky on the station concourse, watching the passengers mill through turnstiles into the street. At 54, the late Michael Thornton's youngest son was stocky and gnarled from years of work at Gundungurra. Tufts of thick, greying hair protruded from his battered felt hat as he scanned the throng. George had always regarded James as a tribal elder; part of the legendary Thornton dynasty pioneered by his grandfather, old Mick Thornton himself. He hadn't seen his uncle for a few years, but had been looking forward to his arrival, even though the occasion was a sad one.

He saw them and waved his whip in the air. James acknowledged, and they headed toward the sulky.

'Welcome home, Uncle James, Aunty Sarah.'

After hand-shaking and quiet condolences, George loaded their bags and nudged the horse into Peisley Street.

While the two men talked of the coming grape harvest and the price of stock feed, Sarah took in the sights of her home town. Orange was busier than she remembered. Honking automobiles had asserted dominance over the streets–pushing through wandering horses and bicycles as if they were a cloud of annoying blowflies. She recognised most of the buildings–the ones that had risen in the more sedate Victorian years. But others had appeared like new teeth in an old set of dentures–shinier, sharper and brasher. She could see a faint high-tide mark of the 1916 flood on their facades, when Blackman's Swamp Creek had broken its banks yet again.

Young girls giggled with each other on busy street corners, whispering behind gloved fingers as young men in slouch hats swaggered by on their way to become heroes. Dress hems were higher, hats were sharper, and lower collars bared alabaster skin. Sarah knew it was no different to any street in Randwick, but she had somehow expected Orange to remain chaste and wholesome, frozen in the ice of her memory.

The sulky jingled up to the Empire Hotel and turned left into Summer Street, and before long they'd cleared the town's outskirts and were heading for Gundungurra along the Cargo Road through a patchwork of farmland. The traffic was light–a cart loaded with hay rumbled by, and the occasional automobile issued blue smoke. Here and there a farmhouse would appear, standing back from the road with chimneys poking demurely from a ring of shade trees. The sun was stooping lower, and three miles to the south, Canobolas cast lengthening shadows as it settled into the afternoon.

The day was still warm and the scent of moist earth and straw lifted on a northerly breeze as the horse clopped along the road. James breathed deeply and felt a pang of nostalgia for the place he'd been born and bred so many years ago. His thoughts returned to the family.

'How's your mother?'

'She's holding up. Dad kept telling her he'd go on the 15ᵗʰ, but I don't think she really believed him. She woke up that morning and he was gone–she feels like she deserted him at the last minute.'

James glanced at his nephew. 'I heard his voice from out in the hall that morning. I knew the old bugger had cashed in his chips.'

'Doesn't surprise me–I'll bet Uncle John heard him too.'

'What about Katy and Mike?' They were George's older siblings.

'They're all right–but the place isn't the same without Dad.'

'I know - it was the same when your grandfather left us in '83, remember? You were what, 25? It was like the place didn't have a soul anymore. But he's still there, you know, and so's your father.

George smiled. 'Yeah, you're right, Uncle James– but it's gunna get a bit crowded out there with all of us, I reckon.'

They swung off the Cargo Road in twilight to a chorus of droning cicadas. High in a snow gum, a pair of kookaburras laughed at the halo of a dying sunset.

Another half-mile up a gentle rise, the gates of Gundungurra stood open, and as they rounded a curve in the gravel drive, homestead lights glowed through the trees. Mary stood framed by the open door. Her eighty years had been kind; her deep-umber eyes shone brightly from a face crafted by years of hard work and good humour; her one concession to age an ebony cane. A shadow of grief grazed her brows, marking the passing of her husband of almost sixty years.

James embraced his sister-in-law. 'How are you, Mary?'

She smiled wanly. 'As well as can be expected, as the doctors are fond of saying.'

Mary and Sarah dipped into quiet conversation while James carried the bags inside. His parents had saved every penny to buy this land, and it wasn't until they were in their 50s that they slept under a roof they could call their own. James grew up in the original house that burned to the ground in the bushfires of 1870. The Thornton men built the new homestead brick-by-brick around the old fireplace; the only thing still standing after the rains put an end to a two-year drought. As the family grew, more dwellings were built, but the soul of Gundungurra was in these walls–and as he'd said to

George out on the Cargo Road, the spirits of Mick and Cate were palpable.

Later that night after dinner he sat in a rocker on the back veranda nursing a glass of old shiraz. A three-quarter moon cast the landscape in silver, silhouetting black angus cattle huddling against a cool wind, and from a nearby waterhole, frogs croaked in deep harmony. They would hold the funeral the next day, and friends and family would gather at the homestead for the wake. His brother John was coming up from Cadia, and they'd all drink a toast or two to the late Michael Thornton Junior. He drained his shiraz as the frogs' chanting set his mind free, and he drifted back to Galway, 1841, to the story passed down by his parents.

They stood arm-in-arm on a wind-swept jetty under scuttling grey clouds; their two young boys, Michael and John, hugging their parents' legs for warmth. Mick balanced a sea chest on his ample shoulder as the steamer made ready to cast off for Southampton and the Great Southern Land. He turned to his young wife.

'It's not too late, love, we can still go back.'

'No Mick, our boys deserve a better life than to till someone else's land until they drop from overwork–our future is on that boat.'

He nodded with a smile and followed his wife up the gangway.

James shed a tear for his mother–a strong woman who led without fanfare–especially when it mattered.

~   ~   ~

The next morning, clattering pots and rising voices filled the house in a squall of activity for the wake. Mary's daughter Katey had come down from Parkes on the early train, and Sarah was battling an unco-operative fuel stove. Clouds of flour drifted in a shaft of sunlight, and butter sizzling in an iron frypan sounded like heavy rain on tar. Out on the back lawn, George and his brother Mike were hefting garden furniture from the shed, while James did what he did best–setting up the bar. Mary was thankful for the swirling ocean of activity– it stole her thoughts away from the reality of the funeral.

After the early rush, the hubbub died down and the house reverted to an indistinct murmur while the family dressed for the funeral. Mary hated black. She stood before the mirror and muttered to herself. *'I look like some old Banshee about to go haunting.'* At the last minute she took the scissors to the black veil on her hat. *'To hell with this,'* she thought. *'Michael hated me in black, and anyway, it was only to keep the flies away.'* With the alterations complete, her eyes shifted to the bed where her husband had fulfilled his prediction of dying on time. *'He always **was** punctual,'* She thought, as a tear, which she swore would be her last of the day, dropped silently to the carpet.

In keeping with Michael Thorntons' egalitarian ways, the funeral at St. Joseph's Catholic Church was attended by a wide assortment of Orange's townsfolk. Aside from a tribe of Thorntons, the Byrnes family was well represented, old Bill Dalton from Dalton's General Store shuffled in on the arm of his grandson, and a coterie of regular drinkers from the Wellington Inn wore black armbands in memory of Michael's legendary beer drinking records, back in wilder days. In his sermon, Father Flynn noted that while Michael Jr, like his father, was no regular church goer, he was nonetheless a benevolent donor to the building fund. Mary noted the fact that her husband's accurate prediction of his own demise wasn't mentioned. She assumed, correctly, that the good Father thought it best to keep such matters in the realm of the Holy Trinity, for fear of undermining the faith.

~ ~ ~

Sunshine angled through the smoke of a spit roast under red gums. The hum of conversation and children at play flowed over the back veranda as food and drink was relayed by willing friends. This was not a sombre wake–people were enjoying themselves, secure knowing that old Michael Thornton would expect nothing less. Everyone at Gundundurra that day had a place in their heart for the man, and a story to go with it - usually involving wit and wry humour. Many recalled the Thorntons' infamous Federation Party of 1901 when the outside dunny went up in flames from a wayward skyrocket–what's more, as the flames took hold, Michael had burst out the door and taken off like a champion sprinter, but with his pants at half-mast, didn't get very far.

Mary sat in a swing seat with Sarah, sunlight ebbing and flowing through the shadows as they swung back and forth in a gentle arc. 'The Thorntons know how to throw a party.' Remarked Sarah as a pair of young boys ran past, whooping like wild Indians. Mary rested arms on her cane, wishing she could throw it on the fire and race the boys to a standstill. 'Not just the Thorntons, my girl– the Byrne's and the MacDougall's have been doing this for centuries.'

She was right–the celebration of remembrance and good fortune had been hard-wired into the Celtic clans over millennia of struggle–wars, harsh winters, plague and pestilence had forged within them a stoicism harder than granite, but come the opportunity for a party, they snatched the moment greedily, knowing that good fortune fades faster than footprints in the tide.

The two surviving sons of old Mick Thornton nursed their beer on the back veranda. James took a pull from his glass as he gazed over rolling paddocks.

'One down, two to go, Johnny.'

'Yeah, I'm only a year behind him, so I reckon I'll be next–but not yet. I hope to see our young Bill come back from this bloody war before I turn up my toes.'

James presented his glass, and they touched for a toast.

'May he have better luck than our John, or Danny for that matter.'

'Yes–you and Sarah have paid a greater price than you deserve.' They took a swallow. 'How is the boy, by the way? I hear he took off for the bush.'

'He was gone six months - working odd jobs, sleeping rough most of the time–even got into a bit of trouble, but it did him good. He's almost his old self again.'

'I'm glad. The three of us were lucky not to fight a war.' His attention was pulled away for an instant, and he grabbed a piece of folded notepaper from his coat.

'Mary's giving me a wave–I think it's time for me to give the eulogy - if we can get this mob to shut up for five minutes.'

John ambled over to a corner where the veranda rose above the crowd. Someone handed him an old school bell, which he shook vigorously, and the clamour dropped to a murmur.

'Ladies and gentlemen, boys and girls, for those of you who don't know me, I'm Michael Thornton's little brother, John.' A wave of applause and a whistle or two followed. 'Many years ago, at my wedding here on Gundungurra, Michael was my best man, and as tradition dictated, he made a speech about me wherein he slandered me most unjustly–so this afternoon I'm repaying him the complement.' A few chuckles resounded.

'Most of you would know that Michael and I were 6 and 5 years old when we sailed with Mum and Dad from Galway to Sydney in 1841. On the ship, we'd always be fighting, and Michael would terrify me with threats of selling me to pirates. Well luckily, we encountered no pirates, and when we docked at Circular Quay after months at sea, all we could think of was getting back on dry land. But when I started down the gangplank, the Captain roared from the poop deck. "Where do you think you're going, Cabin Boy? I've paid good money for you!"

'We lived for a few months in The Rocks. It was a rough and tumble place that made its own rules, and to hell with everybody else. Gangs of boys roamed the streets looking for trouble, and one day they jumped me on the way home. Just as I was about to cop a hiding, who should show up in the alleyway but my big brother. In he came with fists flying, but they were big kids and I wasn't much help. Michael was getting the worst of it, so I looked around for some kind of weapon. As luck would have it, there was a sanitary wagon standing nearby in the street. I grabbed a half-full dunny-can and upended the whole stinking sludge over the lot of them. Well, that stopped the fight, but didn't I get a hiding when Michael came home smelling like a shit-carter.'

'When we were in our early twenties, we rode down to Ballarat, dreaming of riches on the diggings. Well, we worked like navvies for six months, with nothing more to show than a few specks of gold dust. It turned out there was a boxing troupe in town, and Michael threw his hat into the ring. If he went three rounds with one of their boys, he'd win ten quid to take home–a fortune in those days. Well, come the night, this bloke, about the size of a prize bull, gets into the ring. He was like a giant meat-safe on legs. The bell goes for round one and Michael dances around this bloke and lands a few left jabs that give him a bit of a surprise. Round two they both cop a bit but stay upright. Come round three, this gorilla comes out throwing everything at Michael except the referee, and the two are getting pretty tired. Out of the blue, Michael cops a haymaker from the gorilla and drops like a lead balloon to take the full count. Afterward, Michael says to me, 'Oh well, that's buggered it–ten quid's up in smoke.' And I said, 'No mate–I bet a fiver on the other bloke and won twenty.'

'Well, I reckon I've made my big brother laugh a bit this afternoon. I know he can hear us, because James and I heard his voice last Monday as he left us–I was in Cadia, and Jimmy was in Sydney.' A low hum rippled across the crowd in affirmation.

'The Thornton family thanks you all for coming here this afternoon, in memory of a fine man and a wonderful brother. I'll finish now with an old Irish poem that I hope says what is in our hearts today:

'He's not lost, our dearest Michael,

Nor has he travelled far.

He's just stepped inside Heaven's gate,

And left it ajar.'

~   ~   ~

Henry Wong flicked through the Herald, trying his best to ignore the surrounding chatter. Running his finger down the sporting columns, he found the boxing results: *'At the Stadium on Saturday night, Tom O'Malley, 11st 6lb, beat Pat Moran, 11st 3lb'*, and slapped his thigh in delight. 'Hah! I'm five quid richer–better nick down to the bookie later, to collect my winnings.' Victoria scurried past, brandishing a cleaning cloth. 'That's nice darling, but please go and put your tie on–they'll be here any minute.' He sighed and eased from his armchair. 'Yes dear, right away.'

It was Monday, February 4, 1917, and the Wong house was in a flurry for the Tea Ceremony - the curtain-raiser for Tom and Cath's wedding in three weeks' time. In Chinese tradition, the bride and groom serve tea to both sets of parents, signifying two families being joined; and although Tom was blasé about ceremony, Cath had insisted on learning the fine art of Chinese tea-making from Victoria. She was busy fussing over an ornate tea set when Pearl came in from the kitchen, wearing a slate-grey tailored suit and devouring a Granny Smith apple.

'Cath, sweetie,–it's just a cup of tea–not a royal banquet.'

'Yes, I know–it's just that I want to do it right, you know–perhaps the "Gweilo-girl" can at least pour tea like a Chinese.'

'Darling, I think they must have switched us at birth.'

Tom carried a plate of steaming chicken and pork rolls. 'Where do you want these, Cath?'

She cleared a space on the table. 'Right here.' She glanced at her watch. 'Where's Mum and Dad gotten to?' And as if on cue, a knock sounded.

Henry walked down the hall; checking his tie in the mirror. He opened the door to James and Sarah.

'Good morning to you both!'

'G'day Henry–I hope we're not too late–the tram was as slow as a wet week.'

'No–you're right on the button–welcome to the chaos.'

Much had happened since Tom and Cath's engagement. The two families had drawn closer since Grandmother Yvonne's passing; bringing to an end the barrier she'd created with her acid tongue. Henry and James had struck up a friendship over a shared passion for golf, and Sarah met Victoria now and then for lunch in the city. Cath and Pearl had leant weight to the 'opposites attract' theory, hastened by Cath's appreciation of 'Chen's Millinery' and spiced by their good-natured banter.

They gathered in the sitting room as Cath rested an iron kettle on a reed mat; a ribbon of steam curling from the spout. The tea-set was decorated in a Jingdezhen 'Ice Plum' pattern - a twisting white plum branch against cobalt blue porcelain. She had boiled the water to 180 degrees Fahrenheit, and it would cool a couple of degrees for the pouring.

Sarah examined a cup. 'What a gorgeous set. Is it very old?'

'Yes—it's been in the Chen family for generations. It was my great grandmother's.'

Cath spooned Tsao Chun tea into the pot; a step known as 'The Black Dragon enters the palace' and poured the water; replacing the lid. She took a pair of cups and dropped two red dates into each. 'Mum, Dad, the dates symbolise the sweetness of married life.' Then she dropped a pair of seeds into the cups. 'These are seeds from a lotus flower.'

James spoke. 'And what do they symbolise?'

She reddened as Tom replied. 'The lotus flower is a symbol of fertility.'

Pearl broke in. 'In other words, if the seeds work their magic, Cath will soon become the old woman who lived in a shoe.'

Cath gave a sardonic smile. 'Thanks for that wonderful cultural insight, Pearl.'

After they'd drunk the dark, aromatic tea and toasted good fortune to Tom and Cath, Henry produced a tray of glasses and a bottle of Bushmills Single Malt Irish Whiskey. He winked at James. 'I've always said that one good ritual deserves another, don't you agree, James?'

'Absolutely, but only in the interests of racial harmony, you understand.'

When the Bushmills had achieved a dash of cross-cultural empathy, Henry called the group to order once more. 'As we know, my mother passed away not long ago. A week before she died, she called me to her room. She told me her time was short, and she wanted me to pass something on to you, Cath.' A look of surprise crossed Cath's face. She'd seen very little of Yvonne since their infamous first meeting, and their brief interactions since then had been polite, but strained. She shuddered inwardly. *What on earth would she have to say to me from beyond the grave?'*

Henry produced a battered old cardboard box secured with twine. 'She instructed me to give you this.'

Cath stared at it a moment, torn between curiosity over what was inside, and a horror of what she might find. It disturbed her that such a private and confronting moment would be on show for all to see. Tom read her mind, and joined her at the table.

The box felt heavy as she undid the string and lifted the lid. Her first glimpse was of a heavy metal ring, which she grasped, but needed Tom's help to lift it onto the table. It was an old brass bell, about 18 inches high and 12 in diameter; richly decorated with writhing dragons breathing fire. The metal was tarnished with a patina of greens and greys; nicked and scarred by the knocks of untold years. Only the rim maintained its rich ginger-gold sheen, as if polished by generations of hands. It was beautiful.

Tom retrieved a sealed envelope from the bottom of the box; tattooed with the imprint of the bell's rim. It was marked 'Catherine Thornton' in spidery handwriting. She opened the envelope, took a deep breath and read aloud:

'Dear Catherine,

When you read this, I shall be cold in my grave, but being particular about tying up loose ends, I wanted to give you these few words. Centuries ago, in the bloody wars of feudal China, armies issued commands on the battlefield using bells. Each bell had its own unique sound that was well-rehearsed. The emperor Qianlong used this bell in the wars against Mongol tribes in the 1750s–and its sound tolled the command to retreat.

And this is my message of surrender to you, Catherine– given by way of metaphor because I'm too proud, and, yes, afraid, to say these words to you face to face. I go to my death in the fourth month of your engagement to my grandson, and I don't need a fortune teller to know the two of you will become happily wed, despite my insults when we first met.

I am weak; imprisoned by the chains of my own prejudice. That is not a defence–just a fact. I wish you and my dear Tom a long and loving life, and hope that when you look at this bell, you will remember me–if for nothing more than someone who knew when they were beaten. Beaten by a love that conquers fear and ignorance.'

Wong Yu Yan.

~ ~ ~

Balla breathes deep draughts of sea air, remembering the Illawarra, and she's eager for the gallop along Maroubra beach to Malabar Headland. Clouds sift across morning sun; light checkers over drifts of wet kelp. Danny heels her forward, and she responds with an eager whinny. She's getting on, this one, but she'd still match a two-year-old over this half-mile as she hugs the shoreline where ripples drain to hard sand.

She's at a gallop now, looking the champion she'll always be–sunlight glowing from muscled shoulders, body lunging forward; her jet-black mane flying wild as hooves beat the sand like distant war drums. Clods fly in her wake, scattering gulls to the air in loud protest. A couple of brawny lifesavers at the clubhouse cheer her on. She's worked up a sweat now, her big heart pounding a tattoo as she nears the Malabar dunes where banksia and wattle rise to the headland. She eases back to a canter and Danny strokes her chestnut neck, whispering, 'Good girl, Balla'. She snorts softly in reply.

~   ~   ~

February 1918. More than a year had passed since he'd ridden through heat haze to the Royal and the frayed threads of a former life. At first his old mates at Coogee Surf Club looked anywhere but down at his wooden leg, their conversation tiptoeing through the safety of weather and rugby. But he understood, and it was only by his daily lap-swimming and jokes about white-ants that the ice was broken. In fact, his one-legged kicking style had made him something of a legend on the beach–earning him the nickname of 'The Dolphin'.

As he swam through rolling emerald water beyond the break, he'd ponder the past; weighing his fortunes as if they were specks of gold dust on a set of delicate scales. On one side was his precious, hard-won survival: on the other side, a sickly childhood and the desecration of war. But his six-month odyssey had made him realise there was a third variable involved; something that could tip the scales like a butcher's concealed thumb–one's own reaction to events. He'd stared death in the face and sunk to unfathomable depths, but had survived by finding answers within himself, and fighting back. Life had thrown a lot at a boy named 'Lucky', but instead of breaking him, it had strengthened him.

~   ~   ~

The GPO clock sounded midday as Danny exited Prouds Jewellery Store on the corner of Pitt and King. He'd returned to a scarred workbench on the lower ground floor among tweezers and oil cans while a chorus of clocks ticked away time in orderly seconds. A steady breeze funnelled harbour salt up Pitt Street and the sky burned hot. Pedestrians hugged shade under shop awnings; pub windows gaped open for a breath of wind.

He turned down Pitt Street to Martin Place, heading to the Angel Hotel for a quick counter lunch– perhaps a walk over to Wynyard Park afterward. A figure emerging from the Colonial Mutual Building caught his attention - a young woman. He'd not seen her face, but there was something familiar in the walk - the sway of dark hair and the purposeful stride. Emma? Nurse Emma Parkinson? He quickened his pace.

THE END

If you enjoyed 'Breaking Lucky', Volume 1 of the Thornton Series is also available on Amazon. Join the Thornton family where it all began, on an epic journey from Ireland to Sydney and beyond in 1841. It's the story of the women and men who saw a wide sky full of promise, and turned a colony into a country.